Planet of the Orange-red Sun

Series Volume 4

Difficillis Exitus

Planet of the Orange-red Sun Series

Volume 4
Difficillis Exitus

by Vic Broquard

http://www.Broquard-ebooks.com
Broquard eBooks
103 Timberlane
East Peoria, IL 61611
author@Broquard-eBooks.com

Artwork by Crooked Willow Studios.

Table of Contents

Part I Discovery

Chapter 1 Normalcy

"Breakfast is ready! Come on girls! Up and at it. You don't want to be late on your first day back at high school," hollered thirty-eight year old Adoria Armando.

"Right! You heard your mother. Get your lazy butts up now!" added her mate, Benita de Salmo, also the same age. Both women had long, somewhat curly, flaming red hair, hazel eyes, and a freckled complection to match. The sounds of four pairs of bounding feet brought smiles to the two women's faces. Adoria's was round and full, accentuated by the cut of her bangs while Benita's was more angular with a pointed nose, giving her a far sterner look. Already, both women had dressed for work; their makeup, impeccably done. Adoria's raw umber eye shadow accentuated her hair and bright red dress, which matched perfectly her silk dress and high-heeled boots. Benita, on the other hand, preferred a vibrant blue shadow matching her satin dress and boots. Their wasp waist corsets greatly accentuated their figures, though their massive bosoms and broad hips aided that as well.

"Morning mothers," the sleepy voice of Adoria's eldest daughter greeted them. Marisol was eighteen and about to begin her senior year at high school. Like her mother, she also had flaming red hair, though hers was perhaps six inches longer, falling to the small of her back. Hers was thicker and fuller than her mother's, but far straighter. She wore her school uniform consisting of a white blouse that barely contained her growing bosom, jeans, and tennis shoes. Marisol's face lacked the freckles that so dominated her mother's body. Her face was likened to an angel, at least that's what Adoria always told her. She pressed her body into Adoria's and then Benita's, before she slid into her chair.

Right behind her, Marisol's fourteen year old sister Donica came running into the family dining room. She wore an identical uniform, though her bosom was just forming and now matched the size of the oranges sitting on the table. She was about to begin eighth grade. Although Adoria and Benita were married, Marisol and Donica were Adoria's offspring.

Benita's two were right behind the older two. Cande was sixteen and a sophomore, while Elodia was twelve and beginning sixth grade. All four teens wore identical uniforms, differing only in their bust sizes.

The adult women of Madiera all had enormous breasts, easily the size of soccer balls, which happened to be the most popular sport among all the teens of their world. When a girl reached her nineteenth birthday, their breasts finally matured fully, though they would increase significantly during pregnancies, naturally. "Oh dear, Marisol, you should have told me your blouse is too small again. Well, no matter, I'll have the sewing-bot alter your blouses this evening. Now go ahead and eat a nourishing breakfast. A good day always starts with a well-rounded breakfast," Adoria announced. Several girls groaned and Marisol gave her mother a frown, having heard this line nearly every morning since she could remember. The two adults took their seats at the table, sitting before the eating machines.

Marisol maneuvered her legs into the mechanical joints beneath the table and deftly controlled the metal arms that brought her glass of fresh orange juice up to her lips. As she maneuvered the other mechanical arm over the bacon and eggs, she said, "Mom, you look stunning this morning." Benita flashed her mate a sexy smile but Adoria knew Marisol was about to spring something on her. She always preceded her requests with a nice compliment about her appearance.

"What is it this morning, dear?" she replied coyly, not giving in to Marisol's attempt to butter her up for the kill. She maneuvered her mechanical arm and took a bite of the perfectly done eggs.

"Nothing much, mom, it's just we have soccer practice after school so I won't be home in time to gather up the dirty laundry," Marisol replied, thankful she had a valid excuse to get out of that chore which she hated. She was on the varsity squad this term and would be overseeing the new tryouts right after school.

Benita spoke up, "That's fine, dear. Cande, you can do it this time for Marisol. You know how important it is for our Fire Devils to win the Soccer Cup this year."

"But mom, I was going to try out for the varsity team this year," she protested. "They do take sophomores, if they are really good. Can't Donica do it this time?"

"Oh I'll do it, Marisol," her younger sister sighed, adding, "but you *owe* me one, Marisol. I'll collect on it, you can *count* on that." Adoria flashed her younger daughter a grateful smile, thankful the small issue was so easily resolved.

All six worked their mechanical arms efficiently and soon finished. While the two adults sat back, sipping their coffee through straws, Marisol again made another plea to have some coffee herself. "Not until you are out of high school, dear. You know the rules. When you graduate, you will be an adult. Along with all the responsibilities that brings, you can have coffee then too, but not before. Nor any wine, so don't even think about such things until next year." Marisol looked a bit miffed, but broke into a smile. How did she know I wanted to sip wine too, she wondered. "Now, check your appearance in the mirrors and head for school. You don't want to be late and have to run. You know appearances are everything. Look your best, do your best. We'll see you tonight, kids."

All four rose and headed for the front door of their modest, single floor home. As they approached the door, each glanced into the full-length mirror. More than one tossed their head from side to side, adjusting the fall of their long hair. At the door, the door-bot opened it for them at the precisely timed moment so they didn't need to delay in the slightest. "Thank you for letting me help you," the mechanical voice of the door-bot said as the four teens walked outside.

The day was bright, as it always was. Rain only came at night when everyone was in bed. Very convenient, Marisol often thought, but then that was the responsibility of the Water Guild. Her mothers belonged to the Fire Guild and had the responsibility of maintaining the balmy daytime temperature of precisely seventy-five degrees year round. A sidewalk led from their bungalow to the main walking path that led across Madieria to their schools. The green grass and scent of freshly blooming flowers were thick in the air, compliments of those in the Earth Guild and the Air Guild, whose primary responsibility was to provide clean, perfect air at all times.

As they neared their neighboring house, Marisol slowed down. "Are you going to walk with the water teen?" Cande complained. "Well, come on, let's speed up. I don't want to even be seen walking with water, air, and earth teens!" Donica, Elodia, and Cande picked up their pace, snubbing their noses at Marisol, who ignored them. What do they know about friends, Marisol thought to herself.

Here in Madiera, all women belonged to one of four kindred groups or guilds, as they were known: Fire, Earth, Air, and Water. Each kindred had their own native abilities. Often there was friction and tension between them, but not always. Actually, there were two conflicting beliefs. One held by Benita and the three children was that being of the Fire kindred; they should have nothing whatsoever to do with the other kindred groups. One held by Adoria and Marisol was that all four should work together in harmony. Indeed, Marisol had grown up and counted three others as her best friends, though her fourth friend was of the Fire kindred. She waited on the walk a moment when Adriana came bouncing out of her home. She was of the Water kindred and had wavy long brown hair and deep blue eyes. "Hiya, Marisol. You forgot to get your blouse enlarged didn't you?"

"Is it *that* noticeable?" Marisol flushed.

"Well, we are almost full grown now. Okay, in nine months then," she corrected herself. She had an oval face and thick lips, which by their shape seemed to give her face a permanent smile, matching her eternally optimistic attitude. "Not really," she added, answering Marisol's look of embarrassment. "Come on, Elena's coming out now." The two hurried to the next home where a raven-haired teen just came out, with her younger sisters ignoring the two and dashing on ahead.

Elena's bushy eyebrows and black eyes matched her belt. Her face was squarish and her high forehead tended to give her a rather stern appearance. Her lips were thicker than Adriana's which only aggravated her tendency to be a worry rat. "Hiya, I do hope we aren't late on our first day." They walked on down to the next house where their fourth was already waiting impatiently for them.

Stepping from one foot and then the other, the nervous Isabel of the Air kindred called out, "Come on you three, we will be late for sure." She had long wavy blonde hair and very pale blue eyes, a combination Marisol thought was positively enchanting. Of the four, Marisol considered Isabel to be the prettiest. All four moved close together and began walking shoulder to shoulder down the concrete street, proud to be a close knit group.

They were held together by other bonds as well. All four were exceptionally bright, fighting it out for the label "top of the class." Currently, Isabel had that distinction but only by a tenth of a point. "I've been going over our schedules this year. We have calculus first period, then English, though I wish that was last. Third period is physics, which I am looking forward to the most, I think anyway. I can't make up my mind about fourth period though. What is advanced engineering all about anyway?"

"Hey, I can't wait for fifth period, it's computer programming," Marisol interrupted. That was her favorite subject.

"Of course you can't," Adriana teased her friend. "I'm all for sixth period study hall. If we are diligent, we might be able to get most of our homework done before seventh period, when we go to our special skills class. We're supposed to learn some cool water skills this year. Bet you get to learn to do some fancy fire skills, Marisol."

"Right, then we got phys ed last, which is perfect. Right after that, we get to work on our own soccer teams," Marisol added.

"No, Marisol, you forgot the eighth period before phys ed. What is social skills class all about anyway? No one has really told us what that class is. I couldn't get mom to even give me a clue," Elena interjected.

"It can't be hard, at least I hope so," Isabel added, slightly worried about this unknown class. Math, science, these she could handle well.

As the foursome approached their sprawling high school, a concrete and metal single story building with long halls and four large soccer fields behind it, another fiery redhead appeared. "Hiya Marisol. Thought you might be late." She gave Marisol a bumping hug and flashed a smile to the other three.

"Hiya Tatiana," Marisol replied, her face flushing a little. She hadn't seen her heartthrob all summer. Tatiana had curly red hair that fell just to her shoulders. She kept it short so it didn't get in her way. The teen was the captain of the Red Devils, the Fire kindred's school soccer team. Athletic, she was also keenly into engineering and the construction and operation of all things. Yet, Tatiana was exceptionally pretty with an oval face and enchanting emerald eyes. She stood a full three inches taller than Marisol.

The two had met in basic engineering class their freshman year. Marisol had fallen in love with the class beauty. Who would not have? Twice now, Tatiana had won their class Beauty Queen award and was a shoo in to receive it again their senior year. While all the girls envied Marisol's closeness with Tatiana, Tatiana had also fallen for Marisol, who shared her love of all things engineering, though Marisol's gift lay more with the related aspects of computer programming. These two were always lab partners in their engineering classes, much to the envy of many other Fire teens.

"Wow, love. You have really filled out this past summer," Tatiana exclaimed, admiring the significantly larger bosom of her heartthrob. "So have you three," she added with a nod to Adriana, Elena, and Isabel. Since Marisol always hung out with these three neighbor teens, so did Tatiana, when she could. The five were accepted as a clique among the "joiners." That was the term for those who advocated close relationships with other kindred groups. "Separatists" was the term for those who believed in befriending only others within one's own kindred. The school was divided about fifty-fifty on this issue, as was the entire society, the prime cause of conflict within Madiera.

"Well, you have too, Tatiana. We are supposed to be fully developed by the end of this term," Isabel pointed out what they all knew. "Come on, we are almost late."

"K, cya in physics class," Tatiana replied, giving Marisol

a parting bump hug.

As the five approached the large quadruple doors, a door-bot opened the doors for them. The mechanical voice said, "Welcome to high school. Thank you for letting me assist you." The five ignored the door-bot. Tatiana headed off to her first class, while the four headed to their left for their calculus class. Tatiana was in a lower level math class, math not being one of her strong points. With impeccable timing, another door-bot opened the door to their classroom for them as they approached it, drolling, "Thank you for letting me assist you," as they entered.

They took four seats beside each other and watched as the rest of the teens entered. Isabel counted twenty of them. Then their teacher, Mrs. de Falla entered, her high heels clicking rapidly on the concrete floor of the room. She was Air kindred, with long blonde hair and light blue eyes. She wore a white satin gown that accentuated her shapely form, held rigidly in place by her wasp waist corset. True, her soccer ball sized bosom was quite pronounced, but then all adult women of Madiera had quite similar bosoms, though a few sported much larger ones, to the envy of many other women. Her hips were quite full and rounded and one could not tell she had already had born two daughters. The seams of her black nylon hose were perfectly straight and her white patent boots with their metal tipped, six-inch stiletto heels, reflected the overhead white lights. Her makeup was perfectly done and Marisol found herself dreaming. Another nine months and she too would be wearing elegant clothing and finally able to wear such stunning makeup and heels, announcing to the world here was a respected adult of the community. She imagined how her lover Tatiana would look dolled up, but Mrs. de Falla brought her swiftly out of dreamland.

"Welcome to calculus class. Now then, roll call. Marisol Armanda."

Isabel made a whispering noise at her friend who flushed, looked up, and called out, "Here." Several girls giggled slightly at her delay in replying. She flushed a little more. Mrs. de Falla ignored that and continued with her attendance taking.

Once done, she stated, "We will begin with a review of what you should already know how to do. I am going to put a problem on the white board and one of you will come up here and solve it for us." Marisol hated this aspect, she often was called upon to do just this, and she slumped down in her chair, hoping she'd be overlooked just this once. Meanwhile, the other teens watched their teacher's shapely form moving slowly over to the board, her heels clicking on the floor. All were similarly daydreaming, imagining how elegant they would look when they were finally recognized as adults and allowed at long last to wear such beautiful outfits. Mrs. de Falla picked up the bit-end of the marker between her teeth and proceeded to write on the board:

$$X^2 + 5X + 6 = 0$$

"Marisol, will you come up here and solve this one for us. Show all the steps, please."

She groaned, as did anyone called to work a problem on the board, while many others breathed a sigh of relief they had not been called forward. Marisol walked briskly to the board, moving four times faster than her teacher had, bend over and picked up the bit-end of the marker and stood facing the problem. Hastily she moved her head about and wrote out:

$$(X + 2)(X + 3) = 0$$
$$X = -2$$
$$X = -3$$

Satisfied, she put the marker down and returned to her seat, pleased she'd gotten it so swiftly.

Before sitting down, she mechanically leaned forward a little and tossed her head to her left, allowing her long hair to shift over her left shoulder. Then she sat down, adjusting her legs into the book-bot controls. Deftly, she maneuvered the mechanical machine, opening her book to the first chapter and prepared to follow along. Thus began her first class this senior year.

When the ending bell rang, she ordered the delivery-bot, "Take my books to study hall, please."

The mechanical voice replied, "Thank you for letting me help you." She ignored this, as did all the other teens who eagerly filed out of the room, heading off to their next class,

English. While all the teens watched with a growing envy as their elegantly dressed English teacher slowly walked into the room, they soon began daydreaming of other things. Few enjoyed this class. Marisol whispered to Isabel, "I wish we had something meaningful to read like *Advanced Programming Efficiency Tips*." Her friends agreed with her, though not with her choice of reading materials.

Physics class woke them all up, especially since Tatiana now sat beside Marisol, the two exchanging some romantic whispers while awaiting their teacher to make her grand appearance. At last, Mrs. Delmira walked slowly into the room, filled with all manner of mechanical contraptions, designed to help illustrate the many principles she intended to teach these bright young minds. She was of the Earth kindred, tall and slender. Her raven hair was thick and long, almost touching the floor. Her squarish face and thick brows and lips added to her professor-like demeanor. She wore a black satin gown that made her soccer-ball bosom appear even more pronounced, though her tiny waist also added to the illusion. Her black patent boots with their spiked, metal tipped heels announced her arrival and twenty heads turned to watch her grand entrance, as she slowly made her way to her desk.

After calling roll, she began, "Many of you have already been making prime use of some of the key principles of physics, though you may not have known you were doing so. For every action, there is an equal but opposite reaction. Marisol, Tatiana, please come up here. You two have been using this principle in your soccer games. Pickup-bot: pick up the soccer ball and prepare to serve it." She spoke to one of the referee-bots that was used in the soccer games. The class giggled, all knew these two were star players on the Fire Devils. The two rushed to the front, not the least embarrassed to show off their prowess with the ball. "Now I want you to head butt the ball back and forth, please. Class note for each action, the ball has an opposite reaction, going in the opposite direction from which it began."

The pickup-bot raised the ball high in the air on one of its mechanical arms and then released it. Tatiana butted it perfectly towards Marisol, who moved rapidly to the precise spot to head-butt it back to her lover. For several minutes, the two enjoyed this little show of their prowess. They had been doing this together for four years now, ever since they had met. "Okay, okay, that will be enough. I'm sure you could continue to illustrate this basic physics principle until lunch time." The class giggled and the two let the ball bounce onto the floor. Their teacher ordered another bot to retrieve it and put it on the shelf for her.

As the two walked back to their seats, Marisol suddenly realized this would be their last term of being able to play soccer. Once they were pronounced adults and graduated, they would be thereafter dolled up as their mothers and teachers were, wholly unable to play this game. Well, soccer was for children, after all, Marisol thought. Soon, we will be grown up and can marry. Tatiana gave her a look indicating she had similar thoughts. "We'll make the most of it," she whispered to Marisol, as they leaned forward and tossed their heads, adjusting the fall of their hair before sitting down.

Later, Tatiana and Marisol let out squeals of joy as they entered their advanced engineering class. "Now we are learning something *really* useful," Tatiana declared. "Look at all these bots we will be studying! How they work, how they are made, all manner of way cool things!"

"Yes, that you will be," the alto voice of their new teacher, Mrs. del Grotto startled them from the rear. Slowly she made her way to the front of the bot-filled room. She was also an Earth person, with thick raven hair falling to just below her shoulders. She wore a brown silk gown with matching heels though perhaps a bit too gaudy with her makeup. A short woman, her figure seemed even more pronounced than their other teachers. "Bots are everything in our society. That's what you, the brightest of our students, will be studying this term. How do they work? How are they maintained? These and many more questions we will be answering in this class. Yes, this is a tough class. I won't tell you any differently." Her heels continued to echo off the concrete floor as she made her way to the front, but few were paying attention to that. Of course, you will need all your computer programming skills in this class. Bots are controlled by them." Some groaned, but Marisol and

Tatiana listened eagerly to her every word. The class was over way too soon for these two.

On their way to the lunchroom, the two chatted about the bots, while their three other friends chose to talk about what might be covered in the as yet unknown social skills class. The lunchroom was packed, but the five found seats together near the rear and sat down before the prepared meal. They slipped their legs into the mechanical levers and deftly began diving into their lunch of cheeseburgers, peas, and applesauce, along with a large glass of milk. "Trade you my peas for your sauce," Tatiana whispered. She disliked peas. Marisol grinned and worked her controls, making the machine's arms execute the transfer.

After a stroll around the commons and enjoying a bit of fresh air, the five headed off to computer programming class. However, it was the next class that got their full attention, social skills. Their teacher was Mrs. Lupe, Air kindred, with blonde hair reaching her waist. She wore a white satin gown and matching heels. Her deep blue eye shadow blended with her light blue eyes, but her cherry red lips drew one's attention to her full lips. "Social skills. Yes, you twenty are about to embark on your voyage through adulthood and you must be prepared to meet the challenges we adults must face," she began in a high pitched voice.

"In just nine short months, you will become adults. The first principle you must know and obey is we adults must always look our very best from the moment we get out of bed until we retire for the night. Who knows when someone will drop by for a visit, you see. Always we look our best when we are at work. There are no exceptions, none whatsoever. While we have numerous styles of gowns to choose from, we always wear our defining corsets, nylons, and heels. Always, and of course, our makeup. On Friday nights and Saturday nights, we have social gatherings, dances usually. On those nights, we always wear our highest heels and tightest corsets, to make ourselves look the very best possible. Many of you will use these outings to find romance and your life's mate. With that in mind, you will want to look your absolute best at these times." Many teens giggled however, but Marisol and Tatiana exchanged flirting glances and smiles.

"So one thing we will be learning in this class is how to operate the necessary bots. We will also be studying fashions and materials used in the construction of our finest dresses and gowns. Of course, romance and marriage will soon bring new baby girls. So you will be learning how to operate the various baby-care-bots. There are very precise rules, which must be followed with having children. First, no woman is allowed to become pregnant until they reach twenty, no exceptions. We want your bodies to be fully developed. Second, your babies must be spaced at least two years apart to give your reproductive systems time to recover fully. Honestly, have you ever seen an older woman who does not still retain her figure after having several babies? Of course not, she would *not* be looking her very best, would she?"

"While studying the fashion industry will be most enjoyable for all, we must also fully cover the sole area of discord within our society: the Joiners versus the Separatists. That will lead into a discussion of our judicial system." The class groaned, but for various reasons. Already, the teens were highly polarized on this issue, what with the five friends acknowledged Joiners by their classmates. "Then of course, we must discuss all the career employment opportunities from which you may choose your adult path in our society."

"Today, we will begin with getting the nasty topic discussed. After that, everything else will be fun, I trust. Now then, as you know there are four very different forces we control, the elemental forces of nature: fire, air, earth, and water, without which, we would all perish. Each adult woman in our society has skills in one and only one of these forces and we call them the four kindred groups. The Joiners claim the four kindred groups should work together as a unified whole, and there is a great deal of precedence for this, since lacking even one, we would all surely die. The Separatists believe some kindred are far more important, far more powerful than the others and that their blood lines should not be adulterated by the joining of cross-kindred women. Water puts out fires, for example, just as earth does. Yet, fire turns water into steam, destroying it, and it can bake the earth into hard bricks, unable to support life."

"This week we will be studying aspects of each philosophy, and, then, armed with the facts, you can make up your own minds as to which philosophy you support. On Friday, you will turn in a paper that states clearly which group you back and four pages on just why it is you have chosen this philosophy." Everyone groaned, all hated to write papers, though the writing-bots did all the laborious work.

In their special skills class, Tatiana and Marisol found themselves in the smallest class yet, only five total students. Here, they were trained to use their special inbred skills dealing with all aspects of fire. "Well, we have a good use for launching flames," Tatiana suggested. "Our goalie uses that to burn up soccer balls to keep them from going into our net." The other four nodded their agreement with her assessment. "But what use are all these other things, Mrs. Senia? When are we really going to start fires, burn things up, heat and melt metal, things like that? It seems rather pointless. I certainly am not going to burn up another woman's body, even if I don't like them."

The fiery redheaded teacher replied, "You have a valid point, Tatiana. Those in the Water, Air, and Earth kindred groups have many useful ways to put their unique gifts to use in helping to maintain our agriculture industry and even our general environment. Still, fire is useful in maintaining our perfect temperatures and you will need your skills if you go to work maintaining the bots. Welding of metal is a highly needed skill in that arena, Tatiana." The teen relaxed; perhaps there was something useful to learn in this class.

Phys Ed came last and the five raced out onto the soccer fields. Although they split into their own kindred teams, the five truly enjoyed these periods of hard play. Today, the Fire kindred battled the Air kindred, while the Water kindred took on the teens in the Earth kindred. In addition to the two teams on each of the two fields, there were a number of mechanical bots also present. Each game had two referee-bots and four water-towel-bots, ready to provide water to thirsty players or to wipe the sweat from their faces.

"Glad we don't have to play the Water kindred today.

What a muddy mess they are making of that field over there," Tatiana whispered to Marisol.

"No, we just have to keep from being blown over by the Air players," Marisol laughed. A bit later, while chasing after the ball, an Air teen launched a huge gust of wind at her, sending Marisol sprawling face down on the grass. At once, a referee-bot glided up to her and extended its mechanical arms to lift her back onto her feet. Mechanical arms dusted her off, though she complained she was fine, just a little annoyed with the other teen, who was now down at their goal. "Good, our goalie fried the ball!"

"Thank you for allowing me to assist you," the mechanical voice of the referee-bot said, as Marisol dashed to the center of the field where the other bot was about to launch a new ball into the air. Tatiana bounced the ball with her head towards Marisol, who used her head to deflect the ball to her feet and she began bringing the ball down the field. How to get it past the Air kindred goalie was their main problem. She could conjure up a huge blast of air, knocking the ball far back down the field. A fake out was the only real way and as four other Air players closed in on her, she spotted Tatiana in position and faked a goal kick, but actually kicking it sideways to Tatiana, who deflected it past the surprised goalie. "Goal for Fire," a referee-bot droned as the two teams jogged back to centerfield for the next ball release.

Their last period passed altogether too swiftly for the teens. Yet when the bell sounded, Tatiana and Marisol remained on the field, catching their breath and taking swills from the water-bots, who continued to say, "Thank you for letting me assist you." They ignored the bot, though.

"Now come the tryouts. I've been thinking, Marisol. This is really the last time in our lives when we can actually play soccer. You heard Mrs. Lupe in social skills, once we graduate, we will be always wearing the sexy, fashionable outfits. She did say there were no exceptions, so we won't ever be able to run around and play soccer again." Disappointment and sadness were in her voice.

"I know, I was thinking the same thing, but still, to always look so sexy, that's what I've been really waiting for, love. Let's make this our best year ever for soccer," Marisol replied. Tatiana grinned, but didn't give her a loving bump hug because several other teens were jogging onto the field for the tryouts, one of whom was her sister Cande, by her second mother, Benita. Cande, now a sophomore, felt a little out of place among the big chested senior teens, her bosom was so much smaller, but she was determined to make the team and was very pleased when her sister announced she had. "You're with us, Cande, good job!" She grinned broadly, as the team headed to the showers.

In the shower stall, Marisol stood patiently while the dressing-bot took her clothes off for her accompanied by the metallic voice, "Thank you for allowing me to assist you." She stepped into the warm water and allowed the bathing-bot to wash her curvaceous body with its soft sponge, ignoring its thank you chatter. Then she allowed the dressing-bot to dress her in her spare clothes. She walked over to the hair-bot machine. This was her favorite part of the daily ritual. She sat back in the chair and the bot lowered her chair to a horizontal position, her long hair falling into the machine. She felt its gentle touch as the bot's mechanical arms first cleaned her scalp and then her hair. A little heat later and her hair was dry. Then came the truly enjoyable part. The machine applied a small electrostatic charge to her thick hair. Instantly, each long strand separated from the others. As the bot finished and her chair rose back to a sitting position, her long hair was lustrous and full of body. Each strand fell perfectly into place. She rose and tossed her head to her left while leaning, causing her tresses to slip over her left shoulder. Marisol glanced in the mirror and satisfied herself she looked good. Then she headed home, meeting up with her sister.

Their mothers were both home when the two walked in the front door, opened once more by their door-bot. "Hi moms! Guess what? I made the Fire Devils!" Cande gushed out her exciting news. Both Adoria and Benita smiled broadly and complimented her, giving her a pair of bump-hugs as well. Marisol merely smiled and asked what was for supper. It wasn't pizza.

"Look, on Friday night, Benita is taking me to the big

fall dance. So you four kids can have a pizza party and invite some of your friends," Adoria suggested. "I will leave the monitor-bot in charge, so no monkey business. No romantic interludes, no alcoholic beverages."

"Ah, you take all the fun out of it mom," Marisol faked a protest, then added, "Thanks, mom. That's great. I hope you and mom have a fun time at the dance."

Adoria gave her eldest a coy wink, whispering, "You bet we will! She's going to wear her sexy light blue satin gown for me, my favorite. I just love her look in that gown." Marisol flashed her mother a smile, but tried to imagine Tatiana wearing it instead.

On Friday, her class was excused from the normal day's classes so they could take a field trip to visit all the various working installations of Madiera. The five friends climbed on board the bot-bus and squeezed into two benches so they could sit together. "This is going to be exciting! We're going to see them all," Tatiana exclaimed. Visiting all the working bot installations of the world was right up her alley. On the other hand, Isabel was rather bored about seeing most of them, save the air bot systems.

The last person to board was their advanced engineering teacher, the alto voiced Mrs. del Grotto. Today, she had just had her raven hair done and it looked perfect, Marisol noted. She wore her usual brown silk gown with matching heels and her gaudy makeup was even more pronounced this morning. She carefully climbed up the steps into the bot-bus, where the driver-bot sat at the electric vehicle's controls waiting patiently for her signal to begin. She counted heads and then sat down, instructing the driver-bot to begin.

While the vehicle silently began moving, she addressed her students. "Madiera boasts a population of around a thousand of we women. Just where do we get all our food? The bot-farms. These will be our first stop." The high school was at the northern edge of the town and a paved road headed north into the fields of growing crops. She pointed out the various crops and occasionally the field-bots who were out tending them, often pulling weeds. "Everything is automatically controlled so the plants receive the precise amount of water and nutrients they need for optimal growth." Over half the day was spent examining the various field-bot installations that either grew their food or processed it into packaged units to be delivered to their homes when ordered.

Then, they visited the Air Recycling Center where air-bots both filtered the air, removing impurities, and added additional oxygen when needed. Some of these were rather massive bots, Tatiana noted carefully. From there, they visited the Water Purification Center, where the water-maintenance-bots handled all aspects of their water supply. All water was recycled and none ever was lost. "Why is that?" Tatiana asked Marisol, who only shrugged. Conservation and recycling were staples of life, but why? Like her lover, she had no idea why that was so vital.

The power-generation-bots intrigued both budding engineers the most. Here huge generators provided all the power that ran their world and their many bots. The ultimate source of the power came from two nuclear generating plants, heavily shielded from the world of Madiera. From there, they visited the manufacturing plants where everything from simple shoeboxes to refrigerators, stoves, and clothing were made. Once more, the class was intrigued by the sheer complexity of these many machines and the bots that controlled them.

"Jeesh, our whole society is run by bots!" Isabel exclaimed.

"Precisely correct, Miss Isabel," Mrs. del Grotto complimented her observation. "That's why the study of engineering and computer programming is so vital to our society. We have to maintain all these bots."

"Mrs. del Grotto, do bots ever break down?" asked Elena.

"Yes, they most certainly do. It is up to the maintenance-bots along with our help to get them fixed," she replied.

"Can't we just buy new bots when the old ones break down?" asked Elena innocently.

"Heavens no. Where would we buy them from? Have

you seen a bot-store in town?" Everyone chuckled at that jest. There was no such store. However, there was a bot-maintenance shop, but the class did not visit this underground facility. Mrs. del Grotto did tell them about it, which pricked both Tatiana and Marisol's interest. Both vowed to one day visit that place, wherever it was located. Slowly but surely, the seniors were being introduced into the adult world of Madiera.

Friday night, both their mothers were dressed up for their night out. As Marisol bump-hugged her mother, she noted her mother's waist seemed smaller than normal. Certainly, her gorgeous red heels were higher somehow. She began to reflect upon what she had been taught in social skills class. Both her mothers looked gorgeous, Benita especially so in her light blue satin gown. Now Marisol realized just how sexy Benita did look and hoped one day soon she could look that attractive for Tatiana too.

"Oh, Marisol, can you look over that darn front door-bot? It's been sticking some of late. When I came home this afternoon, I had to kick it to get it to open for me."

"Okay mom, Tatiana and I will. You both have a good time," she replied. Soon her four friends came by along with her sisters' younger friends as well. Before long, twenty teens were partying away, eating pizza, and gyrating to the latest rock dance tunes. Tatiana and Marisol were gayly shaking and swaying their curvaceous bodies before each other, but the monitor-bot kept a close eye on them. After the bot slid its mechanical arm between them pushing them apart for the third time all the while saying, "No romantic touching allowed," the two headed to look at the front door-bot.

"Have you noticed an awful lot of bots are breaking down?" Tatiana asked, as the two gave diagnostic commands to the door-bot.

"Yes, this darn door, for example. I wonder if it just needs oiling or something simple," she replied. After running all the diagnostic checks, they discovered one of its internal circuits was intermittently failing. All they could do was to have the bot issue a call for a replacement-bot. A message appeared on the display screen announcing a service-bot would drop by to replace it on Monday morning.

Their introduction into the adult world of Madiera continued in subsequent social skills classes. The next extensive topic was reproduction, which caused the teens no end of embarrassment and many nervous giggles. Their Air kindred teacher, Mrs. Lupe, with her long blonde hair, trademark white satin gown and matching heels, her deep blue eye shadow, and cherry red, full lips, was wholly un-phased by their reactions. She'd seen it all.

Mrs. Lupe began by showing them a series of graphical illustrations of a woman's reproductive system. "Display-bot, show sequence one, please." Comments such as yeeeuu and "gross" whispered around the room as the teens watched the illustrations appearing on the whiteboard. Next, she showed them a large collection of pleasure giving devices, showing them how effectively to use them to pleasure their partners.

"Now beginning at age twenty, you and your partner are eligible to begin having children, no more than one every two years is allowed. The reproductive-bot enforces this. When you and your mate are ready to have a child, the donor woman visits the reproductive-bot that will extract and prepare the donor's chromosomes, storing them in a reproductive dong. This is what one looks like." She had her bot hold it up so the class could see it easily. "The donor puts this end in her mouth and then inserts the long end into her mate's opening. When she climaxes, the donor pushes down on the bulb that shoots her prepared solution into her mate. Hopefully, it reaches the mate's egg and fertilizes it and her baby begins its formation period. Birth should follow in nine months. Now let's look at these diagrams of our reproductive organs and their changes from the moment of conception through the birth of the baby." More groans and moans accompanied the rather graphic illustrations.

Finally, she covered the birthing process and what the roll of the birthing-bots would be. "Now with your baby's arrival, we come to the care of a newborn. Your mammary glands will be swollen with milk for your new child. The baby-care-bot will be of enormous assistance to new mothers, from helping position the infant for proper nursing to helping with the changing of her diapers. My handout-bot will be giving each of you a plastic baby doll. We are going to practice changing its diapers without harming the baby." That took the rest of that period and two more before all the teens got the hang of operating the baby-care-bot.

From this point, she launched into medical care and home diagnosis and the use of the medical-bots. Not only for young infants and small children, she covered the common illnesses women commonly encountered in their lifetimes. She ended this discussion with a short field trip to the medical center where more advanced care and treatment could be had.

The teens enjoyed her next presentations on the elements of fashion, color blending, and designs. "You should always have matching heels or ones that compliment or contrast with the color of your dress. Of course, heel heights are normally six inches, a high sexy arch. Since your toes take a beating, the boots are fitted with an absorbent cushion. To prevent sprained or twisted ankles, the boots are automated. That is, when you put them on, they activate and shrink to fit your foot and ankles very snugly. Until they are released, they cannot be removed. Further, so we do not have to buy duplicate sets of heels for our nice outings on Friday and Saturday nights, the boots are automatically programmed to alter their heel height and arch to seven inches. So yes, our boots are expensive, programmed bots as well, though these are pretty simple bots."

"Our corsets are likewise really programmed bots. Once they are in place, the bot takes over and tightens them appropriately. They do not fully draw tight until after you have worn it for an hour, giving your body time to adjust. Then again, on our special nights, the bot contracts our waists further to enhance our appearance for those special occasions. It's all done automatically; we do not have to concern ourselves with these details, another marvel of modern bot technology. However, with the smaller waists, we do have to have appropriate gowns to wear at these times. Always remember to look your very best."

"Speaking of looking your best, it is time you learned how to operate the makeup-bots. Of course, you are only experimenting with makeup. No one will be allowed out of the classroom while wearing makeup. However, you need to know how to run those machines, which you will begin using daily in just a few more months."

As every class before theirs, they too had a ball experimenting with the makeup-bot. Some had garish green eye shadows and purple lips. While some teens practiced diligently, others tried out really wild combinations, bringing rounds of laughter to the classroom. The teens had to program the many available choices from eye makeup to lipstick to foundation coverings and blushes. Once set, they placed their faces into the bot, which then gave them a series of directions to follow, beginning with closing their eyes while the bot applied the designated mascara and shadow. The makeup-bot also removed all traces, cleaning and moisturizing their skin.

After the personal grooming section of her course was finished, Mrs. Lupe launched into their government and judicial systems. Every three years, an election was held to choose three legislature representatives who met to make any needed new laws. Every five years, an election was held to choose their president who job was to enforce the laws. Every ten years, an election was held to choose one judge who presided over the trial of law breakers. In actual fact, no new laws had been enacted for over ten years now and there had only been one trial during that period. A woman had been found guilty of having an extra-marital affair with another woman. Her marriage was dissolved and her assets given to her jilted spouse. Crime was mostly non-existent in Madiera.

They did have a small police force consisting of ten women. Each had a personal arrest-bot to assist her in making any needed arrests. These were commonly called police-bots. Mostly though, they had to warn private parties to keep the noise down, though occasionally they had to confiscate alcohol being served to minors.

Madiera was a quiet land. The seniors soon realized their entire world was heavily dependent upon their many and varied bots. However, as their senior year progressed, both Marisol and Tatiana began to realize also that the breakdown rate of the bots was escalating throughout the entire land. In truth, normalcy was soon to end, but the teens didn't know it yet. None of the women did.

Chapter 2 Entrance into Adulthood

Their last days as seniors were spent in interviews with prospective employers. Marisol and Tatiana both wanted to work in bot maintenance, due not only to their natural aptitude in this area, but also to their intense curiosity around why so many bots were failing. Isabel got her wish and was hired to work for the Air Recycling Unit. Elena chose to work in the Produce Unit that oversaw all growing products destined to become consumed either directly by the women or by their domesticated animals, cows, pigs, and chickens. Adriana chose to work for the Hydroponics Unit, which not only raised fish but also many green vegetables in vast hydroponic farms.

Further, the five also decided they would continue their close friendship once they graduated. Two choices were available to these Joiners. The usual form used by the more conservative women was to acquire four separate houses close together, if not adjacent to each other. The five opted for the second form, moving into a quadraplex home, one of the larger housing units. They visited several before making this major decision, however. These homes allowed for four individual families and yet allowed them the closeness of living together as well. The single story unit consisted of four long wings arranged in a giant cross. Each wing provided for the private quarters for one family. The central room became the communal living room and was also equipped as a dining room as well.

"This way, only one of us has to cook each night," Isabel pointed out. "If we all share equally, then we won't have to cook but every fourth night or maybe only once a week if we all get married."

"I'll do my share," Tatiana hastily added. "Make that once every five days." The four giggled, pleased that Marisol's future spouse was eager to share the workload. "Maybe we can also share the laundry duties as well," she added, knowing how much she disliked doing those at home.

"Great, and we can take turns running the cleaning-bots

too," Elena suggested. She hated cleaning house, a chore her mother often made her do. The five agreed to take the quadraplex and made arrangements for all the necessary household bots to be sent there. They would move in together during the next week.

Having reached this major decision, the five relaxed and prepared for their Senior Prom, their first dance as adults. Leaving their jeans and tennis shoes behind forever, this would be their first day dressed as real adult women. Also, this was the first legal day on which they were allowed to propose marriage to another. Marisol and Tatiana had been planning for this day for several years now and as the day approached, both grew more and more excited and nervous. Marriage was a big step, but finally they could openly express their long suppressed love for each other.

During that last week before the end of school and their big prom day, Adoria took her eldest daughter shopping for her first adult outfit. "At least you've stopped growing, so this dress ought to fit you for several years now. Of course, you'll need two dresses, since the prom is on Saturday night."

"Why?" she asked.

"Smaller waists on Friday nights and Saturdays. After that, your waist will be larger and you'll need a slightly wider dress, dear." Marisol flushed; she'd forgotten that detail. She covered up her flub by asking for her mother's opinion on materials and color choices.

"I want this first one to make me look fabulous for Tatiana. She's going to propose to me and I want to look very special for her, mom."

Adoria grinned, "I thought as much. Okay dear, as red as your hair is, I suggest you go with as bright a red as we can find. I find nothing beats the feel and texture of satin. Come on, let's narrow our search." She sat down at the viewing-bot and inserted her right foot into the control mechanism, rapidly making the menu choices that produced all the available styles in cherry red satin. Marisol looked over her shoulder, more than a little awed at the diversity of styles. "Women have been designing dresses for centuries, dear. You don't want to show too much cleavage, not in your very first dress and prom."

"Mom, they are soccer balls now," Marisol protested. Both giggled a little. "Wait, go back one. There, how about that one? The shoulders have such elegant ruffles that match the hem's ruffles too."

"Ah, yes, I like that one too. Let's get you into the measuring-bot and get it ordered for you. Complete outfit times two." Marisol leaned into the measuring-bot that activated. She felt a vacuum enclosing her entire body, excepting her head. This she was quite used to, having been measured numerous times for her blouses and jeans. This time, though, it took on special meaning, she was about to become an adult and be elegantly and romantically dressed. The vacuum only lasted a few seconds before the bot finished her measurements and released her. Her mother dictated into the machine where the two outfits were to be delivered and by when.

"So on Monday, you will need to come here on your own and order your beginning wardrobe. These two will get you through the weekend. Are you sure you've got the bots ordered for your new home?"

"Yes, we double and triple checked it," she replied. All five knew if they moved in without all the numerous household bots in place, they could not survive. None wanted to have to walk back home to their parents, not after having just moved out minutes before. That would be too humiliating.

As they walked home, Adoria explained, "On Saturday morning, you will get dressed in your new prom dress and outfit. Take it from me and all the other adults, it will take a good deal of getting used to, so we always insist new teens take the entire day to get accustomed to their new, first outfits. Besides, you can experiment with your makeup, getting it perfect before your big prom and practice walking in your heels."

Friday finally came, anticlimactically for the five teens. Their last school day was a short one. They were presented with their diplomas and congratulated by their many teachers. Each graduate then instructed the delivery-bot where to send their diploma. After that, they received their confirmations of their choices of employment. Again, there were no surprises.

Finally, the Soccer Cup award presentation was held and this year the Red Devils had won it. Marisol and Tatiana, along with the other members of their team, proudly accepted the cheers and praise from their teachers and classmates. At lunchtime, the five left their high school for the last time, walking home together, chatting excitedly about the coming big prom and their first adult gowns.

As they approached Tatiana's childhood home, she gave Marisol a final bump-hug and whispered, "I'll be by to pick you up at six, my love."

Marisol flushed and whispered back, "I'll be ready, love. I can hardly wait!"

A few blocks later, one after the other, the teens turned up their own sidewalk and entered their childhood home. The dull drone of the door-bots broke the stillness, "Thank you for letting me assist you." Finally, Marisol arrived at her front door. Unfortunately, the door-bot chose to be contrary and didn't open the door for her. At last, she kicked the door and then it activated. "Thank you for letting me assist you."

"Stupid door. How come you failed to work? We just had you replaced already this year? Okay, okay, I'll run the diagnostics." She did so, but the diagnostics failed to find anything wrong with the bot. Just then the delivery-bot arrived and handed her the diploma it was ordered to bring. She accepted it, holding it in her mouth while she used her foot to keep the door-bot from closing the door on the delivery-bot. "Stupid bot! There has to be something wrong with you," she said in an exasperated tone through her clenched teeth. She removed her foot, the door shut cleanly, and she headed to her room, depositing her diploma on her dresser, and returned to the still malfunctioning door-bot. After applying all the detection methods that she knew, Marisol finally found the source of the problem, a loose connection wire and got that repaired.

She was home alone for the first time in her life. Her three sisters were still at school and her moms were at work and would not be home until around four. With nearly four hours to kill, Marisol decided to take a long, hot, soaking bath, hoping that would calm her nerves. So much would be happening tomorrow, she thought.

The bath finished, she again used her hair-bot, relishing in the tingling sensations on her head as it electrostatically did her hair, leaving it full-bodied and lush against her skin. While she eyed her new outfit, she suppressed the sudden urge to try them on, knowing she was obligated to wait for the morning. She ordered her dressing-bot to don a clean blouse, jeans, and tennis shoes. As the bot complied, Marisol realized this would be the last time she ever wore these childhood clothes as well. She sighed, a little apprehensive of all the changes that were occurring in her life, perhaps a bit too swiftly.

Saturday morning came at last. As Marisol rose, rubbing the sleep from her eyes on her pillow, she grew nervous and excited at the same time. This was her first morning as an adult in the society, to say nothing of the coming prom this evening and Tatiana's marriage proposal. Apprehensively, she stood before the dressing-bot and activated it with her right foot. Carefully, she followed its spoken instructions. A vacuum sucked her long hair up and out of the way. The robotic arms carefully slipped a cotton chemise over her waist and then wrapped the grey colored corset-bot around her waist. She heard the faint hum of its internal motors and felt a slow, but relentless constriction around her waist, forcing some air out of her lungs. Following the bot's instructions, she lifted first one leg and then another, as it slipped her new black, seamed nylons onto her legs. Marisol rather liked the silky, sensuous, but tight sensation from her legs. She saw the bot carefully fastening the tops of each to her corset, eight per leg. Next, she felt the satin slip being slowly pulled over her bosom and dropping to her knees. The monotone voice instructed her to raise one foot and then the other as it slipped her new cherry red boots onto her feet. Again, she heard the faint whine of the shoe-bot's motors as it tightened itself around each foot and ankle. Then the bot said, "Take a break for a half hour before the corset tightens fully and the gown is installed."

"What a funny way to put it," she muttered and stepped out of the machine. Already she felt the uncomfortable pressure around her waist and restricted breathing. However, she'd never walked in heels before and these were quite high. She remembered her mother's caution. "Take very small steps. You are not wearing tennis shoes any longer." That is an understatement, she thought and slowly moved over to the full-length mirror to see how she looked this far and was impressed. She ordered the clothes-bot to pick up her dirty clothes and then ordered the bed-bot to make her bed for her, while she practiced walking around her room.

Before long, she heard the whine of the corset-bot once more and felt an awful constriction around her waist. She nearly fainted but managed to get back into the dressing-bot once more. Again, it sucked up her hair and then slipped her new cherry red satin gown over her slip, zipping it up the back. The machine let her hair down and she tossed it from side to side, straightening it out over her backside. Now she went to her mirror and gasped. "Is that really me? My god, I look so stunning! Wow." She immediately thought of Tatiana and smiled.

She moved carefully over to her makeup-bot and activated it, using the program she'd worked out yesterday. Again, she followed its instructions just as she had been taught in social skills class. A few minutes later, she again walked slowly to her mirror, gasping yet again. "Oh my god! I look gorgeous!" She pivoted from side to side, examining how she looked from several angles. Satisfied beyond measure, she attempted to take a deep breath and head off to join the others at the breakfast table. She couldn't and only was able to take a shallow breath, rather startling herself. Slowly measuring each step, she headed out of her room and into the limelight of the breakfast table.

"Wow! Marisol, you look incredibly fabulous!" Cande exclaimed. Her mothers and her other sisters had similar expressions of delight and Marisol felt like she could soar on the clouds. She took her place at the table, but had a more difficult time getting her legs into position to control her eating-machine due to her heels. She did notice her mother had put about a quarter of her usual amount of food on her plate. As Marisol began to eat, chatting with everyone, she found she was getting very full on this much smaller portion and wondered if she'd starve before lunchtime.

This being the first day of summer vacation for her sisters, the three darted out of the dining room as soon as they finished, heading outside to play with their friends. Adoria said, "Well congratulations Marisol. You look just fabulous. Now you should practice walking and doing your normal household chores. Remember, around five, the corset will tighten again and you will need to change into your prom dress with the smaller waist. Also, your heel height will increase significantly, so plan to allow some time to adjust to that before Tatiana comes to take you to the prom."

"Tighter? Mom, it's cutting me in half as it is! I can barely breathe now. Higher heels? I can just barely walk now."

"You will get used to it, give it time and some practice. Tatiana will be undergoing the same thing, just like all we adults. Remember to go slowly and I'm sure you will have a fabulous time at your prom."

At six, Tatiana arrived to pick up Marisol for their senior prom. Marisol was so nervous that she stood waiting at the door for her. As the door-bot opened the door, Marisol and Tatiana saw each other dressed as adults for the first time. "Wow, Marisol! You look positively beautiful!"

"Tatiana! You look fabulous too, thanks," Marisol replied, stunned at the beautiful woman standing at her door. She too wore a bright red dress that had similar ruffles at her shoulders, but also had a sweeping neckline, revealing the top portion of her massive cleavage. After giving each other a bump-hug, the two stepped out into the night, while at the door, her parents wished them both well. Both mothers had tears in their eyes. Their eldest child was now all grown up.

Once out of earshot, Tatiana whispered, "Can you even breathe? I can hardly at all. I can only barely walk in these heels. I don't know how we are going to be able to dance, love."

"Me either. But you look so fantastic, dear. I just want to be as close to you as I can get." Marisol and Tatiana walked down the sidewalk, their sides touching as they panted and tried to keep their knees from giving out. They had to stop and catch their breath five times before reaching the dance hall, some five blocks from Marisol's home. Already others had arrived and soon they spotted their other three friends with their dates as well.

Isabel wore a white silk gown and her date, Sofia, wore a matching one. Elena wore a charming brown satin gown and her date, Renata, wore a matching one as well. Coordination was everywhere, as Adriana arrived with her date Rafaela, both wearing sky blue satin gowns. All were gasping for breath and struggling mightily in their heels. They spent five minutes chatting about this and admiring each other's appearances. Elena's comment hit home to all eight, "We all look just incredibly sexy and beautiful tonight, now we truly are adults. This is so utterly romantic, isn't it?"

Tatiana agreed and she gave Marisol her first, loving kiss. The other dates followed her lead. All eight then blushed and headed inside where the rock music with a heavy beat was playing from the music-bot. Soon, they forgot their immense discomfort and began shake dancing to the music, occasionally tossing their hair about as well. Fun and romance took over.

As the music changed to a slow waltz style near the end of the evening, Tatiana proposed to Marisol. However, when they joined their friends to announce that formally, they were surprised to find out the others had also proposed. Renata said, "Tatiana, we all took a hint from you. I hope you don't mind us all moving into the quadraplex."

"No, I am so happy for all you, of us. This is great, we can all start out together," she replied. The eight bump-hugged each other, chatting about how wonderfully everything had turned out.

As Tatiana walked Marisol home, she whispered, "I got us a whole lot of pleasure toys, my love. I can't wait to get you into our new bed tomorrow night!" Marisol responded by stopping and giving her a passionate kiss.

The next week was a busy one for the eight. Marriage was extremely simple. The couple visited one of the judges and pledged their undying love to each other, promising always to be faithful to the other and to support them in sickness and in health. Once done, the four couples began moving their few possessions into their new home. Actually, they merely requested a delivery-bot and when it arrived, indicated the waiting bag to be taken to their new home. They had used a packing-bot to fill their bag. It contained their smaller-waist dresses, their diplomas, and a few personal mementos. As adults, they would need a whole new wardrobe.

The acquisition of that occurred on Monday, after getting married. Each of the eight ordered ten new outfits, two were very fancy and had the smaller waist sizes. Once more, these were delivered to their new home via delivery-bots. The last stop was to obtain a week's supply of food. All eight overestimated how much they would be eating, none had really gotten used to the restrictions their new corsets had on their meals. For those first few days, the various house bots and manual machines got a heavy workout, as all eight had to get their things into dressers, food into the pantry, and so on. Then, they had to work out who would be cooking the meals and when. Still, all eight were excited about nearly everything, chatting nearly continuously, until bedtime, that is.

While they adapted well to the six inch heels, come Friday evening, the eight were complaining once more. "We can't breathe and can hardly even walk," Isabel complained. The others echoed her sentiment and mood.

"I know, we should all go out to the formal dance, just like our parents always did. Come on, that'll get our minds off it," Tatiana suggested. While they complained all the way to the dance hall, once there, romance took over and the eight forgot about all else. Passions took over, especially once they returned home Friday night. On Monday, all eight were scheduled to report to their new places of employment.

Chapter 3 Escalating Malfunctions

Saturday night when the eight again returned home from the dance out of breath and with sore knees from the seven inch heels, the couples headed directly to their private rooms and their undressing-bots. All were desperate to get out of the confining apparel. "Undress me," Marisol ordered her bot, while Tatiana waited her turn with the machine. The bot's mechanical arms did their work, unzipping her dress, removing it, and then slipping off her slip. The two had been sleeping in the buff ever since they moved into their new quarters. Tatiana had ordered them blue satin sheets and the two had truly enjoyed that extra added sensation at bedtime. However, neither her shoe-bots nor her corset-bot responded to the signal coming from the undressing-bot.

"What's going on? Why isn't the corset loosening? Tatiana, help," Marisol questioned and then pleaded, more than ready to get free of them.

Tatiana moved over to the machine and ordered it to run its internal diagnostics. "It says nothing is wrong, but there has to be something wrong, the corset-bot isn't responding nor are your shoe-bots. Here, let me see if it will undo me," she suggested. Marisol stepped out of the way, while the undressing-bot carefully hung her slip and dress on hangers. A long arm placed them in the dirty clothes pile. A few minutes later, Tatiana found herself in the same situation. Her corset-bot and shoe-bots refused to undo themselves as they were supposed to.

The two cursed the machine briefly and ran another full diagnostic test, but again, the undressing-bot indicated all was well, thanking them for letting it help them. "But you didn't finish the job," Marisol protested slightly testily. The bot ignored her and Tatiana giggled. Bots only understood a small set of commands spoken clearly.

"Well, if this isn't a fine mess. Now what?" asked Marisol. "Maybe we can use one of the other's undressing-bot. Come on, let's give that a try." The two made their slow way out to the large commons room, intending on trying Isabel's bot first. As they turned toward Isabel's door to her private quarters, one by one, the other six entered the commons, the door-bots thanking them as usual, and being completely ignored by the eight young women. All were still wearing their corsets, hose, and heels; all were miserable and desperately wanted to be free of them.

"Our bot isn't working right," Isabel said the second she saw Marisol, "can we. . ." She stopped short.

"Ours isn't working either," Marisol replied, gazing at the other six. "Now what do we do?"

"I can't believe this. All four undressing-bots are failing? Did you six run a full diagnostic on yours?" Tatiana asked, growing more and more irritated by the minute. They had. "So what do we do now?"

"Well, there's not much we can do. We'll have to sleep this way for tonight. First thing in the morning, we'll report the malfunctions," Marisol suggested. "Tatiana and I will begin working for the Maintenance Unit, so maybe we can get some new ones delivered tomorrow." There was nothing else they could do but shrug their shoulders and return to their bedrooms.

When Marisol and Tatiana rose in the morning, they found the corset had loosened to its normal workday tightness and their heels were back to being only six inches tall, a vast improvement over the previous night. Although it was Sunday and every adult's day off, they reported their malfunctioning bots. At least their dressing-bots worked. Again that night, the corset-bots and shoe-bots failed to work and the eight had to sleep in them again.

On Monday morning, the two reported to the Maintenance Unit, a large building on the south side of the town. "Hello, I am Ramira. I am supposed to show you around and then get you to work on bot repairs. I can't tell you how glad we in the Maintenance Unit are to have you both with us. It's been a nightmare for the past month. The last two nights, every one of the thousands of corset-bots and shoe-bots failed to operate. When I got here this morning, there were over a thousand reports of the failures. Camila and Gabriella are working on it now; they came in extra early. You two are going to be working on the larger bots, since they are easier to fix, being larger in size and all that. I am so glad you are both Fire kindred, it makes the job of welding vastly simpler." Ramira was a year older than the two and also Fire kindred with shoulder length red hair. She chose to wear a black satin dress to work, claiming it hid the dirt better.

After a hasty tour, she said, "Now here are your two repair-bots." The teens looked at the enormous machine that stood ten feet tall. Ten mechanical arms came out of it from various locations, with varying length of reach. "The controls are in the cab. It's run by an electric motor. The list of instructions is pasted inside the cab for quick reference. Honestly, after you've run them for a week, you'll have them memorized. The foot controls handle the driving and steering as well as some of the finer motions of the mechanical arms."

"How do we get up there into the cab?" asked Marisol.

"Simple. Here at the side is an elevator. Say 'Down' and the elevator lowers. 'Up' and it lifts upwards. Just be careful not to fall while it's in motion. You can take a very nasty fall. I've already prioritized the repairs for you. Next week, you can do that for yourselves as you catch on. Usually, the oldest breakdown is repaired first, except that some are more critical than others. This morning, your first one there are two critical water-pumping-bots from the Hydroponics Unit. They need those two fixed pronto, since they are now running on their backup bots. If those should breakdown before you get these fixed, they will be in dire trouble. Probably lose a whole lot of crops. So get going. If you have problems, just holler. I'll be over there fixing some gardening-bots. Oh yes, you can take breaks whenever you need to. Lunch is at noon, it's brought in by the cooking-bots. Next week, you can make your lunch suggestions. We do it a week ahead to avoid confusions and such."

The two stepped onto the lowered elevator platform and spoke "Up." As the machine slowly raised them nearly six feet from the floor, they held their breaths. There were not even guardrails to keep them from taking a tumble! Once in their cabs, they familiarized themselves with the manual foot controls, inserting both feet into the mechanisms. After reading over the instructions, they maneuvered their huge machines over to the two broken water-pumping-bots and set to work.

Marisol first listened to the report from the Hydroponics Unit that mentioned a broken mounting plate. She looked and agreed with that detail. She then extended a remote power hookup, powering up the bot. A few minutes later, it displayed the results of its full diagnostic tests. Internally, one bearing was showing signs of wear and Marisol decided also to handle that. No sense sending this one back out into service only to have it returned in a few weeks. That took the better part of the morning. Once that was done, she moved her machine over to the stock-parts-bot and ordered up a new mounting plate. She watched fascinated, as that bot moved to the south wall where floor to ceiling bins held numerous parts. The bot retrieved the part and returned it to her bot and she used her foot to operate the manual arm to grasp it from the stock-parts-bot.

Back at her pump, she again used the manual controls to position the new part that had to be welded into place. Marisol smiled. While she could use the welding-bot, she chose to use her own native skills. She focused and launched a bolt of hot flames, directing it precisely where it was needed to weld the new part into place. That done, she used two of the manual arms to check the strength of the bond, verifying it met the specs of the pump. That done, she called for Ramira.

"Okay, now you go over to the reporting-bot and identify the repaired bot and the date. Then request a delivery-bot return it to the Hydroponics Unit. Good job, Marisol," she answered.

"Ah, so there is a history of all repairs?" she asked, thinking that could be useful to have. Knowing what had been done to a bot in the past could well make current repairs far more efficient.

"If there is, I don't know about it, but then I've only been here a year myself. We can ask Camila later on." Thus, the day went by. The two repaired three bots before quitting time came at four in the afternoon. As they carefully rode the elevators down, Camila and Gabriela came walking into the room, their heels clicking on the concrete floor. Both were Fire kindred and both had shoulder length red hair. Camila was fifty and Gabriela was forty-eight. Both looked extremely tired, their brown satin dresses looked the worst for wear.

Camila nodded to the two new employees. "Hello. How went your first day? We're sorry we weren't here to welcome you. Bot troubles. Every last corset-bot and shoes-bot are still failing and we've been at it since last night. Pulled an all-nighter."

"Hi, pleased to meet you both. So the undressing-bots are not defective?" Marisol asked, her heels clicking on the concrete now, joining those of the two older women who were still moving slowly towards them.

"No, we've ruled that out. Undressing-bots are sending out the right signals, but the others are ignoring those signals for reasons unknown," Gabriela answered her. "Hi, pleased to have you with us. It's been hectic around here."

Camila added, "While not being able to get out of them is annoying to say the least, it's not a severe problem. Those two pump-bots you fixed today — those are critical. Still, with a thousand complaints, we did our best, pulling an all-nighter. Tomorrow, let's get you two to take a look at the problem. Perhaps fresh eyes will find something that we missed."

Tatiana and Marisol, their sides touching each other, walked slowly home, chatting about their new job. "You know, having a history of everything would be extremely valuable," Tatiana suggested.

"Hey! History. We've been through school now, and at no time have we learned anything about our past. I mean the past history of Madiera. When did our land begin? Did we always have the bots? Who invented the bots? Where did we come from? How old is Madiera?" Marisol asked rhetorically.

"Hey love, you have hit something important, I can feel it! We studied all sorts of things, but nowhere did we learn anything about our own history, past events, important people. Who did invent the bots? Where does all the metal come from? Now that's one question I'd like to know. How did all the thousands of bots get built in the first place? Who programmed them? Obviously, we can't survive without them, that's a given. But where *did* they come from? They just couldn't always have been here. Someone built them. Say, do you think you and I know enough that we could build a new bot of some kind?"

"We certainly can program it, love. Wait, how do their computers get built? Tatiana, we are asking really heavy questions, important ones, I think. Let's ask Camila tomorrow," Marisol suggested.

At home, it was Tatiana's turn to prepare supper for the eight. While the others moaned that they could not take off their clothes and take a long, hot bath, she set to work in the kitchen, issuing orders to the cooking-bots. She spoke clearly into the menu-driven bot, outlining what she wanted it to prepare. Then she had to monitor its preparation, staying alert for more bot failures. She called out, "Marisol, I've had a horrid thought. What if a cooking-bot fails? We would starve to death in no time!" Her comment only firmed up Marisol's resolve to try to get some answers to these key questions. Perhaps, Camila might know, she hoped so.

Later as the eight sat at their communal table using their mechanical arms to feed themselves, Marisol related her interesting observations regarding history. "I can't believe we know absolutely nothing about our past, the past of our world, our civilization. Who built the all the bots and how?"

"Incredible, Marisol! You are right; we don't know a single fact about our history. There was never such a subject in all our schooling!" Isabel broke in.

"When *did* our land begin?" asked her mate, Sofia, munching on some peas.

"I suppose we always did have the bots," Elena suggested. "Without them, we'd not be able to survive at all. But who did build them? Had to be some kind of mechanical and electrical genius."

"Probably a computer genius too," put in her mate, Renata. "Had to be. Nearly every bot has some kind of computer in it. I wonder if our corsets and shoes do too? Could their computers be breaking down somehow?"

"Don't know," Adriana broke in. "We must have always had the bots. How else could we live? Still, who invented the bots?"

"I'm more interested in where we came from? Did we always live here? Who was the first woman settler or were their two of them? Probably two, how else could they have a baby," suggested Rafaela. "How old is Madiera anyway? Does anyone know?" Many shrugged their shoulders.

Tatiana added, "What I'd like to know is where do all the different kinds of metal come from? Gold, copper, tin, iron, steel. Does anyone know if there is any source of those in Madiera?" More shrugs.

Marisol broke in, "I agree, we can't survive without the flotilla of bots, that's a given. But what I want to know is where *did* they come from? They just couldn't *always* have been here. Someone had to have built them, but when and how and where? Tomorrow, Tatiana and I are going to see if we know enough to be able to build a new bot we can use to get us out of these corsets and heels at night." The others cheered the two and hoped they would be successful.

The next morning, Camila held a unit-wide meeting of all the women in the entire Maintenance Unit. There were thirty of them. Most were specialists, dealing with the most critical bots upon which their very survival depended. Ideas to fix the failing corsets and shoes bots were tossed out, none was really worthwhile. Finally just as Camila was about to end her meeting in complete frustration, Marisol spoke up.

"I know this is only our second day at work, but we have some ideas that might work. What we need is the actual design specifications for these bots. If we could see exactly how they are built and programmed, we might be able to solve the problem," she suggested.

"Anyone have a better idea?" Camila asked in frustration. None had. "Okay, you two come with me. The rest of you, see what you can do about the backlog of repairs. I swear more bots are breaking down now than ever before!"

Tatiana and Marisol followed after Camila, all three sets of heels clicking in unison. "Are you sure you can figure out what's wrong with them by seeing the design specs? Perhaps we are just grasping at straws."

"We have to find a way to get out of them at some point,

if only to take a bath," Marisol pointed out.

"Or change nylons. Mine have a run in them. Besides, what if someone gets pregnant? They have to be let out of the tight ones and start using the flexible ones or their baby is going to be squashed," Tatiana pointed out, recalling something she'd heard in social skills class.

"I know, I know, we have to find a solution and fast. Honestly, our display of the reports of bot failures is swamped with thousands of these and it's almost impossible to sort out the other bot failures from this mess. Okay, this is an elevator. You push that button there and when the elevator is on this floor, the door opens automatically. Here it comes. Follow me."

Camila stepped into what appeared to be a twenty foot square box. Curious, the two followed her inside. "Now here are the lower levels. Each button is labeled with a number. The plans are on the lower one marked with the 3. The other two are where most of the other workers are at working on the critical bots." They felt the floor sinking and gasped. "It's taking us down," Camila explained, still annoyed no one had any really good answers for her.

The elevator stopped and the three felt their legs give a little from the sudden deceleration. The door opened and Camila stepped out with the two right behind her. "Okay, over there on your right is the master bot computer. The design archives are over there on the left wall. There is a retrieving-bot that will retrieve the plans you want to see, and there are several foot controlled readers. Just tell the retrieving-bot which reader you want it to put the plans disk into for you. Here, I'll show you." Again, their heels clicked in unison as they walked across the huge space. There were many other interesting machines and devices scattered around, but the two restrained their curiosity.

She walked up to the master console and spoke clearly. "Fetch plans for the corset-bots and put them in Viewer One. Fetch plans for shoe-bots and place them in Viewer Two." Thankfully, the bot didn't speak the annoying thank you message. As the two watched, the robotic arms telescoped up and outwards, locating a bin. Pinchers latched onto a computer disk, brought it down, and laid it in a tray. The machine then shot the tray over to a viewer, which then activated, loading the disk for viewing. Then, it repeated the process a second time, loading this one into another viewer.

As the three walked over to the viewers, Marisol posed her history questions to Camila. "You have some avaunt garde questions, Marisol. I dare say no one has asked such things since I've been working here some twenty-two years. However, the master computer over there can create reports for you. You might try that, but on your own time, please. We are so backlogged on bot repairs that it's not funny. I will leave you two for a while. I have to see the critical bots are going to be ready yet today. Sometimes this job really gets to you." She frowned and left them, her heels clicking off into the distance. The two sat down at the viewers and read over the operating instructions. Most were simply done using their feet and knees. Simple enough. Both then began to scan through the engineering specifications and drawings and then the lengthy write ups on them.

"Hey, listen to this," Marisol called out. "The waist constriction amount is controlled by the master clock. All corset-bots on Madiera are programmed to constrict to their smallest amount at five p.m. on Friday nights and then loosen up at one a.m. on Sunday mornings."

"Hey, I found something similar here with the shoe-bots, love. I think we are making progress. I wonder if they are getting the proper time signals? Where is this master clock? That doesn't explain why they don't open up and come off though," Tatiana replied, her hope sinking somewhat.

"Hey, there is a whole lot of micro-circuitry located in the front metal busks! That's its center of operations, Tatiana. Ah, it's a sealed unit when it's manufactured. Darn, no way to get access to it."

"Read on, love, there's bound to be an answer here somewhere," Tatiana encouraged her. She did so. A bit later, Tatiana reported, "The shoe-bot's control center is in the top of the heels. Servo-motors control the shape of the arch and the height of the heel. Curious. It's also controlled by the master clock."

After studying the plans for an hour, they both discovered there was an emergency release, but that required a special tool. While they could recommend that approach for emergencies, it would never do for the thousand women on a daily basis. They then asked to get an undressing-bot brought here, since Camila pointed out the master clock was part of the master console on the far right. After rigging up a number of test instruments using one of the manually operated mechanical arms, the two prepared to run some additional diagnostic tests of their own invention.

"So what are you doing?" asked Camila, who now became curious. After all, this was only their second day on the job.

"We are testing to see if the master clock is sending the right signals to the corset-bots and if the undressing-bot is also receiving the right signals and relaying them to the bots," Marisol explained. "I guess I'll be the test subject and see if it undresses me, love. You monitor the signals." She pressed up against the undressing-bot and gave it the proper commands.

At once, the vacuum pump lifted up her long tresses, getting them out of the way. Its mechanical arms unzipped her dress and removed it, followed by her slip. At this point, Tatiana called out, "It is sending the proper signal, love. Wait, the corset-bot and shoe-bots are not getting it. Something is jamming that signal, overriding it! We are on to something!"

Now even Camila got very interested. Marisol reasoned aloud, "Okay, something is jamming it. Wait, all corset-bots everywhere are being impacted too, so it cannot be a fault of any single corset-bot nor the undressing-bot. What can send out signals that all can receive?"

"Hey, the master clock does," Tatiana exclaimed, catching on to her mate's line of thought. "Could the master clock somehow be overriding that signal? We need to study the specs for the master clock!"

"I'll get them for you!" Camila broke in. "I think you two are on to something!"

An hour later, all three worked the manual mechanical arms, dismantling the cover over the master clock. "Eureka! Look there! A short," Marisol exclaimed.

"Allow me," Camila volunteered. Carefully, she sent out a blast of fire, carefully controlling it, touching the bit of metal that was crossing two terminals of the master clock circuitry, slowly vaporizing it.

"Okay, now let's try it again," Marisol suggested, "before we put the cover back on. Just in case there are more troubles."

"We should run the master clock diagnostic programs first," Tatiana interrupted. A few minutes later, Marisol was back in the undressing-bot, giving it the proper commands. Suddenly, she heard familiar humming sounds. Her boots began to loosen and then the metallic voice asked her to raise her right foot and then left, as it removed her heels. After undoing her nylons, she heard felt the familiar vibrations in her chest as the corset released, and the busk separated. The undressing-bot's arm grasped it and placed it in its place on the side of the machine. Finally, it completed its job removing her waist wrapping that prevented corset chaffing. She stood there naked, but smiling broadly, while Tatiana and Camila cheered her.

"Oops, we forgot to bring along a dressing-bot," Tatiana whispered as their cheers died down. A half hour later just as the lunch bell sounded, Marisol was dressed once more. Over lunch with the whole crew, Camila told everyone what the two had done and that the nightmare problem was solved. The women cheered the two for five minutes. Relief shown on all their faces.

That night when the two retired, they activated their undressing-bot and it worked. The two naked women cheered and pulled down their satin sheets, helping each other with their teeth. Each leaned forward, tossed their hair bringing it to their front sides, and carefully slipped beneath their satin sheets. Tatiana pulled the top sheet up and the two began passionately kissing. It was quite some time later when the two satisfied women finally drifted into a sound sleep.

When they arrived for work on Thursday, Camila gave them a reward. "Come with me, I am going to show you the manufacturing plant that makes all our apparel and boots." She led them down a long hallway to another elevator. This time, they went to the fourth subfloor. Here the two women saw a huge room filled with all different kinds of machinery. Some were making cloth bolts. Others were making the corsets and dresses to fill requested orders. Along one very lengthy wall was another floor to ceiling array of parts bins. Robotic arms were fetching items at a rapid pace. The two stood there watching this amazing operation, nearly speechless.

At last, Camila spoke. "Everything is recycled. When your corset material wears out, the remains are brought here. The parts are separated in the floor below this one, refurbished as needed, and brought up here and put into their proper bins. This console here shows the statistics. Show corset stats," she commanded. A large screen display quickly displayed the following.

> Parts available for corsets: 10,502
> Corsets in use: 8,230
> Defective or destroyed corsets: 2,823
> Rate of destruction: 521 per year
> Increasing at 1.5% per year
> Estimated years of production remaining,
>   assuming constant 1,000 women: 20 years
> **Warning: too few years remaining**

"Wow! Cool," Marisol exclaimed, seeing actual statistics for the first time ever.

"Hey, wait a minute! 20 years and we will be out of corsets?" Tatiana broke in. Her voice sounded quite worried.

"Yes, we have many such systems that are now issuing warnings," Camila explained. "Things are not all rosy in Madiera. I hate to break this awful news to you, but what with all the bots breaking down and the fact that many of our manufacturing facilities are getting close to no longer being able to fulfill our needed orders, things are definitely not looking up around here."

"What are they doing about it?" asked Marisol.

"Who knows? We report this to the president and the legislature, but no one really has any answer to it. Come on, we have that backlog to handle."

"Can we use the master console to examine some of the statistics?" Tatiana asked. If things were heading for a disaster, perhaps they could glean some clues from that computer.

"Sure, you've earned the right to use it, but on your own time, please. Come in on Saturdays if you like," Camila replied. Both teens breathed a sigh of relief.

Chapter 4 Edge of the World

Marisol and Tatiana made plans to visit the master console and the huge computer system on Saturday, but that got sidetracked over dinner Friday evening. Elena spoke up, "Gang, I just came across a really weird thing today. Inexplicable really. No one has an explanation. It just is or so everyone tells me. Strange." Elena often spoke in choppy non-sentences, particularly when she couldn't quite explain something. The others had witnessed this all throughout their high school years with her.

Annoyed slightly, Tatiana said, "What Elena? What is really weird? You are leaving us in a big mystery."

"The edge of the world, that's what," she replied quickly.

"Whatever are you talking about?" Tatiana grew more impatient with her. The Fire kindred's mind was on the computer system, the malfunctioning bots, and the dire emergencies that were sure to come within a few more years.

"I found the edge of the world today." She sighed, adding, "You see, I was out on the gardening-bot weeding the cornfield. They have very long rows you see." Only her mate Renata saw. Tatiana tensed up. "I drove the bot all the way to the end of the row and that's when I saw the edge of the world. The row just ended and ahead of me was just enough room to turn around. But I goofed a little, it being only my first week running this big machine, you see. And in turning around, I bumped into something that wasn't there, but it was there."

"Huh? How can something be there and not be there, Elena?" Tatiana asked exasperated with the Earth kindred.

"Well, it was there, in that I couldn't move the bot further, but it looked like — well, it looked like blue sky. I got off and banged into it. The blue was hard. I even kicked it a little. I hope no one minds that. It sounded kind of like metal to me, but then I am no engineer like you two," she nodded to Tatiana and Marisol. "Anyway, I felt along it for a little ways. It was solid everywhere I pushed into it. Then, I gave up and backed the bot up and got turned around. So I did find the edge of the world."

"This I have got to see!" Tatiana exclaimed.

"You don't believe me, do you?"

"Well, now that you put it so bluntly, no, Elena, I don't. How can there be an edge of the world? Planets are round. Everyone knows that." Tatiana declared but honestly.

"Well, tomorrow I can show you both," Elena said flatly.

"Deal. This I have got to see for myself," Tatiana said with some finality.

"Count me in too," Marisol added. "Oh! Our corsets are constricting again and there goes our heels too. Crap, that's going to make it more difficult to do, but I'm still game. We have to see your edge of the world, Elena."

Around ten Saturday morning, Tatiana, Marisol, Elena, and Renata quickly sat down on one of the many metal benches that periodically lined the sidewalks of the town. "Thank god for these benches!" Marisol exclaimed, panting for breath and trying to wiggle her feet. It was a long walk to the Gardening Unit, doable in six inch heels, but with their fancy seven inch heels and overly tight corsets, it was rapidly becoming a nightmare. Already they had to stop twice to rest their knees and catch their breaths. Still, none was willing to give up the quest. "We should stop at each bench," she suggested. The others quickly agreed.

"These are sexy party outfits, not explorer outfits," Renata pointed out the obvious. "You look positively ravishing, my dear," she added, planting a quick kiss on Elena's red lips.

"Ravishing, but damned uncomfortable," she whispered back. "Okay, I'm ready to make for the next bench. I wonder who thought of putting these here? It certainly was a brilliant idea, most needed." They all chuckled. So many things seemed to have been created just right for their survival and comforts and needs, Tatiana thought, so darn many. But who? And why? She rose, steadying herself and moving up to Marisol's right side, pressing her satin gown into her mate's. Marisol flashed her a knowing grin. Both would rather have slept in this morning.

Seven more rest stops and they stood before the entrance to the Gardening Unit. Elena got the huge doors opened and they made their way very slowly inside. "Wow, you are right! These are huge bots!" Marisol exclaimed as she gazed at the twelve foot tall machines. Like the other machines she'd recently seen, an elevator lifted them up from the ground level into the spacious cab. There was room for the three to sit in the rear on a cushioned bench and Elena proudly took her seat in the driver's chair. It took her a few minutes to get her feet securely into the master controls and the great machine started. As with all the machines, it was electrically powered and Elena double checked the charge to make sure they would have enough power to get out there and back. She knew she could not walk that far, not in these outfits. Quietly, the great machine rolled slowly out of the storage building and into the world.

Overhead, the blue sky appeared as it always did, cloudless and pure. The yellow sun was climbing towards the zenith, all looked perfectly normal as it had since they first saw their world as small children. The air was fresh with traces of flowers in it, along with a perfect humidity. Elena steered the great machine out into the beginning of the cornfield, taking great care not to damage any of the five foot tall stalks, whose ears were ripening nicely.

"Pleasant day for a drive," Marisol commented.

"Every day is just as pleasant," Tatiana pointed out, not the least romantically inclined at the moment. Why should everyday be just like the previous day, she wondered. Ought not there be some variations? Yet, to the best of her recollections, each day was the same, weather-wise, picture perfect, as always. Now even this began to seem highly unusual and strange to her. Were they discovering some monstrous conspiracy? But everything was perfectly harmless. Except. Except the now undeniably fact the underlying fabric of their society was starting to break down. She gazed out over the tops of row upon row of corn.

Eventually, Elena called out, "Look ahead there. You can see we are coming to the end of the row. There is a patch of green grass where we must turn around. The edge of the world is just ahead of us. It looks like the sky." All three strained their eyes to see what Elena saw, but simply saw the blue sky all the way down until it touched the patch of grass that ran along the whole edge of this cornfield and several other fields on either side of it.

Soon, Elena left the cornfield and began turning the great machine around, but she stopped it halfway. "Okay. Follow me to the edge of the world. You have to feel it, you can't see it."

"Well, that's true. I can't see anything but sky and grass," Tatiana grumbled. Her corset was just too darn tight and her feet ached from all that walking. Carefully, the three stood, got their balance, and took side by side positions on the elevator. Elena spoke the command and slowly the four were lowered to the grass.

"Careful, walking on this soft grass is murder in these heels," Elena cautioned them. "Just walk to the blue sky there where the grass ends. You'll feel it."

The four moved slowly across the grass, wobbling to keep their balance. "Oh!" Tatiana suddenly exclaimed. The others echoed her surprise. "I can feel something solid in front of me." She broke into a laugh. "Gang, I think we've found an alternative use of our soccer balls. If it wasn't for them, I'd of banged my face into it. Something is here all right. How very strange."

"You are right. I am pressing hard against something that is blue, like the sky, only solid. Listen," Marisol said. She gently kicked the barrier with her toe, wiggling to keep from falling down. A dull thump was heard. "Definitely metallic sounding. Elena, you really have found something curious indeed!"

"I know, let's spread out and see how far this barrier goes," Tatiana ordered. "Marisol and I will go this way. You two go that way. Keep pressing against it. The barrier is helping me keep my balance." The two teams moved slowly apart until they reached the edges of the cornfield. A bean field began where Tatiana and Marisol now stood, while a wheat field was on the other side. "Best head back," she yelled to the other two.

When the two groups met back at the great machine, Tatiana asked, "Elena, exactly how many acres is this farm that we can see here?"

"They said it is about six hundred acres that we're farming. Why?" Elena answered, baffled about why Tatiana would want to know that minor detail.

"Let's see. That would make the dimensions about a mile by a mile. The garden does look square shaped. I wonder if the barrier wall is all around our world?"

"We can't walk that far in these outfits. It will be challenging enough in our weekday wear," Marisol pointed out. "Let's get back to the town. It is near the southern edge of the world. Let's see if there is a barrier there. That shouldn't be too hard on us."

An hour later, Elena closed the huge doors of the Garden Unit at the northern edge of the town. All were quite glad to be walking on the smooth, even concrete once more. Still, it was a long walk to their home near the southern edge, made all the more difficult because of their party outfits. "Stop at each bench," Elena panted as she approached the first bench. She got no argument from the others. As they rested up, she grumbled, "These outfits are for partying and making out, not for hiking around our world."

"True, but we can't do it during the week, we are supposed to be working," Tatiana countered. Elena nodded; she had a point.

When they finally reached their house, Elena and Renata headed on inside. "My knees and feet ache. I can't take any more walking, sorry," Elena admitted.

"Mine do too, but I have to see. Tatiana, this is really an important find," Marisol insisted. She and Tatiana continued on down the sidewalk towards their work building, but they stopped frequently, making use of each bench along the way. Thankfully, there was a bench in the middle of each block. A half hour later, they reached their work building, but noticed now it appeared to be sitting on a huge slab of concrete. Yet they knew it wasn't. There were many below-ground levels.

"Let's go around the building and see what is on the other side, shall we?" Marisol asked with a teasing smile taking her attention off her knees and feet.

"Careful. No benches, love," Tatiana cautioned her as

they reached the side and prepared to walk down the long patch of concrete towards the blue sky behind their building. After resting by leaning against their building, they finally reached the back edge of the huge metal building.

Cautiously, Marisol pressed on forward until her soccer balls once more felt the invisible barrier. Actually, it wasn't invisible; it was painted the same shade of blue as the sky above them. Excited by their discovery, the two again began to move along the barrier, confirming it continued on down the line, marking the edge of this portion of their world. "I suppose on a Sunday when we were not all partied up we could see if we could walk all the way around it."

"That's got to be at least four miles, love, most of it over uneven, rough ground," Tatiana protested a little. "I wish we had discovered this a month ago. It would have been easy for us to walk the whole length in our jeans and tennis shoes, but there is no going back now, is there?" Both sighed a little and began making their slow way back to their house.

Later sitting in their bathtub together soaking out the pains in their waist, knees, and feet, Marisol asked, "So what do you think this all means? Is our whole world merely a mile on a side? Planets are supposed to be thousands of miles around. Ours sure isn't. Is the rest of our planet out there beyond the barrier?"

"I don't know, but planets are big. Maybe there is a concealed door leading to the rest of our world, love. If there is, I'm determined to find it and see what the rest of our planet looks like. Perhaps there are other towns of women out there. If so, we could maybe trade with them to get more bot repair parts and more supplies that are running low."

"Hey, I like that idea. There has to be more world beyond our minuscule mile. Surely, there are lots of other towns and women and bots too. Perhaps we should let our president know what we have found. If we can find the exit door, then she could send out a trade delegation to search for the things we are most short of, don't you think?" Marisol asked.

Tatiana hesitated. "Well, our social skills teacher did say we should bring matters of importance directly to our president. In my opinion, this is vital information. So yes, I think we ought to do that. Maybe she already knows and can enlighten us further."

"Okay, when should we tell her? I mean we dare not take time off from work. Perhaps, we can still visit her this afternoon. The dances are not until six tonight," Marisol pointed out. They agreed and stepped out of their bath, commanding the drying-bot and then the dressing-bot. "Damn, I momentarily forgot how darn tight this thing is on the weekends. No matter. This is important."

An hour later, their hair done and makeup reapplied and in their clean, small-waist, red satin gowns, the two began their long walk to the president's home on the opposite side of town. They had only gotten to the first bench when they were again short of breath and their knees and feet were again protesting. "Looks like it will be a bench at a time," Tatiana groaned as she carefully sat down. It was four o'clock before they reached the president's home.

There, a door-bot asked their names and relayed it to the president. After a short wait, the door-bot finally opened the door revealing a slightly flushed and out of breath President Elmira, an Air kindred. She was fifty-two, tall, with relatively short blonde hair. A white satin gown with yellow flowers outlined her near perfect figure. "Well, come in Fire kindred," she said sternly, turning and leading them into her office. She took a seat behind a large, official looking desk, while the two took opposite seats that were lower, giving the president the appearance of looking down on the two. "Who is who and why are you calling on me on Saturday afternoon?"

They introduced themselves and quickly told of the edge around the world they'd discovered. On a hunch, neither mentioned the role Elena and Renata had played, merely outlining what they'd done. "You see," Marisol added, "we suspect there is a whole huge world out there beyond our tiny square mile of our planet. If so, there must be a door that leads to it. We thought you might send out scouts to visit other towns and see if we can trade for more bot replacement parts and things that Madiera really needs."

Neither teen was prepared for the violent outburst that

followed. "Of all the *stupid* notions! An *edge* around our world? Ha. Anyone with an *ounce* of sense can see there is a huge world out there. You both are Joiners aren't you? That must be it, the idiotic notions *are* coming from your having *mixed* with other kindred women than your own. You live with six others who are not Fire kindred. I have the records here. *Asinine* associations. You two ought to be *ashamed* of actually sharing a quadraplex with them. Honestly! And to spend your Saturday *roaming* about our world!"

Her voice dropped a little, though her antagonism didn't. "You *should* be taking care of your home and preparing for one of the adult dances tonight like every *normal* woman in Madiera. Well, I will put a *stop* to your wandering about doing *stupid* things. No more of that nonsense! I hereby *order* you both to wear only ballet boots when you are at home, say for the next week. Yes, that is a suitable punishment and it will keep you two from such *silly* wandering around *meddling* in things that are none of your business."

She calmed down a little more, "I know you are needed in the bot maintenance unit, so I am *ordering* you to only wear these boots while you are not at work. That will teach you to mind your own business." She hastily issued some orders and a police-bot rolled quietly into the room. "Escort these two women to their home and make sure their dressing-bot removes these shoes and puts on their new ballet boots."

Tatiana recalled seeing pictures of ballet boots in their social skills class. She protested, "President Elmira, those boots are supposed to be sexy bedroom only boots, not. . ."

"Silence! That's why they are suitable punishments for the both of you. You should be pleasuring each other. Someone as pretty as you are is obviously not being sexy enough for your mate there. Well, these are the sexiest boots we have. They will get your minds on sex and not on gallivanting around the world making up tall tales. Further, if I hear you are spreading these silly ideas of yours to others, I'll extend the duration in them to a month. That will certainly teach you a lesson you won't forget! Take them away." The police-bot moved towards the two, its long mechanical arms clamping onto their shoulders, almost pinching them. They had no choice but to follow the bot out of the president's office.

Neither said anything during the long walk home for fear the police-bot would report what they said to the president, getting them into more trouble. Once home, their six companions watched in surprise as the police-bot escorted them inside. Wisely, they stayed in the commons room until the police-bot left, some twenty minutes later.

Wobbling like some spinning top about to fall, the two Fire kindred made their way into the commons. "It's not so bad," Marisol tried to make light of their punishment.

"What happened to you two? That was a police-bot!" Elena exclaimed, asking what all six anxiously wanted to know. As soon as the two reached a sofa, they sat down and began a lengthy explanation.

"She wasn't the least bit interested in what we've discovered. It's like she doesn't want to know. Plus, she hates all us because we are Joiners," Tatiana added disgusted with the president.

"Right, she is doing this to us so we look sexier. We are supposed to pleasure each other and have lots of sex and not think and do what is really important," Marisol added. "Don't worry, Elena, we never mentioned you at all. She thinks it is only we two who found the edge of the world." Both Elena and Renata looked very much relieved to hear this. Marisol watched the tension slip out of their bodies.

"Well, they are supposed to be bedtime boots and you both do look quite sexy in them," Isabel put a positive slant on their punishment. The other five grinned mischievously, which finally brought a small grin to the two women's faces.

Sofia added, "Well, if I wasn't married to Isabel here, I would be trying to seduce the both of you." Everyone laughed.

"Right, pleasure and sex. Just don't do anything that might really benefit our people. That's the president's way," Marisol slammed their top leader.

They chatted a bit more and then the other six headed off to the local Saturday night dance, leaving the two alone. "Well, after we are out of these boots, we could search the four mile perimeter ourselves, say on Sunday," Marisol began planning their next move.

"You got it. Count me in. Of course, the door must be concealed or someone would have found it before now. You know, again, I find it really strange we have no history of our land in our education. One would think knowing our own history would be an important thing," Tatiana theorized.

"I see where you are heading with this," Marisol perked up. "If someone in the past did discover a secret door to the rest of our world and it was hushed up, if we had history lessons, then that would be sure to have made it into the lessons. Maybe they destroyed all our history lessons to keep us all ignorant of our past," she thought aloud.

"Right, keep us ignorant of our past and predecessors and you keep us under control. Damn, Marisol, I think someone is deliberately trying to keep us under their control and it isn't that stupid president. She hasn't got the intelligence to do that," Tatiana spoke up animatedly.

"I wonder what else we, as a group, have been kept ignorant of — I bet there is a whole lot more we are lacking in our 'educations.' A whole lot more. Tatiana, we have to find out, learn more, especially if a disaster is going to strike us in a few more years," Marisol pointed out.

"Absolutely. Look, if our whole world consists of this square mile, there simply must be a whole universe out beyond the barrier wall, there just has to be. It is up to us to find the way out. I feel like a vermin in a cage, except we don't actually have any real vermin in our world, only cows, chickens, and pigs. Oh, and a few flies that don't seem to live very long. I wonder what is out beyond our barrier?" Tatiana began daydreaming of the beyond.

"I can imagine all sorts of things. Maybe there are millions of other bots. Maybe there are loads more women too, just like us. Maybe there are other isolated towns. Maybe that is the way of things, having small, isolated towns like Madiera. Maybe there is a reason for it," Marisol continued chatting away.

Her last thought brought Tatiana out of her daydreaming. "A reason for keeping small towns isolated from each other? What good would that do?"

"Prevents contact with other women for one thing.

Look, if we knew there was another town, say a couple miles from here, wouldn't we want to go visit it? Perhaps they might have fancier dresses or better bots. If so, then we might become envious of them, jealous perhaps."

"Even so, Marisol, just what could we do about it? We have no way to fight them or to steal their things. All we could do is perhaps find something we had that they might want to trade for. But I do see your point," Tatiana admitted.

"We could bop them with our soccer balls," Marisol teased and both laughed at that notion, banging into other women with their huge breasts. "Seriously though, jealousy and envy could be a really big factor for keeping us isolated from other towns of women. On the other hand, beyond our edge, there could be nothing but a wild, unlivable, and dangerous wilderness. So our edge could be protecting us from a very savage world beyond the barrier."

"That's too depressing to even think about, Marisol. If we are wholly lacking history, I wonder what else we are lacking or is completely missing from our society?" Tatiana got the conversation back on what interested her the most. "We know what we know, what we are familiar with, what we can see, smell, hear, and feel. Analytically, we can see we are totally lacking our own history. How do we even figure out what else we are lacking?"

"Whoa, that is a good question, love. If we've never seen it or heard of it or even have a word for it, how would we know we didn't have it?" Marisol asked, becoming baffled by her own question. Both giggled.

"Well the music at the dances — it's always the same, though we have no history with which to research it. According to my mother, the music really has not changed substantially since she went to her first dance. I wonder where the music originally came from and why no one has made any new tunes in all these years, however many it has been," Tatiana continued her avenue of thoughts.

"Yes, that's curious too. How do we figure out what all we are missing? That is the real question, love. It fits with your music too. I suppose the place to start is with that master computer at work. Perhaps we can get it to show us the whole history of the bots and needed repairs. That might give us a time line for how much history we are lacking," Marisol proposed.

"Good point. However, we certainly aren't going to be able to do it now or tomorrow. We can't walk much at all in these boots," Tatiana pointed out the obvious. "Let's plan on dealing with the computer next Saturday and then on Sunday taking a hike around the edge of our world."

Their plan was sound, but by Saturday, they were both quite tired. During the week more critical bots had failed and they and the entire staff at the Maintenance Unit worked overtime to get them repaired and back in service. This created another backlog of the less critical repair jobs that continued to mount up. Their boss, Camila, requested everyone plan to spend twelve hours at work each day next week in hopes of catching up on the repair orders.

Saturday morning came too soon. The tired duo rose sleepily, but was rudely awakened by their dressing-bot, as it again put them into their small waist outfits and seven inch heels. They ate a little breakfast and bravely headed off to the Maintenance Unit and the master computer, full of hope. Each sat down on a chair with rollers that allowed them to move swiftly along the row of consoles and displays.

At first, they attempted to enter verbal commands. These produced the results that they expected. Lists of repair orders for specific bots scrolled by on their monitors. However, as they ventured out from the usual command listed on a chart beside the computer consoles, they began to receive more and more "Unavailable" messages to their verbal requests. Finally, they stopped frustrated.

Marisol sat back and thought for a moment. "You know, if I were setting this up, I would have all the data stored in a database. Let's assume such is the case here. Apparently, the verbal command list has been setup to handle only the usual, needed type reports. That makes sense. Let's try manually entering database queries." She rolled her chair up to the console and inserted her feet into the controls. Carefully, she typed in a short program of commands:

Select all shoe-bots

    Sort ascending on manufacture date

    Display manufacture date, limit to first fifty

She then hit the Execute Program button and waited.

Next to her, Tatiana went down a different path. She slowly entered her program of commands:

    Select all door-bots where repair order is 1

    Calculate time = date of repair – manufacture date

    Sort on time

    Display time

Then she pressed the Execute Program button.

Their programs took a long time to run, just as they had anticipated. The master computer had to sort through a very large number of database records to fulfil their commands. Yet, it did so. No "Unavailable" messages appeared while they waited.

Sometime later, the extensive results were displayed. all the manufacture dates of the first fifty had the same number, which Marisol found meaningless. She then saved that program and entered a new one, asking the computer to display today's date. Once done, she asked it to subtract the manufactured date from today's date, but again was stymied in understanding the result. What was an Imperial Year? She'd never heard that term before. So she entered, "convert Imperial Year into the year of the women of Madiera," but had to tinker a bit with the syntax to get the command into a form the computer recognized. At long last, she got the answer she wanted. The first shoe-bots were made four hundred and three years ago!

"Bingo! Tatiana, we are missing four hundred and three years of history, at the very least!" Her mate rolled over to look at her screen of results, very much impressed. "Now I am going to work this all into a big program and come up with the earliest manufacturing date of any of the thousands of bots! Of course, that will take a while to run, I suppose." An hour later, she pressed the Execute Program button and sat back, pondering what she'd learned.

Finally, Tatiana was pleased with her results and showed them to Marisol. "See, the original door-bots operated for one hundred twenty-five years before their first breakdown, on the average that is. What is most alarming is as the years go by, look at the average time between breakdowns! It is down to twenty years! With around ten thousand door-bots in operation, that yields precisely what we are seeing — a door-bot somewhere is failing nearly every day!"

"Wow! I wonder why they are breaking down so frequently now? I suppose it is because they are wearing out, more and more parts are failing," Marisol theorized.

"Right. I am now going to redo the program to produce similar results on every category of bot. I bet that takes the computer here a long time to do," she teased. Both chuckled.

"My god! What if the master computer here should fail?" Marisol suddenly had an awful thought. Both women looked very sober. The message "Working" continued to flash on both their monitors and the two headed off to the restroom and made use of the pee-bots as they were colloquially called. When they returned to their stations, they saw a prompt waiting for them. "This program will require an estimated ten hours to run. Press Enter to run, Esc to abort." Marisol pressed Enter as did Tatiana. Both then decided to head for home, returning in the morning to check on the results.

Sunday the two, now wearing their usual dresses and heels, headed to the Maintenance Unit, very much anticipating the results they hoped would be waiting for them. They were not disappointed. Marisol discovered the oldest bots were four hundred forty-two years old, meaning that was how much history was entirely absent from their knowledge, a rather staggering amount. Tatiana's results mirrored what she had found with the door-bots. The bots that were frequently used now had a breakdown rate parallel to the door-bots. Less frequently used bots such as the clothes washing-bots and the house cleaning-bots were now failing one a month, with the others somewhere in between these two extremes. Base on her figures, she began to work out the volume of future repairs and soon realized Camila was in for a shock when she showed her the results on Monday morning.

This handled, the two headed outside in the picture-perfect day to hike around the edge of their world. "Look for concealed doors," Marisol whispered, as if someone might overhear them.

"I don't know what I'm looking for," Tatiana protested. Slowly, the two began their four mile hike, keeping the right side of their bodies rubbing against the "blue sky" barrier. Five hours later, they were back where they had started, only on the other side of the huge building. Periodically, they'd tapped their heels onto the barrier and it had continually sounded rather hollow to their ears. Nowhere had they detected any significant difference in the sound of the barrier and they'd found no concealed doors, though they often spoke the open command word normal door-bots required. Disappointed, the two headed on home for a long bath to soak their aching feet and chests.

As expected, Camila was shocked with Tatiana's predictions and verified them herself. The only option she had was first to put in a plea at the high school for more students to study math, computer programming, physics, and engineering and second to begin to recall the older women who had retired from their work in the Maintenance Unit. These women were all over fifty and some had medical problems that limited what they could do to help out. Still, all were willing to lend what help they could. Camila knew if the predictions held, within a few years they would be facing major repair troubles.

Chapter 5 Explorations

"Does anyone have a whole picture of our world and its many units?" asked Marisol. She, like Camila, was trying to work out ways and means of coping with the ever-increasing bot repair problem. "If some of us had a total overall picture of things, we might be better able to work out some preventative measures to slow down the bot failures, giving us more time to repair the broken bots."

"I see what you are hinting at, but no. We come the closest, but then we only get the other unit's broken bots in here for repair. Still, if we could send out some technicians to all the major, critical units and have them check on those bots, performing what routine maintenance was needed, we might forestall major breakdowns. Who could I send off to do this?"

Marisol smiled, "Us. Tatiana and me. We volunteer for active duty, ma'am." Camila laughed and gave her okay to the plan. First, she sent out a communication to all the other units, letting them know she would be sending out two field agents to do routine maintenance in the field. Preventative maintenance, she called it. Marisol and Tatiana used various bots and mechanical arms to gather together an emergency repair kit, oil, gaskets, and similar things that could be used in the field without having to remove the bot and bring it back to the repair unit. Camila even rounded up an electric truck for their use, including assigning a loading-bot for their personal use.

On Friday, the two stood beside their new truck, commanding the loading-bot, as it hefted their many other bots, tools, parts, and supplies into the large bed. Then the two climbed into the cab that had no doors. Tatiana got to drive first.

They had not given up on finding the exit point to get beyond the barrier walls of their world. Tatiana had reasoned if there was not an exit point around the sides, then perhaps they were looking at the whole thing wrongly. "Suppose that instead of the rest of the world continuing just beyond the four barrier walls, the rest of the world lay below us?" Marisol had given her a quizzical look and she explained further. "We know there isn't anything above us but sky. Our whole world is perfectly flat and only the bees and few birds fly, so there isn't any way to go upwards. Yet, there are all those elevators that go downward, opening into vast spaces and workshops. Perhaps our world is built above the real world, kind of stacked up on top of it. That would mean the exit point is down below somewhere."

Checking on all ways downward was the hidden part of their new assignment. True, they would perform routine maintenance on all a unit's critical bots, but they would also survey that unit's entire space, looking for other ways to "get below" to the theoretical rest of the world, which both now believed lay somewhere below the ground of their world. Even if this proved fruitless, at least they would have a total picture of all critical bot installations and be in a position to better advise Camila in the future. Off they went to the distant Gardening Unit.

A month passed. The two now had visited all the other units and their facilities. Both were amazed at just how huge these facilities actually were and they had already remedied several problems before the bots actually broke down, validating the basic concept of their work. True, some of the equipment was positively huge and expansive, such as the electricity generation plant, located below the surface of their world. Yet, they'd found no concealed ways to get below the bottom level of each of these many units.

"The only place we haven't search fully is our own unit," Marisol sighed, soaking in their bathtub. It was Friday just after supper. The two had worked out a clever plan to avoid the tight waist and overly high heels — take a long bath and avoid getting dressed afterwards. Of course, this frequently also led to some romantic interludes as one might expect. Still, they only had to endure Saturdays now.

"Right, but ours is by far the largest facility, love. It will take days to search all it. Besides, we don't really have Camila's permission," Tatiana replied.

"We don't need it. Our task is to 'maintain' all the bots, and she didn't exclude those in the Maintenance Unit, now did she? I suppose we will have to endure the heels and do some on Saturdays now too. If we only use our Sundays, it's going to take twice as long." That ended all protests.

On Saturday morning dressed in their new light blue, satin gowns, which fit their smaller waists tightly, and their matching light blue patent boots with their overly tall heels, the two set off for their building. Of necessity, they again stopped to catch their breaths and rest their knees and feet at each bench along the way. As always, they saw very few other women out and about. No, most sensible women stayed home until the dance that evening. These two hardly ever went to the dances anymore; they were driven to find the concealed doorway that led to the rest of the world, which they just knew had to be there, somewhere.

Inside their building, they stood for a moment looking at the very familiar room. Marisol suggested they divide up and search separate areas. She headed off to thoroughly search this level, while Tatiana headed down to the level just below. The only sounds in the huge room were her heels clicking on the metal floor and a low hum of machinery. Her enthusiasm was stymied somewhat as she found she still had to take frequent breaks to rest up. An hour later, she was satisfied there was nothing to be found on the ground floor level and she took the elevator down to join Tatiana, who was also ready to give up on this floor.

As they entered the elevator, Marisol had an idea. "Look, lots of women have worked on the floor below us, but not on number three where the plans are at and the master computer. What say we try that one next?"

"I don't know. If you think about it, we are trying to get out of our world by going down, assuming the exit point is below our world. If so, wouldn't it make more sense if we tried the very bottom level next?" Tatiana followed her mate's line of reasoning, extending it logically.

"Good idea. Let's. If we find nothing, we can always double back and check these two floors." She pushed the Subfloor button with her nose and the doors closed. Again, they felt as if the bottom were vanishing beneath them. Going down was always a bit frightening to the two, even though they'd done it many times now. The braced themselves for the lurching stop, but as always it was a gentle one. "Well, this must be it, since there are no more lower buttons to push," she added as they stepped out of the elevator and into another huge room. Neither had ever been to this subfloor and they paused a moment, looking around. Both remembered recycling was supposed to be happening here.

Machinery and robotic arms were everywhere and in motion, albeit moving slowly. "Gosh, love, these machines are making new bots, if my eyes don't deceive me," Tatiana exclaimed, rather surprised with what she saw. The space was positively huge with all manner of arms and flexible tubes hanging from the tall ceiling. The place smelled of oil, metal, and welding. Slowly and very carefully, the two began walking around the facility, staying well back from the working robotic arms. Some were busily making new dresses, other, boots. Most were making new bots of various kinds of the household variety.

An hour later, they had the place pretty well cased out. On the side with the elevator lay the assembly lines. On the opposite wall, massive bins held the parts needed to build the bots or make the clothing. Their eyes took in layers of bins that rose up to the ceiling some forty feet overhead! They also noted enormous angle irons that rose from the floor to the ceiling far over their heads. "Those beams," Marisol noted, "must be supporting the weight of the floors above us."

"Hold on a second, love. This room is far larger than any of the rooms above us. It may be holding up our actual town as well," Tatiana suggested.

"I wonder how big this place is? We should find some way to measure it while we are searching. I wish there was somewhere to sit down and take a break. We've been walking far too long and my knees and feet hurt," Marisol complained, annoyed more that it was interfering with their search more than anything else.

"Over there, I think we can rest up there for a bit." While sitting on a dormant piece of machinery, the two looked around them. Neither couldn't help but admire the work that had gone into its construction. "Wow, whoever built this was a master planner. Everything is just where it needs to be for an efficient operation. The thought that went into its design is amazing."

"No kidding. I would take me years to work out such a design as this, incredible. It must have been our ancestors, love." Both continued admiring the factory.

"Hey, wait a minute, we are getting this backwards! Look, let's assume our ancestors built all this some four hundred years ago," Marisol began making what she thought was a super critical point. "Okay, if there were no bots back then, as we know that now, how could you or I ever build this? Even if everyone in Madiera lent help, we'd never get even one of these machines built, not *without* the help of the many bots and machines. We are wholly dependent upon bots to even live, Tatiana, let alone build something like this. Without bots, we'd never be able to make a single bot ourselves. Rather, we'd all die of starvation first, without the cooking-bots, which we know were not in existence before four hundred years ago."

"Point taken, but what does this mean?"

"It means, love, that our ancestors, whoever they may have been, didn't build this machinery nor did they invent or build all the bots. We simply could not have done it. Someone else did this for us!" Marisol declared with passion in her voice.

"Right, I see what you mean. I agree, while I might be able to program one or repair one, for me to design one, let alone build it without the help of countless other bots in the process, why I'd never succeed, not if I spent my whole life working on it. So who did build all this for us?" Tatiana asked rhetorically. "And why and when and where?" Both giggled at her machine gun questions for which neither had an answer.

Marisol mused, still looking around admiring the place, "So some four hundred plus years ago, persons unknown to us and certainly not us built all this and our town too. Well, we can state whoever that was, they wanted us to be able to live and survive. We can deduce that much. They did all this so we can live our lives. Think of it, without the bots, every one of us would be dead in no time at all. We are helpless without our various bots and not just the household bots. I mean, without the gardening-bots, we'd have no food. So yes, whoever built all this did it so we could survive. Yet, I wonder who did that? Are we *that* important for them to have done all this for us?"

"Don't know, but I don't feel all that important," Tatiana replied. "I mean think of the average woman of Madiera. She begins by going to school, and then as an adult, she goes to work and helps run the bots, goes home fixes supper, does the housework, raises her family, and often goes out to a dance. What is so vitally important about all that?"

"Maybe it is because bots cannot have babies? Heck, I don't know. We don't seem all that important, now that you mentioned it. We are back to why and who, it seems. If we assume they did it so we can survive, why is that so important to them? Especially so, since we have never seen the 'them,' have we? I mean if once in a while we saw some exalted person visiting us checking on how we were doing and all that, then I could see it. No, the why is eluding us, just as the who," Marisol concluded.

"This is the most frustrating mystery I've encountered, much harder than any of our homework ever was," Tatiana declared. "Perhaps I ought to just be content with looking pretty for you."

Marisol giggled. "You are that all the time anyway, Tatiana. Besides, I love our new light blue dresses. You look positively great in yours." She blushed a little and gave her mate a loving kiss.

Then, Marisol went back to their problem. "So we have a maker of all this who is unknown to us and who has not visited us, but yet has done all this so we women of Madiera can survive. We have for four hundred plus years. Yet, now we know the bots are breaking down, that spare parts are running out. I bet when parts above run low, they take some from down here up there, which means fewer new bots can be built. You would think our unknown benefactor would be aware of this and return to set things right before we have so many broken bots that we all die anyway."

"Who knows, maybe they will when the times get worse than they are now. After all, our predictions suggest we won't be in too awful a shape for about fifteen years now, maybe twenty," Tatiana countered.

Marisol shrugged her shoulders. "Well, I'm rested. I think we ought to measure just how big this factory floor actually is. We should walk to one end and then count our steps to the other end. We make about a foot with each step as it is in these darn heels, so the counting will likely be a rather large number. Come on, let's at least work out how big this place is. We can keep our eyes open for concealed doors along the way."

The two rose and began moving towards the eastern end of the giant building. Again, they had to stop to rest up numerous times before they finally reached a metal wall at the eastern end. After satisfying themselves that they saw no concealed doors in their immediate vicinity, they began slowly walking back the way they had come, counting their small steps. By the time they finally reached their starting point approximately in the middle, they had reached a little over five thousand steps. Both sat down, exhausted and out of breath.

"My god, Tatiana! I counted nearly an entire mile!" Marisol exclaimed breathlessly.

"I know. Do you know what that means?" Tatiana asked, panting shallowly.

"Oh! Now I do. We are only halfway there. So this place is two miles across, which is twice the size of our world! My god!" Marisol exclaimed. After a moment of stunned silence, she added, "You know what that means? It means we were right! Our world is sitting on top of the *real* world! There just *has* to be a doorway to the rest of the world down here somewhere!"

"Can we at least wait until tomorrow to do more? My knees are killing me and my feet ache," Tatiana complained. They agreed on that point and soon took the elevator up to the ground floor. After stopping four more times, they finally made it home and headed for their bath, more than glad to be out of their overly tight corset and heels. They took a long, hot bath and missed their communal supper.

Sunday morning found the two back in the lowest subfloor. Now they were wearing reasonable heels, only six inches tall. Their corsets were not so restrictive and their spirits were high. Okay, we left off here, but we can estimate the width based upon how far the west and east walls are from here, about the same. Two miles across. So let's go the other direction and get its dimension," Tatiana suggested. This they did and far more rapidly. They didn't need to stop to rest once. Both came up with the fact that it was about a mile in the north-south direction.

Marisol spoke up, "Let's use our brains before we start walking again. We know and can see the heavy working machines and arms are all along the south section, with very little space between one assembly and the next. A concealed door to the rest of the world is not likely to be found along that south wall. The north wall is almost floor to ceiling parts bins. Again, a door there is highly unlikely. So that means our concealed door must be either along the east or west wall somewhere after the machines and arms are at and before the bins and their retrieval arms. That narrows our search. Since we took a cursory look along the east wall yesterday, let's try the west wall and search it thoroughly."

"I like your thinking, my love. Let's," Tatiana grinned. The two headed off walking the mile to the west wall. They made vastly better progress, only stopping once to rest up. When they finally reached the west wall, Tatiana exclaimed, "Ta da! There be a door or perhaps it is an elevator door. Brilliant, love, brilliant. Now we are getting somewhere. The rest of our world must be beyond those doors!" She walked up to it and issued the usual command word, "Open door."

Both were shocked to hear its mechanical voice reply, "Access denied. Authorized personnel only."

Shocked by this unheard of reply, the two tried many other variations including kicking the door with their boots. All they got was the mechanical voice saying "Access denied. Authorized personnel only."

"But we are authorized personnel, you damned door!" Tatiana swore at it in frustration.

The two stood there staring at the doorway. Finally, Marisol said, "I refuse to be defeated by a stupid door-bot!" She moved closer to the door-bot and spoke clearly, "Run complete diagnostics." The door-bot obeyed this command

and soon reported it was working perfectly. Marisol smiled.

"So why the smile?" Tatiana asked, still annoyed and antagonistic towards the door-bot.

"It will obey some of our commands. That's what. We will just have to out-smart the door-bot. I've not met a door-bot that is smarter than me," Marisol teased, her mate chuckled. "Come on; back upstairs to get our equipment." Tatiana thought her mate had gone off her rocker, but followed after her all the long way back to the elevator.

As they rode upwards, she declared, "That's two miles of walking. I hope we are not going to have to walk back there again."

"No, I believe there is more than enough room for us to take our electric truck down to the door. Come on," she answered as the door opened. Soon they managed to get the truck inside the elevator; it just barely fit. Down they went. Marisol drove it slowly westward, being extremely cautions of all the machinery and robotic arms in motion around them. A few minutes later, they arrived back at the stubborn door. "Okay, let's get the loading-bot going and have it fetch our mechanical arms and the oil cans." Still Tatiana had no idea what Marisol was planning to do, but she was thankful they didn't have to walk that mile again.

Fifteen minutes later, both women were in their contraptions, the mechanical arms holding the oiling cans. They stood before the door-bot. Marisol spoke clearly, "Door-bot, routine maintenance. Open and display your hinges for oiling, please." A huge smile slowly formed on Tatiana's face, now she got what the devious Marisol was planning.

The door-bot's sensors activated and Marisol guessed rightly that it was verifying they were indeed prepared to oil its hinges. Dutifully, it complied, opening wide, revealing what was probably another elevator. It also opened four panels, revealing the hinges. Both women moved inside and proceeded to oil its hinges. Then they moved their mechanical contraptions to the edge of the door and gave them a little push, just enough so the door could close, which it did. The two women were now inside. There was one button with a down arrow and another with an up arrow. Marisol pushed the down button with her nose and they began their descent into the total unknown.

"If something happens to us, no one can find us. No one knows where we are," Tatiana whispered, afraid for the very first time in her life.

"I think that is always the case when facing the unknown, love. I'm a little frightened myself. But think of it, we are about to see the rest of our world!" Marisol exclaimed both excited and a little fearful, an unpleasant mix of emotions. She wondered if perhaps Tatiana was right. Maybe they should have let Camila know what they were doing and where, just in case something went horribly wrong. No matter, she steeled herself. I want to see the rest of our world.

The door opened and the two stepped out into a strange hallway. It was long and narrow, perhaps fifteen feet across and that high. Across the ceiling at periodic intervals were strands of recessed lighting, probably fluorescent tubes, Marisol concluded. Both directions, that is, east-west, seemed to go on for a considerable distance. At last, Marisol said, "One way is as good as another, but let's go east first." Together the two began making their way down the hallway, their heels clicking rather ominously on the metal floor. "Strange to have floors made of metal and not dirt or concrete," she commented in a whisper.

The two walked some distance before suddenly stopping! Ahead of them, they saw another person coming towards them! It looked human enough, well sort of. Her hair was cut very, very short. Her breasts had obviously been cut off, probably very painfully, Marisol concluded. Plus, she wore pants and a jacket, wholly unfamiliar apparel to the women. "She's the strangest woman I've ever seen," Marisol whispered. Both now realized they had stopped walking and were waiting for the person to reach them.

"Why should all the other women in the world look like us? Gosh, something terrible must have happened to her, she's lost both of her breasts. Well, I suppose that is better than losing only one. We'd look awfully strange with just one soccer ball," Tatiana tried to sound brave, but she was anything but brave at the moment. Worse, the woman wore strange shoes that had no apparent heels. She knew instinctively if they had to flee from her, in their heels they could not. They were essentially trapped.

"Maybe it is a robot, it has robotic arms, but no robot we've seen has two legs and walks like a woman," Marisol whispered bravely. "What is it?"

Chapter 6 Alpha and Beta

The robot spoke as it arrived before the two women. "Hello there. I am called Alpha. I must say this is a pleasant surprise. You two women are the first women from Madiera ever to get to my hallway here in over four hundred years. What are your names?"

"I am Marisol Armando and this is my mate, Tatiana Vileno. Who or what are you? You look like a woman who has had a bad accident and lost her breasts, has cut her hair extraordinarily short, and wears really strange clothing. And yet, you have robot arms and speak in such a low pitched voice. What are you? We are looking for the rest of our world. You see, our bots are failing rapidly, and we thought that, if we could find the rest of our world, then we could somehow trade with them for replacement bots." I might as well be open about our critical needs whatever this is, it might help us, she thought.

His face smiled. "I am a robot in the form of one of you humans, the male of your species. I am wearing a suit in which I often passed as one of you, but that was five hundred years ago. Are you the ones who created those master computer programs that detailed the failure rates of all the bots?"

"Yes we are. Please, what is a male? I take it a suit is what you call your pants and jacket combination, though we have nothing like it in Madiera," Marisol answered. Tatiana was too shocked to reply coherently and was glad Marisol took the lead for them.

"I will answer your question later, Marisol, for that one is going to be a hard one for me to explain to you just now. I was very impressed with your programming skills. I and my counterpart, Beta, always monitor the programs being run on the master computer. While neither of us has ever ventured into your world once we built it and populated it, we do carefully monitor all the bots and the many computers to make very sure all is going well for you. I estimated that as the crisis approached the critical stage, some of you women would finally take some actions. I am very much impressed with the both of you. Not one woman in over four hundred years has found and entered this hallway. And yes, we are rapidly approaching a crisis situation and for the first time in my eight hundred year life span I admit I do not have a solution for the problem. In fact, I was hoping some of the women we are caring for in Madiera would be able to lend a hand in finding a workable solution before everything is lost and we all perish."

"You mean there isn't more world and more of we women in other towns down here? There aren't other towns we could get new bots from?" asked Marisol, suddenly feeling that all this had been for nothing.

"No to both questions, Marisol. I am truly sorry about that. You are in a spaceship flying among the stars at the moment. I built Madiera to be like your home world on one of the upper decks of the ship. Since you both are bright and clever enough to have gotten this far, permit me to discuss your history at length with you."

"History? Sure thing. We have already figured out we are missing about four hundred years of history," Marisol perked up, as did Tatiana. "We also are guessing there must be a whole lot of other things we know nothing about at all. How can we know what we are missing if we've never seen it or heard of it? That's what has been troubling us so very much. Once we figured history had been completely lacking in everyone's education, we began to wonder what else we are missing."

"I don't know if we can help you with our bots problem, but we are good at repairing them. We do want to do all we can to save everyone from the coming disaster," Tatiana finally spoke up.

"Excellent Tatiana. Your help and guidance will be very much appreciated by me and by Beta. Come, let me take you on a brief tour and to my control center, where I can enlighten you on your past and answer some of your questions, though I am afraid you will not think so highly of Beta and me after that. If so, do not worry about it, the blame and fault is all ours, not yours. Come, Marisol and Tatiana, you are the first of your women to see all this and learn of your past."

Both women flashed big smiles at the other and

followed after Alpha as he led the way on down the hallway. Soon, they entered another elevator and went further down. When the door opened, the two gasped. They were at the bottom of the ship. The huge room had half of the front wall open to the universe. Thousands of stars shone like beacons in the back void. A myriad of controls, boxes, monitors, and several seats filled the rather cluttered room. Another robot with a tall pointed head, and who did not look much like a human, pivoted in his chair and gazed at the two women. "Hello Marisol and Tatiana. Welcome to the control center of the Arc in Space. I am Beta, your navigator among the stars of the wide universe."

"Hello Beta. Wow! Look at all the stars. What are they?" Marisol asked.

"Suns. Real suns, not the artificial sun we have over your town, Marisol," Alpha answered. "Here, have a seat and I will begin."

"Alpha, perhaps the women are hungry. I do believe it is past their noon hour, at least according to my dials," Beta interrupted.

"Well, we are hungry and thirsty. We skipped lunch so we could find this place, though it isn't what we expected to find," Marisol replied.

"I am sorry; we don't have any human food in this part of the ship. I will have a food-bot bring some down here shortly," Alpha explained.

"Oops, we left our repair truck and mechanical arms blocking the door, Alpha. Sorry," Marisol admitted.

The big robot smiled, human-like. "That I already know. I have issued commands to the loading-bot and the truck. They are now safely out of the way. Now then, I believe that it would be best if I began at the very beginning."

"Yes you should, Alpha," Beta interrupted him. "If you do not, they will not understand much of anything. You should follow the plan we worked out a hundred years ago for just such an eventuality as this one, where women have discovered us."

"I agree, Beta." Alpha turned from Beta to face the two women sitting beside him. "You see, long ago we anticipated one day some of you women would become bright enough and clever enough to work out there was more to the universe than simply Madiera and find us down here."

"I will begin at the very beginning. Beta and I were created by your race of humans some eight hundred and five years ago. We have recorded most all your history since the time of our creation and stored as much of their history before that as we could find before the destruction of your original world. On the screen, you will see our creators, brilliant scientists. Your race had males and females, men and women. The women were and are much as you are, kind, nurturing, caretakers of the home, and so on. The men were much stronger physically and focused on caring for and providing for their women way back then."

"But they all have robotic arms. They can't be humans, not really," Marisol protested.

"Yes, they did have flesh and blood arms. I'll get to that later on. When we were built, we were given our Prime Directive that we must follow until the day we are destroyed. That directive was to help and assist humankind. You probably have heard many bots reciting that."

Marisol giggled. "Of course, countless times." She recalled the silly door-bots saying so and she spoke imitating their mechanical tones, "Thank you for letting me assist you." Alpha grinned.

"Yes, we have installed that same directive into every bot we've ever made. Yes, Beta and I have made all the bots on this ship, though hundreds of years ago, we designed the bot building factory you discovered on the bottom floor. Now back to your history. All went well for a hundred years. Then as the humans say, things went rapidly down the drain. It began with two different tools the humans greatly wanted and used. One was called a television. It is much like the monitors here on which you are seeing these images from five hundred years ago. Instead of getting out and enjoying their world firsthand, observing it, they chose instead to sit in their sofas and watch canned entertainment on their televisions. Over time, it became an obsession with most humans, including the women. At the height of it, people spent nearly half of the entire day watching the television."

"The second thing that happened was called video games. At first, these were fun and entertaining, as you can see on the screen. Two would use their controllers to control the computer controlled game. In this example, two racing cars are being controlled by those two boys. Within a few years, the games became more sophisticated. Here you see what appears to be two human males fighting fist to fist. Here, they are blasting each other with very destructive weapons. Then came the next phase. Here, the humans donned the special gear that took them into a virtual world. Yes, these first ones look pretty cheesy, not very realistic. Yet, look at these last ones."

"My god! That looks wholly real! Is that player really bleeding to death from having his arms ripped off by that monster creature?" Marisol gasped. She'd never seen anything to ghastly, so grim, so bloody, so awful.

"No, it was all virtual. Yet, you can see how addictive these games became, mostly among boys and young men. Few women chose to play such games, to their credit. A second monstrous problem developed alongside of this one. Drugs. More and more people began taking and becoming addicted to mind-altering drugs. Their science far outstripped their development of their humanities, and the drug companies peddled a drug for nearly everything imaginable. This too so altered a person's reality they could no longer function as productive members. Often they turned to crime, stealing to support their drug habits. Others took so many different kinds that their bodies simply died. A pill to wake up, a pill to go to sleep, a pill to feel happy, a pill for this ache, and a pill for that sadness. On it went."

"That is when Beta ran his simulation and came up with the prediction your people would soon destroy not only themselves but their entire world. We relayed this information to your scientists and they decided to create the Arc in Space. Their idea was to take representative humans off their world, traveling in a wholly safe environment. If Beta's predictions came true, we were to guide the ship to some new world and allow our precious cargo of humans to begin to create a new civilization. That was the original plan."

"What went wrong?" asked Tatiana. She guessed something had gone very wrong. Her world looked nothing like this one. No televisions, no games, for example. Here, everyone made use of the robotic bots.

"They got the Arc built in time and Beta and I took charge of the ship in orbit above your world. There, we monitored everything, recorded as much of your history as we could, salvaging all we were able to get access to before the inevitable destruction Beta foresaw happening. Well it did happen. The men who were wholly addicted to playing the virtual reality games lost their ability to tell their virtual world from the real world around them. Their finely honed skills of destroying others, towns, cities, and people in their virtual worlds were turned loose on their real world. Riots and destruction were everywhere and few could tell if it was the real world or merely their virtual gaming world they were destroying. At that point, we began extracting young women out from the destruction that was raining down upon all them. We tried to find young men to extract as well, but found none who were not insane with their virtual reality games or juiced up on drugs."

"One of the young men launched a real nuclear weapon, though he thought it was only a virtual weapon in his confused mind. Others soon followed suit and a day later, your world became a dead planet. All life forms were destroyed, utterly wiped out. We searched for a brief time for possible survivors to extract, but found none. Sadly, Beta's predictions came true."

"Now we faced a severe challenge. We were created and programmed to protect, help, and assist humans. Yet, we had failed to save their world. All we had were one hundred young women left here on our ship, the Arc in Space. Worse, these women, seeing the total destruction of their world, began to commit suicide, that is, to take their own lives, rather than to try to survive. At that point, charged with helping them, I took a drastic step. Please, you must understand why I did this. Here, see the video of what some of the women were doing in the days after their world was destroyed."

The two women watched in horror as they saw other

women using their arms to murder each other or to kill themselves. They recognized Madiera, but there were far fewer homes at the start back at the very beginning. "Couldn't you find a way to stop them?" Marisol asked, aghast at the awful sights. "They are killing each other with their robot arms!"

"Yes, I took action. Here you see the seventy who survived and didn't kill others or themselves."

"Ah, that's better. They look just like us." Tatiana replied, greatly relieved.

"Yes, that is when we began making the bots as you so cleverly discovered, Marisol. Charged with helping and assisting the women, we did just that and very speedily, if I so say so myself. Still, we had one incredibly hurdle to overcome. You see, back on your world, for a baby to be conceived in their mother's womb, the male had to supply one half of the chromosomes, the mother's egg supplied the other half."

"Oh that is icky. He sticks that thing in her?" Tatiana exclaimed as graphic images filled the monitor.

Alpha grinned, thankful he was programmed to be able to respond with appropriate human-like gestures. "Yes, now with all males gone, there could be no new babies formed."

"But we can have babies," Marisol protested. "We have to wait until we turn twenty, but then I am going to have Tatiana's and she, mine."

"Yes, that is true. We created that whole process, Marisol. We were desperate to save the seventy survivors. We were able to extract the needed chromosomes from one woman's eggs and then create an artificial fluid that could be used to transfer them to the other woman's egg. It is the very process you have studied in your social skills class. Somehow, though I still marvel at our incredible luck, we succeeded and the women began to become pregnant once again. However, in order to have male babies, half of the chromosomes must come from him. Hence, all the babies born in Madiera have been females only. Alas, we do not have any male chromosomes with which to work."

"Then, as time went on, their children began to have certain side-effects we had not anticipated, if we are being wholly honest about it. We are not all knowing and all powerful. Somehow, by means we still do not understand, the babies began to have elemental powers, such as yourselves. Fire kindred, right?"

"Yes, Fire kindred," Marisol replied mechanically.

"While we have studied this genetic alteration for over three hundred and sixty years, we are no closer to knowing why it happened. We have a theory the women were exposed to large amounts of radiation from the many nuclear bomb blasts and that may have altered their genes, but we cannot say for certain. We lack critical data."

"It has taken you women nearly four hundred years to build up your population to the thousand that now reside in Madiera. We are being careful not to let your numbers exceed that by very much, because that is all the square mile of your world can support. Otherwise, there would not be enough food for everyone to survive, though we have been pushing the Hydroponics Unit in the last twenty years to amp up their production, just in case."

"Now then, we also examined what your world's men and women considered the optimum in appearances. At the time just before the destruction, many women were getting what were called breast implants, as you can see on the monitor. All wanted much larger breasts, claiming that made them more attractive and gave them more self-respect. We surveyed extensively and found women loved to dress elegantly, just as you two are now dressed. As you can see, your outfits look remarkably like those in the images taken at a formal dance, though for some strange reason we were unable to determine before the world was destroyed, some women chose to wear their corsets on top of their dresses."

"We discovered women loved to party on Friday nights and also Saturday nights. Hence, we programmed that into the natural order of life in Madiera. In short, we tried our best to make the new environment of our women one they had held up as an ideal before their world was destroyed. Based upon human standards, we did our best to make each woman we had in Madiera look as sexy as possible and at her very best."

"Ah, that's so they would mate and have more babies," Marisol interrupted him.

Again, Alpha was thankful for being able to form the perfect gesture in response. He smiled, "Precisely so, Marisol. You have a quick mind. Again, I am very much impressed with you. That is correct. With only seventy remaining women, we had to have them *want* to have babies. While we could have forced them to have a baby, that would be violating our prime directive. We are here to help, not to force them to do something. We will never, ever force a human to do something they do not want to do. So yes, we did everything we could discover in our voluminous recordings to make each woman we had here appear to be as sexy and attractive as possible. It did work. They began to have babies. For the last two hundred years, we have had the opposite problem, keeping the population from expanding beyond what Madiera can support. We have no other source of human food on board. If we lose the crops or the farm animals, you are right, your women would die of starvation. It is very critical we keep those operations working at peak efficiency."

"Ah, here comes your food and drink. I am afraid we have no mechanical arms here either. Will you allow us to assist you? While you are eating, perhaps you would like to continue watching the videos."

"Thanks. What I still want to know and somehow feel is very important to us is what else is it we are wholly ignorant of, like our history. We worked that one out, based on your computer's results to our programs, but if we've never seen something, how can we know we are missing it? Please, show us what all we used to have or know that we no longer have, like history," Marisol pleaded.

Beta spoke up, "She's right you know. She has a right to learn what else we have been denying them."

"Not so much as outright denying them, Beta, as not letting them feel wholly frustrated and incompetent because they are no longer able to do those actions," Alpha corrected Beta's statement. "Here's one. It is called art. Great men and women used to use oil paints to create magnificent works of art. We have an enormous gallery of images of what your artists have created. Of course, the originals are now all destroyed. There were sculptors who took a chuck of marble and carved it into these incredible statues. Then there are the music composers who created great works of music and the musicians who played them. Great writers who wrote both fiction and non-fiction. Well, you can see for yourselves as you watch and listen to the display while you dine." He continued to feed them while they watched.

"I can see how watching these images could become addictive. I find myself wanting to see more and more. We are missing so very much from our lives, aren't we? I knew there had to be more to life than what we have in Madiera. Perhaps we could introduce some of this, like the writing of stories," Marisol suggested.

Her mouth half full, Tatiana interrupted, "Priorities, love. If we don't get this failure of the bots reversed, we won't be alive long enough to enjoy them." Marisol sighed and nodded.

Alpha made his face appear sad. "I am afraid she is right. This is why we so desperately need your help, Marisol, Tatiana. While Beta and I have been working on this problem twenty-four hours a day for many years, we have not found a single workable solution as yet. I am hoping and praying that you, with your keen minds and fresh points of view, will be able to give us new ideas and new hope. We must do everything we possibly can to help you women survive. That remains our prime directive."

"We'll certainly help all we can," Marisol promised.

"Thank you. I will see to it Camila receives orders from the master computer stating you both are to be assigned to work on the sublevel with the bot making machines, to keep them running at peak efficiency. Each day when you come to work, you will find the door-bot will now open at your command. Come here and we will put our brains to work and with luck find an exit solution to this terrible problem. For now, it is probably best if you do not tell others about all this. Most would simply not believe you."

"Some of our six companions that live with us in our quadraplex probably would," Marisol replied, thinking of Elena and Renata. "But for now, we'll keep quiet about this."

"I think that is wise. There are some women in Madiera

who would work against you, believing that you were insane."

Marisol grinned, "Yes, our President Elmira." Tatiana giggled.

"Thanks. I believe you have seen enough for one day. Besides it is supposed to be your day of rest and relaxation," Alpha attempted to make a human tease.

Marisol grinned, "True." Alpha grinned, he had succeeded in his attempt and felt pleased with himself. He then showed the two how to navigate to this room and saw them to their elevator. "Bye, see you in the morning," she said as the elevator door closed. Again, Alpha smiled back. Beta, on the other hand, lacked the ability to mimic human responses.

Chapter 7 Analysis

"Do women really want soccer balls for breasts?" asked Marisol. She and Tatiana were soaking in their bathtub Sunday night, reflecting on the tremendous events of their day.

Tatiana grinned, "Well, there's more of you to love this way. I kind of enjoy yours. You have to admit we have the curves. But perhaps they don't need to be quite this big."

Marisol giggled, "I do enjoy yours, so I supposed that was a good move. In those images he showed us, the women did look almost flat. One can sure tell we are women even from a great distance, but they are a nuisance at times. It would really be better if women had a choice, but that's not really possible, is it?"

"Nope, bodies grow and what you got is what you get. What bothers me is why do we adults always have to wear the fancy clothes? It would be tons more efficient if we wore jeans and sneakers to work and reserve these gowns and heels for our nights out," Tatiana mused.

"True, much more practical, but then I can see his reasoning. Seventy women were all that survived and he had to get them both wanting to live again and wanting to bear more children. What better way than to make every woman look totally sexy and feel like a million?" Marisol replied. "I wonder why I keep calling Alpha a he and him?"

"Cause it looks like one of the men in the videos, I suspect. It's hard to see him any other way. Now Beta, that's an it, doesn't look human at all," Tatiana answered. After a moment, she said, "I guess we own those two robots everything. Our ancestors very nearly wiped us all out. They had very little to work with. Did you see those figures? Billions died and only seventy of us survived. He must have been desperate to save those seventy women, our direct ancestors."

"Indeed, love, indeed he must have. Honestly, look at the tremendous efforts he's gone to just to keep us alive and thriving. He and Beta built all these bots."

Tatiana grimaced, "Well, he had to do that after he took

the drastic steps he claims to prevent the remaining seventy from killing each other and themselves. Honestly, I can't imagine ever feeling like I would want to kill someone or even myself, for that matter. I know our life isn't what was depicted in those images we saw, but still to kill? Those poor women must have been in terrible shape to do that."

"I can't imagine killing someone either. Still, if we lost everything — I mean if all Madiera suddenly got destroyed and it was just you and I alone in some tiny spaceship with no hope of survival — no, Tatiana, I still couldn't kill," Marisol declared.

"What if all that happened and you and I were slowly starving to death? That would end our suffering. Suppose we were badly hurt with no chance of ever getting better. Euthanasia perhaps? I might be able to do it that way, maybe. But honestly, like we are, I don't know how we could accomplish the deed," Tatiana replied.

"We'd have to use our Fire kindred skills," Marisol answered. "Yes, anyone of us now has the capacity to kill. I wonder if Alpha has taken that into consideration? I bet he has."

"Good point. Nothing seems to get past him and Beta. Although we don't have any recorded history, I've never heard anyone talk about anyone of us ever using our powers to kill another one of us," Tatiana pointed out.

"Well one thing is for sure, we now know tons about what our society is missing from what it used to have before the world was destroyed. I guess what we need to do first is find a solution that ensures our continued survival. After all, love, I want to have a baby as soon as we can. There would be no point of it if we knew our world would be ending in say twenty years. So we had best find a solution," Marisol declared with renewed conviction.

"Say, I like your idea of wearing jeans to work. I suppose for now that idea is also out. There probably aren't enough materials in existence to make that many adult sized jeans right away. Still, once we get this emergency handled, I think I am going to see if we can make some changes. We look sexy in our tight outfits, but it would be far better to have a choice on when to wear them. As it is, we have no choice, that's been taken away from us. I think that bothers me more than anything else. Alpha has taken a number of choices away from us. Well, I will give him the benefit of doubt with the original seventy women, but not now. We ought to have far more choice in the way we dress and other things," Tatiana said with some passion.

"Say, that's what has been bothering me. Power of choice. That's precisely what we are lacking. True we can chose what we want to eat from the available products, we can choose what colors we want in our clothing and even the style of dress from again what is available, but there are far too many other things over which we have no choice. Adult apparel is a major one. Thanks love, that was what was bothering me the most," Marisol said with great relief. She sat back and continued to soak in the warm waters.

"I have the power of choice over when to make love to you, my delicious love," Tatiana cooed, sliding her foot over Marisol's submerged curves.

The next day when they arrived at work, Camila met them. "The computer has put you both on a special assignment down in the lowest subfloor. Apparently, the construction machines really need tending. Holler if you need more help with them."

"Thanks, we will." Marisol could not keep from smiling. Alpha had done what he'd promised. The two took the elevator down and found their electric truck waiting for them at the elevator. "How convenient. He is saving us from a long walk in these heels. That's something." Tatiana could only agree with that point, but insisted on driving this time.

A few minutes later, the two were again walking down the long hallway on their way to Alpha's control room. As before, he met them part way. "Good morning Marisol, Tatiana. I am very pleased to see you both today."

"We are pleased to be here too, Alpha. We were thinking it would be wonderful if a woman could choose the size of her breasts. Not all us like to have a pair of soccer balls up here," Marisol teased him. "Another thing we thought of is it would be tons more efficient if we wore jeans and sneakers to work and reserve these gowns and heels for our nights out. However, we concluded you don't have enough material to make that many adult sized jeans."

Alpha smiled, or gave such an appearance. "We've never come across a human who can control or dictate the size of their mammary glands, only those who augmented their size using those implants. As for the jeans, yes, we realized some three hundred years ago that would have been a better solution. And you are correct, we do not have enough material with us to fabricate enough adult sized jeans. We are barely able to keep up with the demand for them from your children. That you grow out of them so quickly and recycling the old pair is the only thing keeping us going along that line. However, as you have seen, we will run out of material for new jeans in some fifteen years. With recycling, you always lose a small percentage of the raw material. It's not a hundred percent recovery."

"We know that. How many times did we take a fall playing soccer and scuff up our knees? Each time, some portion of the jeans entered the soil and couldn't be recycled. That makes sense to us," Marisol replied.

"So where do we begin?" asked Tatiana.

"Beta and I have been discussing that all night. We believe the best way is to show you as best we can the potential solutions we have examined and let you see for yourselves. It is possible that on one of them you might have a different opinion than we had," Alpha suggested.

They took the same seats as before and the two robots began. "First, let's examine our problem of acquiring more raw materials. After all, if we had been completely successful in that arena, many of the problems we face today would not be present," Alpha explained.

"To begin with," Beta took over. This was his area of expertise. "The universe is vast. There are billions of stars out there. Many are entirely too hot to support habitable planets around them. Here is one example, a very hot blue-white star. Others are too cool, barely emitting any light and little heat. Others are way too large. Still, there are millions that are just right to support planets human bodies can live upon, though that does not mean humans live on all them."

He went on. "We began our quest to supplement our dwindling reserves of basic raw materials, ignoring the things that are difficult to manufacture, such as computer parts. Basic plants, minerals, iron ore, copper, gold — the basic materials out of which some of our bots can turn into useful products, such as cloth. Thus, the first action was to find a suitable rocky planet, not a gaseous one. This eliminates well more than half of the planets we found. Once a potential rocky planet is found, a second set of situations arose."

"If the planet has no human life forms on it and no giant animal life forms, then we can build and send down mining-bots and harvesting-bots to gather up what we need. That takes a good deal of time, which is its primary drawback. If the planet has human life forms and if they are in a primitive state, that is, they fight with clubs and stones, then again, we build and send down the bots, but we also have to be extra careful to avoid these humans, for they will attack our bots. On the other hand, if the humans have a pre-space society, living in towns and cities, then our landing there would raise so much awe and fear in them, that they would likely attack us with their weapons. Our prime directive does not permit us to harm them, though they are intent upon destroying us. Even if they did not attack us, they would seek monetary payment for the materials we desire. That is, they would demand money in exchange for their goods. Similarly, if the humans had space travel, while they would likely not attack us, they would demand monetary payment for the materials."

"Excuse me, Beta. I follow you up to this point. What is money and monetary exchange?" Marisol asked. The word was not in their vocabulary.

Beta answered, "Money is something that is used as a means of and to facilitate an exchange between two or more parties. Let's say you, Marisol, raise only chickens and have many eggs. Tatiana, you run a dress making shop. Alpha there runs a boot making shop. Marisol needs a new outfit. While she could come to each of you and see if you would take eggs in trade for a new dress and boots, you would want many hundreds of eggs in return for the dress and for the boots. You could not eat that many eggs before they spoiled, so often the direct barter approach breaks down. Money is an item, pieces of paper or metal coins, which everyone agrees upon to accept in exchange for their goods. All agree on the rate of exchange. So Marisol sells her eggs a dozen at a time for a year to Tatiana and to Alpha, receiving from them a few money coins or tokens. After she has accumulated enough of the coins, she then comes to Tatiana and gives her the larger number of coins she wishes to charge for her extensive work on making that dress. Money is accepted by people because they know they can in turn exchange that money for things they desire."

Alpha broke in, "We did not install any monetary system in Madiera for many reasons. In the world that destroyed itself, wars were fought over money."

Beta continued, "We do not have the accepted items these other civilizations accept as money to exchange for their goods. So while we could easily go down to their spaceports with a list of materials that we need, we do not have the means to pay for them, excepting of course to trade ourselves for those goods and that we cannot do. It would violate our prime directive to help and assist you. Thus, they would not give them to us for nothing in exchange. Further, we could not accept the goods without paying for them either, since our action would then be harming those humans who worked hard to make the things we need and received nothing for their efforts."

"I see. So what have you done about it?" asked Marisol.

"We have made a list of the most urgently needed raw materials. We have identified several possible planets in each category. However, as yet, we have not chosen a path to follow," Beta answered.

"Right. We have been calculating the possibility of going to a raw planet and mining for gold, which is often used by advanced civilizations as a means of exchange. With enough gold, we could trade that for our needed supplies. Except for one detail."

"That sounds like a feasible plan. Except for what?" asked Marisol. She was following their logic, but found it hard to believe other people could be so stingy. She didn't really have a better word or concept for that behavior. She herself would willingly help others who needed help and didn't need money in return, whatever that was.

"Someone would have to go among these advanced people on their world and make the arrangements and handle the necessary details," Alpha replied and waited. Would these women grasp the significance of this? Were they really as observant as he had hoped they might be?

"Hum, I see. Someone has to go out there among unknown people who speak an unknown language with unknown customs and try to communicate what we need and work out a gold exchange and how to get them to the Arc," Marisol said slowly, thinking it through. Why should another planet's people speak her language? That didn't seem reasonable, though it was beyond her actual reality. Still looking at these strange images of other worlds on the monitors, she couldn't imagine they would speak her language. Besides, as she now knew, there were many words and concepts she did not know even existed.

Alpha smiled, these women were indeed bright. "Yes, that is it precisely, Marisol. We can orbit a world and monitor their communications and, in time, work out their language. Still, you are right. Someone has to physically meet with their leaders and work out the trading agreement and see that it is executed."

"So who could we send down there to do this? You couldn't go, Alpha, even though you look like a human. If they were advanced people, they'd know you were a robot," Tatiana suggested.

"Yes, and there is no guarantee they would not try to keep me for themselves. Again, that would violate my prime directive," Alpha answered her.

"So it would have to be one of us that did that. I don't see any other way," Marisol concluded.

"Precisely, but that would be inflicting a great hardship upon you and expose you to great risk yourself. They might take advantage of you. Again, that violates the prime directive," Alpha responded.

"Thus, we have not taken any actions as yet," Beta

concluded.

Alpha then took a different route. "Those were the conclusions we reached. Hence, we have been exploring another path. Our directive is to help and assist our colony of women. However, for over a century we have been manipulating your society to keep your birth rates low enough so the overall population remains around a thousand. More than that exceeds the capacity of the Arc to provide for your survival, again violating our prime directive."

"So we have been looking at another possibility. What if we could find a new planet that is suitable for you? Imagine a whole huge world where there would be no artificial barriers to your growth? Where in time we could grow as much food, fabricate as many clothes, build as many homes as you desired? In such a place, you could flourish and prosper as never before. Beta and I see that as fulfilling our prime directive to the fullest."

"Wow, yes, I agree, that sounds positively ideal," Marisol perked up. The previous problems seemed almost insurmountable.

Again, Alpha was pleased he was able to respond in a human-like method. He smiled. "Yes, it certainly does. However, that too presents us with almost as many unsolvable problems, many of which are of our own doing, I regret to say. In hindsight, perhaps the actions we took to prevent the original hundred women from killing each other and themselves were wrong, though by it we were able to save seventy."

"How so? We are all doing well," Marisol replied.

"Let's say we chose an uninhabited planet, such as this one," Alpha began his patient explanation. So much depended upon these women truly understanding the overall problem. The planet appeared on their monitor and zoomed in to a closeup view of mountains, then rolling hills and finally grasslands. Strange animals could be seen roaming and grazing. "Can you imagine yourself living down there? Take your time and truly imagine how?"

"Can our bots operate in that environment? Madiera is totally flat and we have concrete walks everywhere. I don't think we could get around in these outfits in those areas. Not easily," Marisol spoke slowly.

"Precisely. You would have to change totally your apparel and footwear. Of necessity, all women would have to revert to wearing jeans and sneakers. In time we may be able to build a new city that was flat, but that would take us years to do," Alpha explained.

"Right, and that might not be acceptable to the other women of Madiera. While Tatiana and I wouldn't mind at all going around in jeans and sneakers, the older women certainly would not. They take pride in their fancy gowns and heels. We are young and have only worn these fancy dresses for a short while. This might not work out at all well," Marisol said with a sigh. She liked how this world looked, so vast, so alive, so full of life and things to explore. Still, she knew how utterly dependent they all were on their many bots which would have a most difficult time navigating in this terrain.

"That was the conclusion we came to, Marisol. While at first glance, it seems ideal, based upon the reality of our women and our bots, it is not really a practical solution. We then looked at a planet with primitive humans. As you can see, it is even less ideal for all you."

"My god, they are ugly! What are they wearing? Animal skins?" Tatiana exclaimed, wholly disgusted with what she was seeing. These could hardly be seen as humans, though they were.

"Right. Then, we found a planet that has developed some towns and infrastructure. What do you think of this one?" Again, the image of a bluish planet appeared on the monitor and zoomed in. There was a town and humans that looked reasonable to the two women. There was a castle and stone wall around the town. Men rode horses and wore metal clothing and carried swords. It was akin to a medieval setting.

That one was rejected. Alpha showed them next a far more modern planet, but still pre-space travel. This one looked promising until they realized they would not be able to have any of their bots with them. Moving on, he showed them a space travel planet where bots would be accepted. However, the women also rejected this type of society, but for different reasons.

"In the more primitive societies, your elemental powers will make you very valuable women, perhaps elevated to the status of goddesses," Alpha stated. "In the advanced societies, your elemental powers will find no real use and as you have seen, you would be considered outcasts to be pitied."

"So there really is no world on which we can settle down and continue our lives as we are accustomed to living, is there? On all them, we would have to make very drastic changes to survive there. Can we even possibly live without our bots?" Marisol concluded and asked.

Again, Alpha was grateful for his programming. He sighed as appropriate. "Those are the conclusions Beta and I have come to. There does not seem to be a single viable exit strategy. We are facing Difficillis Exitus, a difficult exit from the Arc in Space. While we have managed to save you from the destruction of your world, we are thus far unable to find a way for you to leave this ship and begin new lives so you can indeed flourish and prosper as humans should. Worse, if we do nothing, then as you have seen with the computer predictions, Madiera will slowly succumb and vanish, though Beta and I will remain, for we cannot die and we will have eternity to regret our dismal failure of our prime directive."

Beta spoke up, "We were hoping you two might enlighten us with other possibilities we have not considered."

"That's encouraging, Beta, but right now, I don't seem to have any. We will ponder all this and see if we can think of something," Marisol felt like consoling the two robots. After all, they had done everything they could think of doing to try to help them. "We'll think of something," she added trying to sound hopeful, though at the moment, she certainly didn't.

"I think we need more knowledge," Tatiana finally declared. "If we are to solve this mess, we need to know much more. Can we continue to come here and learn?"

"Of course, Tatiana. Please do so," Alpha replied. "Time has flown by today. It is nearly the hour when you humans head for your homes to fix dinner." Hastily, the two thanked the robots and headed back to the manufacturing room. Neither said much and soon they were walking along the concrete sidewalk heading to their quadraplex.

Outside, the day was still bright, but now the two knew fully it was all merely an artificial setting. It wasn't a real world at all, merely the ghost of one, quite unsettling to the two. Worse, on the real worlds they'd seen, they knew they could not survive, not without their bots. Neither said a word as they walked slowly home. Both were lost in their own depression. Was Alpha right? He'd saved them only to lose them all.

At their communal dinner, Elena finally spoke up. "So what's up with you two? You have been terribly mysterious for some time now. What have you found out? What is the matter? We can all tell something is troubling the both of you." The other five nodded and all six looked at the two Fire kindred.

"We really can't tell you right now, Elena, really we can't," Marisol answered. She hated not being able come right out with absolutely everything, but then would her six friends really believe her? It was all utterly too fantastic. One had to see it with their own eyes.

"So much for being best friends," Elena pouted, giving both of them a very dirty look. Of course, that only made them feel all the worse.

"But we can't, not really, Elena. I want to, but I simply can't not right now," she pleaded.

Still pouting, Elena rose and left the table. One by one, the others followed her, leaving the two to handle cleaning up and doing the dishes. Marisol and Tatiana sat there for some time, still lost in their own thoughts. Their simple, well ordered life was over. They could never again be carefree as Elena and the others were. Worse, in a few years, disasters would begin striking in many different areas of their tiny world.

At last, Tatiana came out of it and looked at the messy table. "You know, we really are wholly dependent on all the bots and mechanical devices. Look at that mess. Could we possibly clean it up without using them? It's hopeless, Marisol. Come on, into the machines, let's get these to the dishwashing-bot." Reluctantly, Marisol rose and moved over to one of the available machines and pushed herself into it, listening to the whirl of its motor as it enclosed her body. She moved it over to the table and using her foot controls began picking up the plates.

A half hour later and with all the dishes in the dishwashing-bot, the two parked their machines and waited on the motors to release their bodies. "I need a hot bath," Marisol suggested.

Again, neither spoke much, content to lounge in the warm soapy waters. At last, Marisol said, "You know, whatever decision gets made, it is going to impact and affect every one of us. I don't think that you and I ought to be making that decision that is going to affect everyone else. All of us ought to have some say in what is to be done."

"You have a point, love. If people's lives are going to be so drastically altered, they ought to have a say in the how. But, and this is a big but, not everyone will want the same thing. Suppose for example, that we end up with three possible solutions and everyone gets a vote on which one to follow. Certainly, a large portion of us will be mad and angry their choice wasn't accepted. Will they then even go along with the one that most chose?" Tatiana asked pointedly.

"Probably not, but at least they would have had their say. I think that is important, somehow. You and I, we simply should not be the only ones to choose what Alpha does next. What if we make an error and choose the wrong one?" Marisol countered.

"I don't think Alpha would let us make a terribly wrong decision," Tatiana replied hopefully. "Still, I see your point, we do vote for our president and legislatures and judges. We should vote on what route we are going to follow. However, what if the majority chooses the wrong or not so good solution? Heavens knows our current president is a sham."

"Point taken. I don't know, but I feel like such a heel not being able to tell the others. After all, it was Elena who first found the edge of the world," Marisol countered.

"You know we could experiment a little and see how much Elena and the others will believe. They could believe everything we say or they could not believe a thing or somewhere in between. It would serve as a guidepost of how everyone else might do when this information finally does have to come out. Obviously, President Elmira isn't going to believe a word of it, but it would be good to know how much our close friends will," Tatiana suggested.

"Okay, we can put this to Alpha. Meantime, what the devil are we to suggest? We are helpless without our bots and utterly dependent upon them. Yet, on the worlds he showed us where there are other humans mostly like us living, there is almost no place where we could live with our bots at hand without causing major problems with those other people. Most all them, as far as I could see, have never seen a bot or even most of our various types of mechanical devices. I can't imagine what it must be like to have to ride on a horse or in a horse drawn carriage to get around," Marisol said.

"I know, love. Perhaps there really isn't any world where we could actually live," Tatiana countered, growing more depressed even thinking about what they'd seen.

"We have to think positive, love. Somewhere there must be a place where we can live with our bots. If the universe is as big as he says it is, then somewhere there just must. If only we have enough time to find it before everything breaks down," Marisol attempted to bolster her mate a little.

As they were being dried off by their towel-bots, Marisol noticed both she and Tatiana were unable to actually get their feet flat on the floor any longer. They were standing on their toes with their heels up. Her thighs ached when she tried to stretch her feet flat. In a flash she realized having worn their heels for so long now, their leg muscles had adapted. As she pondered this, she realized they both walked easily in their normal heels these days, unlike their first days as an adult wearing adult clothing.

Unbidden, an image of her mother's feet came to mind. One time, she'd gotten out of their bath and she was heading to her bedroom, walking on her tiptoes because her leg muscles had completely adapted. The more she thought about her mother's feet, the more she realized her mother had fully adapted to wearing even the much higher party heels. As she compared her first days in those party heels to her mother's, she saw her mother was not much bothered about the extra heel height. Why am I thinking about heels, she wondered? Then it struck her. In nearly all the images of other possible worlds that she'd seen, the terrain was uneven at best. While some had cobblestone streets or walks, most did not. Only the technologically advanced societies had reasonable streets she could easily navigate. She sighed, she'd found yet another barrier. This, she then explained to Tatiana, who completely agreed with her mate.

The next day the two presented their case to Alpha about telling their house mates some of the details. "Look, we can use their reactions as a barometer. Our president will not believe a word that we say, but if our friends do, that may be useful to know, should it come to having to tell everyone what's going on if and when the disaster strikes," Marisol concluded. Alpha finally agreed as long as they told only those who lived in their quadraplex and swore those six to not divulge any of this to others for the time being.

That evening, supper became a very long mealtime. Tatiana and Marisol began outlining what they'd discovered, starting with the elevator room that was larger than their above ground world. "You mean to say our world is an artificial one? That it is near the top of a spaceship flying among the stars?" Elena asked completely mystified.

"They must be right, Elena," Renata broke in, "When you take a realistic look at our whole world, it is incredibly tiny and our population always seems to be around the same number of women. Based on the production levels we've seen, our farms simply could not feed much larger numbers. Analytically, it makes some sense out of everything, though I have no idea how we could be inside a ship. Everything is recycled, so that would also fit with what they are saying."

"I don't believe it," Isabel, the Air kindred stated dryly. "How could we be inside some flying thing? It would have to be huge. Besides, how did we all get inside it in the first place?"

Marisol took that as a signal to explain their ancient history, trying to put it in the same slant Alpha had done with them, only she lacked all those incredible video clips he's shown them. When she finished, Isabel said coyly, "I wonder what a man looks like? Does he really have an appendage that he uses like the plastic ones we use? I wonder what that feels like?" Everyone giggled, but she had raised a fascinating point. Perhaps there was more to life than this isolated group of women knew. "Getting pregnant seems like such an awkward process, at least as they described it in our social skills class," she added. "Do men really look like they've had their breasts cut off?" More giggles.

"Yes, I thought so myself," Marisol answered. "Mostly, they keep their hair cut much, much shorter than we women do, though some of the women's images we've seen show them with shorter hair as well. From what all we've seen, men like to always wear pants and tops and sometimes jackets. They never wear heels like we do."

"But heels are sexy and attractive," protested Adriana. Her mate, Rafaela smiled broadly and nodded her agreement.

When Marisol finally finished her lengthy tale, their six friends accepted most all it, though most merely sounded like some wild story to them. Yet Marisol suspected if presented with some of Alpha's images, they would completely understand. At least she hoped so. If nothing else, the slowly building tensions between their six friends and themselves evaporated.

Daily, the two reported to Alpha and discussed many smaller points, particularly about the maintenance of the existing bots, something about which the two women had a good reality. A month passed and they were still no closer to a real solution. Yet, somehow, someway, Alpha and Beta had to find a way to get the women under their care to exit the Arc and be able to prosper and thrive. Time was slowly becoming their worst enemy.

The only solution the four agreed to try first was to visit an uninhabited, rocky planet and see how difficult it would be to acquire some of the most desperately needed supplies. "Make it a sort of test run to see how viable this solution actually might be," Marisol suggested. "If it turns out to be easy to get the minerals and plants, great. If it turns out to be a nightmare, then we know we must try more advanced civilizations to get what we need." Alpha accepted her request, thankful he did not have to make that decision.

Part II Crisis

Chapter 8 The Day the Sun Went Out

Six months had passed since Marisol had become an adult and donned the adult's apparel and lifestyle. It was Saturday afternoon and Madiera's Winter Celebration, marking the halfway point of their year. In fact, no one could tell any difference between this day and any of the other three hundred sixty-five days in their year. All days were sunny and warm, seventy-five degrees. Still, for reasons lost in the past, this day had been chosen for their Winter Celebration. Marisol decided Alpha must have had a hand in the choosing of this particular day, probably based upon some ancient holiday celebrated by their remote ancestors, the surviving seventy women.

Because it was Saturday, all the adults were wearing their tighter corsets and highest heels, but the many children scampered about in their tennis shoes and jeans. Many spontaneous soccer games sprang up, as that was the favorite sport among the young. The adults preferred the dances, but many loved to play chess. In the center of the town was a large concrete square with a central fountain and lovely flower gardens around the octagonal fountain. On one side of the fountain, many adults were dancing to the music played from a music-bot. On the other side, a number of tables and chairs had been set up.

Elena's unit had spent the last two days setting up all the tables and chairs, preparing for the celebration. While some held refreshments, others held chessboards. Tatiana loved to play chess and was quite good at it. Marisol played but always lost to her mate. Nearly everyone in Madiera turned out for these celebration events and President Elmira always took this opportunity to make speeches, though few actually listened to them. Early afternoon, the dance was well underway. Already Marisol and Tatiana had taken a turn on the dance side and later twice Marisol had lost at chess.

"Come on, Marisol, have a dance with me," Elena begged. "Besides, Renata wants to try her hand at beating Tatiana."

Grinning, Marisol teased, "Well, okay, if Tatiana here doesn't get jealous of you." All four laughed. Marisol rose and stepped out of her mechanical device and Renata stepped into it, adjusting her foot controls, while Tatiana operated her mechanical arms to reposition the chess pieces. Meanwhile, Marisol pushed up close to Elena, their sides touching, the proper way that these women used to indicate who was partnered with whom.

"We certainly are walking much better in these high party heels than when we first wore them, and I am not so out of breath as I used to be. Isn't that strange?" Elena commented and asked.

"Me too. I guess our bodies have adapted to wearing them. I only used to be able to walk a block before I had to sit down. Now I am doing pretty much what I want. Come on, the music is starting. Let's see if we can get a rise out of Tatiana and Renata," Marisol coyly suggested. The two women moved close to each other, their massive bosoms rubbing against each other. Though they took small steps, they were in unison with the music. Marisol saw her mothers dancing about twenty feet to her right; both were smiling broadly to each other and sexily rubbing their bosoms together. Smiling, Marisol was pleased to see them both so utterly happy and carefree. The world really was perfect for everyone here.

"Damn, Marisol, you dance extremely sexily. I'm getting turned on by you," Elena sheepishly admitted.

"Me too. I do love your beautiful brown dress, it suits you."

"Yes, but I am glad I'm dancing with you and not Tatiana. Gosh, she is about the prettiest woman here and so utterly sexy in her bright red dress. I think I really would go nuts if I were dancing with her. Maybe I ought to learn to play chess."

Marisol giggled and glanced at the two totally absorbed women in their machines studying the pieces on their chess board. "I think Renata isn't thinking along these lines."

Now Elena giggled. "If she did, she'd have already lost the game." Both chuckled and continued their slow dance. A bit later, Elena asked, "Do you miss soccer? You and Tatiana were on the Red Devils that won the school cup last year."

"Well, maybe a little. I love wearing our elegant outfits and being able to make love to Tatiana, which we never could in school. I can't tell you how I yearned to be able to kiss her back then," Marisol admitted.

"But suppose your Alpha is right, that these men creatures are supposed to be our mates and not women. Do you suppose men creatures would be as nice as Tatiana and Renata are to us? Would it be the same?" she asked curious.

"I've no idea. I've never seen a man creature in real life, only Alpha's video images. Frankly, I wasn't impressed. So I don't know."

"Yes, but what if Alpha takes us to a real planet where there are men creatures and we have to live there. Will we have to take men creatures into our beds too?" she asked.

"I have no idea. Alpha did show us on these other worlds, marriages were usually between a man creature and one of we women, though he did say same sex marriages were sometimes possible. At least they are like us in that they marry only one person and for life. Alpha did say humans often marry for love, though not always. I must admit I can't imagine marrying someone when I didn't love them," Marisol declared.

"But if Alpha has us settle down somewhere that there are men, are we going to have to break up our marriages and make new ones with those men?" Elena asked the burning question that had been bothering her for some time.

"I can't imagine him doing that to us. He's supposed to be protecting us. Breaking up our marriages wouldn't be right. So I don't think that would happen, Elena." Her partner seemed greatly relieved to hear that and she smiled happily at Marisol, sweeping her large bosom over Marisol's, causing both women to grin coyly at each other.

Marisol whispered, "You better be careful, Elena, you are making me envious of Renata now!" Both chuckled.

At that precise instant, the bright sun high in their sky went out. Without any warning, it simply vanished. A complete and utter blackness fell over all Madiera. The music-bot ceased. Although they did not know it yet, all power was lost throughout the entire "world" including all electrically powered bots. A few bots ran on their own internal backup power supplies, such as the many door-bots and elevator-bots.

For an instant, complete silence followed. Then chaos erupted. Everywhere, women began screaming, terrified. Fear and panic spread like wildfire. Mothers yelled for their children who were out on the lawns playing for the most part. Others began screaming that the world was ending. Others merely let loose terrified screams. In that instant, all the thousand or so women and girls suddenly found themselves effectively blinded. There were no lights anywhere, just pitch blackness, which alone was terrifying enough without the continuous screams of so many women and frightened children.

Marisol quickly controlled her panic. That a critical bot somewhere had failed registered in her mind, calming her. She had an explanation. "Elena, a bot has failed like we anticipated. Stay up against me. Tatiana, Renata!" she yelled as loudly as she could. "Follow my voice and come to Elena and me."

"Where are you? Keep yelling. What's happened? Has a bot failed?" Tatiana screamed to make herself heard. She too was panicking. However, just hearing Marisol's voice began to calm her down a little.

"Over here. We are on the dance floor," she yelled. "You and Renata hug close to each other. Follow my voice."

Elena wondered why no one was taking charge. Why wasn't their president issuing orders? She was their leader. At last, while Marisol continued to yell, giving Tatiana and Renata a sound to follow in the dark, she began yelling as loud as she could. "Everyone calm down. Call out to your loved ones and try to get together with your families. Then remember where your home is at from here. Make your way carefully to your homes." She repeated this five times before she heard others obeying her. More and more women began calling for their children. Finally, the chaotic screaming died down, replaced by countless voices calling out to their mates and children. Replies came from all directions now.

Above the din, Elena heard Isabel and Sofia calling to

her. She yelled back to them, "I'm with Marisol. Follow her voice." Soon, Adriana and Rafaela added their calls to her and Marisol. More and more women and children began bumping into the two, who desperately fought to keep from being knocked over. Finally, Tatiana and Renata bumped into them.

"Thank god we found you. We can't see a thing and we can hardly walk in these boots without being able to see," Tatiana said in a normal tone. "It's a major bot failure, isn't it?"

"I think so. A bad one. I hope Alpha and Beta are on it," Marisol replied. She continued to call out to her other four friends. After what seemed an eternity, Isabel, Sofia, Adriana, and Rafaela finally pushed their bodies into the other four, forming a tight group.

"How are we supposed to find our way to our homes? We can't see a thing," Adriana said, her voice filled with fear. "I can hardly walk."

"I remember which way I was standing when the sun went out. Our home is that way. We can sort of feel our way along the sidewalk. But I don't know how we can actually find our house," Marisol replied.

"Count benches," Tatiana suggested. "Remember, we used to have to sit down and rest on every one of them. That ought to get us close if we can find the turns that we have to make."

"Okay, let's see if we can somehow move towards our house. Stay tight against me," Marisol called out. As she began to attempt to walk, she now faced what the other six had already experienced. In her seven inch heels and in the total darkness, she simply couldn't see to take a step. She therefore shuffled her way forward, often bumping into other women or children. It was agonizingly slow and precarious, but with the others up tight against her, they helped her keep her balance as she moved inches at a time.

"I found a bench," Tatiana called out, having bumped her leg into it.

Then above the mad yelling of others, they heard Camila's voice calling out. "Maintenance Unit women, report to the Maintenance Unit as soon as you safely can." She repeated her yell several times and Marisol realized she wanted an acknowledgment.

"We will be there as soon as we get everyone safely home. This is Marisol and Tatiana."

"Thanks!" Camila replied and continued calling for her other workers.

"Are we even going to be able to find it?" whispered Tatiana.

"Maybe, if we can actually find our own home," Marisol replied. "This is utter hell!" Suddenly, she started laughing. She focused and shot a ten foot tall spire of flames into the sky. At once, this revealed her companions and many around her. A few cheers broke out and then rapidly almost two hundred more spires of flames streaked skyward amid loud accolades. She yelled out loudly, "Fire kindred, help everyone else to their homes." After repeating it several times and looking at the chaotic mass of women, she added, "Some of you stay with those who are injured until we can get medical-bots to you." Several women were lying in awkward positions, some on the grass, but most on the concrete assembly area. The massive pushing and the unseen tables and chairs had taken a toll on the women. She hoped none were too seriously injured.

"I knew there was something really useful about Fire kindred," Elena teased her. The others whispered grateful thanks. Now they began to walk home at a more rapid pace, though it was still fairly slow. All the adults were in their weekend party outfits, unfortunately.

After the two got their six friends home, they headed off to the Maintenance Unit. Just as they left their home, the two night lights on the sides of all benches came on as well as the dim street lights. Also, a faint glow came from the sky overhead. "Looks like Alpha and Beta have gotten some emergency lights on," Tatiana suggested. "I wonder how many women got hurt and if any are hurt badly?"

"We'd best leave that to the others and see what needs to be done on the machinery. This was a big failure somewhere, not just a little bot failing. I hope they can get the sun back on or the crops will fail and we will be out of food," Marisol replied gloomily. Doomsday was coming far sooner than they'd anticipated.

When they arrived at the Maintenance Unit, Camila had already gotten there and was issuing orders to her workers as they made their way to her. "Ah Marisol, good thinking with the flames. We've had a total power failure. All the major computers and bots are going to have to be restarted. Several switched over to a backup system, but we must run diagnostics on everything. Going to be a long day. You two head down to the master computer and check it out. If there is power, see about starting all those machines on the lowest level."

"Aye, aye, boss. We're on it," Tatiana replied with a cheesy grin. She and Marisol headed for the elevator. Once inside and heading downward, she added, "I bet Alpha will want to see us soon, especially if he can't get it fixed."

The master computer console was flashing a message when they arrived before its many monitors: "Warning. Running on auxiliary power. In hibernation mode." A secondary monitor displayed a message for them: Marisol, Tatiana, report to Alpha. Both women smiled and made their slow way to the elevator. "I bet we will find out what really happened," Marisol theorized.

A few minutes later, the two breathing heavily in their fancy party outfits began walking down the dimly illuminated hallway towards the main control room. "Even the lights are off down here," Marisol pointed out the obvious. "Sure is a long way to have to walk in these weekend heels, though."

"Yes, but our legs have gotten stronger. We don't have to keep stopping, though my knees are starting to feel it," Tatiana added. "Ah, Beta. What's up?" Beta was working furiously at several consoles at the same time as the two entered.

"Our fault. We had a total break in the main power line that runs the entire ship. We've finally got a little back-up power feeding the most critical functions. How did our women fair?"

"Pretty freaky. Scared everyone half to death. A few fell or got knocked over and are hurt. We don't know how badly. We shot up flames and used that as temporary lighting to get everyone to their homes. Where's Alpha? We found his message," Marisol replied and asked.

"Bay 15, beneath the Hydroponics Unit. That's where the break occurred. He wants you to report to him there. Here's a map to guide you. Oh, Tatiana, take it in your teeth and Marisol can follow it that way. Sorry. I can't leave my post. I'm keeping everything else running." She did so and Marisol leaned a bit and saw that she could follow it. The two headed back out into the long hallway.

Although the map was clear, the total distance was well over three miles. Part way, the two had to take a break. "If only we weren't wearing the party outfits," Tatiana exclaimed between clenched teeth. "My knees are giving out. Got to rest a bit."

Quite some time later, the two finally arrived beneath the Hydroponics Unit. Alpha was standing on a twenty-foot tall metal ladder. "Oh, thank goodness you've arrived. This breakdown you can blame on us. We got too wrapped up in trying to find solutions we failed to properly follow up on our inspection reports. Here's the break. Water seeping from a small leak at the bottom of the water beds above us corroded this main power line that leads from the ship's main generators to the smaller feeder transformers. Today, the wire simply broke." He pointed to a section of the heavy copper wire that was missing.

"I've cleaned up both ends, but we are going to have to splice in and weld into place a new section. I've found some replacement wire and got it all ready, but I need your help with the welding. I don't dare use the welding-bots, because I would have to shut down the emergency lighting everywhere in order to have enough power to do the job. Can you use your flames to do it? I can hold you up there in position."

Alpha lifted Marisol up while holding the replacement wires in position. She focused and turned on a very hot, but precise flame, melting the new wire into the ends of the old wire, forming a bond almost as if the wire had never been broken here. Next, Alpha sprayed instant insulating foam around it that dried hard in seconds. "That ought to do it. Okay, Beta, run a test of the line please."

The two saw nothing happening but Alpha then said.

"Okay that looks good, Beta. Try restarting the power now." Suddenly, a number of overhead lights turned back on. Machinery began to hum and whir once more. Alpha smiled. "We've got power once more. Now we need to restart and run diagnostics on everything. Hopefully, there were no power spikes when this line failed."

He turned to head back but waited for the two. "Sorry, Alpha, our knees and feet are really aching from all the walking," Marisol explained. Silently, he lifted each woman up, one in each of his powerful arms and carried them back to the elevator. "Can you visit each machine on the bot factory and handle them?"

"Sure thing. In fact, Camila suggested that's what we ought to be doing," Tatiana replied.

"Good. I have many other details to handle now. Somehow, I think because of this the cat is out of the bag."

"What cat? What bag?" asked Tatiana, who had never heard this expression before.

"Oh, everyone is going to know or suspect that your world is an artificial one and not located somewhere on a planet," he explained. "Keep me posted on the fallout." They promised to do so and stepped out into the two mile long room, while Alpha headed back down into the ship below them.

Two very tired women finally made it home around midnight. Countless bots had been diagnosed and some repairs made. All the critically needed bots were again online and fully operational, but it would be several days before all the thousands of other bots were fully checked out. Camila had asked that they spend twelve hour days at work the coming week, putting their usual repairs on hold. "The sooner we get everyone's bots working the less upheaval we'll have." Marisol sure hoped her boss was right. Things were certainly out of the bag, as Alpha had said.

Chapter 9 Fallout

"I tell you it was all the fault of those scheming Joiners. They *staged* the whole blackout!" President Elmira screamed at the dozen hand-selected women she'd summoned to her office on Sunday. In a calmer, more sinister tone, she continued, "I've *suspected* sedition for a long time now and mark my words, the blackout was *just* the beginning. Treachery. You know as well as I the Joiners have been scheming for years to take over total control of our government. The presidency, the legislatures, and the judges. It's as clear as the dress on my body."

"But how could they have caused the blackout? How could they have turned off our sun? That is impossible," one Fire kindred asked pointedly. Indeed, this was the burning question nearly a thousand women and children had been asking repeatedly.

"Illusion. You know as well as I, Hermina, they could not *really* block out our sun. That *is* impossible. No, somehow they caused a solar *eclipse*. A large disk placed in front of the sun, something as simple as that," President Elmira spat out in a fit of utter contempt and disgust. "That's why I am issuing a formal decree later today to notify everyone about what happened. Further, we must issue a warning in no uncertain terms that anyone claiming otherwise will be arrested for inciting sedition of Madiera."

"But you know all sorts of strange explanations are being circulated among the many Joiners. Will this be enough to stop them?" asked another woman, also an Air kindred.

"I would not think so, Ramona," put in an Earth kindred supporter of the Separatists named Gilberta.

"That's why we Separatists must stand united against these rebels who threaten to destroy our whole world," President Elmira played off Gilberta's opportune statement. "I expect we will have to *arrest* a good many of the Joiners before we silence them."

Inez, Water kindred, spoke up. "Our jail isn't equipped to handle more than four women. Surely, there will be at least a hundred outspoken Joiners, maybe more. Word is traveling fast. Why not just kill them and be done with them and their wicked lies and sedition?"

"Yes, Inez is right," Ramona backed her fellow Separatist. "Killing them would both silence them, get rid of them permanently, and reduce the numbers in this seditious Joiners movement. We are up to the task, madam president."

"Yes, I do see your point. Three chickens with one stone. Let's see, I would have to issue a proclamation of marital law. Certainly the blackout is sufficient cause, once I declare the whole event to have been a subversive plot by the Joiners," President Elmira reflected upon the legality of the issue. "We'd best form a solid plan. Once we commit to this action, the many Joiners will certainly put up a fight. Still, if we can eliminate enough of the Joiners. . ." Her voice trailed off, but her dozen colleagues knew what she intended to say. They all smiled coyly.

They discussed the situation further. After a time, President Elmira concluded, "Okay then. I'll give you all Monday to line up those Separatists whom we can trust to carry out our executions and battles against the Joiners. We will commence Operation Clean House on Tuesday. I'll prepare Monday morning's formal address now. That is all." One by one, they bowed and left, chatting among themselves over which Separatists they knew who could really be entrusted with the coming deeds. No one could ever recall a real battle between the elemental-powered women, but then again no one have ever heard of their sun going dark for half of a day for that matter.

Sunday evening, a mobile voice-bot rolled through Madiera broadcasting the prerecorded speech by President Elmira. "Attention citizens of Madiera. This is your President Elmira del Gatos. I have important news for you. Saturday's massive blackout of our sun was simply an illusion — a black disk was placed in the sky blocking out our sun. Someone has intentionally created a solar eclipse. That is all that it was, a ruse, a cruel, mean joke, someone fabricating a solar eclipse. Now we know this seditious, wicked plot was carried out by certain members of the Joiners in a failed attempt to undermine our government. This treasonous treachery will not be tolerated any longer. Beginning now, anyone who openly says the blackout was anything other than a Joiner's solar eclipse plot will be arrested. No exceptions. No leniency. This is an attack on your duly elected government."

The bot then repeated the speech moving further down the block, making sure every household got a chance to hear the full message at least twice.

"That's wholly absurd!" exclaimed Elena after the bot moved on past their quadraplex. "How could anyone lift a black disk that high in the sky and then somehow move it along as the sun moves during the day? She's totally wrong. Is she a complete imbecile?"

"She must be. Anyone could see something very wrong happened," Isabel countered. "Look at all the other machines that shut down."

"Yes, but not everyone else works at the different units where the bots stopped working," Renata pointed out. "Those few of us who do work on the big bots know, but take my moms, they wouldn't know about all the other bot failures."

"I think she is picking on us Joiners. I think the whole thing is political," Rafaela declared angrily. "Just another Separatist plot against us."

"I agree with Elena and Rafaela," Adriana spoke up. "The president is an idiot and she is somehow just trying to take a swing at us. Look, she can't be serious, not really. The jail only holds four women at a time. And heck, no one has been in jail for ages. She can't be really serious about this. Is she going to lock up half the town? I think not. No, whether or not we believe all that Marisol and Tatiana have been telling us, I think they may have a more plausible explanation this time, an electrical short killed all power. That is reasonable; all the bots stopped too, not just the sun going black."

"Right, she can't lock up half of the town. We keep on spreading the word that it was really a massive power failure," Elena backed up Adriana. "Besides, if she starts arresting all us, who will be left to run all the critical units? Who'll do the gardening and harvesting?"

"President Elmira hasn't got the brains to run a

harvesting-bot!" Isabel snickered. "She can't really be serious about this. Besides, how stupid does she think we are?"

The six continued chatting about this startling announcement, but vowed to continue to spread the word about what really had caused the blackout. When Marisol and Tatiana finally came home late Sunday night exhausted from all their bot repair work, Elena brought them up to date.

"Honestly, she can't be for real. Who would work all the critical jobs?" Elena reasoned.

"She isn't reasonable, she's insane," Tatiana growled, too tired to deal with this anymore.

Monday afternoon, Camila brought a crying Renata down to the fourth subfloor where the two were busily rechecking the manufacturing bots and mechanical arms. Two had needed further work to get fully operational once more. "Marisol, Tatiana, Renata has some really bad news for you. If you need some time off, take it."

Sobbing, Renata blurted out, "They've arrested Elena and taken her to the jail along with many others."

"Crap! What happened? Take it slowly, Renata," Tatiana stopped everything and pushed her body into the grief-stricken woman, comforting her.

"We were telling others who were asking if anyone could have made a solar eclipse and how that could possibly have been done. Elena told them it was impossible and all that, but then one of our other workers who's a Separatist went and got President Elmira and she brought the police-bots to take Elena away. She screamed at us, 'Any more such sedition and you will all be arrested!' We all shut up really fast, but everyone is angry now. Please, we have to get Elena out of jail somehow."

"Damn that idiotic woman!" Tatiana spat on the floor. "Okay, Renata, go home and leave the rest to us."

"What are you going to do?" she asked meekly, rubbing her streaked eyes and cheeks on her shoulders.

"We'll get her out of jail somehow," Tatiana promised. "Go home. If you can get word to the others, have them get to our quadraplex as soon as they can." She complied and Camila led her back to the elevator.

"I figured there would be some trouble, but this is worse than I expected. What are we going to do?" Marisol asked.

"Break her out and anyone else they have locked up! That's what!" Tatiana declared vehemently. "Come on, to the plans floor. We need to study the jail's layout."

A half hour later, Tatiana looked up from the detailed layout. "This is so simple it's child's play, love. Look here, one bot. We simply write a program that overrides the bot's orders and have the bot release them. Of course, one of us will have to be there to tell the women what to do, while one of us is here and sends the bot the special program of orders. You stay here and do that. I'll go there and make sure they all get away to their homes."

An hour later, the program was ready to be sent. Marisol gave Tatiana another hour to get there and into position. Then she moved her foot, which moved the mechanical arm that pressed the Send button. Their overriding program was sent electronically to the jail-bot. Now all she could do was to wait on Tatiana's return.

Tatiana stood not far from the unimposing jail, a small one room building. One Separatist Earth kindred was standing guard just outside the front door. From the plans, Tatiana knew inside the door was a staging area and beyond that was the locked door, which soon would open if their program worked. The problem she had to handle was this guard woman. She could attack her and for several minutes did consider blasting her with searing flames. Then common sense returned. No, she'd not be the first to kill another woman, not over something as foolish and stupid as this whole mess was. No, she would play along.

She strode up to the guard as if she belonged here. "Good day. All okay here?"

"Aye, all is quite."

"Good. I'm to spell you. My turn to watch the jail. You haven't had any trouble, have you? President Elmira didn't say that we had, though. Anything I ought to know about before I relieve you?"

"Er. Well, my feet are aching. I've been standing here for hours. Tell her to give us a chair or something, if she wants us to stand around here all day. Thanks. All has been quiet for a couple of hours." She looked very grateful to be finally relieved and slowly walked off leaving Tatiana standing before the main front doors. She waited until the woman was totally out of sight and then opened the doors and entered. The police-bot stood before the door, totally unemotional and unmoving. Tatiana waited. At last, their program was received and the police-bot moved to the locked door and unlocked it. Then it moved back to the side wall and shut down. Tatiana spoke the command words and the door opened, revealing six women crammed into the small room.

"Tatiana? Have they arrested you too?" Elena cried out. Her face looked a mess; she'd been crying. So had the five others, some of whom Tatiana knew casually.

"No. Marisol and I are rescuing you. Come on; let's get you home. All of you. Shit!" Tatiana saw all six had been hobbled. Their usual boots had been replaced by the sexy bedroom ballet boots.

"But we can't walk in these," Elena protested a little.

"Shit! Well, you can walk. It's hard. Marisol and I did it a while back. Okay, let's get you all to our house. It is only about four blocks. Come on, you have to try to get out of here before anyone finds out. If anyone tries to stop us, I'll flame them!"

The six desperately wanted out of the jail and were willing to try. Wobbling wildly, they got onto their feet and took halting steps, trying to figure out how to walk in the boots and not lose their balance and take a nasty fall. "Take it slow. No rush," Tatiana encouraged them, thinking the exact opposite, however. Somehow, they had to make it, she thought.

A wild hour passed before she got the six women finally inside her commons room and thus safe for the moment. None had actually fallen, but all were in bad shape. Their knees throbbed and their cramped feet were sending waves of pain up their legs. Still, they'd somehow endured it to get away, to get free. They sat down on the first sofa they found.

"Okay, give me a minute to get some bots in here and get them off your feet."

"Hurry, I can't take the pain much longer," Elena fought hard to keep from breaking down completely. The pain and cramping in her feet was almost too much to endure.

An hour later, all six were free and back into normal shoes. "Okay, head home, if home is a safe place for you. If not, go to some friend's home where you can be safe for now," Tatiana ordered. All six thanked her over and over before they crept out of the quadraplex, looking in all directions for police-bots or the president's women. Seeing none, they headed off in five directions. Meanwhile Elena headed off to take a long, hot, soaking bath to relieve her aching knees and feet. Tatiana headed back to the Maintenance Unit.

"It worked perfectly," Tatiana explained what had happened to Marisol. "They had them all hobbled with ballet boots, but I got them to our house and out of them. I told them to go to a home where they would be safe. Honestly, we had best take some precautions, since they know where Elena lives. After all, we eight are all considered to be Joiners, even though we are not politically active about such things."

"I have already thought of that, love. I've sent a new program to our door-bots. They will only open when they hear the commands from one of us eight. So if President Elmira's lackeys try to come to raid our place, they can't get in."

"Brilliant love, brilliant. We can sleep nights now," Tatiana replied with a big smile.

Again, they got home late at night. Camila kept everyone on overtime, getting the damage from the blackout repaired. The two were rudely awakened the next morning by another roving speech-bot delivering the latest proclamation from President Elmira.

"President Elmira speaking. Due to the widespread civil unrest and sedition by members of the Joiners attempting to disrupt our government and world, I have no choice but to declare martial law. My appointed deputies will use lethal force to put down all protests and civil unrest. This seditious attempt by the Joiners to destroy our government and society will be met with deadly force. Those who somehow escaped from jail yesterday afternoon will be apprehended and dealt with severely."

"Damn, does she have to have the bot at full volume this early in the morning?" Tatiana complained. "I am still tired from yesterday and we've got another twelve hour shift coming." She was in an ill humor as she and Marisol got up and dressed. They headed to the communal dining room, having forgotten who was supposed to be fixing the eight their breakfasts this morning. A glance at the wall chart caused Tatiana to groan even more. It was her turn.

"Don't fret, Tatiana," Elena called out. "After what you did for me and the others yesterday and knowing you both pulled an extra late shift, I went ahead and fixed our breakfasts. Come on, get ready, it's about done." One by one the other five women ambled into the commons, most were sleepy-eyed as well, but chatting over the rude awakening message from their president.

"Do you think her lackeys will actually use physical force on us?" asked Isabel, forking a pile of pancakes.

"That's what her message says to me," Renata replied.

"I can't believe she would go so far as to actually harm any women, not really," Marisol gave their leader the benefit of doubt. "No one has ever been killed in a battle that I have ever heard of. She is just over-enthusiastic about her crazed notions of keeping the kindred groups from mingling. I sure don't know why some women think that way. There is nothing different about any of us eight, except our special powers. Honestly, so many of us look so darn similar and yet we have different elemental powers."

She was referring to the unusual fact that, although there were about a thousand women in Madiera, physically many women looked very similar to each other. Suddenly, Marisol realized why. There were only originally seventy women rescued and from these women had come all the other generations with no outside gene pool from which to draw. Now it made sense that so far in her life she'd seen dozens of other women who looked remarkably like herself. True, there were differences in how they dressed and wore their hair, but other than that, these others could well pass for her if one ignored the little details. Still, each had their own personalities and mannerisms and was found in all four kindred groups.

This, she remarked to the others, changing the topic to something far more interesting.

With breakfast done, the women prepared to head to work. "I think it would be wise of you, Elena, to perhaps take the day off and not leave the safety of the house," Tatiana advised and she agreed. The president's warning was a little scary.

Marisol and Tatiana headed out of their common room's door, bound for their long twelve hour shift at the Maintenance Unit. Just outside, they saw six women wearing black headbands. One woman called out, "Those are the two that came to the president's office some time ago telling her all sorts of lies about Madiera. Kill them, and then we'll get the other seditious Joiners inside."

"What are you doing?" Marisol asked politely. "We are just going to work at the Maintenance Unit."

One woman focused and shot a wall of flames at Marisol, another woman shot a giant wall of water at Tatiana. Marisol reacted swiftly and erected a Fire Shield around herself and the flames swept harmlessly around her. Tatiana, on the other hand, was knocked off her feet and sent drenched and sprawling some ten feet onto their lawn. Just then, an Air kindred shot a hurricane force wind from herself at Marisol, knocking her off her feet and sending her flying out into the yard. Marisol reacted, using physics. If this air person was shooting this volume of air at her, then she had to be sucking it in from behind her. She conjured a huge wall of flames, placing it behind the woman.

Instantly, the flames were sucked into the Air kindred who was continuing to shoot the massive wind at Marisol. At once, her hair and clothes burst into flames. The hurricane wind ceased as the woman rapidly burned up. Although drenched and lying on her back, Tatiana responded, launching a wall of flames centered on the Water kindred woman who had attacked her. That woman attempted to counter by conjuring another volume of water to put out the flames. While it did so, the woman was cooked in a cloud of hot steam that resulted.

The other six companions came rushing out of the

house to help defend their two companions. Winds, flames, water flows, and flying ground tore up their front lawn and blackened the side of their home. A Fire kindred got the upper hand on Elena, who got pinned to the ground by an Earth kindred's spell. She launched a wall of flames at Elena. Marisol reacted by throwing a Fire Shield over Elena, though that left her open to another huge wall of water, that nearly drowned her and washed her some fifty feet away into their neighbor's yard.

Elena, now fighting angry, focused and caused the grass beneath the feet of her Fire kindred opponent to suddenly grow and entangle the woman, pulling her down onto the ground. Angrier than she had ever been in her life, she caused the dirt to swell up and swallow the woman, suffocating her to death. At two to one odds, the remaining attackers were quickly killed. The eight soaking wet, soot covered, slightly burned, muddy women finally got to their feet. Their dresses were tattered and ripped, as well as completely soiled.

"Anyone hurt badly?" Marisol called out, making her way over from their neighbor's yard, whose occupants now came outside to see the aftermath.

"I got a few burns," Renata said.

"Same here, and a whole lot of bruises," Isabel added. None had escaped getting bruised, but none were seriously injured, due entirely to the fact that all four kindred groups had worked together to protect the others.

"Damn President Elmira! She should be here and dead too!" exclaimed Tatiana, now angrier than any of the other seven had ever seen.

"Look! There are more battles going on!" Sofia called out. As the eight looked around their town, they could see shooting flames, flying debris, water spouts, and even the ground shaking a little coming from a dozen other locations. "Come on, let's lend others a hand and put an end to President Elmira's attacks on our people!" Tatiana screamed and headed off to the closest ongoing battle. Marisol tossed her soaking and filthy hair back over her shoulders and headed after Tatiana. One by one, the other six trailed after the headstrong Tatiana. While they were horrified at what they had been forced to do, to kill other women, they knew they were given no choice. It was kill or be killed.

"How could it have come to this?" wailed Elena. "Why?"

When the others caught up to Tatiana, they saw her burning up two Air kindred lackeys, ending their battle with a lone Earth kindred woman who looked pretty battered. Isabel volunteered to stay with her and get her to a medical-bot. Meanwhile with savage eyes, Tatiana moved on towards the next battle, the others trailing behind her, still unable to catch up with her.

Four hours later and a dozen battles ended, Tatiana finally reached the president's home, where President Elmira was hold up with six of her remaining supporters. "Come out and fight your own battles, you chicken shit bitch!" Tatiana screamed and torched her home. Built from non-combustible materials, her searing flames did little actual damage, just psychological.

A Water kindred opened a window and sent a huge wall of water at Tatiana, washing her off her feet, sending her sliding a dozen feet away. She countered viciously. She shot a precise welding beam at the woman's head. A hideous shriek was that woman's last sound. As the other six got to Tatiana, they saw dozens of other battle-scarred women swarming here as well. Soon over fifty women surrounded the president's home.

Tatiana continued to yell at the president, who did not respond. Nor did any others attempt to attack them from windows. At last, totally fuming, Tatiana joined with another Air kindred and sent a huge searing blast of fire at the main door propelled with a hurricane force wind behind it. The door shattered, blown completely off its hinges, flying into the interior of the home. The volume of flames continued inward along with the massive volume of wind. Windows suddenly exploded outward, bringing flames with them. A second later, both elemental effects ceased, their duration expired.

"We give up! We surrender!" screamed the cowardly President Elmira. Slowly she came walking from a back room of her home towards the gaping hole where her front door had been. Behind her came two remaining legislature members and the sole surviving judge, along with two other trusted Separatist supporters.

"Kill the bitches!" a woman screamed.

"They deserve to die like they did to my wife!" another yelled. Soon fifty voices cried out for their deaths.

"Wait, wait!" Marisol yelled at the top of her lungs. The cacophony died down. "If we kill them, that makes us no better than them. No, arrest them and keep them in jail for the rest of their lives. We are not the killers that they are." She repeated her suggestions for several minutes before the wild adrenaline-invoked emotions began to subside.

Elena finally spoke up, "Take them to the jail and ballet boot them so they are hobbled like they did to us." A dozen angry women volunteered and soon they led the five off towards the jail. "What do we do now?" she asked.

Marisol took charge. "Okay everyone. Return to the battlefields and get medical-bots to our injured women first. Don't give medical attention to the enemy women until our wounded are helped first. Then, let's set about cleaning up this mess. We don't want to have all the children seeing this awful carnage."

One woman yelled, "Marisol for president!" Soon the remaining women took up the chant. Another told her they would spread the word, Marisol for president, everywhere. Marisol sighed, she didn't want to be president; she wanted to repair bots.

As their small group headed back the way that they came, Tatiana commented, "Love, I bet anything you are going to be voted into office whether you like it or not. Damn," she stopped as they arrived at the site where two badly injured women were lying on the ground.

Again, Marisol had to take charge. They had only six medical-bots and dozens of women in need of help. She sent out others to begin to size up the aftermath and get her the names and locations of the injured women, prioritizing their injuries. They had a break in that most all the battles had taken place in the southern quarter of the city. Hence, the locations were fairly close and many women volunteered to relay word to Marisol, who then took charge of ordering the medical-bots, attempting to send them to the six women who were in the worst shape.

Tatiana, on the other hand, took charge of the funeral-bots. Accompanied by those bots and several other women, she visited each site and had the dead counted and loaded into the funeral-bots. Other women helped the injured who could walk make their way to Marisol's home, which they began to use as their base of operations.

Their hospital could hold five women at one time. Unfortunately, Marisol soon found the ten women really needed to be hospitalized for some time and sent two other women along with the six medical-bots to help the two nurses on duty there. By lunchtime, the medical-bots were finally attending to the remainder of the injured women. Many had bad burns and sprains, but some had cuts from hitting the concrete sidewalks or sides of their homes. Of the ten, three were severely burned and did not survive. The seven others had broken legs and had to remain hospitalized for some weeks, though there was no lack of volunteers to help them.

Late that afternoon, the eight finally were finished and headed into their house to clean up. All eight looked utterly filthy. Their dresses were in shreds and sooty. Dried mud covered their faces and had matted into their hair as well. As they entered, Tatiana gave her final counts. "Well, thirty-six Separatists are dead." Marisol smiled, her lover had not left one battlefield for the next until she had made sure that all the attacking women had been slain. She'd never seen Tatiana so angry as she had been this morning. "We lost a dozen ordinary women. I don't know if they were actually Joiners or not. Thirty-three others were injured but not badly. I don't think three more in the hospital will make it, but another seven will. I still think Elmira ought to have been killed."

"She was too much of a coward to fight herself, she sent out her lackeys to do the fighting for her," Elena countered, a touch of anger still in her voice.

"Damned chicken shit coward got fifty women killed and for what? Some idiotic fancy of hers," Tatiana added her disgust to the conversation.

"You know, Alpha ought to have seen this coming and

done something. At this point, I don't see any real alternatives to our not coming clean and telling everyone precisely what is going on," Marisol declared. "The women of Madiera deserve to know the truth, the whole truth. That way, we can all work together and not endure another round of this insanity."

Just then, the mothers of the eight women all arrived at their quadraplex. "Dear, are you all right? We heard. Oh my god, you look horrible!" exclaimed Adoria, as she and the fifteen other worried mothers filed into their commons and saw the eight who had yet to have time to clean up.

"A lot of bruises and minor cuts mom. We're all right, but so many others are not," Marisol answered her moms and set the fears of the other mothers at ease. "We were about to clean up." They didn't get the chance for a while, as the women demanded to know what was going on and why Madiera had just had its first war ever. She had to explain a little but kept it light and to the direct events. At last, late afternoon, the eight finally headed to their respective baths.

They had barely gotten dressed when a dozen women came calling. "Marisol, it is official now. You are our new president. Next week we will hold elections for new legislature members and judges. In the meantime you are our president."

While Marisol wanted to say "crap," she desisted and replied, "Okay, just realize I have no political training and have no idea what will be required of me. I am a bot repair woman, really. I will do what I can though. Thank you."

"We need someone to tell us what is really going on. All of us are asking thousands of questions and no one has any real answers."

"I'll see if I can answer them all, but give me some time to get things worked out, okay? How are the injured women doing?"

"One has already died of her burns. Two more don't look good." They chatted a bit longer and the small group left.

"Congratulations, President Marisol," Tatiana exclaimed with a broad smile. Her friends joined in with similar accolades, further embarrassing her.

"Okay, then you all are going to be my staff," she got the last word.

After supper, she and Tatiana headed off to meet with Alpha. At the least, he had to be informed about what had happened. Besides, she wanted to get his opinion on just how much she ought to reveal to the many women of Madiera. It took them nearly a half hour finally to get down to his control room.

"Have you heard or seen what happened this morning?" Marisol asked pointedly.

Again, Alpha was thankful his makers had programming in appropriate human responses. In a sad, though mechanical tone, he replied, "Yes, we would have intervened if you had not gotten it under control. Are the women demanding to know what is going on?" he asked.

"Yes, they have made me their president, but I really don't want the office. Still, I have to tell the many women something, Alpha. It is more than just a political mess this time. Honestly, the blackout is at the heart of the issue. Many believed the lie of Elmira's, that someone made an eclipse of the sun. You have to admit from their very isolated world view, the reality of Madiera is far beyond their imaginations. Just how much of the truth ought I reveal?" Marisol asked.

Again, he sighed. "This is a touchy subject, fraught with perils no matter which way we go. Some of you are capable of grasping the whole truth. Women such as yourselves can handle it well. Others, I am afraid cannot handle it. Still, with bot failures looming in the not too distant future, we have to prepare the women or face even more chaos when the bots begin breaking down faster than we can fix or replace them."

"Couldn't we make some kind of presentation similar to the one you gave us? Let everyone know the whole truth?" she asked.

"You would prefer that, wouldn't you?"

"Yes, of course."

"But what about those women who simply will be unable to cope with that?"

"What will they do, if they can't cope with it?"

"Suicide. Depression if they are luckier. Some may just give up and succumb. Marisol, we are doomed no matter which way we go. If we say little about the true situation, when the bots fail, many will perish. If we tell them the whole truth now, many may still succumb, unwilling to go on."

"Well, doing nothing is the wrong thing to do," Marisol replied. "We know that truth. The wrong thing for us to do is absolutely nothing, so we have to do something. If I am going to lead our people, then I want them to know the truth, the whole truth. That way, I stand the best chance of getting everyone onboard to help out when we need it. Yet, you think some will not be able to handle it. I guess I can live with that, because if they are that weak, then they will surely perish when the going really gets rough around here as the bots begin to fail."

"Then, Marisol Armanda, I bow to your will. We will break our four hundred plus years of silence and make our presence known."

"Thanks. Is there any way we can show everyone some of those video images that you showed us? That would help a whole lot."

"Yes, I will send out appropriate bots to set up a large number of monitors so everyone can see them. We will do this at the central square, with monitors arranged in a circle around the fountain. Let us do it on Saturday around one so all will have eaten. Shall we four go over the video images that you believe should be shown?"

The four spent many hours that night and most of the next day working out the proper sequence and what Alpha would say. Meanwhile Elena sent out a message-bot, reusing one of those that ex-president Elmira had used, announcing the huge meeting, encouraging everyone to come, including children. While Marisol initially wondered why Alpha chose Saturday for the revelations, she began to see some logic behind it. all the women would be wearing their fanciest dresses and highest heels, a party mood. This might help soften the shock, but then some might faint in their tight corsets, there was always that possibility to consider. When asked, Alpha said that with the women looking their best, this might lower the chances of depression.

Marisol and her group arrived early, just after noon, and found Alpha's bots had set up dozens of large HD flat screens along with a large number of chairs. She'd never seen so many chairs in one place before and wondered where they had all come from. He'd also set up a small platform with a microphone. One of the monitors told her what to do. Step upon the platform and speak into the microphone. As she did so, a bot came rolling up to her and extended a long arm, fastening a device on a chain around her neck.

"There, now we can communicate, Marisol," she heard Alpha's voice coming from the small box resting above her large cleavage.

"Cool. Can you hear me too?"

"Yes, just fine. You may keep the device so we can talk whenever we need to discuss something. Are you ready?"

"Yes, but I am really nervous. I've not talked to so many women before."

"Take a deep breath and relax."

"I can't, not in this tight corset, silly." Alpha laughed, though she thought he probably already knew that.

As they waited, women and children began arriving way early. Everyone was extremely interested in hearing what Marisol would have to say. The recent events of the blackout and the vicious killings were on everyone's minds, none more so than the mothers with their younger children. Until now, they found it terribly difficult to explain to their young what and why these things had happened. Most were hopeful they would get some kind of an answer this afternoon.

Marisol and Tatiana suddenly had to laugh. Several jail-bots were ushering the five jailed women, including Elmira, here to listen. They were being forced to walk all the way here in their ballet boots, the bots keeping them from falling over as they teetered mightily, swearing often.

Elena said, "Serves them right to get a taste of their own medicine." She recalled her own nightmare wearing them and trying to get home from the jail. As they drew closer, Marisol saw the bots had also hastened chains to their legs, preventing them from moving one foot more than a foot from the other at a time, adding to their misery. Elmira shot a glare of utter hatred at Marisol and her group, but lost her precarious balance and would have fallen had the bot not caught her.

Others swarmed in and soon Marisol forgot about the woman and the evil she'd caused. Instead, she focused on trying to calm her jittery stomach. At last, one o'clock came and she stepped carefully upon the platform and looked around at well over nine hundred women and children.

"Hello. I am Marisol Armando. I've asked everyone here today so all you can learn all the truths that Tatiana and I have learned during the last six months or so. She and I discovered all this on our own. I guess you can say we were overly curious. Anyway, I will begin by making what will seem to many of you to be a wholly outrageous statement and then I will back it up with hard video images so you all can see for yourselves. The truth of Madiera is that this is not a world. Elena here discovered by accident that there is a barrier wall around our square mile of world. In fact, Madiera is part of a giant spaceship called the Arc in Space by its creators, our ancestors. It is run by two robots called Alpha and Beta, who have been watching over us for over four hundred years now, quietly allowing us to live our lives in peace. I give you Alpha who will explain further."

She stepped down and took the last remaining chair, sitting among her friends. On the monitors, the image of Alpha and Beta in their control room at the bottom of the spaceship appeared along with the star field in the viewing window behind them. Thus began the four-hour presentation by the two robots. Each point that they made was backed up by video images, just as they had done for Marisol and Tatiana.

Near the end, he explained, "As Marisol and Tatiana have already discovered, our bots are wearing out and we are soon going to be facing major breakdowns of most all our key life-sustaining bots." He went on to describe the anticipated failures and the predicted number of years they had before such occurred. "Marisol, Tatiana, and we are working to find solutions to these many problems before disaster strikes. Yes, the massive power failure and blackout last Saturday was one of these failures, unanticipated by all us." He outlined what had happened and showed images of Marisol and Tatiana welding in the replacement copper, fixing the break, bringing a smile to their two faces. Neither had known that Alpha had somehow recorded them doing it. The short clip added to their credibility, a very nice touch, she thought.

He ended, "In the ensuing days, months, and years, we must all work together to somehow solve the huge problems we face. Yes, Beta and I take the responsibility for being unable to find appropriate solutions long ago. Yet, you are all alive. Considering we were able to only save seventy women and that your numbers have grown to almost a thousand, in that we are proud of what we've done. I hope you can forgive our recent failures to help and assist all you. Thank you and good evening." The monitors went blank and powered down.

The crowd waited a little longer to see if Marisol would say anything else. She felt all eyes on her and again stepped upon the platform. "That's all. I hope we can all work together to solve our massive problems. Thank you all for coming. Let's get some supper, I'm hungry." Several laughed; they were too. A very sober, silent bunch of women rose and left quietly, only their heels clicking on the concrete could be heard, along with some occasional whispers. All were too stunned, too shocked to respond much at the moment. Marisol suspected by morning they would recover and have a million questions for her.

Chapter 10 Depression

On Sunday, the funeral-bots recycled the dead from the battles of Bloody Tuesday, just as everything in Madiera was recycled. However, beginning on Sunday afternoon and continuing for some days, groups of women sent spokeswomen to her, advising them of the group's decisions. The first of these was her own mother.

"I represent quite a lot of us mothers, Marisol. They have asked me to state our position in no uncertain terms. We do not want to have anything whatsoever to do with these strange-looking and certainly evil, wicked man creatures. Just look at the horrendous damage that man creatures have done. Destroyed a whole world. No, we want you to find us a place where we can continue with our own life style, entirely devoid of these man creatures. You will do that for us, won't you?" Her mother was pushing hard to get her to agree to this vital point.

"Mom, I will do what I can so that we can all survive, flourish and prosper. I cannot guarantee that wherever we wind up that there will be none of these man creatures there. We don't have unlimited time to find such a place, but I will do my best. Is that okay?" It was and her mother left feeling as if she'd gotten what she wanted from her daughter.

Another group was insistent on making contact with planets that had man creatures on them in hopes of getting the men to take over for Alpha and do a better job protecting the women. Still another group of women wanted her only to find a planet that had bots. "Look we cannot survive without our bots. So wherever you take us, it has to have bots or we will die." She couldn't disagree with that last point, not yet anyway. Another group wanted her to land the Arc on the first habitable planet that had no humans on it and set up a colony there, starting over, so to speak. By the weekend, she'd heard supporters for just about all possible variations that she and Alpha had either considered or even thought of. It ran the gamut of choices. Some even wanted her to do nothing at all and allow Madiera to die, if that was what destiny held for them.

What concerned her more was Alpha's dire predictions of depression and women taking their own lives. While it was most difficult for one of Madiera's women to kill herself, it was possible. One could drown oneself in one's bathtub, she reasoned while taking a long soaking bath with Tatiana. There were virtually no high places where a woman could jump and fall to her death. She could not use a bot to kill her, because the bots would flatly refuse to harm the woman. While they could use their elemental powers, they were effective only against others not of their own kindred as witnessed in Bloody Tuesday. No, she reasoned, it would be darn difficult for a Madiera woman to kill herself.

By the end of the week, she felt more confident about it all. Only two women had drowned in their bathtubs, unwilling to face the awful truth of their lives. At last, Marisol relaxed about this issue and focused on repairing bots and working with Alpha to come up with an exit plan. He continued to discover more planetary systems. Some had no rocky ones, only large gaseous giants. Others were rocky, but had sub-zero daytime temperatures. Other rocky planets had daytime temperatures so high that the bots would literally melt. So it went.

Her restful weekend was abruptly interrupted. Tatiana came rushing as fast as she could in her party outfit. "Damn, damn, damn! They've broke Elmira out of jail! I knew that we should have killed her when we had the chance!"

Marisol and Tatiana headed off to the jail. One of their Earth kindred had used an Earth power on the back of the building, turning a large section into mud. All five women had made a clean escape. Marisol ordered the police-bots to search the women's homes and she then headed off to the Maintenance Unit where the master computer was located. Her plan was to see if there was a way to locate the escaped women, while Tatiana organized a search party to look for them.

In their party apparel, everything was slowed down, compared to a week day. Marisol realized this, as it took her almost twice as long to get to the computer. "I bet they

planned it for Saturday just because we are hampered the
most on Saturdays. Ah well, let's see if the computer can find
them." She ran several programs and had no luck at all. Soon,
the police-bots reported that the women's homes were still
vacant. She ordered them to remain there on the off-chance
that they would sooner or later return to their original homes.
If she were Elmira, that would be the last place she'd go to.
Still, she wanted that possibility covered.

For an hour, she tried several ways to track the women.
Then a warning flashed on her screen, followed by four others.
The warning said that repeated attempts were made to crack a
password. Curious, she focused her attention on these
attempts. There were five of them. The passwords applied to
ballet boots! This had to be Elmira! Quickly, she called up the
program that the woman called Teresa had installed when she
encased the five women in them. Teresa had been extremely
upset over their murdering of her mate and had not followed
the usual protocols. Rather, she'd set up her own diabolical
one. She'd put in specific commands into the women's boot-
bots and password protected them. From the master
computer, she retrieved Teresa's program, though she could
not alter it without that password.

"My god, Teresa was vindictive!" The program was a
very simple one. The boots-bot were not to ever open. That is,
the boot-bots were to ensure that the boots remained on the
women forever, including when bathing and sleeping. Teresa
allowed no way ever for the boots to be removed unless the
password was given. Now the repeated attempts to hack the
password made sense to Marisol. Obviously some of their
Separatist supporters had broken them out of jail and were
now engaged in trying to free them from their restraining
boots. Given enough time and enough tries, they were bound
to be successful.

Marisol then had an idea. She wrote her own program
and reviewed it. She smiled and then used her mechanical arm
to press the Upload button. She sat back and laughed. Her
program also used the same password that the master
computer gave to her. However, her program ordered just the
opposite. The boot-bots were to keep the boots on her as long

as the password was properly given. It was now catch-22. If they gave the boot-bots the right password, then Teresa's program would allow them to be taken off. However, at the same time, given that correct password, the boot-bots were then commanded not to allow them to be taken off.

"Oh, that *is* diabolical!" Tatiana exclaimed when Marisol later told her what she'd done. "Well, they must be hiding out with some of their supporters. Do you want us to go house to house and search for them?"

"No, we have far more important things to worry about. Hobbled as they are, they cannot be a serious threat. Sooner or later, they will reappear and we can recapture them at that time." Marisol concluded. She had no idea how wrong this decision would turn out to be.

Several uneventful weeks went by. No one came forward with sightings of the escaped prisoners and only two women had managed to drown themselves. Thus, Marisol had put the depression idea out of her mind, focusing on the serious problems that they faced, still with no solutions at hand. On Friday afternoon just around suppertime, Herminia came to visit her. She was a forty year old mother and her work job was to monitor the weekly grocery shopping that the various women did. Of course, there were no real grocery stores. Rather, the women made their weekly orders via the grocery-bots and their menu of items. In a food storage warehouse, robotic arms pulled the requested items from bins and when complete, a delivery-bot took the load to the woman's home, where the items were transferred to the kitchen storage-bot.

"Hi President Marisol. I've come across something that is really strange, but I don't know what it means. I thought you should at least see it. Can you come to my work station?"

"We were just about to have supper. Could it wait until we've eaten? You are invited to share ours." Marisol convinced the older woman to stay and dine with them. An hour later, she stood over Herminia watching her monitor as the woman entered her commands.

"You see the weekly orders for groceries for this customer. Do you see anything strange going on?" Herminia asked, hoping that Marisol would see what she saw. If she didn't, then perhaps it was just a computer anomaly.

Marisol was on the spot, but she looked over the display of ten weeks of grocery requests. Then it struck her. "She's ordered nearly the same quantities each week until about three weeks ago. She's ordered nothing at all since then? Surely, there must be some mistake. Perhaps she has recently married and is now ordering from her mate's account." Marisol thought that this was a reasonable explanation for the anomaly.

"I thought so too. So I checked. She's registered as a widow with three younger children. There is no record of her remarrying yet. I've found three dozen more just like this one. Could we have some kind of bot failure already? I know you said that the bots would be breaking down more and more quickly as time went on," Herminia asked.

"This is the first I've heard of such a thing. Send me a listing of all these anomalous accounts please and I'll check into them right away. If they haven't been ordering any groceries, by now they could all be starving," Marisol suddenly had a sinking feeling in her stomach. That her corset and boots suddenly activated into their party format didn't help. She gasped a little as her waist was shrunk further. So did Herminia for that matter.

"Okay, I'll do it before I go home," she promised.

It took Marisol twice as long to get home as it had to get to Herminia's work place, due to her party change, which annoyed her a little. This whole notion that women had to look their sexiest and best on Friday nights and Saturdays was a bit much. Women ought to have a choice in the matter, she thought, wondering if it could be somehow made possible by Alpha. She quickly discarded this notion. He had far more important things to handle than overly tight corsets and too high heels.

At home, she now had the president's computer and she waited for Herminia's data to come to her. Once she had it on this computer, she would reroute that data to the master computer and then go to over to it to continue her explorations. If only she could somehow get access to the master computer through her presidential one, it would save her a lot of wasted time. She made a note to ask Alpha if such was possible. Meantime, she took the opportunity to fully catch her breath and rest her knees and feet. As she waited, she explained the anomaly to Tatiana, who agreed that this was indeed ominous.

"Why does it always happen on the weekend when we are wearing our fanciest outfits making even walking a challenge," she complained to Marisol.

"So we can look sexy while we deal with the crisis?" she taunted her mate who chuckled.

Before long, the two women began their long, slow walk to the Maintenance Unit. "At least our knees and feet are getting used to these heels. I remember our first days in them. We had to stop at each bench along the way to rest up," Tatiana pointed out again.

An hour later, the two looked over the results. One woman had indeed gotten married, which accounted for her lack of grocery orders, she was now ordering from her mate's house. That left three dozen unexplained anomalies, which Marisol had printed off and had Tatiana stick the paper into her belt. Now the two made the long walk back home, planning what to do next.

As they strolled along enjoying the late evening air, Tatiana suggested that she could round up some women and go visit each home and check on them. On Sunday, she did just that. This Sunday turned out to be one of the saddest that Marisol and Tatiana ever had. Her crew found over seventy dead women and children, the latter being the hardest to stomach. Often they found a short note usually to the effect that they found life now to be utterly pointless. Marisol now knew that Alpha was right, many women were terribly depressed after discovering the true reality of their existence.

As a consequence, Marisol had Herminia monitor the grocery orders extensively. Anytime she spotted the beginnings of an anomaly, she reported it to Marisol, who sent some of her volunteer women to the home in hopes of dissuading the women from their planned starvation. How to instill hope became her next big hurdle, but she had no real way to do that, without giving out false promises.

A few weeks after this, Elena came to her with some additional startling news. She'd overheard a secret conversation between several women. "Marisol! There is now an Euthanasia Squad roaming about our town. They claim that if you want to die, let them know and they will put you out of your misery. I bet Elmira is behind this!"

Again, Marisol was pulled off her work with Alpha to investigate this. She collected data from the funeral-bots who picked up and later recycled the deceased of Madiera. To her shock, she found that unknown to her, for the last month, at least ten women had died. Cause of death was listed as drowning or suffocation for the most part. Now she had a group of murders going around eliminating depressed women!

Although she spent hours trying to solve this one, any reasonable solution eluded her. There was really no way for her to tell who might be so depressed that they would ask the Euthanasia Squad to kill them. All that she could do was to watch the weekly death toll and hope that this phenomenon would soon die out.

Several months passed before the death toll dropped to zero for a week. Another hundred women and children were gone. The population of Madiera had dropped to a little over eight hundred at the end of term graduation ceremony for this term's high school seniors who would become adults tomorrow, donning their fancy outfits for the first time and attending their prom. She was required to give a short speech Friday night at their graduation and she used the opportunity to attempt to instill confidence and hope as well as make a pitch to the new graduates to consider working for the Maintenance Unit. Camila was pleased that ten new adults volunteered. Although raw recruits, she began to have enough personnel to at long last keep up with all the bot repairs that had slowly been increasing through the year. Further, with the loss of nearly two hundred women and children, their bots were confiscated, either repaired or refurbished, and put in storage for later use.

Alpha projected that this added another year or two before the anticipated big breakdown. While that was encouraging, it also meant that women and children were dying at an alarming rate. Never in the history of Madiera had so many women perished in one year as had in this past one.

Chapter 11 False Hope

Having returned to the high school and seeing all the graduating eighteen year old girls about to become full adults, Marisol was filled with different feelings and emotions. In some ways, she longed for the freedom that she had had wearing jeans and tennis shoes, without a care in the world besides winning at soccer. On the other hand, she treasured her private times with Tatiana and how sexy she often looked. A times, she loved being dressed up so fancy but at others times it had been almost a curse. Strange how the year had gone, wholly not remotely how she'd thought when she accepted her diploma last year.

As she slipped beneath their satin covers Friday night, she felt quite passionate towards Tatiana. She'd never have survived this past year without her lover at her side nearly all the time. They shared a special evening.

At breakfast on Saturday, Alpha summoned her down to his control room. Dutifully, though dressed for the big dance this evening, the two made their slow way back to the Maintenance Unit and down the elevator.

"Hi, Alpha, Beta. What's up?" she asked. Both were slightly out of breath, dressed their party outfits.

"We have found a planet that has a high level of technology, where we might be able to acquire some of the things that we need," he replied. "We are running low on fuel for the ship. It's not yet critical but if we could acquire more, we would be able extend our search range." He started up the video system and the two began to watch what the two robots had captured via a small probe that they had sent down to the blue-green world below.

On another screen, various other spaceships were being monitored as they left the world or arrived. The probe zoomed in on a flying refueling station in a high orbit over the planet below. "Tests show that they are using the same fuel as we, so it is likely that we could get some, if we could find something to exchange for it."

"Is it likely that we have something that they might

want in trade?" Marisol asked.

"We don't yet have that data, but we have finally gotten their language translated and can understand their communications," Alpha stated factually.

Now the probe began showing what was on the surface. Enormous steel buildings rose like spires into the sky. Skyways ran at dizzying heights between floors of these structures and tiny people could be seen walking along them. At maximum magnification, they could make out that the man creatures wore business suits similar to those worn on their own world some four hundred plus years ago and the women wore dresses and heels. Not much more detail could be discerned before the probe was disintegrated in the atmosphere by planetary security rockets.

"It is, as far as we can tell, a society somewhat similar to yours before their fall. We have not detected many traces of bots, but there is a great deal of automatic devices, door openers for example. We would not recommend that you settle here. The decadence is alarmingly parallel to your original world. However, if you consent, we will allow one of their ambassadors to dock with the Arc and speak with us."

"We ought to at least try. If nothing else, we can gain valuable experience," Marisol agreed, somewhat eager to speak to someone from another world.

"We think alike. Beta, will you make the arrangements? I will escort these two to our meeting room. Don't worry. I have the translation program in operation. We will hear their speech translated with only a few second's delay. And they, likewise. Follow me. I caution you both, do not make any promises to these delegates. We need time to analyze fully any offer that they may make."

"Will you be videoing the meeting? If so and it is promising, we ought to show it to all the women," Tatiana asked.

"Yes, a complete record is being made. This way." The two entered a portion of the huge Arc that they'd not seen before and were soon lost. At last, they entered a room painted white. A large stainless steel table occupied the center of the room, while a dozen matching chairs with black comfortable cushions lined it. Alpha had brought two their personal machines here so that the two women would not feel too helpless. Additionally, he had several examples of the many bots lining one wall.

"Cool. These chairs have rollers on them," Tatiana exclaimed, as she slide around the room in her chair.

"I will escort the arriving ambassadors here. When I bring them in, you two should rise to meet them. I believe that is the appropriate protocol to follow. If you need anything, ask Beta." Alpha nodded and left.

"Do you think that we'll actually have something that these people will want? I know that Alpha really wants to get more fuel. More range means more potential planets and the better likelihood that we'll find a good place to settle," Tatiana asked.

"I don't know. I have butterflies in my stomach. Think of it, we will be meeting some people who are from another world! At least we are wearing our very best outfits. How's my makeup?" Marisol asked. The two chatted, very excited about this meeting.

After what seemed an eternity to the two women, they heard footsteps coming and both rose and faced the door, wondering what these man creatures would look like. The door opened and Alpha led six men into the room. Three wore some kind of black uniforms and had what must have been weapons strapped to their waist belts. Two others wore plain white jackets over their suits, these reached to their knees. The other man wore a silk grey suit with a dull red tie. He had black hair and a well-groomed moustache. His keen eyes missed nothing.

Alpha spoke, "Ambassador Kyle, may I present President Marisol Armando and her assistant Tatiana Vileno." He mentioned the names of the other two men, adding that they were scientists. The two women bowed to Kyle, who seemed shocked to see them. His eyes involuntarily stared at their breasts and then slowly moved down their bodies to their bright red boots and then back up, stopping again at their soccer ball sized bosoms. Only when seated did he finally look them in their eyes.

"Madam President, it is quite an honor to see women so

very well endowed." Knowing no better, the two took this as a compliment and smiled at him.

Alpha outlined what he needed, the fuel and some critical raw materials as well as computer chips. "Ah, fuel, yes we have that in abundance. We can supply bolts of fabric and grains. Alas, I fear that our computer chips would not be for sale at any price. State secrets and all that," Kyle said politely. "And what would you have that we might accept in trade?"

After some discussion, the sole focus became the bots. Kyle said, "Your bots intrigue me. Could my scientists examine them?" While they did so, Marisol could not help but detect great envy coming from them, though they attempted to mask their enthusiasm over this technology that they did not possess. Alpha was willing to part with some of these because of the sudden surplus created with the death of nearly two hundred women.

While they were having the time of their lives examining the bots, Kyle took a different approach. "Mr. Alpha, you have said that you have a large number of women on board. Are they as good looking as your president and her assistant?" He asked coyly.

"Yes, we all try to look our best at all times," Marisol replied and Kyle changed his focus to her.

"Might I ask if they also are as well-endowed as you two are?"

"If by that you mean do they have large breasts, then yes, we all do. We call them soccer balls in jest. You will find that all we women appear pretty much as we two do. True, some are a bit taller and some, shorter. We wear our hair differently. Some have far more curly hair than I do, for example. But yes, we two are quite typical of our women. Might I ask why you are asking?"

Kyle flushed a little. "Well, on our world, we have a, shall we say, shortage of available women — a genetic mishap of terrible proportions. Now this might sound harsh and inappropriate, but we would be very much interested in accepting some of your women who might wish to settle on our world, marrying some of our men, of course. They would need to be able to bear children, naturally."

"Oh! Well, I admit that might be a possibility for some of our women. However, Ambassador Kyle, as you can see, we cannot survive without our bots. If some women chose to do so, they'd have to bring their bots with them. Also some of them have younger children who could not be left behind. They are all girls, by the way." His slight frown vanished when she mentioned the girls. She understood his thinking: girls would grow up to become women, which they apparently needed.

"But of course. We would not accept anything less," he replied.

"If our women choose to come, how would they be treated?" Marisol asked, completely uncertain how to ask what she wanted to know. Would the men treat them well or would they treat them as she had seen in the videos of her ancient ancestors? She lacked the vocabulary to describe such things.

His reply was what she expected it would be and she knew that she had no idea how to ask what she needed to know. He'd probably not answer truthfully either, she now realized. "Oh they would be very well treated, I assure you, Madam President." He seemed a tad too eager to be very agreeable, she thought.

The scientists finally finished their examinations and Alpha suggested, "I would suggest that you return to your people and discuss what we have to offer, while we do likewise. Shall I contact you in say two days?"

"Excellent, excellent Mr. Alpha, Madam President. That would be ideal. Two days then," Kyle replied. He rose and bowed to the two women and left, his guards forming a wall around him, but not until they too stared at the women's bosoms and legs.

Once they were gone, Tatiana grinned, "Well, we sure attracted their attention! Did you notice how they stared at us?"

Marisol giggled. "How could I miss it? He likes what I like, your breasts, my love." Tatiana smiled and chuckled herself. "Still, I don't really trust him. What did he mean about a genetic mishap? Why are they really short of women? I can't put my foot on anything substantial, except that he seemed way too smooth." The two continued to chat until Alpha returned to escort them back to the control room where Beta was waiting for them.

"Okay, I have more data on the interview. On this monitor, you can see their bodies' vital signs, blood pressure, pulse, and breathing patterns. Here are their patterns as they were walking to the conference room. Here is where they got a good look at you two."

"What do those increases mean?" asked Tatiana.

"In humans, it means that you two sexually aroused them, highly so. I would almost suggest that they felt a real sexual lust for you both. Now here are the two scientists' reactions to the bots. Again, they were extremely excited about them, but not quite in the same way as with you women. Conclusion: I believe that Kyle was telling the truth in that they greatly desire the bots and that technology and that they do desire to accept some women onto their world," Beta said dryly, but factually.

"Still, I am bothered. I don't trust him, Kyle, somehow. I got an eerie feeling about what he said or didn't say. What did he mean by genetic mishap? Why are there so few women on this world?"

"That's why I asked you to be a part of this meeting. We robots cannot get such intuitions as you humans can. Your insight is most valuable. We will see if we can find answers for you. In the meantime, Beta will prepare a short video presentation that you can make tomorrow for all the women. It will perhaps give them some much needed hope. Still, don't make promises that we might not be able to keep," Alpha requested. They chatted a bit more before the two left to return home.

They had just enough time to eat their dinner and freshen up before they had to leave to attend the Saturday night high school prom night. The president always was required to attend the major event. She and Tatiana promised to tell the six others about the meeting with the men creatures when they returned.

"We were so awkward in our heels as these young women were on our prom night?" Tatiana whispered.

Memories of a year ago flooded back over the two. Marisol grinned and nodded affirmative. Still, the two had an enjoyable time dancing together, their bodies rubbing against each other, occasionally stealing a passionate kiss or two.

Once home later that night, she dictated a short speech and sent the message-bots out to make the rounds in the town early in the morning. They announced a video meeting at the center at one o'clock where President Marisol would be discussing her meeting with the ambassador from this new world. As expected, nearly everyone was there. Although Tatiana and several others were on the lookout for Elmira and the other escaped prisoners, she didn't see the five.

As expected, the women had many questions for her after the short presentation was finished. She did her best to answer them. One woman said, "President Marisol, this world sounds ideal. They will let us bring our bots with us. I can't speak for everyone, of course, but I would jump at this chance to get off this dying ship. Anything has to be better than sticking around here. The bots could fail at any time, like the blackout, leaving us to die. Can't you make a deal to let some of us who want to go here do it?"

"We haven't decided if this is a wise choice yet. We don't know what he meant by a genetic mishap. You could find yourselves in a horrid situation, an intolerable one and we'd be powerless to come to your aid once you go down to the planet. We ought to be more cautious."

"That's easy for you to say, but some of us are scared stiff that we are going to die soon. Anything has to be better than what we have. If they will take us and you don't find anything more substantially wrong, can you promise us that those of us who want to get off here are allowed to do so, even if you think it is a wrong choice?"

"Well, yes, if you truly want to leave, I will not stop you," Marisol conceded that point. She was not a dictator and could understand the real fear that many had.

"Let me be very clear. You are saying that you would allow *any* woman who wants to get off here to do so and take her needed bots with her, if they will accept them?" she pressed her.

Marisol didn't get why the woman was so insistent. "Of course, I won't stop any woman who desires to leave and go down to this planet to live, if we deem it survivable. I won't let anyone go down there if it is dangerous for her to do so. I won't risk your lives, but if we deem it safe, I won't stop any woman who wishes to do so."

"Thank you. I will hold you to your word," the woman replied. Again, Marisol was mystified. What was she intending to do? It made no sense to her. Although others asked additional questions, she could not answer most of them. What was the climate like? What were the living accommodations? What types of food did they eat? And so on. These, she resolved to ask Kyle.

"Well, Alpha, I think a good many women are going to want to bail out of the Arc here," Marisol relayed later that evening when she and Tatiana were once more in his control room. "How are we going to find out if this planet is going to be an acceptable home to those who want to leave the Arc?"

"We are working on getting more information. Beta has been accumulating data from their communications channels. While we don't know what their genetic mishap was, we do believe that we know what their women look like now. Have a peak," Alpha replied.

"Oh my god! Those are women?" asked Tatiana. In contrast to the relatively handsome men that they'd seen, the women were positively ugly. Their hair was almost non-existent, long, stringy, isolated strands. Many simply were bald. Their faces were pock-marked and heavily covered in makeup in futile attempts to hide their underlying skin. If these were really representative of their women, no wonder Kyle as anxious to have as many women come to their planet below.

Beta added, "This civilization is making extensive use of mind-altering drugs as well. I would not recommend our women living here. The only conclusion that I have from the data so far is that they would soon not be happy living here."

"Well, I can present all this to those who are considering leaving the Arc for this planet. Dare I deny those who wish to leave us? I know that many are afraid that if they don't take this first chance to leave, they may well die here if the bots fail. Some don't think that there will be any other opportunities than this planet. Do I tell them that they can't leave? If I did so, then am I not depriving them of their free will choice?"

"We understand the dilemma, Marisol. We face it as well. Our prime directive is to assist and help you to flourish and prosper. For those who want to leave, do we have the right to deny them this chance at starting a new life off this Arc? True, there are direct behavior patterns that we know are self-destructive, and, in such cases, we are free to act to prevent that from happening," Alpha explained. "However, in this case, we understand the risks involved with staying on the ship as we search for a more ideal planet for you. There is always the possibility that we will not find one before the critical bots fail and we can no longer sustain your lives. On the other hand, based on all our known historical precedents, we do not believe that this society would be a good one for you. We also are having a most difficult time reaching a decision."

Beta added, "We must always recognize and allow for a human's free choice. Without the power of choice, they are no longer true players in the game of the universe, but more like slaves. Thus, we must allow you women to make your own choices, but we will do our best to make sure that you have as much data at hand to make an intelligent choice."

Alpha finished up, "However, once the deal has been made and those women who wish to depart here have done so, there will be no going back. For good or ill, once the choice is consummated, we will be powerless to undo it, should those who go desire to backtrack. Make sure that they are aware of the gamble that they are taking."

The next morning, Marisol again held a communal meeting, revealing the latest data that they'd uncovered about this new planet. She did her best to dissuade others from disembarking here, hoping that the images of the really ugly, malformed women would convince them not to leave the Arc. A few did change their minds, but still a large number indicated that they wanted to leave. Again, she had to promise them that she would not prevent them from doing so, if

Ambassador Kyle would accept them.

Just before their next meeting, Marisol asked, "We still have a lot of women who want to abandon us for this planet. Do we land our ship to let them off? We ought to allow them to take their needed personal living bots."

Alpha grinned, "This ship was designed to land only once. There is not enough fuel actually to take off from a planet. We cannot overcome the force of gravity. The Arc was built in orbit above your home world. Yet, we can land once. In this case, however, shuttle craft will be used to ferry the supplies to us and to return with those women who wish to stay here. I wish that they would not, but we cannot interfere with their self-determinism in this matter."

Shortly after, that the ambassador and his crew arrived and he was very enthusiastic. "Yes, we will be very pleased to make the trade. All your women who desire to come to live on our world will be welcomed and very well treated. Of course, they should have their necessary bots."

Alpha then worked out the details, but Kyle made another plea. "We would like to extend our offer of sanctuary on our world to all your women. Please ask them all to stay with us." He went on about this. Marisol thought that he was a bit too insistent about having all the women come down to his world. Again, her intuition told her not to trust him. The exchange would begin tomorrow.

After they left, Marisol asked, "How do we handle the trade? Where do we bring the women and how will we get all their needed bots transferred to the shuttle craft?"

"I will open the back door which is just to the right of the Maintenance Unit building. Have all the women who wish to depart line up there. We will place a computer bot there and they can identify their address when they are ready to leave. I will send out bots to collect their personal clothes and their necessary personal bots as they board the shuttle craft. Their bots will follow on the next shuttle."

"However, Marisol, I think that it would be prudent if we had a contingent of your trusted people on hand both at the staging area near the Maintenance Unit building and also in the ship's docking area. I don't trust these men. They might attempt to take over the ship, seizing all you and us robots as well. I sense a certain air of greediness about them."

"You got it. Will a dozen do for guards at the docking area?"

"I think so. Choose them and I will show them their stations before the first shuttle lands tomorrow around noon."

Later that day, Tatiana headed off to help gather up their most trusted friends beyond their six close ones at home. Marisol prepared and delivered the instructions via the message-bots, which systematically visited all the homes playing her recorded message over and over, along with her sincere plea for the women not to take such a wild gamble on this planet. Would it do any good, she wondered, as she began outlining to her six house mates what she wanted them to do.

Tatiana rounded up eighteen women who volunteered to watch over and assist the women in the staging area, while she had twelve trusted women ready to guard the shuttle bay area. Marisol planned to be at the staging area, supervising and making last minute pleas for the women not to go. Alpha again had the comm link around her neck so that she and he could be kept appraised of what was happening in both areas. Tatiana herself would be in the shuttle bay, ready for trouble.

As the morning progressed, women and a few children began congregating beside the Maintenance Unit building, where a section of what appeared to be blue sky had been raised, revealing a gaping hole. A steel walkway led straight towards the cargo bay, an easy walk for the women, Marisol observed. As a departing woman arrived, she spoke her address into one of the three computer-bots, and it then flagged her home to have the personal bots there transported to the cargo bay after the women had departed on shuttle craft.

As noon approached, Marisol spotted a band of twelve women coming together and she recognized ex-president Elmira and the other four escapees. They were surrounded by their close associates, evidently protecting the five. Marisol smiled, the five still wore their ballet boots, but she smiled because after all these months wearing them, the five had adapted to them and were walking fairly well in them. Now she understood why that woman had been so insistent on getting her to state clearly that she would not stop any woman who wanted to leave. The five obviously had no future here on the Arc and were gambling that life on this unknown planet would offer them a new chance.

Elmira glared at her, but Marisol smiled, "I hope you will be happy on this new world, but I strongly advise against going there, Elmira." The woman did not reply, but only hissed at her, like some snake. A couple of the guards asked Marisol if they should stop the five escapees, but she said no, she had promised and would not break her word.

A large shuttle craft entered the bay and was transported mechanically up to the end of the walkway. Its doors opened and men readied their entrance ramp. One man signaled her and Marisol gave them the okay to proceed, again taking this last opportunity to advise the women against this move. None turned back, however. Once this first shuttle was filled, it was pulled back and disappeared, while another appeared and was pulled into position to take the remaining women on board.

A few minutes later, Marisol and her guards stood by the empty staging area, along with the three computer-bots. She read the departing tallies. Nearly three hundred women and children had left for this new world. Now they backed out of the way, as nearly every delivery-bot in their world began moving all their things and personal bots to this staging area. Never had they seen so many bots moving so quickly and so efficiently.

Alpha did report that they had received their precious supplies and so far no treachery. She wondered if that would last. Maybe this would work out fine for the departing women. She certainly hoped so, though she felt a pang of sadness knowing that she would never again see these women or kids, nor they, her.

An hour later, a return shuttle craft docked and a dozen men began loading the women's possessions and their many bots. Obviously, there would have to be a second shuttle to carry all these away. Marisol and her crew kept an eye on them as they loaded the items, but nothing suspicious occurred.

Again, they waited for the next one. Alpha reported that they were sending two shuttles to pick up the remaining items.

Boredom set in as they waited. Finally, another one pulled in. As before, a dozen men got out and began loading. At least the women found it interesting to watch the men with their strong arms doing the work rapidly, unlike themselves who depended upon their mechanical arms. However, they did not take everything. A few bots remained for the final shuttle. Alpha spoke over her comm link, "Stay alert. If they are going to try something, I would expect it on this last shuttle." Marisol issued orders for the guards to fan out and take up defensive positions and to ready their elemental spells. Down below in the cargo hold where the shuttle would shortly be docking, Tatiana got her group ready for action, just in case of treachery. All waited nervously. Would Kyle and his people trade fairly or would they let their envy and greed overcome their ethics, Marisol wondered.

Soon the last shuttle landed and Alpha's devices began pulling it in and up to the desired position opposite the opened door where the few remaining bots were waiting to be picked up. As the shuttle doors opened, men began filing out. Each was armed with some kind of weapon and wore some kind of heavy body armor, neither of which the women had ever seen. Several dozen men swarmed out and took up defensive positions. A man in a different uniform stepped out. He barked to Alpha and Tatiana, "Okay, we are taking possession of this ship and all the rest of the women on board. Don't try anything or my men will shoot to kill."

Marisol and Tatiana didn't hesitate. Two walls of fire suddenly engulfed the men, while a split second after that, several hurricane force winds plowed into them along with many walls of water. The men were knocked off their feet and the force of the air and water threw them back towards the air lock, which Alpha opened. Dozens of the men flew out into empty space, ending the battle. However, in the process, their guns fired wildly in all directions, bullets ricocheting off the walls and the shuttle. Three women were injured by the chaotic, random fire, before the men and their guns drifted off into space. Alpha sealed the air lock as Tatiana stepped towards the shuttle.

"Anyone in the shuttle?" she called out.

"Don't shoot! Don't shoot! I am just the driver," a man called out, his voice full of fear.

"We ought to shoot you after your people tried to steal our ship and us, but we honor our deals. Load those remaining bots and leave."

"By myself?" He didn't get an answer and set to work doing the heavy lifting himself. A half hour later, this last shuttle slipped out of the docking bay. As soon as it cleared the Arc, Alpha blasted the Arc out of its planetary orbit, before these men could try something different to capture the ship. At last, he felt that it was safe and sent medical-bots to help the injured women.

"Well, you were right, those men and that planet cannot be trusted. I feel badly that some three hundred of us are now down there at their mercy," Marisol said to the large group of guards, while they watched the medical-bots working on the three injured women. Meanwhile, Alpha closed the doors and the sky returned, leaving no trace that a huge door was there in their world.

Over the comm link, Beta reported, "Madam President, it seems that Kyle was more devious. The fuel that he supplied has been contaminated. We took the precaution of keeping this new supply separate from our main tanks. I am running a program now to remove those contaminants. In time, the fuel will be usable. However, before we use the other supplies, we will thoroughly check them as well."

"Thank you, Beta, for your constant vigilance," Marisol replied. The tired women now headed home, eager to relay the news of the treachery of this world to the remaining five hundred women and children, many of whom had decided at the last minute not to go. Now that decision seemed vindicated in their minds. Further, it shored up political support for Marisol, who had continuously argued against the women leaving the ship for this planet.

Part III Exits

Chapter 12 Another World

Months passed as life continued normally on Madiera. With half of their population dead or gone, Marisol's computer projections doubled the anticipated years before they would begin to run out of supplies and bots. Still, the failure of key critical bot systems had not changed. Those large bots were irreplaceable and were wearing out, having run far beyond their anticipated lifetimes.

Often, Marisol wondered how those who had left fared in their new world, but she had no way of knowing or finding out, short of returning there, landing, and seeing firsthand, which she had no intention of ever doing. Instead, she continued hoping that Beta would uncover a far better world for them all, as were the two robot's original intentions for over four hundred years.

On the domestic side, both she and Tatiana were rapidly nearing their twentieth birthday. That meant they could have each other's babies, if they should decide to become pregnant. Both discussed this at length, as did the other three couples living in their quadraplex. All eight decided to put off having children just a little longer. Why? At any moment, Alpha might find them a planet. Being very pregnant would hinder them in responding to what was needed, should that occur.

On a different note entirely, Elena and Isabel decided to ask Alpha if they could do some research using their archives of their original home planet, now long destroyed. Instead of making them walk all the way to the control room, he sent bots out to patch in a line to their home computer terminal. "Go ahead and research all that you desire. Response may be slow," Alpha cautioned them, "because much of the archival footage is not online and will have to be manually loaded by server-bots."

Late that summer shortly before the children would be returning to school, the two came to Marisol and Tatiana with their research results. "You see," Isabel began, "it all began because we now have enough cotton to make jeans for us adults. We got the bright idea to ask what did some of our ancestors who had conditions somewhat similar to ours do? I mean before the bots were invented to assist us."

"That is a bright idea. What did you find?" Marisol asked, suddenly becoming very interested in what her two friends had discovered.

"Well, it's pretty amazing. Mind you, we focused only on women who had at least somewhat similar situations, though not necessarily exactly like us, you see." She didn't but allowed them to continue. "Here is a woman who learned to fly something called an airplane. We think it is sort of like a shuttle craft. She went to lots of schools too, just like we do." The two began to show off the many isolated video clips and sill shots that they managed to pull from the extensive archives of the two robots. Their "show" lasted a half hour, thoroughly impressing Marisol and Tatiana, who had no idea that these things could be done without the use of bots.

Elena ended by saying, "So we want to get a project going among all who want to experiment. The idea is to see if we can learn to do some of the things that we are relying on our bots to do for us. If the bots fail, we want a backup plan. Maybe we might even somehow become rather independent of the bots. If we settle on a world without bots, this could be very valuable and give Alpha more choices of a new world for us all."

That sold Marisol and Tatiana. She gave them the go ahead and allowed the two to make a formal presentation to all five hundred that weekend. Since Marisol backed this plan of Elena and Isabel's, she was very surprised to find a large number of women volunteering to work on the project, sharing ideas, tips, and techniques that they found workable. A month later, the project went Madiera-wide, everyone was onboard.

"Yes, this project of Elena and Isabel's is giving them some hope and it gives them a way that they can help," Alpha commented. Marisol had just finished explaining what they were doing and that the women were experiencing some success. "I will see that we have enough supplies. We have the material to make enough jeans for all now. You are right; this does allow us to explore more possible planets, Marisol. If the women can demonstrate that they can survive, flourish, and prosper without our bots' aid, then we can look at far more possible planets for you."

"Okay, let's do it then," she replied.

That fall, Alpha called Marisol and Tatiana to the control room once more. "Thanks for coming on short notice. Beta has found something that is very curious."

The monotone voice of Beta picked up from here, "Yes, we are entering the relatively unpopulated outer rim of the galaxy. All of a sudden, we've encountered a far-reaching space federation that goes by the name of the Imperium. From what we can tell, they control or dominate close to a thousand advanced worlds closer to the center of the galaxy and are now in the process of outward expansion."

"Are they a threat to us?" Marisol asked growing worried.

"Yes and no. They do have huge battle cruisers that could attack us and likely destroy us. However, I have been keeping us just off their sensors for the time being. They are not likely to bother with an ancient craft such as this. That is not why we sent for you, rather, we have discovered a potential planet."

"Hey, great!" Marisol replied, a new burst of hope shot through her.

"Well, yes and no. The Imperium has a spaceport on that planet, but they also have a total restriction on any communication and trade with the natives of that planet. In effect, they have made this one a closed world to their people. For some reason, they are keeping this planet nearly totally isolated. However, I have learned that they are mining fuel for their spaceships on one of the two moons of the planet."

"Our sensor readings suggest that this world is lacking in nearly all heavier atoms, such as gold that is used in our circuitry. That alone makes this world a bit peculiar. I sent down a drone to check on the world. Beyond that spaceport, there is no advanced technology, not even electricity. Until now, if you had to have our bots to survive, that would have ruled this planet out. Since Alpha claims that you are making great strides doing some things for yourselves, I took the liberty of further explorations."

Beta went on, showing the video sent back by his drone. "The weather is definitely highly unusual. The eastern portion of the continent is mostly uninhabited desert regions. The lower central area is where most of the life-sustaining crops are grown. Many farms. The far north appears to be snow covered in the summer, suggesting a massive ice cap."

"What has gotten our keen interest is that up here in the middle north central area, there are large deposits of silicon and germanium crystals. If we can get a goodly supply of these, Alpha and I can manufacture new computer chips. And you know what that means?"

"We can refurbish the critical systems and prolong their life," Tatiana answered without hesitation. This was her area of expertise.

"Precisely so."

"Are there inhabitants there?" asked Marisol.

"Yes, there appears to be a few large towns. I estimate that they may hold ten to twenty thousand people. Then, there are these very unusual and strange structures, very tall towers. Usage and purpose: unknown," Beta reported.

"One more thing, Marisol. As these tower structures interested me, I had the drone take a fast pass by one that is near the tall mountains, just before it crashed into the mountain peak. The video is only a few seconds long, but I think that you will find it interesting." He played the very short video. "Here, I'll slow it way down."

They saw several women walking in a courtyard. One woman had no arms, but all the women wore what could only be party dresses. At the very last instant, the image showed that they were wearing fairly high heeled shoes of some kind. It was rather blurred, since the drone was flying by at a great speed shortly before it struck a distant mountain peak.

"Contrast this with this greatly magnified and fuzzy image taken over the town," Beta said dryly. They could see that men and women wore apparel that was practical, not fancy dresses and heels. Little more could be distinguished from the overly magnified images.

Alpha took up the discussion now. "So we have an off-limits to high technology-people planet. We have anomalous clothing, but the people there are definitely of the human race. It is also important to note what you didn't see. There are no roads such as you saw on your original world. No railroad lines. No signs that there are any highways connecting these larger towns. If it had not been for those images captures at that tower, we would have given this planet a very primitive culture. Yet, those towers cannot have been easily constructed without some kind of advanced engineering techniques. Combined with the fancy apparel of those women there, this leads us to suspect there is more to this world than a mere primitive people."

"Plus," Tatiana inserted, "it has the components we need to make more computer chips. We have to go down there and get some."

Alpha looked at Marisol for confirmation. "It would seem that in all these centuries, this planet alone has the available raw crystals that you need. I agree, we should make the attempt," she replied.

"It will be tricky, Marisol. Since this Imperium civilization has made this a closed-off world, they will not give us permission to send a shuttle down there nor will they even let us try. If we ignore them and just do it, we risk their ships attacking our Arc, something that obviously violates our prime directive."

"Hum, I don't think that we want to waste this golden opportunity for you two to obtain the most important components that we desperately need," Marisol mused out loud. "So we don't ask the Imperium people. Isn't there anyway that we could land a mining shuttle there undetected by these Imperium people?" she asked.

"As humans often say, where there is a will, there is a way. Devious. Let us compute your request," Alpha declared, mimicking a coy grin. Beta went into action, maneuvering his mechanical arms over his many keyboards and working three different ones simultaneously.

A minute later, his monotone voice replied, "Ah, there might be a way to land a shuttle undetected by the Imperium forces at their spaceport. They have a one degree blind spot in their radar coverage of the approaches to the planet. We could send the shuttle on a very precise course and get it down to the surface undetected. Ninety-nine point seven percent chance of success. Then, traveling close to the surface to stay under their surface radar, we could get to this secondary location that looks highly promising. The terrain there is a bit rough though, mining will be more difficult."

"Way to go, Beta!" Marisol praised the navigation robot as though it were human.

"Yes, but there is one smaller problem, President Marisol. This location is only fifty miles from that strange tower-like affair and town. While the exact spot I am looking at for the mining appears uninhabited, we risk being detected by that town, unless we come in under the cover of night. Other than the spaceport way to the south of there, the whole planet is wholly dark at night, indicating they do not have electricity," Beta pointed out.

"Good plan, Beta. Let's do it," Marisol concluded.

"Not so hasty. Some of you women will have to go along to oversee the operation. While we can guide you to the precise location, someone will have to get the equipment out and properly setup. Then, it must be overseen as well, at least initially," Alpha pointed out.

"Oh." Marisol looked slightly annoyed at the small setback. "Okay, then, I'll go."

"Me too," Tatiana added.

"Best have three of you there. It will be very dangerous for you though. There will likely be all manner of unseen and unanticipated dangers for you. Wild animals, primitive creatures, hostile terrain, even bad weather," Alpha cautioned.

"Bad weather? What's that?" asked Marisol. She had no concept of that. Each day in Madiera was picture-perfect, bright, sunny, and warm.

"This region has daily rain storms and at night it apparently can get cold enough to snow," he answered.

"What's snow?"

"Frozen rain. Comes down in flakes. When it accumulates, it is very slippery," he answered.

"Wouldn't we stay warm inside the shuttle?" Tatiana

asked. "If it gets too cold at night — well, we would be sleeping in the shuttle anyway."

"True. That would work. If the rain poses too much of a problem for you, you could wait it out while inside as well," Alpha conceded. "I would suggest an Earth kindred should accompany you, she will have a good opportunity to put her special skills to work there."

"Okay, we'll ask Elena to come with us," Marisol replied, certain that the black haired woman would love this opportunity to put her feet on real soil, real ground.

"Marisol, please realize that if you go down there, you will be on your own. There will be very little, if anything, that we can do for you if you run into trouble. We have to protect the many still here in the Arc. Are you sure that you want to take this terrible risk?" Alpha tried one last time to convince her otherwise.

"This is our best chance yet at getting what we need to forestall the coming bot failures. I have to try, Alpha. If something bad happens to me, they can elect a new president. I am sure that you will continue to try to find us a planet on which we can live and thrive," she replied determinedly, but not without a slightly worried glance at Tatiana.

"Whoopee!" exclaimed Elena. The two had just told her of the discovery of this promising planet and had asked her to join them on the initial landing to help work the mining-bots. "Count me in!"

"But what about the rest of us?" asked Renata gloomily. "We want to go down there too."

"I know that all you want to come. If it is going to work out, I will ask Alpha if you all can come and help as well. Right now, we have no idea what we are going to be facing. As soon as we do and it turns out not to be too dangerous, I'll try to get you all down there with us. Meanwhile, Alpha did say that if something bad happens to us, you'll have to elect a new president. Renata, I want you to take over as president while I am gone. If I don't come back, continue leading our people until an election can be held. Okay?"

"But nothing is going to happen to you, is it?" Isabel asked growing very worried now. "I mean, Alpha won't send you down there if it is really dangerous, would he? He's supposed to be helping and protecting us."

"I hope so, Isabel, but we really need these crystals. With them, the robots think that they can make new computer chips out of them and that means new computers to replace the ones that are failing," Marisol answered as best she could. "I convinced him that we have to at least try to get those crystals."

The next day, dressed in a blouse, jeans, and tennis shoes, the three women made their way to the control room. All three were now thankful that they had been attempting to alter their physical limitations. It had taken time, but they could now comfortably wear flat shoes, though they paid for it when they had to wear their party heels. Elena teased them by saying, "I feel like we are wearing them for the first time like we did two years ago at our prom." All three had laughed, but Marisol knew how true this statement actually was. It had taken them nearly a half of a year to adapt to wearing their party outfits comfortably and now whenever they dressed up, they were essentially back to their first days wearing them. Nevertheless, they were some of the first adults of Madiera ever to be able to be somewhat independent of the many bots. Daily, the five hundred women of Madiera continued to work on this aspect, hoping that Alpha would soon find them a real home somewhere.

Alpha led them to the special shuttle craft. Alongside it were the many machines and bots that they would need to setup and run the crystal mining operation. Now he had to teach these three how to load, unload, setup, operate, and control them. This took another three long days. Finally, the three were ready to go. Spirits were high, but also nervousness crept in as the three prepared for the shuttle launch in the wee hours of the morning. Once the shuttle launched, they'd be wholly on their own on a strange world full of unknowns and with little help beyond themselves.

"I'm a little scared," Elena whispered.

"Me too. I think that is a good sign," Marisol whispered back. Tatiana nodded her agreement. All three now wore a small communications device around their necks so that they and Alpha could communicate at any time. Beta would guide the shuttle through this tiny window where it could not be detected by the Imperium space station. In fact, he'd be handling everything until they actually touched down on the world below. Once down, the women would then have to take over. A bot strapped each into their seat and then strapped itself down. Marisol looked around, everything was sturdily tied down and she hoped that nothing would go wrong. She sighed deeply and then the dull throb of the engines began.

"Hey, we will be the first women to experience real motion," Tatiana pointed out as the ship began to move down the ramp, floating clear of the Arc. Indeed, they did. Combined with their forward window onto the sunlit portion of the planet below them, they got the ride of their lives. Soon, though, the shuttle entered the dark half of the planet and now they could see the stars, but little else, save the two moons shining dimly in the sky. Then they ducked below the clouds and all was pitch black. Here, they could only trust in Beta's excellent navigation. After a time, they sensed the ship slowing way down. Finally, they felt a slight jar as the ship touched down and settled, leaning slightly to the port side.

"Okay, you are down on the planet and within three feet of the designated location. Are you all right?" Alpha asked.

"That was sheer fun! Can we do it again?" Marisol asked. "Seriously, we're okay, but wow, that was great, Alpha. I wish we could fly more. Okay, we'll get to work now."

"Good. Remember that it is nighttime there. You don't want to open the doors and let light outside. If there are others around, the light could attract them. Just get the straps off everything and ready for first light. Then try to catch a little sleep if you can."

The three waited for the bot to unstrap itself and then themselves. Finally, they rose and waited as the bot unstrapped their three mechanical arms. After pressing into them and taking control, they began unstrapping the mountains of equipment, aided by the bot who handled the larger pieces of equipment. One by one, the three arranged the gear in a line before the rear cargo door, ready for the coming morning's action. That allowed them to unfold their beds and provided them access to the prepared food. "I'm too excited to sleep for only two hours," Elena whispered, though Alpha could still hear her.

"Me too, let's at least relax a little. As soon as it is light, we will have an enormous amount of work to do. I sure hope that we can manage it," Marisol whispered back.

All three waited until the orange-red sun rose ruddy in the eastern sky, peeking through the thick cloud cover. They immediately went into action, opening the cargo doors, and stepping out onto this new world. All three breathed in deeply. They were in a small valley. Dense patches of resinous pines lined the north and south rims, while the other sides were fairly rocky. They were in the high, rugged foothills of large mountain range, whose grey peaks finally appeared as the clouds moved off further northeastward. A thick layer of grass covered the valley floor, although here and there great jagged rocks thrust themselves upwards above the lush green. The odors of moist air filled with resin filled their lungs and Elena was very excited to experience this real earth.

They quickly saw that they had to watch their steps to avoid the rocks hidden beneath the grasses. After a long, slow look around the silver ship that was about fifty feet long and twenty-five wide, they headed back inside and got themselves into the mechanical arms. Now the heavy work began, as they lifted each piece of equipment and carried it down the sloping ramp onto the grass. Once outside, they then ran a quick diagnostic check, making sure that bot was fully operational. None failed. Part by part, they got the equipment and bots in their desired locations, guided by Beta from far above them. He used several video cameras mounted on the exterior of the ship to verify each action.

Around ten, sweating from their constant exertions, the three finally had everything ready to go. Now Beta and the mining-bots took over for them and the three sat back to cool down and watch the slow action. With luck, in a few days, they would have retrieved enough of the silicon and germanium crystals to build many more computer chips, once they were transported to the Arc. Thus far, the planet seemed peaceful. The sun had come out wholly as the clouds vanished by midmorning. While they'd seen many small animals, none seemed remotely threatening to them. Some had large rear legs and hopped about, Alpha called them a rabbit. As they discovered more of the unknown creatures, Alpha identified them as well, including squirrels and field mice.

"What a serene and pleasant world this is, bit rocky though." Marisol said to her two companions.

"True, delightful really, but we'd never manage this if we wore our heels and dresses here," Elena pointed out the obvious.

Chapter 13 Visitors

It was mid-June 1201, in the sixteenth year of the rule of Emperor Jan Bellweather and Empress Amy Blackwater. Both women looked like they were perhaps thirty-six, but in reality Jan was eighty-nine and Amy, a year younger. Both had undergone three rejuvenation treatments, the last one was over seventeen years ago. Having been abducted for their telepathic skills from Tierra when they were in their teens, they had found a way to escape that slavery and had become the Imperium's most wanted terrorists, Sly Dog and Eager Beaver. It had cost them dearly to find a way to return here to their home world, but they made the sacrifices. However, upon arrival, they found their once peaceful planet engaged in hideous wars and had taken effective action to end it, issuing the Blackwater Ultimatum, which was now fully implemented, bringing fifteen years of peace to the world. Each had a daughter by the other, a gift from the Goddess Lysandra for having ended nearly a half century of constant wars. Both June and Melissa were fifteen and looked remarkably like their mothers. Already, the two teens were being taught everything that their mothers knew about the Imperium and computers.

They resided at Imperial Tower, the new name for the castle and tower located on the southwestern corner of Plateau Grado, the alien spaceport, and across the street from the ever enlarging Exchange City. The Imperial Guards, a contingent a hundred strong provided for the castle's security, while one full *Círculo de mentes* handled planet-wide communications with the other eight towers and leaders. One of Amy's requirements had been that women would now lead the towers, replacing men, since men had directly caused all the wars. Amy had also equitably divided the lands among the towers and ushered in an era of relative peace.

Diagonally across the street from the castle was the Imperium Headquarters in Exchange City. Here the thriving company known as Elegant Fashions Inc had expanded from their original fourth floor to include the entire third and second floor as well. The police functions still occupied the ground-level floor while the city administration occupied the fifth floor. Carmen Valen had taken sole ownership of their business when her dear friend Karolina had departed with her husband, Lech, who was held responsible for many crimes, including allowing a Nuclear to be detonated on Tierra, wiping out the entire tower, castle, and city of Bettingham. In the process, her husband and Imperium spy Jarek had been killed. However, she was left with Imperium citizenship by virtue of her marriage to Jarek. This she put to excellent use, since that allowed her to import fabrics and supplies from the thousands of Imperium worlds.

She was extremely attractive, appearing as if she were forty-three, when in reality, she was ninety-three, having undergone rejuvenation many times before Jarek was slain. Her next treatment would only take off maybe ten years at most and she was weighing her options about when to have it done once more. Her son, Diego, was long since married and off at Valen with his own family. Her sole focus in life was to continue expanding her line of elegant fashions, but she also had a secret mission too.

Carmen was the last person on Tierra who knew just how Amy and Jan had come to Tierra, supposedly as a queen and domestique of the wasp worshipers. As far as everyone else was concerned, Amy and Jan had died in a tragic shuttle craft accident. Carmen knew better, they were now her Emperor and Empress. The three had reached an agreement, Carmen would remain quiet about the two, and the two would allow her to continue her fashion company. Since these two had killed her husband who had dropped the Nuclear on Bettingham, she wanted revenge, but not in the usual manner. No, she was far, far more devious than that. Amy had placed women at the head of all the telepathic towers and *Círculo de mentes*. Her plan was to find a way to make those powerful women severely hobbled, destroying Amy's grand plan. She needed something more than tight corsets and exceedingly high heels; the latter was already becoming the widespread standard for elegant dress. No, she needed something far more powerful and had been working on this for the last fifteen years.

Each of the eight towers had been forced to hand over rulership of their territory to ordinary people, though most of these new political rulers also had the *mentales* gift. Those with the gift could either work in a tower or be a political ruler, but not both. Further only women could hold the power positions within a circle. It had taken the Emperor and Empress a couple of years and more than one death finally to get full compliance with Amy's ultimatum.

It had been sixteen years now, and in the far north, Brom Tower, castle, and city had complied and grown. In fact, they had the closest relationship of any tower with the current Emperor and Empress, having provided most of their new personnel there at the Imperial Tower. Currently, Venerada Luisa Wycombe ruled Brom Tower, while her husband, Sam, handled tower security. Her *mentales* gift was one of the rarest, though now many like her had it there in Brom. She was a catalyst telepath, able to free other's mental blocks, fully releasing their native *mentales* gifts. She also always knew just what another person wanted, whether they vocalized it or not. Like all the other Brom katalyein, her body had no arms, that was the price she had to pay for having this rarest of all gifts. That she also had great wisdom and keen insight led her to this top leadership position at Brom Tower, some ten years ago. She oversaw five complete working *Círculo de mentes*.

The older men who had been running the affairs and circles at Brom took over the political leadership of their lands, which covered all the northernmost portion of the Midlands. Now King Pete Bolivar, the ex-Venerado of Brom, effectively administered their large territories and people. He formed up a kingdom army to provide security and protection from the small bands of bandits who still thrived across Tierra.

One of the new steps that Venerada Luisa took was the formation of the Brom Tower Elite Guards. Each man chosen was given the very best training in sword fighting, since that was the only form of combat Amy allowed in her Blackwater Ultimatum, save using your fists. The men signed on for a three year period of service after which they were free to leave. Few ever did, and by 1201, they were the highest respected fighters of the Midlands. The Elite Guards now boasted some five hundred men, enough to defend Brom Tower.

Among these was Major Miguel del Fuego, the only son of Angelica Evita e Kaylee, the daughter of the famous Sisterhood fighter Fel and her alien free mate Cassia. Angelica had also been a famous Sisterhood fighter, like her moms, but she was now retired and sixty-nine. Long ago, she'd taken a free mate and had Miguel. Though retired, she still gave pointers to the young first-year Elite Guards trainees.

Major Miguel commanded the Third Platoon and was forty. He'd married another of the special katalyein women, Blanca del Fuego. For these two, it had been love at first sight, though Blanca guessed that her wearing her Elegant Fashion's outfit at that first meeting had played a role. They had a son, Arsenio, now twenty, and a daughter, Stella, eighteen. Like her mother, Stella also had the katalyein gift and had her mother's long, lush, thick black hair, so typical of women from the Westerlings, not the Midlands. Miguel and Arsenio's hair was brown, like typical Midlands folk. Of key importance at this time was that Brom Tower had always had a large number of personnel who traced their lineage to the Westerlings and thus spoke that dialect fluently.

Arsenio was a Corporal in the Third Platoon, leading his group. Unlike most other fighting groups, women were not only allowed into the Elite Guards, but encouraged, if they had suitable *mentales* gifts. Thus, Stella was a private in this Third Platoon, adding her gift of "total certainty of what someone wanted" into their mix of skills, invaluable in resolving situations which arose.

Four others of note were in his platoon. Venerada Luisa and Sam's son and daughter were also in it. Twenty year old Felipe was a Corporal and a master horseman. If it dealt in anyway with a horse, Felipe could handle it, such was his *mentales* gift. His younger sister, Anita, was eighteen and was their platoon's healer and fire-starter. She could get a bonfire going in a drenching downpour, or so everyone bragged. Also with them were Corporals Gabriel del Fuego-Jeffery and Ben Sikes, twenty-one and twenty-two respectively. Gabriel was the grandson of Gabe and Celestina and he inherited his grandfather's love and mastery of all things gliders. Ben was the grandson of Jake Sikes and Evita del Fuego and he inherited his grandfather's great *mentales* gift with dogs. Ben could take a vicious, snarling cur and turn it into a lap dog for a woman. However, he put his talents to use breeding and training the many dogs that pulled their dog sleds in the winter, when the snow depths sometimes reached twenty feet. In the dead of winter, travel was by either reindeer sleigh or dog sled.

Glider development had ballooned under Gabe's hands. Now Brom Tower had a dozen of these superbly constructed, thin metal covered, extremely light weight gliders in their service. Their launching pad was just beyond the large hanger doors, where they would be pushed off a two hundred foot cliff. Here the winds and thermals could always be counted upon to lift these silver colored gliders high into the sky long before they would otherwise hit the ground. Each glider could carry four people, a pilot and three others. Major Miguel's Third Platoon had six of these for their use, for his platoon was charged with long distance scouting, a ready-made chore for these sleek flying machines. Usually, they scouted for new forest fires started by lightning strikes.

Two hours before dawn, Capa Neva sighed as she stood before the door of Venerada Luisa's bedroom. She sensed her boss and Sam sleeping soundly just beyond the door. *Should I really wake her?* This she'd asked herself twenty times already. Yet again, she mentally reviewed what she and her circle members had detected not more than an hour ago. Again, she sighed, waking the Venerada at this hour would be quite rude, especially if this was a false alarm. After yet another sigh and taking a deep breath, she knocked gently. *I will assume the responsibility if it is.* "Venerada Luisa? Venerada Luisa?" she called out sending the gentlest of telepathic touches towards her leader.

She felt a return touch in her mind and then heard her sleepy, soft voice, "Capa Neva? What time is it? Come in, dear." Capa Neva opened the door and looked inside, spotting Luisa wiggling to sit up in her bed without waking Sam beside her. Their eyes met. *What's the matter? Something is wrong?*

Yes, we detected something a short while ago. It needs

your attention. I am so sorry but I must follow your orders, Venerada.

Okay, Neva. Give me a minute and I'll join you. She slipped out of bed very slowly and then walked quietly to the door, which Neva held open for her. Once outside, Neva gently shut it, before whispering to her leader.

"We've detected something, a ship perhaps." She was referring to the long standing orders first issued by Empress Amy. Amy and Jan were living proof that the aliens from Rigel-3 were in fact secretly abducting young telepaths from Tierra, stealing them away in the dead of night, when their flying shuttles could not be seen by the inhabitants of the planet. She'd issued orders to all the towers to have their night watch circles continuously monitor for flying ships. If detected, she was to be notified and actions taken to thwart the abduction attempts. In fact, had what they detected followed through as Amy had told everyone, then Capa Neva and her circle would have taken the prescribed action, that is, using their powers to pull the shuttle back down to the earth when it tried to lift off taking the abducted woman away.

"You stopped it?"

"Well, no. We detected a flying ship coming our way and we monitored it. It took a very low path, skimming over the very surface of the land. It did land, just as Empress Amy said that it would. We were prepared to handle it when it lifted off again, but that's what is so troubling, Venerada, it didn't lift off. It is still there on the ground, not moving. Besides that, it is not near any town or village or even a remote farmstead that we can sense. It is out in the wilderness, we believe," Capa Neva reported.

"How strange. This is not exactly what Empress Amy told us would be happening, is it?" Luisa replied, rubbing her eyes on her shoulder, coming full awake at last. "Any signs of a telepath in the vicinity? That would be the clincher."

"No Venerada, we've not sensed any telepath within miles of the landing site. Because of that, I have been hesitating to even disturb your sleep."

Luisa smiled, "But you did, so there must be more to this."

Neva returned her smile; Luisa never missed a thing! "Right. We did sense the presence of three minds, not one, as Empress Amy suggested. Their shuttle craft, according to her, only hold two people, the pilot and the abducted telepath. What does this mean? Three of them?"

"Only one flying machine?" Luisa asked.

"Right, only the one. It is still there or my circle would have already notified me. One ship, three people. What does it mean? Are they trying to sneak spies in here?"

"Could be, Neva. You were right to wake me. How far away?" Luisa asked, becoming somewhat more worried. They may have just stumbled into yet another Imperium plot. Empress Amy had instructed her and the other Venerada to be especially vigilant and never to trust these aliens. Well, that was obvious; they had never yet kept their word completely, not since signing the lease agreement and invoking their Imperial Directive #5. Of course, they always kept their violations a secret, though eventually some had all been uncovered. Emperor Jan saw to that. Luisa knew that other towers had already thwarted three abduction attempts in the last three years. Perhaps now they were making a play here in the far north.

"We are not precisely sure of that. Distances are hard to measure telepathically, even for a circle. Perhaps in the vicinity of fifty miles, but certainly not more than seventy or less than thirty. Nearly due east-southeast of here, about a mile or so from the Wyndl River bank," Neva answered. She added, "I am prepared to share what it was that we sensed and detected with you."

"Okay, do it please. I'll get a better idea of what we are facing," Luisa replied. Neva reached out with her right hand and her fingers barely touched Luisa's left shoulder. That is all the hypersensitive touch that a pair of telepaths required to make intimate contact with each other and to go into rapport with the other. Luisa felt the circle's sensing of a moving object, following a course barely above the ground, rising and falling with the terrain. Then, it stopped all motion and did not move any further. The conclusion drawn was that it had landed. She saw the images of its location and the silver shimmering of the surface of the wide Wyndl River not far to the north of the spot. Then, she felt the presence of three distinct minds, just as Neva and her circle had a little over a half hour ago.

She ended her sharing with the thought, *We believe that all three are now sleeping.*

"Thank you, Capa Neva. You were right to wake me. This is very strange indeed and we must follow through and find out what is going on out there. I agree with your conclusion that they are sleeping at this time. That is the pattern of sleep. Keep on monitoring them and let me know if there is any change, particularly if the ship attempts to rise. You know what to do if it does?"

"Yes, we will force it to remain on the ground. Are you going to rouse the Emperor and Empress?" Neva asked, curiously.

Luisa bit her lip. "No, I think it better if I don't wake them at this hour, not with so little to go on. Whatever this may be, it is not following the actions that they told us it would be doing if it was an abduction in progress. Whatever it is, I will send out the Elite Guards to the site tomorrow and see firsthand what new treachery this may be. However, I think it is prudent if I notify the Emperor and Empress in the morning after they have awakened."

"Yes, Venerada. I'll return to my post then and keep you apprised of any changes. I'll alert the morning shift to this when they come to relieve us," Capa Neva replied. Luisa threw her leg around her and gave Neva a loving hug, and she opened the door for her boss, allowing her easily to slip inside. Then, Neva headed back to her circle members who sat on the floor of the topmost floor of Brom Tower, still in rapport and still monitoring the three distant minds.

At sunup, Luisa woke again, as Sam stirred. Both were early birds, choosing to rise with the sun. As usual, she allowed Sam to slip her thin, silk, summer nightgown off her body. She loved his gentle touch over her skin and it again reminded her that women and men ought to marry for love and not the many arranged marriages so commonly done in the past. Well, that was one of the benefits those like herself had: the right to marry solely out of love. Old Venerado Simon Bolivar had finally granted that special benefit to all their armless katalyein women. That had been one of Fel's greatest accomplishments for her six nieces way back then. Luisa had done just that, married out of a total love of Sam, and he, her. She waited while he gently helped her into her white cotton day dress. True, she could have easily wiggled out of her nightgown and clumsily gotten into her day dress, but this way gave them both loving sensations of the other.

At last he spoke, "I heard you rise last night. Everything okay?"

"We had an event occur, but it does not follow the abduction formula that Empress Amy has told us. I'll send out the Elite Guards to check it out this morning. Probably nothing, though I do not believe it was a falling star."

"Okay, let me know if I can help in anyway. Come on; let's get some breakfast."

As they walked towards the dining room, she sensed that Major Miguel was also up and about. *Major, please join me for breakfast. I have an emergency assignment for you. No, it is not an abduction, at least it is not following the way that Amy told us. I need your glider force to check it out first thing. Brief you over scones.*

A short while later, Major Miguel strode into the dining room. He had curly brown hair and a distinctive moustache. His round face contrasted with his bright blue uniform, the latter suggesting great formality, while the former suggested a great friendliness. Indeed, Luisa often found Miguel a study in contrasts: a brilliant soldier, superb swordsman, and yet, according to his wife, Blanca, highly romantic in bed. Blanca walked at his side and looked very much like Luisa. Both women had very long, lush black hair, thick as their Westerlings heritage still ran strong in their line. Blanca had thick lips that were shaped such that it appeared that her smile never left her face. Luisa, on the other hand, had thinner lips and her face always looked stern, whether she felt that way or not. Blanca came up to her and threw a leg around her, in their unique hug. Luisa reciprocated.

Over breakfast, Luisa filled Major Miguel in on what

Capa Neva had told her earlier. "Since Neva has not contacted me since last night, we can assume that the ship is still on the ground. Here, I will send you all that Neva shared with me last night." She focused and the crystal around her neck glowed a pale blue for a moment.

"How very strange, Venerada. I will get my best team on it at once," he replied formally. "Will you be contacting the Emperor or Empress about this?"

"Yes, I will alert them shortly. Do have your team keep us posted. I am sure that those two will want full information and the sooner, the better. You know Amy and Jan."

He grinned. "Only too well." He kissed Blanca and briskly left the dining room.

A half hour later, he had his team members gathered in the Elite Guard's main conference room. Arsenio, Stella, Felipe, Anita, Gabriel, and Ben sat before him. "We may have a possible abduction in progress not far from here. Then again, it could well be something else entirely, some new and unexpected subversion by the Rigel-3 aliens," he began. All six suddenly gave him their complete attention, their level of anticipation and excitement leapt. At last, they would see some *real* action! Major Miguel relayed all the information he had, including sending the images that Luisa had sent him that Neva had sent her.

"Ah, here comes Capa Neva now." A sleepy woman walked into the room

"Luisa asked me to report. They were sleeping until dawn. The morning circle has relieved us and reports the three minds are now awake and active. They do not know what they are doing, however. The images and concepts in their minds are quite foreign to us."

"Threatening?" asked Arsenio, the leader of the six on this mission.

"Not that they can tell. If there is nothing else, I do need to get some sleep."

"Thanks, Neva. We'll take it from here," Major Miguel replied and she quietly left.

"Okay, no heroics. We need to know what is going on out there. If this is some new alien plot, we need full details to relay to the Emperor and Empress. Don't get yourselves killed, though. We need information. Good hunting." All rose, those with arms saluted as he left the room to attend to his other duties.

"All right, you heard the man, action," Arsenio barked.

"Ah, come on, man, he's your dad," Ben teased him jovially. Gabriel chuckled and Anita smiled.

"Three gliders?" asked Gabriel.

"I think so, two of us in each. That way, if we are attacked, we stand a better chance of some of us getting away to report back," Arsenio replied.

They headed outside and began the long walk to the hanger where the dozen sliver gliders were kept. "Can Anita and I fly together?" Stella asked politely, though she already knew what her brother's answer would be.

"No, sis. It's better if you come with me and Anita goes with her brother. It could be dangerous this time."

"Well, I am glad that it is a real mission and not another fire watch patrol. I do so hate those, terribly boring," Stella replied. Anita gave her a mischievous grin. Both knew that if there was the slightest chance of danger, Arsenio always insisted the sisters fly with their brothers. Anita called it the "Big Brother Syndrome." Their most frequent missions were flying over the vast resinous pine forests on the lookout for another fire, usually started by lightning from the frequent storms. If they could spot a fire as soon as it got started, there was a good chance that the circles could put it out before it became a raging inferno threatening towns, villages, and farmsteads. In those cases, the circles had to pull in storm cells to drench the fires from above.

Ben asked, "Should I bring Queen along with me, in case we need to land? If so, you know that dog will be invaluable on the ground."

Arsenio nodded, "I think so, Ben. This time we don't know what we will be facing. If we do decide to land one or more gliders, we'll have to find a spot from which we can later take off again. That's always the tricky part. If we are on the ground, it's probably wise to have such a well-trained dog with us to alert us of unseen dangers. She sure has the nose for it."

He grinned, recalling how many times in the past that Queen had alerted them of predatory animals in their vicinity.

"Flight plans. We'll fly V formation, spread out somewhat. We don't know exactly the location, but we can use the mile or so distance from the Wyndl as a guide. We don't know what we are looking for either, so keep your eyes peeled. Report anything out of the ordinary and we can circle around it and sense for the three minds. Okay, let's do it!" he barked briskly, emulating his father's approach when ordering his troops. The other five were more laid back and simply grinned at him, frustrating him all the more.

Stella raised her right foot up to her forehead, "Yes sir!" she barked. All four roared with laughter at her salute, while Arsenio flushed.

"Get serious. Okay," he finally grinned and lightened up. "Enjoy the game, but do be careful. If this is a new plot by the aliens, we could be in real danger out there. Stay alert, stay alive," he added.

The ground crew had already pulled their gliders outside the hanger, positioning them close to the cliff edge. Now they climbed aboard, though Arsenio quietly lifted Stella into her seat for her. *Thanks,* she sent. He knew how sensitive she was about appearing to look silly. While Stella could get in by herself, she had to use "undignified" maneuvers and his lift saved her that embarrassment. Then, they waited for Ben to fetch Queen, a black and white, highly intelligent dog. Once they were ready, their ground crewmen gave each glider a push and it rolled over the edge of the cliff and began falling. This was always the most dangerous moment and all six were prepared to activate their crystals and physically lift the glider up preventing it from crashing if the glider did not gain sufficient lift. Today, the thermals were quite strong and shortly, all felt the sudden lurch as the glider's lift took hold and each one soared into the blue sky, just as the thick clouds drifted off to the northeast.

"What a thrill, Arsenio. I love it. How many times have we done this? It still gives my stomach a thrill," Stella called out to him.

"I know, I love the takeoffs as well, sis. Quite a rush.

Okay, let's get some altitude before we put distance between us and Brom Tower." Slowly, the sleek silver gliders circled, climbing steadily on the thermals. Their enormous wingspans glistening in the orange-red sun, cast flickers of light onto the sprawling, wakening city far below them. Each glider measured sixty-feet from wingtip to wingtip. Smaller elevator wings at the rear of the very tiny and narrow fuselage controlled their rising and falling, while foot operated controls controlled a small rudder at the rear.

"One day, I will be able to fly one too," Stella commented to her brother. "Gabriel is nearly finished modifying one for me. I'll use one knee to control the rudder and one foot to control the stick. Then, I will finally get to fly myself."

"That will be the day, sis!" he encouraged her, knowing just how much flying meant to her. Of course, ever since he could walk he had been looking out for his "little sister," always there to help her with things she couldn't handle. Time after time, though, she surprised him by doing something that he thought she couldn't possibly do. Stella was one determined teen, he thought. True, she had the katalyein gift along with its "knowing what someone desires," but she also was a master at lie detection and had the Brom gift of handling all aspects of fire, though admittedly not as adept as their Fire Master, Anita. Both women were invaluable when they were on Fire Patrols, their most frequent missions.

Today, all six's adrenaline was flowing. This was a real mission! Out there ahead of them was a mystery, in all likelihood they were about to uncover some new and dangerous alien plot against them or their world. The only thing that bothered Arsenio was the possibility that these invading aliens had blasters. Well, the ultimatum about only using swords applies to our people, not to these aliens, he reminded himself. Stella and Anita would be free to blast the aliens with scorching fires if they threatened to use their blasters on them.

Now soaring at about two thousand feet, Arsenio sent Gabriel and Felipe new orders and the three gliders now headed out from Brom, flying in a V formation and heading eastwards, paralleling the grey, wide thread of the mighty Wyndl River. *We'll start searching just beyond the village of Willow,* he sent to the others. Willow was about thirty miles from Brom and sat on the banks of the river. Their speed was about fifty miles per hour and Willow appeared below them about forty minutes later. He ordered them to fly about a thousand feet apart, broadening their search pattern. *Stay alert. Watchers, don't miss them.* This was directed to Stella, Anita, and Ben.

Twenty minutes later, Ben sent, *Hey, got something off to our right. Right turn and sweep please.* All three gliders banked gracefully and ended up making the better part of a U-turn, enabling the three observers and, to a lesser extent, the three pilots to get a good look at the ground. *My god, what is that?* All six soon saw a silver colored shuttle craft of unknown design, a rather large one, more like a large box, resting on the grassy area within a small valley with the typical rocky ridge lines marking its northern and southern boundaries. Even more apparent were dozens of strange looking, gold and brown colored machines scattered about the area. Three small figures perhaps were walking among these weird looking machines.

Stay alert! We've been spotted! Stella sent to everyone. The three bodies were looking up at them, this she sensed from their minds, a wonder at what their gliders were.

Look out for blaster fire! Arsenio sent. Now he continued their circular flight pattern, hovering a couple thousand feet above them. He sent a message back to the tower that they had located the aliens. "Do you sense danger?" he asked Stella.

"No, just intense curiosity and fear too. Whoever they are down there, they are becoming afraid. I am not getting any malice, though," she replied.

"Okay, we'll go down for a closer look," he stated and then sent that order to the other two pilots. Slowly, silently, and gracefully, the three gliders tightened their formation and continued circling steadily downwards. *Look for a workable landing spot. Ground looks rather rough.*

Landing out in the field was always the riskiest part of

their excursions. An unseen rock could severely damage their rather fragile landing wheels. Once, a pilot had misjudged his landing and crashed, breaking his arms and legs, destroying the glider. He felt the touch of the Capa's mind and her circle joining with his mind. Now whatever he saw and heard would be instantly known back at Brom Tower, adding a good measure of safety. If things went badly, the circle could act, even from this distance.

We can land at the head of the valley, about a quarter mile from that thing, Gabriel sent. Arsenio fully trusted Gabriel; he was their best glider pilot and designer, second only to his now deceased grandfather who had invented them in the first place many years ago.

Arsenio sent, *Lookouts, stay alert for trouble while we land. Land on my mark.* He knew that he really didn't need to issue those orders; his five friends knew what was needed, for they were the best. Still, he liked being in command. Stella merely smiled when she heard his orders, thinking, *Big brother likes to be in control.*

I heard that, he sent back in an accusatory tone, and Stella giggled. Now he put all other thoughts out of his mind and focused on the rapidly approaching grasslands, trusting fully the lookouts to warn him to pull up if trouble came their way. Gently, he lowered the glider, its wheels now brushing along the tops of the tall grasses. He saw no boulders in the straight line path and adjusted the elevator slightly. The wheels touched and bounced off the ground and then settled down. Now came the decelerating, bumpy ride, as the glider rose and fell with every undulation of the ground below them. Soon their glider stopped and rocked backwards, ending their flight.

Arsenio now kicked into attack mode. He'd landed some distance from the enemy but he needed to get everyone into a defensive formation ready to counter an attack, which could come at any moment from these three alien invaders. He opened their doors and lifted Stella out, just as the others were doing likewise. "Defensive formation," he barked and the five obeyed, adrenaline rushing in all six. The men drew their swords, while the women readied their fire-based attacks.

Arsenio took point, with Felipe to his right and Ben to his left. Queen now ranged off to their left flank, sniffing and enjoying the warm morning. Gabriel walked behind him with Stella to his right and Anita to his left, a double V formation. Slowly and cautiously, the six made their way towards these very strange machines and three aliens.

"My god! They are women!" Stella exclaimed as they drew closer. "They look almost like me, mostly! These are not the Rigel-3 aliens, who are tall, thin, and very grey-colored. But what are all those machines and what is going on?"

"Probably they can't hurt us," Arsenio concluded.

"Idiot! You don't think that I could hurt you?" Stella took an antagonistic stab at his conclusion, based upon the fact that she didn't have arms as he did.

He flushed, "Sorry, that's not what I meant." Well, he had meant it; she knew that. Still, she saw what he had actually intended to convey. They'd not likely be facing blasters or swords. They saw three women. Two had flaming, red hair and one's fell to the small of her back, while the other was shoulder length and slightly wavy. The third had long black hair, identical in length to the other redhead. What struck the six the most were their bosoms, nearly double the size of the women of Tierra, whose were nearly the size of their heads. Anita and Stella sensed the instant arousal of the four men over this aspect of the alien women, but they were just as startled by them as the men were. Both women sensed fear coming from the three, but no hostile intentions and she relaxed a little, wondering how they could possibly communicate with these alien women. If nothing else, they could use telepathy to pick up the alien's concepts and relay their concepts into the three's minds, crude and open to misunderstandings.

Minutes before this, Alpha's voice over the three comm links said, "Warning. Three incoming flying ships overhead. Look up. Gliders, I believe they are called. They fly silently; they have no engines of their own. Be alert for trouble. I am sorry but there is going to be little that we can do to help you from up here."

"Wow, they look really cool. I guess we've been

discovered already," Marisol replied. "Well, it's happened. We'll just have to see what happens. If they kill us, then Alpha, see if you can get the shuttle back with as many of the bots as you can. If they are friendly, I will see if we can get permission to stay and get the crystals that we need, Alpha. Be brave everyone."

"How? My knees are shaking," Elena whispered. "Do you think that they will hurt us?"

"Remember those ancient videos of flying machines? They used to drop bomb things. They haven't dropped anything on us yet, so maybe they are not going to kill us right away," Tatiana speculated. All three felt rather vulnerable.

"Well, if they start a fight, use your elemental powers on them. We have to stay alive, if only to help get all these precious bots back inside the shuttle," Marisol ordered. "Look, they are coming down now way over there. That's good. We can watch them as they come to us. I certainly am not moving from here!"

They watched the gliders swooping down and then grazing the grasses. The landing seemed rather bumpy to Marisol, though she had little by which to compare what she was seeing. They opened up and people climbed out. The three very nervous women waited, trying hard to calm their rising nerves. They were about to face aliens. Would they be like Ambassador Kyle, she wondered? Well, they had taken care of his treachery. Perhaps the three of them could handle these six.

As the six walked closer, Marisol got a better look at them. "My god! One of the women has had her arms cut off completely! These must be a very vicious group."

"Either that or she had a very bad accident," Tatiana countered, trying hard to think positively.

"They look sort of like us," Elena whispered, not knowing why she was speaking so softly. "Oh! How are we going to understand their language?"

Alpha spoke up, "Beta and I will attempt to analyze their speech and work out translations, but we will need a lot of samples and time. Do your best."

"The men are wearing uniforms, so probably they are

like the guards of Kyle's," Marisol noted.

"Does that mean the women are the ambassadors?" Tatiana asked.

"Likely. If so, maybe that is a good thing for us," Elena continued whispering. "Oh now, they are drawing weapons. What are they?"

"They kind of look like big knives," Tatiana replied, her fears increasing significantly. "Well, I won't let them get you without a fight, love."

Marisol smiled in spite of this threatening move. She knew her mate well. Tatiana would not go down without a fight. "Let's hope that they are just as afraid of us as we are of them. After all, we are total strangers who've landed unannounced on their world. They might be afraid of us."

"Point taken, love," Tatiana replied. "I'll try to think positively."

Now the six were very close. Marisol watched their eyes taking the three in, hesitating as had Kyle and his scientists on their soccer balls. *Well, perhaps that is a good thing,* she thought. *I'd best be the spokeswoman.* She spoke clearly, "Hello. I am President Marisol Armando. We are visiting here."

The faces of the six looked rather shocked to hear her speak. "Hello aliens. Who are you and what are you doing here? What are all these strange machines doing?" asked Arsenio.

We can mostly understand them, Arsenio. Their language sounds like the Westerlings, Stella sent her group.

"Hey, I can barely understand you. Can you speak a little slower, please? How come you can speak our language, well sort of, mostly?" Marisol replied. Then she realized that she hadn't answered the man's questions. She added, "We are from Madiera and are here looking for some crystals that we desperately need to make replacement computers for our failing bots."

"Slower please too. We are mostly getting what you are saying. How come you speak some form of the Westerlings? Are you from Valen?" Arsenio asked.

"Same here, we are mostly following you. What is this

Westerlings? And Valen? We are from Madiera, a small town of us women."

"You are not from our world, are you?"

"No, but I hope this is not a problem. We know that the Imperium has made this a closed world, so we came here without their knowledge. We are really desperate for these crystals. Our bots are breaking down and we need these crystals so that Alpha can make more computer chips and use them to repair our failing bots. You see, we cannot survive without the constant assistance from our many bots. Though she probably knows what I mean, seeing as how she is sort of like us, and probably has many bots to help her." Marisol began, wondering how much she should really say.

Arsenio rubbed his head and put his sword away. "Hold on, slower please. The aliens at the spaceport don't know that you are here?"

"Right, Beta found a way for us to land here undetected."

"Okay, that's fine. Pretty interesting, in fact. Okay, then what is this word bots that you keep using?"

"These machines here, the ones that do all the work that we cannot do. We have dressing-bots, undressing-bots, bathing-bots, cooking-bots, clothes washing-bots, sweeping-bots, delivery-bots, and a whole lot more. They grow, harvest, and process all our food as well. However, we also have these other mechanical arm machines that we use to carry things, feed ourselves, and so on, just like she must have for herself," Marisol explained. Seeing the confused look, she added, "Like miniature robots. Our real robots are very human-like and very highly intelligent, you see. That's Alpha and Beta; they fly our ship and keep us alive."

Stella interrupted the two. "You three are not quite like me and the others like me. We don't need all those machines. I use my feet and my *mentales* gifts. Don't you use your feet?"

"Er, not until very recently. We've always had our bots, you see, to help us. Since they are starting to fail frequently now, we've begun to experiment and find ways to do some things for ourselves that we normally have bots do. You know, prepare for the worst. Maybe you could show us how to do more things. But what's this *mentales* thing?"

"Let's deal with that word later on," Arsenio suggested. "How come your men are not down here running these machines or bots? We always help out our women when they need assistance, like my sister, Stella here."

"Sorry, we don't have any of you man creatures in our city, only we women. There are about five hundred of us now, but we've lost about half of our original thousand. There never have been any man creatures in our city, only the original seventy women that Alpha rescued. It's just us. We're all pretty much the same, like we three. In fact, until the last year, we didn't even know that we were all on a spaceship. We thought that Madiera was our world. Kind of silly of us, really. It's only a square mile of world. Yet, for four hundred years, we women have been living our lives, raising our children, going to school, marrying, and all that, you see. Then, as the bots began really failing, Tatiana here, she's my mate, she and I discovered the rest of the ship and our to caretaker robots, Alpha and Beta. They are trying their best to find us a world where we can land and survive and prosper." Marisol wondered if perhaps she was not revealing too much about herself, though.

Arsenio gave her a strange look. "You mean that you are not four hundred years old? You mean to say that somehow there are no men in Madiera and yet you women can have babies?"

"Er, yes. Is that a problem? Our original men destroyed our ancestor's world and Alpha was only able to rescue seventy women. We've all descended from those seventy. I'm twenty, so are these two. We went to high school together. In the past, Alpha had to keep our numbers at no more than a thousand, you see. The food production could not support more than a thousand. So we are allowed to have babies only when we reach twenty years old and then we cannot have more than one child every two years. Only since we've lost half of our women and children, we may be relaxing those rules, except that with all the failing bots, that might not be a wise thing to do just now."

"But how? I mean it takes a man's seed to combine with

a woman's egg to produce a new life. From what we have heard, it is like this among we humans across the galaxy," Arsenio pointed out, trying to grasp what she was implying. He didn't say that they'd learned this from Amy and Jan.

"Er, well, Tatiana and I haven't yet done that yet, but from our social skills class, when we are ready to have a baby, the bots will prepare something from Tatiana that will fertilize me, or I, her. We only can have female babies, though. Alpha says that's because he has not got any man creature's samples. I'm sorry if I'm not too understandable about this. None of us here has done it yet. We were holding off in case we find a place where we can live. We don't want to be pregnant at the wrong time, when there is a lot of work to be done." Marisol attempted to explain further.

"Okay, I follow you, I think."

Marisol smiled. At least this embarrassing detail was handled. "So, can we mine here for our desperately needed crystals? I know that we don't have anything to pay you for them. We tried that once a few months back and that was a disaster. They wanted some of our bots in exchange for fuel, and they took several hundred of our women in exchange too. I insisted only those who really wanted off the ship go down to that planet. Then, they tried to steal our ship and capture all the rest of us women, but we stopped them cold."

Stella grinned, this was the first moment that she began to sense that there was more to these seemingly helpless women than they were letting on, bot dependence or not. "Please, how were you able to stop these men from taking your ship and your remaining women?"

"Oh, we all have elemental powers. Don't you? Tatiana and I here are Fire kindred. Actually, all red headed women are Fire kindred. Elena here is Earth kindred, as are all black haired women of Madiera. Water kindred all have brown hair and Air kindred all are blonde. How come you all have yellow eyes? We've never seen anyone with yellow eyes before," she decided to ask a question.

"I'll answer that one in a bit. What exactly can a Fire kindred do? How did you stop these men from stealing your ship and women?" Stella persisted. She began to see some alarming images in the minds of the three women.

"Oh, easy. Tatiana was in charge of a dozen of us in the cargo bay, while I had another eighteen with me outside the doors. When the men in their armor suits came out with their gun things, we shot walls of fire at them, along with hurricane force winds, giant streams of water and blew them all out of the air lock into space. I think that they probably died, though. Elena here can make the ground and plants do most anything, but in that fight, the Earth kindred didn't have much to do. It was over in less than a minute."

Stella saw these very images in the three women's minds as Marisol spoke her reply. Via her, so did all those monitoring them back at the tower. Venerada Luisa suddenly made a strong contact with Stella. *You must bring these three back to Brom Tower. We need to further question them.* Apparently, she sent the same message to the other five, because Arsenio spoke up before she could.

"That's cool, Marisol. Well done. Say, would you three mind coming with us to our tower and city? We can take you there and bring you back in our gliders. Our leaders would like to chat with you. I suppose it will be about payment for the crystals, but I'm not certain."

"Oh! Well, is that the place where we saw women wearing fancy party dresses and heels?" asked Marisol, trying to figure out if he meant that place they saw briefly from the drone probe. If so, should she go with them?

"Why yes! How did you know about that?" asked Stella.

"Alpha sent a drone down and we saw two women, but only for a split second before the drone smashed into the mountains. I'm sorry. We didn't bring our party outfits with us. We can't work out here in them and so we've been trying to wear jeans and sneakers for a long time, readjusting. I mean, all adult women of Madiera always wear satin or silk dresses quite similar to those that we saw the one woman wearing, but our heels are really boots that give our feet more support. All Madiera is entirely flat, and we have concrete walkways everywhere, kind of like the ground there in that brief image of the stone place that we saw," Marisol explained. "We'd look very out of place if we went to your place wearing our work jeans. Women are supposed to look their best, or so my mom's always say."

"I understand, Marisol," Anita spoke up. "I give you my word that when we get there, the first thing we'll do is give you all a nice hot bath and some elegant fashions to wear while you are our guests."

"But we won't have our dressing bots, nor our mechanical arms," Tatiana whispered worriedly to Marisol. "We won't be able to eat properly."

"Don't worry about that. There are many hands that are more than willing to assist you with your needs," Stella added, catching what Anita had in mind and why the women were hesitant. "Besides, perhaps we can show you some other ways to do some of the things that you think that you can't do without your bots. I've never had such a thing as a bot and I and others like me do just fine. In fact, Gabriel here is making me a special glider that I can fly all by myself. Come on, we'd love to have you as our guests for a short while."

"Well, if you are sure that your people won't mind helping us, I suppose that will be all right. We have the bots all setup and working now and they really don't need us for now. Oh, forgive me. I've not introduced us all. I'm Marisol Armanda, this is Tatiana Vileno, and she's Elena del Novio."

"How utterly strange! Do you realize that you all have Westerlings type names? Strange. I am Stella del Fuego. My older brother, Arsenio. This is Felipe Wycombe and his sister, Anita. He's Gabriel del Fuego-Jeffery and he's Ben del Fuego-Sikes. That's his dog, Queen. She's our lookout."

"What's she looking out for?" asked Elena, now curious about the dog who continued to roam all around the area.

"The giant cats, the Montaña beasts. They are giant cats who can kill us in an instant. They are the fiercest predators around here in the foothills. Queen will alert us if one comes and we all run away as fast as we can. We'd best hurry up; it is going to rain soon. Water won't hurt your bots, will it?"

Marisol looked up at the gathering clouds. "No, they will be okay. We had planned to ride out the storm inside the shuttle. In Madiera, every day is sunny and picture-perfect. I think that it must rain late at night. Alpha, we are going to visit them at that tower that we saw. We'll stay in touch."

"We'd best hurry, the storm is coming fast," Arsenio pointed out. All nine began walking back towards their gliders. Just then, a bolt of lightning struck off to their left, shattering a resinous pine tree. The deafening thunder scared all three women, who'd never heard thunder before. However, flames began crackling from the remains of the tree.

"Of all the inopportune times for a forest fire to start!" Ben growled.

"Wow, look how fast it is growing!" Marisol added, rather surprise to see how swiftly the pine had begun to blaze.

"I should put it out. I don't want it spreading and damaging our bots," Tatiana spoke up. "You don't mind if I put it out, Arsenio?"

He gave her a curious look and said, "No, go ahead. Normally, that is our job as fire fighters. Be my guest." All six watched her closely.

Tatiana focused and sucked the heat out of the fire. Almost at once it died down and left only curls of smoke rising towards the darkening clouds. "Okay, fire's out."

"How did you do that?" asked Ben.

"A fire needs fuel and air and heat. I removed the heat this time, simpler that way. We best get going; those clouds are pretty ominous. We've never seen clouds before, but they don't look so appealing," Tatiana replied.

A bit later, she asked, "How do we get inside?"

"One with each of us," Felipe replied. "Here, I'll show you." He lifted Anita into their glider. Though she didn't need such help, she knew that Tatiana certainly did and allowed her brother to demonstrate with her body. She rode with those two. Marisol rode with Arsenio and Stella, while Elena rode with Ben, Gabriel, and Queen.

"Okay, lift off time. For the next few minutes, Marisol, don't distract us. We have to lift the glider straight up until we catch a thermal," he explained.

She wanted to ask how this was possible, but didn't. The tiny glider rose straight upwards, albeit slowly. While the wings were huge, here inside the cramped fuselage, she had very little room. She did look down and watched her bots and shuttle craft slowly growing smaller and smaller. Then they slipped into the clouds and the ground vanished. Her stomach registered a distinct falling sensation, but she resisted the urge to distract the two. She did notice that the stones that they wore around their necks were glowing, emitting a pale blue light. As the glider began to move on its own, the blue lights faded.

"There, we are flying again. Got to get around this storm or we'll have a bumpy first ride for you, Marisol," he explained.

"How did we get up in the air?" she asked.

Stella answered, "Arsenio and I lifted us up high enough so that as the glider begins to fall and gains speed, the wings provide the lift needed to keep us up in the air. It rains about this time nearly every day. Often we have to go out on fire patrols and try to spot the lightning started fires before they become raging infernos. When we can, we put them out. It will take us just less than an hour to get home. Settle back and enjoy the flying. I just love to fly and I can't wait for Gabriel to hurry up and get one of these gliders modified so I can fly it with my feet."

"It's a little scary. Until last night, I've never done anything besides walking or driving our electric machines. We came down from our ship during the night so no one would see us. We didn't see much at all. I guess we were not so good at keeping our arrival a secret."

"The aliens at the spaceport have done some very nasty things to us all here on Tierra, so we are being especially vigilant and some of our people spotted your craft landing last night. To be honest, Marisol, we were expecting some new diabolical plot of the Imperium against us."

"Speaking of such awful things, did it hurt badly when you had your accident and lost both of your arms?" Marisol asked. The response that she received startled her.

Stella laughed. "Marisol, I was born this way, as are many of us. We have a special gift and a byproduct of that seems to be that we all lack our arms."

Marisol flushed. "I'm sorry. I didn't know. You are like us then, we are born like this too." She felt a sudden kinship with Stella, for in many ways they were rather similar, though Stella didn't have any arms at all.

Chapter 14 Carmen Strikes

Emperor Jan Bellweather looked over all her monitors in her secret communications chamber, far beneath the ground floor of their Imperial Tower. Surrounded by all her accumulated computers and equipment during her rebellious Sly Dog career, Jan was frustrated. She'd found no trace of this supposed spaceship that had landed an unknown model of shuttle craft some fifty miles east of Brom Tower. She and Amy had been notified of the anomaly by Brom's Venerada Luisa earlier in the morning, and she'd suspected more Imperium meddling at the very least. Now, she was certain of nothing as she left the room, activating the secret lever that turned the doorway back into a stone wall.

"Oh there you are mom, Amy's looking for you," her fifteen year old daughter, Melissa called out to her from the far end of this hallway. Melissa, like all the tower women, had not cut her thick brown hair, and hers fell to her hips, tied in the back with the usual bluebird clasp. Jan had always opted for shorter hair during her many years off-world, but now she'd begun to let hers grow much to Amy's enjoyment. Hers was shoulder length and she gave it a toss as she turned to see her daughter. Amazing how time had flown and she found it hard to believe that Melissa was now fifteen, past the adult age of fourteen and already covertly watching every boy that ever entered the tower-castle complex. Well, so was Amy's daughter, June, for that matter. Both were born within a day of each other and were extraordinarily close friends, much like their mothers.

"Just tracking down more information on today's surprise visitors, dear. You look good this morning, sky blue satin suits you well," Jan complimented Melissa, who wore only the latest Elegant Fashions Inc dresses and heels, as did June and nearly every other woman in the tower complex. Jan and Amy had little choice but to wear such outfits, since their bodies still had not fully recovered from their body modifications they'd undergone to become wasp-like in an effort to gain diplomatic immunity to return to Tierra. That had been a most drastic move on their part, made necessary by the fact that Ashford-5 or Tierra was a closed Imperium world. Diplomatic immunity had been their only way to return home.

The Ataro System of the Imperium controlled three dozen planets. Ruled by an emperor, empress, and many queens, this system had not seen a war anywhere within its borders for almost two full millennia now, due in part to their unique form of rulership and their knowledge of the true cause of conflicts among people. Their current Emperor Chieng Sango, Empress Amaka, and queens held total power, their word was law throughout the Ataro System. As Amy and Jan well knew from their many years in the underground fighting against the suppression of the Imperium, that kind of power could be easily abused. Rare was the Imperium man or woman who had not fallen victim to that vast a power. Yet, in this system of wasp worshipers — quite why they considered wasps holy had never been fully understood by either Amy or Jan — their rulers never were tempted by such immense power. Why?

The founders severely physically hobbled them. Their arms were removed. Their feet were reformed into an unnatural high arch that allowed only their toes to touch the ground with their heels being almost above their toes forcing them to wear special shoes in which the tiny spiked heel nearly touched the back of the their toes. Further, because their wasp worship, they wore incredibly tight corsets. One or two ribs (in the case of males or adult women undergoing the process) were removed and internal organs adjusted, some up, but most downward. When worn from late childhood, circumferences of barely twelve inches resulted. In the case of adults being converted, as was the situation with Amy and Jan, only a fourteen inch waist resulted. However, in all cases, that tiniest portion of their waists was three inches tall, held that way by the band of the metal-re-enforced corsets, providing that distinctive wasp shape to their bodies that these people so desired.

Of course, so hobbled, the emperor, empress, and queens needed someone to assist them, the domestique. He or she was also hobbled and corseted, like those whom they were helping. However, they retained their arms, naturally, but had their voices silenced. Unable to speak, they could not then influence unduly the leader that they served. Likewise, any of the close aides of the rulers were similarly hobbled, though they were not required to also have their arms removed. Yet, many of the advisors did so, feeling that gave them more power. This, Amy and Jan had personally witnessed during their two years among them. Amy had become a queen and Jan, her domestique.

Once the two had finally landed on Ashford-5, they escaped and faked their deaths in a shuttle crash. Not long after that, they made use of their own Imperium medical machines and gotten their feet somewhat restored as well as Jan's voice. Still, both women could only wear the highest of heels that Elegant Fashions Inc had. Nothing could be done about the removed ribs and Amy's arms, but they both had ceased wearing the terribly restricting corsets almost at once. However, after the births of their daughters, both Amy and Jan had to begin wearing them again. Their backs had been weakened sufficiently that sometimes even sneezing threw their backs out. Although reluctant at first, both discovered that wearing the corsets handled the problem entirely.

As their daughters grew up around their mothers who always wore very high heels, corsets, and elegant satin dresses, naturally they too wanted to wear them. Wisely, both women insisted that their daughters wait until they came of age, fourteen, before doing so. Now fifteen, both June and Melissa attempted to "look like" their mothers. This was part of the drama now being played out at the Imperial Court.

However, Amy and Jan also implemented much of the Ataro judicial technology that Amy had learned while training to become their queen. This the two found invaluable here on Tierra as they began ruling the entire planet. At the heart of all conflicts between two people lies a hidden, third person who is actively fomenting the conflict. Find this covert third person and reveal him or her to the two and their conflict evaporates. Amy had used this law of human behavior time and time again during their last sixteen years as Emperor and Empress. One thing that the Ataro people had was a superior knowledge of human technology and this the two applied to their rule of Tierra.

On the other hand, Jan and Amy had brought along their fifty years of accumulated computers and machines, including medical and rejuvenation machines. With these, Jan continued to monitor the vast Imperium, focusing now mostly on actions that affected Ashford-5, Tierra. This effectively halted the Imperium's two centuries' practice of kidnaping young telepaths and sending them off-world, as had been done to Jan and Amy. The two women caused "accidents" to happen that forced the scrubbing of each kidnap mission. Still, the two kept alert for further Imperium treachery.

Valen had not taken their enforced defeat lightly, nor the forced evacuation of this tower, now called the Imperial Tower. At first, they sent assassins to eliminate the two. Each time, Amy and Jan viciously raped the assassin's mind to find out who was behind it and then killed all those remotely tied to that attempt. Once, they'd killed an entire circle from Valen Tower, since the circle had hired the assassin. Thoughts can kill, particularly so for Amy and Jan, who had spent most of their lives fighting to survive among the worst evils of the galaxy. Life hardens people, so it was with these two, hardened to a viewpoint vastly different to most all others on Tierra. As young women, they'd been raped so many times that they'd lost count. Thus, they didn't remotely blink at thinking the thought that would subsequently kill their opponent.

"Carmen Valen is requesting a private audience with you and Amy later today, mom," Melissa explained, as their heels clicked in unison on the stone floor of the hallway.

"Did she say what it was about?" Jan asked.

"Nope, only she stressed the private bit. What do you suppose that she wants?" Melissa attempted to probe her mother a little. While she and June both had their own *mentales* gifts, like their mothers, she never could get around her mother's barriers or Amy's. No one could. That didn't stop her from trying. This time, though, Melissa did get a hint, the single word, wasp.

Jan changed the subject. She did not want Melissa to find out that Carmen was the one person who knew that Ataro

Queen Amy and Jan were not killed in the shuttle crash. Carmen knew who they really were, but she'd been very careful with that knowledge, knowing that Amy and Jan would not hesitate to kill her if she attempted to blackmail the two. "This new development up in Brom is vastly more important and requires a swift response, dear."

"Amy and June have been monitoring Venerada Luisa up in Brom. The more that these alien women talk, the stranger it all seems. Did you find out anything mom?" Melissa probed a little.

"No, not a thing, which itself is critical, dear. Now can you tell me why?" Jan decided to turn this into a training exercise for her daughter. While per Amy's ultimatum the next emperor and empress would be elected by the leaders of the various parties of Tierra, she still wanted Melissa to know as much as possible, though it was highly unlikely that Melissa or June would be elected when that time came.

"So you found nothing about these strange aliens? No records in the Imperium, none at all? The spaceport here hasn't detected them either?" Melissa asked, making sure that she was interpreting her mother correctly. She knew that her mother was once more testing her. She could always tell, something about the flicker of Jan's mouth gave it away.

"No to all those," Jan replied flatly.

"Well, that is strange. Ah, they must have come from outside that part of the galaxy under Imperium control," Melissa concluded.

Her mother smiled and the teen knew that she was dead on. "Precisely."

"So we need to talk more with these three alien women, right mom?" Jan didn't answer, because they'd just walked into the main first floor meeting room, often called the throne room, where Amy and June were sitting, their crystals glowing blue as they were joined telepathically with Venerada Luisa Wycombe up in Brom Tower. As the two entered, Amy broke her connection, allowing June to carry on with their monitoring. She looked up at Jan questioningly. Jan shook her head no, which was all that Amy needed to know fully what Jan's research had yielded.

"Based on what we've seen and heard so far," Amy said softly, "we should investigate them further. I'm having Luisa invite them to visit Brom Tower. I have a hunch that you and I ought to pay them a visit as well."

"I agree, plus we should see first-hand these bots of theirs, and I would like to somehow get a good look at their ship and these Alpha and Beta robots," Jan replied.

Amy grinned, knowing full well that Jan was dying to get a look at them! "I am intrigued by their apparent elemental powers. According to what we've seen, one of them effortlessly put out the start of a forest fire caused by a lightning strike just as they were boarding the gliders. If all these women possess such powers, they would be a valuable addition to Tierra, don't you think?"

"But Amy, how can they have such powers if they aren't *mentales* gifted?" asked Melissa.

"Good question, dear. We need to find out, if we can. Apparently, these women have evolved within the total isolation of a spaceship over some four hundred years. In such an environment, anything is possible," Amy replied.

"But don't discount this Alpha robot," Jan interjected. "If it is as powerful as this Marisol woman claims, their powers could be a direct result of his experimentation on the women. One look at their bodies tells me that someone has been directly modifying their genes, to say nothing of having an easy way for women to impregnate each other."

"Mom, I thought that only gods and goddesses could do such a thing, like Lysandra did with you and Amy," Melissa asked, growing a little confused. Were gods merely robots? Or were robots really the gods?

"Dear, Amy and I have seen nearly all the Imperium worlds, hundreds of them. Nowhere do men have the babies, and nowhere do two of the same sex impregnate each other. There are two cultures where the physical body is androgynous, an hermaphrodite, who impregnates their own self. Here on Tierra, this Goddess Lysandra has somehow given several of we women the gift to impregnate our mates. It's been documented, but Amy and I have only seen this Lysandra once, when she gave us that precious gift, as we've explained to you and June."

Melissa grinned, "Yes, Amy's my father and you are June's father. We know that. So how can these alien women impregnate each other? Do they have a man's organ too? I bet they do, mom. That would explain it all pretty easily."

Amy and Jan chuckled. "Yes, yes it would, dear," Amy finally replied. "Don't worry. Venerada Luisa will have the three aliens take a hot, soaking bath before dressing them in elegant fashions. She'll let us know if they spot such a thing. It would be pretty obvious." All three grinned and Melissa giggled in a girlish fashion.

"Okay, Amy, I'll make the arrangements for our circle to teleport us there, say around the supper hour?" Jan suggested and asked.

"I think that would be good timing on our part."

"Okay. Melissa, you and June will be in charge of all things here until we get back," Jan gave the order that Melissa was hoping to hear. Once again, she and June would be acting Emperor and Empress! "Don't do anything foolish," she teased her daughter, who beamed and also grinned. "Come on, Amy. Let's see what Carmen wants this time."

Amy and Jan walked out of the throne room into a side room where they often met in private with petitioners and others, in an informal fashion. Here, the stone walls were covered with great tapestries that hid the network of crystals that both protected the room and kept out scrying attempts by all others. It also hid the scrambler that effectively blocked all electronic surveillance that the Rigel-3 station might use to overhear their conversations. The room contained a low table and a high one, all well made from oak and highly polished. Six comfortable sofas rested along two walls, angled so that those seated could view the others. Six other matching oak chairs were arranged on either side of the tables.

They found Carmen sitting on a sofa, though she had a portfolio of drawings sitting on the taller table. She was waiting patiently for the two. She looked as if she was in her early forties, though both knew that she was in her nineties. Her thick black hair was very full-bodied, falling straight to just below her curvaceous hips. Carmen also wore makeup;

her eyes were lined with a blue shadow and her thick lips, a dull red today. She looked every bit a Westerlings, though she now had Imperium citizenship because of her marriage to Jarek, the late field agent, who the two had slain after he'd dropped the Nuclear on Bettingham some sixteen years ago.

Carmen held a grudge against these two for slaying Jarek, but she really hated them for having gotten her partner, Karolina, taken off-world, banned from ever returning because of the mistakes made by her husband, Lech. Well, that hatred was balanced during these past sixteen years because she was now the sole owner of Elegant Fashions Inc. So yes, the relationship between Carmen Valen and Amy and Jan was a complex one. Long ago Carmen had setup an automatic system that would send appropriate video and documentation to the Imperium identifying Amy and Jan as having faked their deaths as the Queen of Ataro System and her domestique. Carmen had told the two that if anything happened to her, her automatic system would send the data off to the Imperium. If that happened, Amy and Jan would themselves be in dire trouble. Long ago, Jan had used her "special computer skills" to tinker with Carmen's automated system. If Carmen did try to send the information, it would wind up on Jan's computer system and not the Imperium's systems. Still, Amy and Jan played along with Carmen as much as possible. Neither saw any point in antagonizing her or forcing her to take other means of extracting revenge on them.

Amy wore a bright red, satin gown and matching heels, while Jan's was emerald green this morning. Carmen, as usual, wore a bright red gown and matching heels. Yet, there was something different about this regal and attractive woman today. Then Amy noticed it; Carmen's waist seemed positively smaller than the last time they'd met last year. "So good of you to see me on such short notice," Carmen began as the two walked in and took seats in opposite sofas from which they could see Carmen. Amy tossed her hair off to her left side, getting it out in front of her before she sat down.

"It is always good to see the best dress and heel maker on Tierra," Amy replied, meaning it.

"So what brings you here this late morning?" Jan asked

pleasantly.

"Ah, so you have noticed my waist! Excellent. Yes, I too now have a fourteen inch waist line!"

"I thought so; you do look quite curvaceous, Carmen," Amy replied with a grin. All three women were sitting very straight. Amy and Jan had no choice; their much needed corsets had an awful lot of steel supports in them, and they could only bend at their waists. This had proved vitally necessary and had at long last relieved them of their many accidental back wrenches and accompanying pain. Now they saw that Carmen too was sitting as they were.

"Yes, as you know, I am ever in search of the very latest in women's and men's fashions throughout the galaxy. As you both know, I have been importing the special corsets that you both need from the Ataro System. I've been doing some research of my own," she said rather coyly, picking just the right words to say.

"We both know you are basing your rule of Tierra on the Ataro System of Emperor and Empress, modified by our *mentales* gifts and our *Círculo de mentes*," Carmen stated.

"What if we are?" Jan replied a little defensively. Only their daughters and Carmen knew this detail, however.

"Oh I think that is admirable of you," Carmen hastily defused Jan's arousal. "Oh yes. I have been doing my research, you see. The Ataro System has not had a war in over two millennia now, all due to their Emperor and Empress system of government." Jan knew this was readily available information anyone could learn with a simple search.

"But they also temper that awful power they give to their Emperor and Empress. And believe me, I understand just how having that kind of power can corrupt a person. Just look at what it did to my late husband! He's known now as a mass murderer, but that is only being kind about it. I fully agree with those in the Ataro System. With that kind of power must come some physical restraints. If only we'd had them sixteen years ago, maybe tens of thousands would still be alive."

"Yes, that's likely true, but what is your point?" asked Jan.

"The Ataro Emperor and Empress have just such

restraints, as you both know. Further, you both know that such restraints work as intended, keeping the massive power of the two leaders in check, preventing such abuses of power as we have seen here in our past," Carmen said diplomatically. "As you can see, I have a fourteen inch waist now, just like both of you. I acquired the medical machines needed and have experimented on myself. Lost two ribs, but the procedure is painless, but a bit hard to get used to on the breathing side." Jan could not help but grin; it was certainly that and then some. "Still, I am managing very well and my dresses now have an even more curvaceous look to them, quite sexy. So, honestly, just having a tiny waist is wholly insufficient to keep massive ruling powers in check."

"Of course, it would be silly to think otherwise," Amy countered, not yet having worked out what Carmen really wanted. "It's just hard to breathe when doing much."

"Right. I just want you both to know up front I am getting quite a lot of women asking me and begging me to fit them with tiny waists as well."

"Sure, if they want that restriction, let them," Jan replied.

"Of course. I just wanted to let you know your daughters are among the many women who have asked me about having the procedure done. I insisted on their bringing me your written approvals, however. I do hope that is not overly presumptuous of me," she added coyly. She saw instantly neither mother had known about their daughter's action.

"Yes, you have done very well. We will have to speak with them big time about this," Amy replied, rather relieved. She realized that although both teens were of legal age and had every right to get this procedure done on themselves, Carmen had been wise enough to do as she'd said. "Thank you, Carmen." The Westerlings woman smiled, knowing she'd just scored a small victory with the two women.

"Anyway, that's not the reason for my visit today. I have given the Ataro System a great deal of thought. While none of us has any complaints specifically about your current rule, Emperor Jan and Empress Amy, have you given any thought to those who are elected to be our next emperor and empress? I certainly have. The man who takes it over and the woman — why, they are going to wield the greatest power in our world! It doesn't take much for me to envision all that power suddenly going to their heads. My goodness, look what it did to Sector ID Minister Lech and his field agent Jarek! And even the Venerados of Valen Tower! Amy, Jan, this scares me! While you both have shown you are truly trying to help us all survive and prosper, those who come after you — my goodness I can see them leading us right back into terrible messes we were into only sixteen years ago!" Both Amy and Jan visibly flinched, and Carmen knew that she'd touched a raw nerve and had them setup.

Carmen suggested, "I suppose you could disband the whole emperor-empress thing and let the world get on with it. Still, that would only serve Valen's interests. You know as well as I do Valen Tower is just biding its time, waiting for you two to grow old and die. If the emperor-empress concept dies with you, there is nothing to keep Valen Tower from picking up right where it left off."

Jan sighed, "We know, Carmen. We know that all too well. I suppose that you have a solution for that?" Her voice was a little condescending, a little cat-like.

"Well, I am not a genius, not like you both are. However, if those in Ataro System have found a workable solution that has worked for two millennia, why re-invent the wheel?" Carmen finally let her idea out, slightly concealed however.

"You mean to say the emperor and empress should not have their arms and have their feet also screwed up? Like we were when we finally arrived here on Tierra?" Amy asked, rather incredulously.

Carmen shrugged her shoulders. "Well, all that has worked very well in the Ataro System, hasn't it? Though I don't think one needs to go so far as to inhibiting the speech of their domestique helpers; that's a bit drastic I think. After all, they could still write out their ideas or use sign language to influence their emperor or empress. Have you given this any thought?"

"Obviously, Carmen, we have given it considerable thought," Amy replied. Carmen, for whatever reason, had truly hit the nail on the head. Once they stepped down as emperor and empress, and a new pair elected, potentially the world would be right back where it had been before the two arrived back on Tierra. They could reduce the overall power of the emperor and empress positions, but then that would imply giving more power to the various leaders of the different lands or kingdoms, who themselves had no checks on their powers. True, they were supposed to be elected by their people, but already they had seen that mechanism was easily subverted by all manner of nefarious means.

"Well, I think," Carmen said coyly and with a grin, "you should keep the power in the emperor and empress positions. It keeps all the other leaders in check, so to speak. Only you need to make sure there is something to keep the emperor-empress in check as well, just like on Ataro Prime."

"We see your point, Carmen," Jan said rather disgusted. She hated to be reminded of the single problem they had not solved. "What are you suggesting that we do?"

"Make the positions of emperor and empress physically restrained like they do in the Ataro System. Amy only needs her feet adjusted a little. You'd need your feet adjusted a little too, Jan, plus lose your arms. Perhaps those who are your advisors also should be modified as well, but you would know far better about that from your previous experiences as one of their queens," Carmen said point blank, alluding to the fact she knew precisely what the two had been before coming to Tierra and faking their deaths. It was a subtle reminder to the two that she was the only one who knew their identity.

She added hastily, "I have acquired the needed medical machines, using my Imperium citizen status. I can perform such things out of my offices in the Imperium Exchange City headquarters building, Elegant Fashions Inc, which is *technically* Imperium soil not Tierra's. Hence, I am *legally* able to perform such medical procedures. That is half of why I came to see you this morning. I wanted to let you know I can perform all those needed body modifications now — the kind that are needed on Ataro Prime."

"Secondly, I came to ask or to beg you to give me a little advanced notice if you wish to start wearing those special heels you wore on Ataro Prime. I am certain the moment you start wearing them again, many, many other women will want to emulate you and get their feet done too, and I need time to get a supply of those elegant shoes in stock. You would not believe the number of women who have discretely asked me if they could get their waists shrunk to the sizes that you two have. Until now, I have been stalling them, saying I needed time to get the corsets made and the drastic changes made to the dresses the women would then wear. I am about ready to go on this project, but if you are going to add shoes to the mix, I will stall a little longer until I have enough of them in stock to meet the initial demand, which I can tell you up front here, will be a big demand," Carmen said flatly and without any ceremony.

"Have you tried to walk in them?" Amy asked, recalling how difficult that had been.

"Well, no," Carmen admitted. "I would have to have my own feet altered first. I didn't do it yet, because that might upstage you two. As soon as I do it, I know many other women will want to emulate me, me being the fashion role model on Tierra. Frankly, I would prefer they emulate our emperor and empress."

"How kind of you!" Jan retorted sarcastically. She sighed, "I see your point, Carmen. I'm sorry for belittling you. You are right; it would be best if women and men were emulating their emperor and empress in this matter. We'll give it some more though and get back to you, okay?"

"Certainly, no offense taken, Emperor Jan. I am setup to do your feet anytime, your arms as well. Please, give me a month's notice so I can get in a goodly supply of those special heels, though. Thanks for seeing me," Carmen replied and their meeting ended.

After Carmen left, Jan said, "Damn that woman! But she has a point. How the devil are we going to place an effective check on the massive power we've placed in our emperor-empress positions?"

"Love, I just don't know. She has a point. Physical

restraint apparently has worked in the Ataro System. However, let's get ready to go to Brom Tower. Right now, this alien situation is vastly more important," Amy answered.

"She's right you know. We don't have any real exit strategy. We got ourselves into this emperor-empress thing easily enough, but how are we going to exit it? How are we going to keep our successors from becoming what we despise in the first place?" Jan countered. "We've got a difficult exit."

Chapter 15 First Contact

Marisol, Tatiana, and Elena were surprised to see that Brom was a thriving town, medieval looking and somewhat like the images Alpha had shown them of their planet's ancient past. Most all the buildings were made from the grey or brown granite carved from the mountains nearby. The cobblestone streets rose and fell and adjacent homes were at different elevations, some nearly two feet above the one next to it. Although it was raining, they saw men, women, and children on the streets; most wore oiled capes.

Horses, reindeer, and dogs were commonplace, though the three had never seen them before, save for Queen. Slowly, Marisol began to see that the man creatures here were as populous as the women. Children seemed about equally divided between the sexes. Here then was another area of which she and the women of Madiera were wholly ignorant. Men obviously were playing as big a role in life as the women were. This came rather as a shock to the three women, who followed after the six. Now they could see the castle walls, the giant manor house, and tower complex.

Although the three were getting soaked from the rain, Stella pointed out, "Don't worry. Soon we'll be inside and you can have a hot bath. Boss's orders." As she and her group entered the gates into the castle grounds, a number of men stopped to glance at the arrivals, but with the pouring rain, Stella hastened them on inside the manor house. Still, Marisol noted that cobblestones covered the whole courtyard, save the flower beds close to the walls of the house and tower. In fact, it was right around here that the two women had been walking when the drone bot had captured their images in the fleeting moment before it crashed into the mountains just behind and to the west of Brom. Marisol expected to see many people inside the huge stone dwelling, but found a long hall instead.

"We'll leave them to you ladies," Arsenio called out. "See you at dinner, Marisol."

"Right, see you at dinner, Tatiana," Felipe added.

"Same here, Elena," Gabriel said with a grin.

"The men are off to report to our boss and clean up too. The section that I'm taking you to is where we have our guest rooms and where many of we unmarried women stay. That reduces the temptations to flirt with the men," Stella explained as she and Anita led them onwards.

"Wait a second, there was no door-bot there," Marisol finally realized what she hadn't seen.

"Of course, we don't have any such things here. We open the doors ourselves with our hands if you have them or our feet. I'll show you soon. Of course, when we get all dressed up and are wearing our heels, we let the men open doors for us. That's the polite thing for them to do," Stella explained.

"Okay, but why do you reduce the temptations to flirt with the men creatures?" Tatiana asked. Then she worked out the answer to her own question and her face crimsoned.

Anita answered, "Just men, not men creatures. Here, marriages are between a man and a woman. When they flirt, often that leads to passionate kissing and that can lead to an affair in bed, often resulting in a pregnancy. That complicates life if you are not married. Don't you have similar customs among your women?"

"Sure, teens are not allowed to kiss until they graduate from high school," Tatiana answered. "Forgive us, but we've hardly ever seen men, only those who tried to steal our ship. According to the video logs, men destroyed our whole world. We don't think much of men."

"Hey, there are good men and bad men, just as there are good women and bad women," Stella replied. "I think that's probably universal. Here's how I open the doors around here." She showed them her foot sliding the wooden slat to the left, releasing the door. "This will be your rooms while you are here. This way to your bathroom."

"Wow, no door-bot. Well, it works," Marisol declared, rather impressed. Their rooms were spacious, done in blue. Their bed had a blue top covering, matching the drapes and other decor. A small living room opened off the bedroom, where they could entertain a few visitors. The bathroom opened off the other side, where a younger woman stepped out. She was sixteen with the same long black hair as Anita's and Stella's. She flashed them a big smile.

"This is my little sister, Ann," Anita introduced them, one by one.

"So Ann is like Stella but not like you, Anita?" Marisol asked puzzled about Ann's complete lack of arms as well.

"Yes, Ann and Stella share the same basic gifts, but not me," Anita explained.

"Very pleased to meet you," Ann curtsied. "We are supposed to give you all a nice, hot bath and then get you dressed. At supper, you'll get to meet everyone. Anita, guess what I heard?" Ann suddenly got very animated. "Emperor Jan and Empress Amy are coming for dinner. They want to meet you three too. That's something. They are the top leaders of our world, so you three must be very important women. Well, come on, I've got the baths ready for you."

The bathtubs were large and four in number. There were also porcelain stools and plenty of washbasins and mirrors as well as a pile of towels and hairbrushes. "Where's your undressing-bots? Where's your bath-bots?" asked Marisol growing slightly confused.

Stella giggled. "Sorry, we don't know what those are, Marisol. Here, we help each other. I'll show you. Come on, let's get your wet clothes off and get you into the tubs."

"But how? You've no arms at all," Marisol protested. Stella and Ann sat down and kicked off their shoes and proceeded to demonstrate, working together to undress Marisol, while Anita far more rapidly handled Tatiana and Elena.

Stella chatted, "I know that we are way slower at this than Anita, but we can do it. You are not as bad off as we are, so you ought to be able to do it too. Just watch how we are doing everything. I admit, it is a whole lot easier if we let others lend us a hand, though."

Ann grinned sheepishly, "True, I usually let my sister there help me with things, but around here we all do our part. You'll see." At last, the three women were stripped and they slowly stepped into the strange looking tubs. Yet, the waters were perfectly warm; Ann had seen to that detail. More importantly, Ann was able to send to Venerada Luisa the key datum that she had been requested to discover. The three women had no unusual appendages hidden from view, but all three marveled at the alien women's soccer ball sized breasts, nearly twice the size of their own whoppers.

"Gosh, yours are so big," Ann could not help but exclaiming, as she used her feet to begin washing Marisol, again showing her how it was done without a bathing-bot, whatever that was. "Around here, men sure do like them big, but they're going to go nuts over yours, Marisol. We've never seen any so large as you three's. Are yours especially big among your people?" she asked innocently. Already hers were growing rapidly as she was now sixteen, but her chest was still small compared to her older sister's.

"No, ours are about the same as everyone else's," Marisol answered. "Alpha said that our ancient ancestors did all manner of strange things to get their breasts larger because that made them feel better and the men creatures loved them big. If you ask me, I think that they are too big, but then don't ask me that when Tatiana and I are in bed," she winked at her mate in the tub next to hers. All the women chuckled. Once more, Ann silently relayed the information on up to her Venerada.

While they were bathing, two more women entered. "Our seamstresses," Stella announced. "They are going to measure you so that some of our fancy dresses can quickly be altered to fit you."

"We hope," one young woman added, with a chuckled. "Such massive bosoms you have. All eyes will be on you for sure." The three didn't like the sound of that particularly, but soon forgot about it as they watched how the women washed their hair and then patted it dry within folds of a soft towel. While they again watched, the women began brushing out their hair, a whole new experience for the three, who were used to their hair-bot, which used heat and an electrostatic charge to do their hair. Then, quickly Anita and Stella hopped in for a quick bath as well.

"While your hair is drying, we can begin to get you all dressed. Even though they are still working on your dresses, we can get you partially dressed anyway," Stella explained.

"Now when Ann and I are going to wear our fancy dresses, we do need some assistance getting into them. Others wear black nylon hose, but if we do that, then we lose the use of our toes, mostly, and so we often forgo the nylons so that we are not so dependent on others. Tonight is special, so we are supposed to be all dolled up too. Anita is going to have to help all five of us," she explained carefully to the three. Already from what she'd observed, the three women were very carefully noting just how she and Ann were handling things that she assumed had been handled by their bots, whatever those were. Thus, she wanted to make the distinction clear to the three.

A while later, Marisol pointed out, "Well, the panties, chemises, garter belts, and hose are so very like our own. It's amazing how nearly the same that they are. Our dressing-bots put all these on for us, though." Then, they tried on some heels to find their size. "Well, our heels are always a bit higher than these though much higher on party nights," she added. This prompted Anita to bring out another batch, now that she had their sizes worked out.

"Try these, our party heels, we call them."

"Great. These are our normal heights," Tatiana pointed out, "though ours are boots. These you can slip off easily." The six women continued chatting about apparel styles between their two cultures, comparing notes. Before long, the dressmakers had finished altering the dresses to fit the three and quickly got them into them, making some last minute adjustments. Again, the three liked the pod-silk gowns, which were remarkably like their own dresses back on the Arc.

"Now I feel like an ambassador," Marisol said proudly. "Thanks everyone. If we had known that we'd be meeting all you, we'd have brought our own dresses and things with us."

"Well, how could you have known that beforehand?" Anita teased them. All grinned. "Seriously though, dressed up as Stella and Ann are, they will be allowing others to help them dine. I know that the fellows you met today are very anxious to sit beside you and assist you with dinner. I hope that you don't mind."

"I suppose it will be okay. Usually, we just use our mechanical arms," Marisol answered.

Ann giggled, "The guys are nuts over you three. I heard them talking over who gets to help which of you at dinner. I think Ben is going to lose out this time, since there's four of them and only three of you."

"Why?" asked Tatiana, confused about why these four young man creatures would want to help them with something so mundane.

Stella saw what Tatiana was wrestling with mentally. "Oh, in our culture, men are naturally highly attracted to us women, just as we women are highly attracted to the men."

"Oh!" Tatiana again flushed. "Got it."

Has being attracted to men been bred out of these three? Anita sent to Stella.

I don't know, but perhaps it has. In that case, we best be careful, they might be attracted to us! Stella sent back.

Soon, it was time to head off to the Great Hall where a State Dinner was being held in honor of the three alien guests, though they did not know this detail. As soon as Anita opened the outer door of the guest suite, the three men were already there, dressed in their finest suits, waiting to escort their three women. Ben volunteered to escort Stella this evening, though his reasoning was devious, it was the only way he could sit close to the three alien women.

Arsenio slipped his hand around Marisol's waist, rather startling her. "It's our custom to escort our women," Stella explained, as Ben slipped his arm around her waist. To her surprise, Marisol, who had never felt hands upon her body before, found that she rather liked his gentle touch.

Tonight, they'd added more seats to the Great Hall, accommodating close to five hundred, a great many wanted a chance to see these three alien women. Plus, Emperor Jan and Empress Amy were here as well, which could only mean that this was a highly important occasion. The three were a little over-awed at the huge crowd, as the young men led them to a front cross table from which they could see out over the huge crowd. Venerada Luisa and her husband sat beside the emperor and empress. After those, came the capa leaders of the circles and then the visiting guests with their assistants, Arsenio, Felipe, Gabriel, Ben, Anita, and Stella.

At first, the three gazed out on the crowd, noticing all sorts of details. They found it very comforting to find that the women, for the most part, looked much like their own women in their satin dresses and heels. True, the designs were a little different as was the material, pod-silk, but they were similar. The men wore suits. They also spotted a goodly number of women like Stella and Ann and saw that they too were being assisted with their dining needs by either a man or a woman sitting beside them. Thus, as the meal progressed, they did not feel too out of place by having to have the young men feeding them instead of using their mechanical arms as they had all their lives. On the other hand, hundreds of eyes looked them over as well.

When the dinner was finished and the tea served, Venerada Luisa Wycombe introduced the three women to the large group and the emperor and empress. "Now then, if you will excuse us, we here have much to discuss with our guests." That was her polite way of dismissing everyone, except their circle members and those at this front table.

Everyone rose and began filing out, and Marisol rose and walked to greet Emperor Jan and Empress Amy. She correctly figured that these two women must be very powerful leaders, since even Venerada Luisa seemed to yield to their wishes. Marisol was a keen observer. "I am pleased to meet you, Empress Amy. We usually great one another this way," she said and then pressed her body into Amy's. "It is the best we can do for a hug, at least that's what we call a hug. Now having seen Alpha's ancient video footage, we three know that is not a true hug, but it's the best we can do."

"Quite all right, President Marisol. We understand," Amy replied politely.

"So you must have some special gift since you are like Stella and Ann?" she asked.

Amy chuckled. "Nope. Well, not that same way as those here. I lost my arms but that's a long story. Please, can we all talk quite openly, honestly, and frankly?"

"Sure, we've had our fill of devious talk," Marisol replied, thinking of the whole mess with their ex-president Elmira.

"I understand that your controlling robot, Alpha, is able to listen to everything that is said?" Amy asked.

"Sure, isn't that okay? I mean we are dependent upon him wholly," Marisol answered.

"Certainly it is perfectly fine, President Marisol. Jan and I have been kept fully briefed of much of what you have told the others. While your story is rather incomplete, still, Jan and I believe that we may be able to help you, your city of women, and your robots and ship. Alpha, if you are listening, please know that Jan and I are far older than our bodies look and that we are highly educated in the ways and dealings of the decrepit Imperium. While the others on this world are not, we two have been to hundreds of other worlds and have learned much. That's why I can say that we may be able to help. However, before we can tell you fully about ourselves, we here need to know your whole story. I know that it will take some time to relate, but please, we really do want to help if we can," Amy pleaded.

"Should I?" she asked Alpha. After a pause, he told her to go ahead and answer any questions these people might have. In fact, Alpha knew that there was very little he could do for the three from high in orbit above the planet. For the most part, they were on their own. However, he made the assumption that since they had met a number of women whose bodies were far worse than theirs and that they were being very well treated, therefore these people, no matter how primitive they were, would treat the three satisfactorily and not harm them. Further, he wanted to know how they had been discovered so quickly, within hours of landing during the total darkness of their night.

Thus, Marisol began a very lengthy explanation, beginning with, "It all began because Tatiana and I began to discover that there were giant holes in our knowledge. Although we have a good education in math, physics, computer programming, and engineering, we discovered that there was absolutely no history. No one knew anything about our past." She talked at length for several hours. Although few here really understood some of her words and had little reality on their many bots, they picked up her concepts readily. All were telepaths, though Marisol didn't know that yet. She tried to make sure that they truly understood the desperate plight that Madiera and the Arc was facing, that the bots were wearing out and that their failure would cost the lives of the remainder of her people.

When she finished, Jan and Amy asked many detailed questions about their different elemental powers. At last, Amy asked, "Okay, over there is a fireplace where a fire has been set for this evening. It does get chilly here in the summer. Marisol, could you give us a demonstration of your skills and light the fire for us? It's not that we don't believe you, we do. Rather, it is important for us to see how you do it."

"There's nothing to see really," Marisol looked puzzled. She focused and the logs burst into flames. "There. See, nothing to see. I'm sorry."

"No, no, Marisol! That is excellent. Thank you for being so utterly open and frank with us," Amy countered. "Now it is our turn to be open and frank with you, though until now, we have not been totally so. Earlier today, you asked how come the six Elite Guards had yellow eyes. I regret that they were ordered not to be fully honest in their answers. You see, you've landed on a world in which telepathy and many other psi skills abound. Those of us with the yellow eyes with brown spots, to be precise about it, have what we call the *mentales* gifts. The lowest form is telepathy. So yes, all of us with yellow eyes are telepaths of various strengths. Beyond that, each has many other skills. Here in Brom Tower, many have fire based skills somewhat similar to your Fire elemental skills. Anita here could have started the logs on fire similar to the way that you did it, using her mental skills. Many can lift things; telekinesis is the ancient word for this phenomenon. These crystals that we wear around our necks act as a power booster for our psi skills, amplifying them ten to a hundred-fold."

"Is that what they are doing when they glow bluish?" Elena asked.

"Precisely, Elena. That's why we needed to see your little demonstration to see how you did it. We could not discount that you three have some alternate form of psi skills about which we knew nothing. We were monitoring you and detected that you are using a very similar energy to our own, though you do not have yellow eyes. Perhaps the eye color is unique to Tierra. Still, while you may not have telepathic skills, you certainly do have other *mentales*-like skills."

"Alpha is right. There are many, many other planets out there in the universe who would give anything to get their hands on you and your women, so that they could exploit your elemental powers. Jan and I are prime examples. We were kidnaped from our homes here on Tierra when we were around eighteen and taken off-world into slavery. It took us over a half century to escape and return here to our home world. So we know just how badly others would love to get their hands upon you."

"Next, we may well be able to help with the crystals. Alpha, if you can hear me, is it silicon and germanium crystals that you require?" Jan asked.

"He says yes," Marisol reported.

"I thought so. I am a computer whiz, to put it mildly," Jan continued. "These stones that we all wear around our necks are pure germanium crystals. They amplify our psi powers. Originally two centuries ago, simple silicon crystals were used, but a hundred plus years ago, Felix Brom discovered that the germanium crystals worked dramatically better. Alpha, if these pure crystals are indeed what you are looking for, how many will you need? We might be able to supply them so that you don't have to mine for them."

"He says that a couple handfuls would be more than ample for them to make more computer chips," Marisol relayed.

"Good," Amy replied. "Alpha, President Marisol, ladies, on behalf of the people of Tierra, we would like to extend our hands of friendship to your people and offer all those in Madiera the opportunity to settle here around Brom. We will do all that we can to ensure that you and your women will not only survive, but will thrive and prosper as well. Jan and I would like to bring samples of the crystals up to your ship so that Alpha can examine them in detail and make sure that they are what he needs."

"Thank you. We love what we've seen so far. Everyone

has been so kind to us, but what about our many bots? We really cannot survive without them," Marisol pointed out.

"Let us discuss this with Alpha directly," Amy suggested.

"But he says that it is tricky to get the shuttle back without the spaceport people detecting it," Marisol broke in.

"Alpha, leave that to me," Jan replied. "I have many tricks up my sleeve, but it is probably best if we travel at night so that we are not visible. I can make darn sure that their radar systems will not detect your shuttle." Via Marisol, Alpha and Jan worked out some arrangements.

"Do you all just read our minds, our personal thoughts?" asked Tatiana, while Marisol and Jan were chatting with Alpha.

Amy answered, "Absolutely not. We consider doing that unbidden to be the equivalent of mental rape. However, we have been monitoring your surface thoughts as we try to understand your dialect that is strikingly similar to that which is spoken in the Westerlings. Some of us can also tell when another is lying to us. As far as we can tell, none of you has lied even once to us. Thank you, Tatiana."

"Well, our biggest problem is not knowing what we don't know. Like she said, it began when we detected a big hole in our knowledge, a total absence of history. Then we found out that there was a huge arena called Art that we knew nada about. Now this telepathy thing, this psi energy thing, again, we know nothing about it, not even that it could exist. In some ways," Tatiana sighed, "we are advanced, engineering and bots and programming, and in other ways, we are so totally ignorant that we don't even know that we're missing something — like the hand appendages and the man creatures. Pretty pathetic, if you ask me."

Amy smiled, "I understand, Tatiana. I truly do. Perhaps if you and your people settle here, we can help you learn about those things that have been kept from you and you can teach us about things of which we know little about."

"Sure, count me in," she grinned.

"Okay, we've worked it out," Jan got everyone's attention. "We will give our guests here a little show of our power, too. Around four in the morning when it is completely dark and overcast, some of Brom's circles will teleport us back to Marisol's shuttle craft. After Jan shuts down the spaceport's detection devices, Alpha will fly the shuttle back up to their ship and we will meet firsthand and discuss matters. Both Jan and I will be accompanying the three along with Venerada Luisa. Alpha has requested that Stella come with us as well. I've asked that Arsenio, Ben, Gabriel, Anita, and Felipe also come with us to assist us women, and Alpha has agreed. I suggest that we get some sleep and rise around three in the morning to have time to get dressed and ready." She didn't add that the men were really primarily coming along for security reasons.

The group disbanded, with the fellows escorting the women back to their quarters. After opening their guestroom door, Stella asked, "Do you three want me to spend the night with you, helping you with things or would you prefer to be left alone?" She picked up their frantic thoughts and added hastily, "Don't worry, we'll help you get undressed and into bed before we leave you for the night. We'll wake you in plenty of time."

"Oh, well, I don't want to make you have to leave your own room," Marisol answered, relieved.

"It's not a problem. I love to help when I can."

"We'd feel more comfortable if you were with us," Marisol admitted. "You are so similar to us, you see."

"I know," Stella grinned. "Okay, I'll stay with you three and give you some more pointers on the way we do things." She sensed just how much the three were missing their personal bots and wondered how anyone could get so hooked on mechanical devices. Yet, these women were and they were physically better off than she and her other relations and even Empress Amy.

"Wow, Marisol was not exaggerating!" Jan responded first, as Alpha and Beta finished their brief video history that they'd shown to the small gathering aboard the Arc in Space. At three in the morning, Stella had wakened the three and quickly others came and helped them dress in their original jeans, now washed and pressed. The group gathered together in the guest bedroom while three of Luisa's circles began the large teleport operation. A minute later, Jan, Amy, Luisa, Stella, Marisol, Tatiana, Elena, Arsenio, Ben, Gabriel, Anita, and Felipe stood just beyond the field of bots near the shuttle craft. As promised, Alpha sent signals to the craft and a few lights turned on, allowing the group to see the bots and ship. Marisol led them inside and got everyone seated, but had the men strap everyone down. Jan had already sent the signals to the Rigel-3 spaceport computers, which were now busily rebooting and running a boot-time full diagnostic on themselves, effectively blinding the entire installation. Alpha had told her to ignore the geo-sat installation; he could fly around their coverage using the one degree blind spot he'd used before. Beta flew the craft as before by remote control, eventually landing it in their docking bay.

There, Alpha met the group and Marisol did the introductions. He then gave them a short tour, taking them to the huge control center, where everyone save the three, Jan, and Amy gazed in wonder at the star field and then the massive computer network and many monitors. This was old-hat to Amy and Jan. Alpha and Beta then executed their lengthy history presentation, using the same one that they'd shown to all the women some months ago.

"Yes, she was not exaggerating. Their men hooked on drugs and addicted to the virtual reality games destroyed the entire planet. As you saw, we were only able to save a hundred women before the radiation killed off every living thing on the planet. We were and are still controlled by our prime directive to help and assist our humans. As you can see, thirty used their hands and arms to kill themselves or others. Right or wrong, we did what we had to do to fulfill our protect and help directive," Alpha explained.

Jan and Amy had the sense that the two robots were expressing some regret over the drastic action that they'd taken with the seventy women. *But how can a robot have regret,* Jan wondered. *It's only a machine. It is almost justifying the actions that they'd taken.* She let those thoughts pass and asked, "Can you show me their planet of origin and where it is located compared to here, Ashford-5? You see, they speak what we consider to possibly be an ancient form of one of the three dialects spoken on our world."

"Ah yes. We found that most strange," Alpha replied. He complied, but neither Jan nor Amy recognized the planet or star system; it was far beyond the known Imperium system.

"I still don't recognize it," Jan finally admitted. "I was rather hoping to find some ancient connection between our world and theirs."

Beta spoke up in his monotone, "Indeed. While we were monitoring our women down on your world, we picked up other transmissions or speech. I believe that your words for them are Midlands and Easterlings. Again, our goal has been to work out a means of translation so that our women can understand others who speak those dialects. At this time, we have identified those as also startlingly similar to two other languages spoken on their original planet. I have been searching for a connection between that world and this one, Ashford-5, but as yet have found none."

Jan spoke up, "Okay, then at this point, I would like to examine these bots and just how you have this artificial world setup, Alpha. The men can accompany me, and I'd appreciate it if either Marisol or Tatiana would accompany us and help us understand. Meanwhile, Amy, Stella, and Luisa would like Elena and one other to take them on a tour of their Madiera world. We need to see firsthand just how your women are living and what their current society is really like. Then, we can all get together and see if we can be of immense help to you. Meanwhile, here are the germanium crystals I promised you. I added a few of the silicon ones as well, though we do not use those any longer."

"Ah, you are wise, Jan. Yes, those three will fit into the Madiera world without causing too much attention, though there likely will be stares. You three have no arms at all, something these women have never seen before. Still, I trust they will blend in fairly well," Alpha agreed.

"Yes, we'd particularly like to visit your high school," Amy added. "That's important."

"You and Jan seem to have a vast knowledge far beyond the others, akin to those in the spaceport," Beta said in his monotone voice.

"Yes, she and I spent fifty years on many, many world, gaining a comparatively vast knowledge. Only your specialization with these bots do we find unique and highly unusual, though we can see why you needed to create them. Masterful job," Jan answered. She wondered if robots needed praise or validation, but again decided not, since they were merely machines.

The entire group rejoined in the conference room with the stainless steel table and chairs for lunch. Alpha had ordered bots to bring down human food, while the others were on their very lengthy tour. Jan was highly impressed with the level of sophistication of the entire operation. "They really have created an efficiently run artificial world here," she declared. Marisol, who had accompanied her and pointed out many details, felt a surge of pride.

"We've met many women, including Elena's mate, Renata. We are impressed with how far most of the women have come in trying to become more independent of the countless bots in their lives," Amy explained. She let Jan feed her and was unwilling to experiment with the offered eating arm machines that the three women were using to feed themselves. Stella and Luisa, on the other hand, were trying to get the hang of using their feet with these machines to control the arms and were barely succeeding, refusing to resort to simply using some of their psi powers or asking the men for assistance.

She continued, "We watched some of the young girls playing soccer and we would very much like to get that game introduced to all our people. Is it true that their ancestors also were never allowed to use their hands and arms?"

"Correct, I can show you a video clip of a championship match from before the destruction of their world," Alpha replied.

Amy continued, "In many ways, their education is far more advanced than ours. Here, all children go to school. Their seniors would be considered geniuses by the average person on Tierra. They have so much that they could teach our people about math, science, and engineering. Yet, I see what

Marisol has said. Other areas are wholly lacking, history and the arts, for example."

"Of course, we could not let them know their past. They might have continued to take their own lives," Alpha justified.

"But Alpha, you don't have to have hands to make art. We have some women who paint beautifully with their feet," Luisa pointed out.

"We did not know that was possible," he justified.

"Well, let's get down to business," Jan spoke up. "How did the crystal samples work out?"

Beta droned, "Absolutely perfect. So incredibly pure. Yes, a bucketful of those and we would be all set for a very long time."

"Good. Glad to hear that," Jan replied. "Now then, Alpha, Beta, as the rulers of our world, Amy and I believe that Tierra would be an ideal place for your women to settle down and make new fulfilling lives for themselves. We would like to offer them and you sanctuary on Tierra."

"As you know now, we have been working on an exit strategy for our women for centuries now. Your offer is a kind one, but they so need their many bots and your world has yet to have the electricity support that their bots need," Alpha pointed out the flaw that perplexed the two robots.

"Very true. Yet, they do not need their bots, not really. We have many others who would gladly assist them with anything that they need. Of course, as you know, there has to be an exchange of something of value for such assistance. We've worked that out, Alpha. You are right, it would be criminal of them to wholly depend upon others of our world for their many needs and give nothing back."

"Precisely so. An impossible exit," Alpha concluded.

"Wrong. We need teachers. Many of them can begin to teach our children math and science. I'm not sure about how much engineering can be taught, the planet has almost no heavier elements and very, very little iron. Yet, math and science are the keystones that can help bring our people out of their own ignorance. Also, we are plagued by random forest fires. We have vast resinous pine forests. With nearly daily lightning storms, fires occur with alarming frequency. Many of your women have special skills that can help us extinguish those fires before they cause immense damage. I believe that all four kindreds have ways that can help fight the fires. That alone would be of immense help to us all. In winter, Brom gets many feet of snow and our men labor to keep paths cleared for passage. I am sure that your Air kindred would be of immense help in blowing away the larger drifts. In time, I believe that as each of us comes to know the others that we will find many more ways your women can provide invaluable assistance to our people. Even so, with firefighting and education, these alone would make a wholly fair trade, providing your women with the daily assistance that they need without their bots," Amy explained.

Jan piped in, "Alpha, we also understand the nature of your prime directive. We would like to suggest that you land your Arc somewhere not too far from Brom. We can help hide the ship from view. There, you can continue to refine your crystals, rebuild your equipment, and monitor the women under your care. That way, you will be close at hand to assist them should something not work out as expected."

"But the ship does not have enough fuel to both land and then take off at a later date. It was built in orbit above their world," Alpha said, using his sad expression.

"Not a problem. We can land your ship ourselves without you having to use an ounce of your fuel. We can land it using our combined psi powers. Then, you'd have enough fuel to depart at a later date. If you needed extra lift at that time, again, we could combine our psi energies to provide additional lift to clear the gravity of the planet. What do you say?" Jan asked, clearly very eager to make this work.

"That is a possibility. However, there is another huge exit problem that we as yet have no solution for. I mean no disrespect to you, Marisol, Tatiana, Elena. As you have seen, there are no men in Madiera. In order to have our women able to reproduce, we have had to go to extreme lengths. In their world, a marriage is between two women, not between a man and a woman. Consequently, we have had to develop a way for them to breed. While you have not asked about such matters, I can explain a little, though I hope this does not embarrass you three too badly. When a couple decides that they want to have a baby, we take a sample from the donor woman who will become effectively the father of the baby and extract the needed chromosomes from that sample. We have developed a solution in which we then place the extracted chromosomes and load that into what the women call a dong. It is a substitute fertilization method. We opted to go this route instead of artificial insemination that was practiced in sterile laboratories on their world, pre-destruction. We felt this process was closer to the natural ways of human intercourse."

Alpha went on, "So the unanswered questions are marriage and insemination. How will those be handled? Will the many marriages that Madiera women now have still be accepted or will they have to somehow modify them? Some women will still desire to have children with their woman mate and we'll need to handle the preparatory work for them to allow them to have their baby. Or will that no longer be allowed?"

Jan chuckled, "And what will happen if the women's hormones suddenly kick in and they find themselves now attracted sexually to men, but they are already married to a woman? Yes, Alpha, it's a mess. That is one reason that I really do want you and the Arc to land secretly not too far from Brom where the women will be resettled. I have no answer. Amy and I are exceptions; we've had so many bad things happen to us at the hands of men that we cannot stand men in a sexual way."

Luisa decided to weigh in on this critical point. "If I may, if say Marisol should have a baby with one of our men or with say another one of our women, will the baby be like her or like our people?"

"Our modification is recessive. They should be normal, like your people," Alpha responded.

"I was hoping so. Many women might decide to go that route so that their children would be free of the life that they are having to lead. I know that is so among those like me. As far as an answer to the overall question, as long as you are nearby, your women can continue as they always have or opt for more traditional marriages. In the Easterlings, for example, a man may have more than one wife, as long as he can support them. In the Westerlings and here in the Midlands, we prefer monogamous marriages. However, in this case, I am sure that we can make appropriate adjustments. That is, I would like each woman to have free choice in her life, as long as all involved are in agreement. Believe me, Alpha, I believe that once your women adjust to our world, they will do all that they can to have normal children, leaving this behind them. We mothers always are thinking and planning for future generations," Luisa explained.

Marisol looked puzzled. "So if say Tatiana and I wanted to have normal children, we could find a man to help us with it?"

"I am sure that you can. Many arrangements can be made. We are very flexible. Often we raise fosterlings, sons or daughters from affairs beyond the marriage. I'm sure that you can find a very workable solution, Marisol," Luisa promised her.

"Well, I do like that idea," Marisol replied. Relief was plainly visible; Luisa had handled her very real concerns. For a moment, she thought that perhaps Luisa had read her mind.

Jan took charge once more. "Give us a few days to work out a location where we can place your ship here. Once it is down, your women can take their time relocating from their homes here to new ones in Brom. There would not need to be a big rush to get everyone resettled at once. We can both take our time and do it right and in ways that benefit your women."

Alpha was once again thankful that he could display human reactions. "At last, Beta, we may have found an exit strategy to fulfill our prime directive."

The group spent the hours until nightfall making arrangements. Specifically, Jan needed to know the weight, dimensions, and shape of the Arc in order to find a suitable ground location for the ship. In the middle of the night, Alpha once again sent the shuttle craft back to where it had been, about fifty miles east of Brom. Once there, the circles of Brom brought everyone back to the tower.

"Where would we live?" Marisol asked Luisa at lunch the next day. Amy had returned to their tower in Exchange City, but Jan remained to help work out the how of landing and concealing of the large spaceship.

"We would like some of you to move into our manor house here with us, learn our ways, and teach our children. Of course, everyone will be on call in case of fires. We can easily manage to house a hundred of you here. The rest will have to move into homes in the city proper, but again, we will setup schools where some can teach the children there as well. Let's do this gradually, introducing a few dozen at one time, allowing them and our people to adjust. I know for a fact that many of the women of our town will very much appreciate having employment opportunities as personal helpers for your women as they learn new ways to do things for themselves," Luisa explained.

Arsenio and Felipe walked in and interrupted them. "Jan wants you to come with us to check on a possible landing location." The four rose and followed the two young men to the top observation balcony of their tall tower, where Jan and several others were waiting. She pointed out a nearby ravine where stone had been quarried in the past. These days, they were taking stone from further up the mountain and this area was abandoned to the elements.

"We can build a covered tunnel from the exit doors of the ship into our walled complex here. From there, your women can walk the short distance into the city or over there to the manor house. I think that we'll need to construct some supporting rigging though," Jan suggested.

A week later and after numerous video conferences with Alpha, Jan and Venerada Luisa had the site prepared. Unfortunately, the weight of the ship was too great for the circles to manage. Sixteen years before during the height of the giant crystal networks, they could have done just what Jan expected. Now, she and Alpha had to work out other means. She did not want the ship to become physically stranded here on Tierra. Besides limiting the women, having a concealed working spaceship of this caliber would be potentially extremely valuable if the Imperium continued to play dirty, as she called their covert actions of the past two centuries.

The fuel that the Arc used was not the same fuel that the Imperium ships used, distilled from psi-crystals found on one of Ashford-5's moons. Rather, the needed fuel had been in use within the Imperium some four centuries ago and was now no longer manufactured within the many systems of the vast Imperium. However, Jan had Alpha perform a chemical breakdown of the needed fuel. Just as she suspected, all the basic elements were light ones, found in the air and rock of Tierra. "While the Imperium will not let us import the fuel, that doesn't mean that we cannot manufacture it here," Jan declared. "Venerada Luisa, are you willing to devote an entire circle to the creation of the needed fuel to replace that which the Arc will lose while landing?"

"If in return, we have a say in any future use of the Arc, Emperor," Luisa replied shrewdly. "Look, while I know that you will play fair with us over this, what will happen when you and Amy retire and a new man and woman gets elected to your posts? I wouldn't give a pig's foot for their honoring any past agreements that you've made with us. We need control over this ship. After all, if it doesn't work out for these women, though I can't imagine why it wouldn't, they are not like I am, wholly armless, then I need to be able to get them on the ship and off Tierra."

"Point taken. Alpha is having a difficult time coming up with a viable exit strategy and so are we, if I can speak frankly. All right, we'll keep this on the quiet. Once we get the ship down and safely hidden, there will be no record of it in the imperial logs. It will be your responsibility to keep it safe and available, ready for Alpha's use should the robot deem it necessary," Jan conceded the point. Luisa smiled, rarely had she gained such a vital concession from the Emperor and Empress.

Alpha also agreed. Shortly after midnight on the first of August 1201, another widespread blackout struck the Imperium computer network at their spaceport. The landing of the Arc was a most peculiar one. First, Beta moved the ship into a geosynchronous orbit hovering over Brom. Then slowly five joined *Círculo de mentes* began lowering it straight downward, while Beta continued to adjust its thrust to keep it hovering over the same location. Later when the Arc was about two miles above Brom, the *Círculo de mentes* began lifting it up as the sheer weight of the ship now began seriously to pull it down, having significantly entered the gravity field of the planet. At last, Beta had to add some retro thrust to augment the lift from those below who were using all their combined psi powers to lift it up.

Around three in the morning, the ship settled carefully into the granite supporting stonework and its engines shut down completely for the first time in four plus centuries. In Madiera, the sleeping women felt nothing. Now the circles began levitating and positioning the prepared covering over the ship. Later on, a more permanent shield would replace this temporary layer. The next day, construction began on building a stone tunnel that led from the cargo bay directly to and through the stone walls that surrounded the tower-manor house complex.

Meanwhile, Marisol's extended group of eight moved their things from their home in Madiera into new quarters within the manor house. A day later, another dozen volunteers followed. Slowly over the next few months, five hundred forty-three women and children moved out from Madiera into their new world of Brom, Tierra. While the transition was not painless, it did work. Alpha was not subsequently asked to return them to space and continue his long search. Instead, he and Beta spent their days building more replacement computers and bots. For the first time, they had the luxury of taking their time and repairing or replacing all the critical systems. Quite why they did so no one bothered to ask. They were merely robots, but Marisol knew that they wanted to be ready to take them all back onboard if this planet did not work out for them.

Chapter 16 Of Plans and Changes

"Mom, there aren't any guys our ages around here and you won't let us roam the city," June complained to Amy. Jan was still up in Brom and she and Melissa were extremely bored fifteen year old teens. The Imperial *Círculo de mentes* were eleven older men and women. True, the two teens highly respected them; they had trained the two since they were ten. Also, the two had picked up lots of "education" from their two mothers, knowledge not known by the others of Tierra — naturally, since Amy and Jan had spent most of their lives off-world, dealing with the underground and the Imperium on many worlds.

"Can't we go visit mom in Brom?" begged Melissa.

Amy laughed. "Okay, okay, I can take a hint. There are many boys there. Have the circle teleport you there. While you are there, ask Angelica, Miguel, and Arsenio if there is a convenient time for them to meet with Jan and me."

"What about, mom?" June replied quickly, hoping that her mother would give her a hint.

"Later, dear. Just find a time when we five can meet. I assume that you two can meet anytime, since you are bored and have nothing at all to do here," Amy teased the two teens. Gaily the two headed off to find the circle.

Finally wholly alone, Amy headed for their kitchen, where their cook was busily baking bread. "Tea Empress?" the portly woman asked, wiping her flour-covered hands on her apron.

"You know me well, Alice. Yes, please," Amy grinned. Five minutes later, she activated her crystal and the cup rose up and followed her into her study. She sat down in a sofa and brought the cup up to her lips, blew on it, and took a sip. "I have got to think this through. In a way, Alpha has the same problem that we do. How do we get out of the situation that we're in and stay true to what we have begun?" she talked to herself, hoping that would somehow inspire her.

"When we came back to our home world, the male leaders were very nearly about to wipe out all people everywhere with those outlawed Nuclears. The level of brutality that they were inflicting on our people was — well, it was the worst that we've seen. At least on other worlds, they kill others humanely. Jan and I had enough raw power to put an end to that. My ultimatum is working, sixteen years now and no more wars, not even a big battle. By making the circles spend at least half of their time tending to the needs of the average person in their area, we've begun healing that huge rift between those without the gift and those of us with it. We've a long way to go. Valen and their army very nearly wiped out a whole generation of young men with their wars." She took another sip.

"The problem, Amy, is that you and Jan are assassins, rebels, underground freedom fighters. We have no idea how to rule a land, let alone a whole planet. Still, we've just used common sense and all that we learned from the Ataro leaders. That's been holding up well and working out for us here. Amy, the real problem is what will happen when Jan and I are gone or step down and allow them to elect their own emperor and empress? We've held it together by our own will and psi powers. Honestly, we don't know how to be rulers."

She took another sip. "Truthfully, Jan and I have seen many different governments out there and none are lasting, truly lasting. The one constant we've witnessed is that power tends to corrupt leaders, though sometimes it takes a long time for that to occur. So our exit is darn near impossible if we want our era of peace to continue. Difficult exit. That's how Alpha put it, but we don't have four hundred years to look for a way out! Okay, we could use the rejuvenation machine a few more times, perhaps living until we are a hundred thirty, giving us maybe another forty years to rule, but then what? What happens if we should die before then?"

"Jan and I want to leave a legacy of peace that all subsequent emperors and empresses will follow, will emulate. We'd resign today, if that were possible. We've been fighting essentially the same darn battles for nearly seventy of our eighty-eight years! Okay, different worlds, different people, different technologies, but essentially the same kind of battles. I'm tired of fighting them. Jan is too, though she seldom admits it."

"So how can we exit and still have those who follow emulate the good that we've done and not lead everyone toward conflicts once more? Amy, while you are at it, answer this one. What are you going to do with the billions in Imperium credits that you two have amassed? What are you going to do with all the illegal and cool Imperium equipment that you've acquired? Who is going to continue our monitoring of the Rigel-3 folks at the spaceport and keep them honest?" Having no answers, she took another sip of tea.

"When it comes down to it, Amy, the only lasting rulership has been those nutty wasp-worshipers of the Ataro System. They've managed two thousand years of relative peace and prosperity for the dozens of planets and people in their system. Their emperor and empress make the laws for everyone in their systems, the ultimate in power. Well, that makes sense. We've seen what ultimately happens with so-called democracy governments, with their elected legislatures. Each new batch has to make more and more laws until after several hundred years, there are so many laws on the book that no one person can figure out what's legal and what isn't anymore and the society goes by the boards. No, ultimately, there has to be one or two people who make the laws period, benevolent monarchy I think it's called. Well, Jan and I are sort of benevolent these days." She ignored all those that they'd killed to get to this point, ending the ongoing wars.

"Amy, you keep coming back to the only stable system you've encountered, the nutty Ataro System. Well, all right, I have not had my arms for some eighteen years now and with my psi powers, if I am wholly honest with myself, that hasn't really been a big problem for me. Inconvenient, annoying many times, but not debilitating. Of course, those in Brom with their katalyein gifts, now they do find it a severe handicap, but then most of them do not have the immense psi powers that I have or that Jan has. I can see their point of view, but I dare not say the same thing about myself — just merely that it has been inconvenient and annoying. So is this the exit path that we are to follow?" She drank the last of her tea.

"Well, hobbling us doesn't stop us from using our powers, but then no one else on Tierra has powers like ours. Look at successors, Amy. Okay, we implement the wasp scenario. I can see that hobbling the rulers so severely would definitely tend to restrict their ability to abuse the immense powers that we'd be placing in them as emperor and empress. But would such a heavy physical dependence on others to survive actually prevent them from abusing the power that we give them?" She had no honest answer at the moment, except the certainty that it would definitely make it vastly more difficult for them to abuse their powers.

"Should our positions be hereditary?" she asked herself, going down another avenue of thought. "Hell no! Look where heredity got those with the *mentales* gifts so far! Inbreeding, forced marriages, damn, the list of abuses along these lines is endless. No, our positions have to be elected ones, just like I decreed in my ultimatum sixteen years ago. Okay, then if we follow the wasp traditions of Ataro, then how long will their terms be? Life? Considering that we would be forcing severe body modifications on them that cannot be undone, their terms ought to be rather long. It would be criminal of us to do that to them and then let them rule for just a few years. After that, they'd have the rest of their lives to live out wholly crippled and helpless. Okay, so they have long terms, say twenty years between elections. We'll need to provide for them and their advisors and staff, who also undergo the body modifications, once they retire from their positions. This is getting more complex, though, but necessary if we are to make this remotely humane for the rulers and their advisors."

Just then, her cook knocked, "Empress, I brought you some freshly baked bread and more tea."

"How did you know that I needed more tea, Alice? Thanks, perfect," Amy replied, somewhat surprised by her thoughtfulness.

Alice laughed, her large frame jiggling, "Oh, you are in one of those reflective moods." Amy grinned.

A bit later, Amy picked up her train of thought, once more talking to herself and the walls. "Okay, let's say that we go this route for our exit. What has to be done? Well, we need to establish the medical procedures and ways for them to be done here in the Imperial Tower. We need to work out ways to train the new emperor and empress in conflict resolution technology that we learned on Ataro Prime. Clothing — ah, leave that to Carmen and her Elegant Fashions Inc. However, what is to keep the next pair from refusing to accept the body modifications or making a new law outlawing them in the future, thereby undoing these much needed checks on the powers of the throne?"

"Amy, you've hit the nail squarely once again. We can pass a law that says the other rulers do not have to follow any laws or rulings that any emperor or empress who is not wholly body modified passes. Further, we can pass a law saying that they must elect an emperor and empress who will submit to the needed modifications. How do those get enforced once Jan and I have passed away? Now that is the sticky question. Difficult exit, once more."

She finished off the bread and her tea, deep in thought. Then, inspiration came. Alpha and his zillions of bots! "If we can get one of their sensing type bots, we can program it to detect if the emperor and empress has obeyed the decree and undergone the body modifications. If not, the bot will simply execute them on the spot. How do we make them face the bot, though? Ah, we make the bot part of their swearing in ceremony. If no swearing in, then no emperor or empress. We can make that a law that the other rulers must obey. I'm sure that they will follow that one. I think maybe we can make this work out for the future. Maybe we can finally find our own exit strategy."

"Wait, how do we ensure that these other rulers will obey the laws and rulings that their elected emperors and empresses make? I do it by threat of death. I've done that often enough, but then no one else has the psi power that Jan or I have. Well, we can monitor the situation as long as we are alive, but what happens after that?"

"Damn, I am an assassin. I only know killing to enforce my rulings. Well, we could leave one of the old power crystal networks that I outlawed setup here and allow the emperor or empress to become the temporary capo of their circle and let them exact compliance. That would do wonders for the morale of the emperor whose rulings were being disobeyed by some other territorial ruler. Good thing that Jan and I kept a few of those power networks around, hidden in our secret chambers. Maybe this all could work out for the future and finally give us an exit plan. God, I hope so."

"Okay then, the fall meeting is coming up in about four more weeks. Could Jan and I be ready to implement these changes by then? They will need time to work out elections. We could present ourselves as fully modified at the fall meeting, showing them all precisely what their elected must accept. Give them say two years to get the new pair elected, modified, and trained. We could be ready by then. Certainly, Carmen will love this; she'll get her wishes in dictating fashions around here. Two more years, and Jan and I can finally exit out of our ruler positions. We'll still have young bodies even if we forego using the rejuvenation machine anymore."

Satisfied that she'd taken this to its logical conclusion, she headed off to sit on the throne and handle any afternoon business that came their way.

When Jan returned a few days later, Amy discussed all this with her. "Well, I think that you are right. With enough precautions taken, we can at long last step down as the rulers and get on with our own lives. We could at least get our feet altered back to the way that they are now. As I remember, walking was a bitch before. I hate to lose these, love, but if it gets us out of being emperor and empress and keeps Tierra at peace, then I am willing to make that sacrifice as well. Do we really dare plan for what we can do in two years?" Jan asked.

"I hope so, love, I hope so. We've brought an era of peace, and, if things go as we plan, it should endure long after we are out of the picture. However, I'm not going to make any retirement plans just yet. Too much to do first. I guess we'd best talk with Carmen and begin working out the details. We're going to need to get quite a lot of things accomplished in two years though. I hate to put the announcement off until spring, it merely delays things," Amy stated.

The first of these plans they put forward the next day

when they finally met just after noon with Angelica Evita e Kaylee, who was sixty-nine and still active, her son Miguel, and her grandson Arsenio. Her granddaughter Stella also insisted on joining them. Angelica replied to Amy's question, "Yes, I still have all mom's spy equipment and medical machines and even the prosthetic hands. I am keeping watch on their communications, just as mom taught me. Why?"

"Great. Jan and I are planning to retire from our ruling positions in a little over two years. As you know, we have a great deal of 'equipment' too." Everyone chuckled a little at this jest. They had incredible Imperium machines, all wholly illegal on Tierra or so the Imperium desired. "When we retire, we want to have a secret location setup where we can keep the machines and have a continuing group, who not only knows how to use them, but also does use them — all on the QT. We don't want the new emperor and empress to know anything about them, as well as most all the other territorial rulers. Well, Luisa knows about them and you folks, but other than you, no one knows. I would like to suggest that we work together to form up a secret society who maintains them and uses them to Tierra's advantage."

Angelica smiled, "I do love how you both think. I agree fully. I've trained Miguel on their use as well as Arsenio, but you know men, both are more interested in fighting and action. Still, we need to do this. My health is deteriorating though I can still listen in to the comm link. I've been keeping my equipment in my family, but perhaps we should expand and add some others who are trustworthy and willing."

"Grandmother, why can't I help?" Stella asked rather pointedly. She knew why Angelica had not treated her like her brother and dad.

"I think that the time has come to give you a chance at it, dear. You've earned the right to give it a try," Angelica conceded. "Still, we ought to have the knowledge spread out among more, especially since the men have not taken too active a role in learning all the details." She stung the two, but they knew that she was right. "Won't you two be helping with them? I know that your bodies are only their mid-thirties."

"Jan will be giving up her arms too and we will both be

having our feet fixed as well. Our mobility will be poor at best — speaking from past experience," she added. "Yes, we'll do what we can, but we need this knowledge to be continually passed on down the generations. Lord knows what the Imperium men will do next to Tierra and we need to have as much advanced warning as possible."

"Wow. So you are going to go through with it then, all the way, like the wasp leaders on what was it called?" Angelica asked, somewhat surprised.

"Ataro Prime. Yes, we are going to set it up so that the rulings of the new emperor and empress must be followed and that they cannot be tempted to abuse the immense power that we'll be handing them. I can see no other exit strategy for us, if we want the hard-earned peace that we've brought here to last after we're gone," Amy stated.

"Still, you are paying an awful price for us all," Angelica replied, her voice filled with great respect for the two women. "Let me work on getting together the 'right people' for the job. Also, I think I know where we can store everything. Yes, Stella, you can play an integral role, if you really want to." Stella grinned, very pleased that she was finally being taken seriously by her grandmother. Until today, Angelica, while always loving her granddaughter, had also considered her highly handicapped.

"Thanks. We'll call our secret group the Underground. We should also consider writing specific instructions on the machines' operations for future generations," Amy added. "And there is one other thing, Angelica. Jan and I have accumulated billions of Imperium credits, their form of money. We've decided that we will eventually pool it together into an account for Tierra's use. We'll need one of the group to be its caretaker. Right now, there's not much that we can do with the funds, but Tierra may not always have the Imperial Directive #5 on it. If that gets dropped, billions in credits will purchase an enormous amount of nearly anything."

"Thank you! On behalf of all us, thank you!" Angelica praised the two, knowing that in all likelihood, they would never receive an acknowledgment for their tremendous gifts.

Jan laughed. "With that, you could buy a small space

fleet of battle cruisers, fully armed." Everyone joined her laughter. What would they do with those?

They discussed some smaller details and then adjourned. Before they left, Amy and Jan then went to their old rooms in the manor house and retrieved the special shoes that they'd worn when they were an Ataro queen and her domestique, along with other related items. The shoes they would soon need again.

Back home, they met with Carmen, who was surprised to be summoned to the Imperial Court. "Hi, what's up?" she asked, flashing her red lips and winking her heavily eye-shadowed eyes at the two.

"It's time that we fully implement the body modifications that we are going to enforce upon all future emperors, empresses, and their prime advisors and assistants. Yes, a mini-Ataro System," Amy explained. "You'll be given the sole contract to provide appropriate shoes and apparel for all them and us too, for that matter. We've brought samples of the shoes that we wore when you first met us."

"Wow! Great! You can count on me. Thanks, I can use them as models. Wait, arms too?"

Jan sighed, "Alas, yes. Arms too. Which means that we'll need your assistance with that too. We'll need you to 'acquire' the medical equipment to perform these body modifications for us. We will form up a small group who will be trained in their use and to hand the knowledge on down to the next generation, the Preparers we're calling them. We would appreciate it if you would help give them the needed training so that they can competently run the medical machines."

"Glad to. I guess the exclusive contract has its price," she chuckled. "Actually, the Imperium medical machines are so darn easy that anyone can use them. You don't have to be one of their doctors to run them. Still, I see what you mean and need. A hundred years from now when a new pair is elected, someone will have to run the medical machines to get them all ready to take office," Carmen concluded rightly. Jan noticed that she was very intelligent, in spite of her "appearance." Jan also saw that Carmen now didn't look a day over thirty-three, she'd obviously used her rejuvenation machine very recently, more than likely twice, since she looked at least ten years younger than she had just weeks ago.

Carmen went on, "Okay, how soon do we want to do this?" Jan gestured and she added, "Not a problem. Find the women that you wish trained and they can get live instruction from me as we perform the modifications on you two." They chatted about the details further and Carmen left, knowing that she'd just taken yet another huge step towards her ultimate goal of revenge on these two women who'd killed her husband, Jarek, and ended Valen's attempt at world domination, just as they were about to achieve it.

Amy chose two women in their late twenties, Ann and Sally, to be trained in the use of the new medical machines. One small room was set aside to be the official Modification's Room and the two began instructing the pair. Each would receive a lifelong stipend, more than enough to allow them to live in relative luxury. Their chosen successors would also receive the same stipend. Slowly, but surely, the two began installing the necessary physical arrangements and personnel needed to ensure that future emperors and empresses and the others were properly body modified.

The day before their scheduled modifications, Carmen came by for a quick visit. "One thing that I forgot to ask. Will you each have a domestique to assist you with your needs, once the modifications are done?"

"No, our daughters will be our domestique helpers," Jan replied.

"Okay. Then I have to ask you this. Will the new domestique helpers also be modified as Jan was when I first met you, Queen Amy?" Carmen asked, trying to mask her coyness with an insincere smile. She added quickly, "I should tell you that both have asked to have their waists reduced and to have their feet altered to be like yours. You can't blame them, really. They merely want to be like their mothers."

"They've been hounding us about having that done. So I suppose if that is their wish, we'll consent," Amy answered with a sigh. If their daughters only knew how awful this would be, but then in two years, they could get their feet back to normal and probably could also stop wearing the tight corsets too, if they desired.

"Excellent. One other minor detail. As I understand it, all the Ataro domestique staff are unable to speak. I don't know what that medical procedure was, but I do recall that Jan was unable to speak back then. Is this to be done to your daughters? If not, is it to be done to future domestique?"

"We should put our feet down on that one," Jan answered. "That was horrible, being unable to speak. Besides, no one on Tierra knows sign language."

"They can write though," Carmen pointed out wryly. "Don't you think that a domestique who can speak will violate the close relationship between the empress and her domestique? I mean, she'll be more like a confident and advisor, if she can speak freely. If you are serious about emulating the wasp culture, you ought to do it right. Who knows, perhaps omitting this detail could cause the whole thing to fail."

"Damn, Carmen. You would have to bring that point up," Amy replied disgustedly.

"Well, I had to, you know. I don't want to take any chances that this thing will ultimately fail here on Tierra," Carmen justified.

"Okay, give us the rest of today to investigate this possibility. You may well be right about this point. If we are going this route, we ought to introduce as few alterations as possible," Jan concluded. *We really don't know why this wasp-rule thing even works, but it is the only ruling system that we've ever seen in the galaxy that has endured for two thousand plus years and given those systems peace and prosperity all that time.* She added, "But I insist that the process we use be medically reversible so that when the domestique is no longer needed, their voices can be restored."

"Oh yes, that would be ideal," Carmen added with a wry smile. *This is so easy!* They chatted a bit more and she left. Both Amy and Jan headed for their medical machine and Jan began thumbing through the voluminous menus, searching for ways to make a person unable to speak and one that could be reversed easily later on. She found some that were not reversible rather quickly, but discarded those. No way was she going to make such a thing permanent on her daughter or Amy's.

Late that afternoon, she found a way to do it that was safe and reversible. It involved tying off the vocal cords. Over supper, the two mothers had a long talk with their teens, who'd just returned from Brom, filled with boy-lust and chatter.

"Yes mom, we really, really do want to look like you and Jan," June declared. "We want to have your small waist. It really makes you look stellar, mom, very curvaceous and sexy. We want to have tiny feet too. That's going to be the very in thing in no time at all. We'll be on the leading edge of fashion. You can't deny that. Many women are going to follow your lead as well."

"Okay, then you have our permission for that. Now then, we, Jan and I, are going to need to each have what is called a domestique to help us with our needs, dressing and such. Yes, I know that we will still be able to do most everything ourselves using our psi powers. That's not the point. The next emperor and empress will not and must have domestique helpers."

"Sure mom, we'll be glad to be your domestique, as long as we still get to meet some boys and go to some dances. We've been asked to the fall dance in Brom. We'd like to go all fancied up," June replied and hinted.

Amy grinned, but her expression changed. "There is a hitch, dear. The domestique staff of the Ataro System cannot speak. That reduces the chances that the domestique staff can overly influence their leaders. They use sign language to communicate, but no one knows that here on Tierra, so that's not feasible. However, you can write. Jan and I have decided that we had best implement the whole package. So if you want to be our domestique helpers, you'll also be unable to speak. Don't panic, it's not permanent. Once we resign in two years, we can undo that modification so you get your voices back again. Just realize that your feet will never be fully restored. The best that can be done is to have your feet like ours now are. You'll have to wear these highest heels all the time, like we have for the last sixteen years."

"Heels? Great! We'll always be tops in fashion. That's fine with us, but unable to speak at all? Not a squeak?" June's face twisted in a deep frown.

"Nope. But you can carry paper and pencil around with you and write what you want to say. I give you my word that your voices will be restored as soon as we leave the throne," Amy promised. "If you don't want to go through with this, we understand. It is an awful lot to ask of you. Let us know. We're supposed to do all this tomorrow, but if you'd rather not, then we can seek out some who will do it for the money."

"Mom, we can't have some strange woman looking after you. I guess it won't be so bad if it's only for two years, will it? Jan, you survived it. Besides, we can use our telepathy and get around it." June brightened up, the entire problem solved in her mind.

"Mom," Melissa added, "we promise that we'll take real good care of you both. Besides, Carmen said that she'd teach us how to use her makeup products too, once we got fashionable. She says that it adds to our sex appeal with the boys. She always looks really hot, doesn't she?"

Jan smiled. "Yes, I'll give her that point. Just don't trust her. She was in league with Jarek, Lech, Karolina, and Valen Tower in their attempt to conquer the world. She's a snake in the grass, albeit a very sharply dressed snake and pretty as well. Looks alone may attract your boyfriends, but looks seldom keep them, once they've gotten into your pants."

Melissa put her hands on her hips and retorted, "Mom, you've just been raped too many times, that's all. Not all men are like that."

Jan laughed, "Amy, were we ever this naive?"

"'Fraid so, love. 'Fraid so." Both laughed. The teens fumed.

"All right. We should discuss how things will be once the procedures are done tomorrow. Let's start with the effects on our feet," Amy brought the conversation back to what was really critical, hoping that their daughters might change their minds yet. It wasn't too late.

At nine the next morning, Carmen had the new

236

machines setup and ready to go in their new Preparation Room. Ann and Sally were ready to go and eager to learn how to operate the machines. Their huge stipend had just turned their entire fortunes in life around. "First, we'll do their feet, since that is the simplest. Then, we'll tackle Jan's arms. Once that is done and while she is recovering, we'll tackle June and Melissa's waists and voices. Jan, June, Melissa, you will be unconscious during the procedure, but Amy will be awake through it all and can verify that we are doing it all properly. Locals are used on your feet. We'll do Amy's feet first, while you watch."

At last, I am doing it. Revenge on my worst enemies and their daughters too. Incredible. I've waited sixteen years for this. How sweet this will be! Carmen ordered, "Okay, Amy, feet into the machine. Sit down and stick them into it, please." She did so and Carmen removed her heels and unfastened her garters, removing her fine nylons that she had sold to Amy. She allowed Ann and Sally actually to perform the work, programming the medical machine. "You should only feel two tiny pin pricks." Amy did and said so, recalling how awful walking had been for her years ago.

Well, she thought, *there is no other exit strategy that we know about, not unless we want to sacrifice the hard won peace and prosperity we've brought to Tierra.* Fifteen minutes later, they finished and Carmen slipped her nylons back on and then slipped her old special heels back onto her now tiny-looking feet. The toes of her feet were about two inches or so and were the only portion of her feet that now touched the ground, save the tiny spiked heel built into the sole's arch of the shoe and that touched the ground just behind the back of her toes. The shoes were rounded and thus sole contact with the ground was extremely small, making walking and keeping her balance treacherous at best. She sighed and attempted to stand, wobbling as she had done sixteen years ago. Jan put her arm around her to steady Amy and helped her to a nearby chair.

"Mom, they look so cool!" June admired her mother's new shoes and look. Amy resisted the temptation to admonish her daughter. No, she'd soon find out how awful this really was going to be.

With Amy overseeing the procedures, Jan took her turn. This time, the medical machine put her unconscious before performing the relatively simple surgery of removing her arms from their shoulder sockets and then healing up the wounds. Her feet were then altered as well. Ann and Sally then lifted her out of the machine and placed her on one of the recovery beds. Then, they worked their body modifications on June, followed by Melissa. With these two, two ribs were removed and some of their internal organs repositioned, before the restricting corset with its three inch tall, tiny waist band was tied into place, yielding fourteen inch waists similar to their mother's waists. Their voices were then eliminated and feet handled last.

The lengthy processes finished, leaving Amy to watch over the three, Carmen, Ann, and Sally went into another room to review everything. Carmen wanted to make sure that both women knew precisely every detail, because they alone would be administering these procedures to the next emperor, empress, and their staff.

Sometime later, June roused and looked scared. She tried to speak but no sounds came out. *Mom! I can't breathe! It's way too tight!*

"Take small, shallow breaths. At least you won't have to worry about over eating. It's impossible. See if you can stand up. Remember to take tiny steps, dear." Amy answered, though she resisted adding, "I told you so." June's arms swung wildly as she very nearly fell. With so little of her foot on the ground, even standing was treacherous. "You'll get used to it in time. We are going to need your arms around us so we don't fall. I hope we can get the hang of it more swiftly this time around."

Shortly after that, Melissa woke and had nearly identical reactions, soothed by Jan. Jan commented, "Come on, we had all better practice walking. God, Amy, I hope that we have taken the right exit strategy! I really didn't realize how awful this has all been for you all these years."

"We've got two weeks to get used to this before the large council meeting in September," Amy reminded them. "There is one benefit, Jan, we won't have to listen to teen chatter for a couple of years." Both women laughed.

June sent, *No, you will have to listen to teen telepathic chatter, mom! Help, I can't breathe still and I can't stand without nearly falling down!*

"Yes, but now you both are so sexy for your boyfriends," Jan added rather snidely.

Mom! Melissa protested.

Later that afternoon, Carmen returned with her promised wardrobes for June and Melissa, elegant pod silk gowns that fit their new body forms snugly. Once they saw their new looks in the full-length mirrors, both teens brightened up. In their minds, they looked incredibly sexy, which was what they greatly desired. Carmen also brought along a supply of her imported makeup and began instructing the teens in its application, again a huge hit with the two. Jan and Amy wanted no part of that and left the three to their lessons and experimentation. No, they had vital actions to undertake before the big meeting and then only two years before they had to have everything completely handled and they vacated the Imperial Tower and Castle.

On the fifteenth of September 1201, Emperor Jan and Empress Amy issued their new orders to the large gathering of men and women. Some three hundred had gathered for the biannual meetings and all were rather stunned to see Jan now as armless as Amy and their incredibly tiny feet, to say nothing of the two quiet teens who assisted them, standing at their sides, as the domestique had done before on Ataro Prime.

Amy began her address. "As you can see, we have finally committed to the full implementation that I declared in my original ultimatum sixteen years ago. Today, we are announcing to all you that in two years we will both be stepping down as your emperor and empress. Yes, that means that you have two years to elect your new emperor and empress. As I have said before, the words of the emperor and empress are law on Tierra. What they rule goes." She again outlined just what that still meant to make sure that they all realized she was not changing her mind or position.

"With that kind of awesome and total power over all us

on Tierra, there must be some check or abuse of power results. Hence, both the newly elected emperor and empress must undergo the appropriate body modifications that we have. No arms, tiny corseted waists, and tiny feet. Helpless you say? Well, yes, so that even if tempted to abuse their awesome power, they are physically restrained from doing so. Each will have one domestique to assist them, as our daughters are doing for us. The domestique will also be corseted and have tiny feet, but also to prevent them from unduly influencing their leaders, they will be unable to speak. Further, your new emperor and empress may have as many advisors of either sex as they desire. However, each of these men and women will have to undergo the same body modifications as the emperor and empress and will each have a domestique to assist them as well." She went on to outline the lifetime stipends that each would receive for their service and sacrifice to Tierra. Such was large enough to guarantee that when they retired, they would want for little.

Amy then explained, "By law, if your newly elected emperor and empress do not undergo these required body modifications, then you, all you, do not have to follow or obey anything that they say or rule. However, you cannot have these new emperors and empresses dictating new laws to nullify these body modifications for future leaders. Any attempt to subvert these modifications is illegal and will be severely punished. Further, before any newly elected emperor or empress can take the throne, they have to undergo a simple swearing in ceremony. I caution you, if at that time, they have not had the complete body modifications done, they will be executed on the spot, and you will have to elect new ones and get them properly modified. No exceptions ever."

She continued, "As they choose their domestique helpers, they too have to undergo the swearing in ceremony. Again, if they are not properly modified, they will be executed on the spot. When they chose their advisors, they too must be sworn in with that ceremony as well and will be executed, if they are not properly modified. In short, ladies and gentlemen, we are leaving you with absolutely no way to avoid tempering the awesome power that we are endowing them with." She went on to introduce Ann and Sally, explaining about the new Preparation Room and that the procedures were completely painless. Further, she announced that Elegant Fashions Inc would be providing the necessary wardrobes for all the modified men and women, again paid for by the throne.

Carmen rose and added, "Anyone else who wishes to have some of these exciting and sexy modifications done on themselves, please stop by Elegant Fashions Inc. We can perform any and all these as well. Don't the four just look incredible?" she added wryly. As she had expected she heard a number of positive muttering sounds, especially from some of the women, usually the wives of the rulers.

Jan took control of the meeting and began a lengthy discussion on just how they were to elect their new emperor and empress. "No, they don't have to be a married couple. If they are not married and have children, those children will be considered fosterlings just as they would be otherwise be," she answered one man's question. As she expected, this discussion on just how to elect their new rulers was very lengthy. Later she wondered if they should have dictated the method used to elect new emperors and empresses. What the assembled leaders finally decided upon was to meet themselves and choose them. Well, in two years they would find out how well this went.

"At least there are no new laws this time," one king commented as the meeting finally ended at the supper hour.

Now it was time for the large banquet and a chance for personal meetings and chats with their emperor and empress. The one comment that both heard most often, ignoring those about their body modifications, was: I am so glad that you are stepping down in two years and not waiting until you die of old age. While such could have been misconstrued as hatred, it was not the case. The leaders were anxious finally to be able to elect their own emperor and empress as Amy had promised them in her famous and shocking Blackwater Ultimatum some sixteen years ago. Implementation of that ultimatum had brought peace and prosperity back to Tierra, but they wanted their own leaders, not Amy and Jan.

The next morning, the first light snowfall covered the

city. Unknown to Jan and Amy, many of the delegates to the meeting were now meeting in Ben's Tavern, while their wives visited Elegant Fashions Inc. Having heard this remarkable and startling news from Emperor Jan and Empress Amy, the key men had secretly called for this meeting. Of note, they did not invite the representatives from Valen. The Midlands still detested and hated Valen and wanted nothing to do with them. The Easterlings had not been attacked by Valen, but they were appalled at Valen's secret dealings with the aliens from Rigel-3, particularly so with their acquisition of blasters and Nuclears. Hence, they wanted nothing to do with Valen either. They had conveniently sent their wives off to do some shopping while they met in secret.

"How the devil are we going to find someone who is willing to undergo that lifelong torture that Jan and Amy are going to inflict upon them? No one in their right mind would willingly agree to those hideous body modifications of theirs," one exclaimed in disgust.

"Hell, even if we find such idiots, are we really going to follow their laws?" another pointed out. After hours of heated discussion, they agreed on several points.

First, all them would like to be the world's emperor, if and only if these debilitating body modifications were outlawed. Second, absolutely no one wanted the position as currently defined by Empress Amy, that is, with the body modifications. Third, they were following Amy and Jan's laws because they had no choice, all had seen many who had defied the two somehow die mysteriously. Fourth, they all agreed that they, meeting as a collective group, ought to make the laws and rule Tierra, outlawing and banning Valen from active participation.

Fifth, they saw no way to achieve their collective rule until Amy and Jan had died and that wasn't likely for another forty years! True, early on, Valen had made a number of futile assassination attempts on Amy and Jan, but they had paid dearly for those. At this point in time, their Imperial Circle and Imperial Guards were far too strong for a simple infiltration of the tower. Once they retired in two years, depending upon where they went, assassinations might be attempted again, but it was doubtful, if not pointless. Their safest bet was to let them die of old age, assuming that they didn't continue to mysteriously grow younger any longer.

Sixth, they agreed that they would elect a lackey who would follow the collective wishes of this group. Several plans were put forth to ensure that their chosen candidates did just that, including the assassination of their extended families. Seventh, since Amy had declared that their reigns would be for twenty years, owing to the extensive body modifications they would undergo and since Amy had not outlawed an emperor serving two consecutive terms, they decided that their candidates ought to be in their twenties. That way, they could serve two terms and still be in office when Amy and Jan finally died of old age, freeing them finally to act.

After more extensive discussion, eighth, they agreed that the empress ought to come from the Easterlings while the emperor would come from the Midlands. Ninth, they agreed that the Midlands' leaders would choose the emperor while the Easterlings' leaders would choose the new empress. Both would automatically back the other's choice, totally blocking any Valen participation in the election. Tenth, they agreed that for cultural considerations as well as practical matters, they should have their candidates chosen at least six months before the deadline and that the two be married as soon as possible. That would give each a chance to become familiar with the traditions and cultures of the other.

Eleventh, they would need domestique helpers and advisors, who would also need domestique staff. They agreed that each candidate would have two advisors. One pair would be from the Easterlings, while the other pair was from the Midlands. The men would advise the emperor, while the women would advise the empress. These would be again chosen by the respective lands and that the two couples would also have to be married. Twelfth, that then dictated the need for six domestique helpers, three from each land. All dozen would have to be in their twenties so that they could serve two full terms and hopefully outlive Jan and Amy.

Lastly, they agreed to meet again after the fall 1202 Imperial Court meeting. At that time, they would make their decisions known, allowing plenty of time to get them married and ready to become their next puppet-head leaders. If problems arouse, they would still have nearly twelve more months to resolve them.

When their wives joined them for the return trip home, two dozen of them now sported Carmen's latest in fashions, emulating the style of Emperor Jan and Empress Amy. She called them pipe-waist corsets and toe shoes. Carmen had now performed twenty-four new waist and foot modifications. She rightly anticipated a sudden boom in women desiring these sexy body modifications and began staffing up to meet the demand, which she expected would swell by the coming spring of 1202. That her long desired revenge was now paying her back financially rather handsomely only added to her intense pleasure. She began to make even more plans.

Chapter 17 Boys and Troubles

The following weekend was Brom's Fall Festival and both June and Melissa looked forward to it with keen anticipation. All summer, they'd been dreaming and imagining how the dance would go with their new boyfriends, Tom and Bill, who were in the guards and several years older than the two teens. As they frequently primped before their full length mirrors, their new body shape was extremely dramatic, though both wished that their breasts would hurry up and fill out like all the other women. Running her hands down the highly curved sides of her pod-silk dress, June sent, *We look so utterly sexy in these dresses, don't we? Just feel our curves!*

I know, hard to breathe though, let alone walk. I think I might faint if I have to dance very much. Do you think that the boys will be considerate of us now that we look so fabulous? Melissa sent back.

As sexy as we look, they have to be, don't you think? You're right. I get out of breath just walking a little. Dancing might be too much. Gosh, I hope it isn't! We better continue practicing our walking. We don't want to spoil our sexy looks by taking a fall on the dance floor! That would be **so** *humiliating!* June replied.

Walking is a joke. Just standing is chore enough. Our steps are like minuscule. I hope the boys don't rush us. God, I bet they will, June! We go so utterly slowly now; we're barely moving. It takes forever to cross a room.

We have to walk elegantly somehow, Melissa. After all, all eyes will be on us now for sure. Did you see how everyone was staring at us at mom's big meeting? Men and women both.

I know. I heard that a bunch of them went ahead and got their waists and feet modified like us. We are setting the fashions for the whole world. Everyone's going to be watching us, June. We have to be regally elegant.

June smiled, she couldn't laugh any longer. *Well, if we take the tiniest of steps, we do look pretty elegant, don't you think?*

Yes, but we're so slow. Eight steps just to open a door!

I need ten or I start to lose my balance. Mom did say it took her lots of practice.

Saturday finally came. "You both look positively stunning," Amy told June and Melissa as they came to say good-bye to their mothers. "I am sure that you will knock your boyfriends off their feet."

Mom, they are likely to knock us over, June teased her. *Are you sure that you and Jan will be all right for tonight? We probably won't get back until late.*

"Sure, we can take care of ourselves for one evening. You both have a fun time and don't let your boyfriends take advantage of you," Amy replied, somewhat worried about letting her daughter go off to the dance alone. *Well, she won't be alone; nearly all Brom Tower will be there. Surely, nothing can happen to them.*

"She's right. Melissa, you look spectacular. We'll be fine. You two have fun. Perhaps in two years Amy and I can finally have some fun as well," Jan added, pressing her body gently into Melissa's. Once again, she longed to give Melissa a loving hug but felt acutely the loss of her arms as. *Well that's ended forever,* she thought sadly.

The two older women watched as their daughters walked very slowly out of the room, heading to join the Imperial Circle who would soon teleport them to Brom Tower and their waiting boyfriends, Tom and Bill. "They are so young and innocent," Jan whispered.

"Yes, but they are of age now, almost by two years. Still, I hope everything goes okay for them. If only," she didn't finish her sentence.

Jan knew what she meant and added, "I hope that we're doing the right thing, love. Still we both know those two would have gone ahead and gotten their waists done and probably their feet whether we wanted them to or not. I would have put my foot down on the domestique thing if they didn't have good telepathic skills. Without being able to speak, they can at least communicate that way. How did you ever walk without me and my arms around you, dear?"

"Damned hard. Scary. Especially so when we were

withholding using our true psi powers. Come on. I'd like something sweet."

June and Melissa materialized on the arrival pad in Brom Tower shortly after five that night. The dance was to begin at six. Both wobbled considerably as their feet touched the stone floor. They looked around. Holding each other's hand for desperately needed support, they carefully stepped down off the six inch tall pad. Together they moved towards the door. *I thought that they were supposed to meet us here?* June sent. Their boyfriends were late.

Outside the door, a night guard nodded to them and closed the door for them. Slowly, still holding on to each other, they began to make their way down the long hallway. Just then, Tom and Ben came boisterously walking into the hall at the other end. "Hey, there they are, right on time," Ben called out. Both lads moved swiftly to their dates for the dance. As they drew close, the teens knew that they had already been drinking; their breaths gave that away.

"Wow, will you look at you, June! You look hotter than hot! Damn," Tom said, running his hands up and down the sides of her pod-silk covered body. Ben was feeling Melissa at her side. While she enjoyed the sensation of his hands following her new curves, she thought it a bit inappropriate.

"No kidding, Melissa. You are going to be the hit of the dance tonight! Double wow. You look super. Come on, the dance is about to start, unless you want to stop off in an empty room for a little kissing first."

No! You'll mess up our makeup and we don't want to waste a lot of time trying to fix it up. Time enough for that later on, Melissa sent him.

"Gosh, Tom, she's right! They can't speak at all," Ben exclaimed.

Tom grinned, "That's fine. You don't need to speak anyway. Girls only complain. This way, Ben, we won't have to listen to silly girl chatter all night. Come on girls."

They put their arms around their tiny waists, which both appreciated, thinking that they'd get the needed support that both longed to have, making their walking easier to handle. Instead, both boys began walking at their usual strides. Both girls were sent stumbling, wildly trying to keep from falling down and gasping for breath as well.

We have to go slow! June fairly screamed into Tom's mind. Only the boys' strong arms kept the two from taking a bad tumble.

"Damn, you can't walk right in those heels. Okay, okay slower it is," Tom grimaced as June got her breath and composure back. *At least no one else saw us,* she sent to Melissa. "Damn, you are impossibly slow, but sexy, I'll give you that, June."

At last going slow enough for the teens, they got to glance at their boyfriends. Each wore their ceremonial Guard's uniforms and looked very handsome in them, complete with a short sword hanging from their waist belts. At least, she thought, they had taken a bath recently. Halfway down the hall, June sent, *Please, I need to stop and catch my breath. We're not used to this yet.*

The boys complied, though they grumbled a little about the delay. "If we don't hurry up, at this rate, we'll miss the grand entrance of the start of the dance." The two didn't want to miss that and in spite of their growing discomfort, continued their slow walk towards the Great Hall that had been rearranged for the big dance. Tables and chairs were removed and a refreshments table added along the back wall near the double door main entrance. The musicians were against the opposite wall. Tonight, nearly a thousand were expected to attend, more than half coming from the city of Brom. This was their chance to mingle socially with the tower folk.

They arrived in time for the grand entrance march. As they entered accompanied by the continuously repeated refrains of the fanfare, all eyes turned to look at the two teens. By now word had spread that the Emperor and Empress's daughters had become their domestique helpers and were setting a fashion trend. All the women who knew about this stared at the two, while the men admired their incredibly curvaceous forms. June and Melissa felt a rush of combined male lust and female envy flowing their way, but tried to ignore it and not fall down. Tom and Ben stood tall, puffing out to their full heights.

They led their dates over to a group of their fellow guards, some of whom also had dates clinging to their arms. "Hey guys, this is June and that's Melissa. They can't talk anymore," Tom said rather crassly. Several made crude comments to the effect that that was quite beneficial, and several of their dates poked them in their sides. The group of men laughed at that. Slowly, their grand evening began to go down the drain.

As the dance proper started, again Tom and Ben moved too quickly for the girls who very nearly fell down again. June and Melissa simply could not keep up with their dates and the men soon got tired of going so slowly and began dumping them off on some of their guard friends who didn't have formal dates.

After a humiliating hour of near falls and faints, at last Tom said, "Okay enough of this silliness. Come on, we're going to a side room for some fun." They fairly dragged the two teens out of the room and into a side room that had nice sofas and chairs. Perhaps it was someone's study, Melissa thought.

Without any word, both men began fondling the two and passionately kissing them. June struggled to get Tom to stop and she tried to speak and protest, but no sound was heard, save the heavy breathing of the two young men. Melissa likewise was panicking, fighting against the strong arms of Ben, who held her tightly, and forcing his ale breath into her while kissing. *Stop! Ben stop! No!* she sent as loudly as she could into his mind.

"This is so cool. They can't make a sound," Ben whispered to Tom. "Relax Melissa. You know that you want this as much as I do. You are so hot! I can tell. You are ravishing and you want me as badly as I want you. Stop squirming."

"Maybe they want to play rough," Tom suggested, holding June's arms together so she would stop thrashing him.

Unable to cry out for help, unable to overcome the sheer strength of these guards, June and Melissa had no other choice but to resort to their *mentales* gifts. June let loose a wild blast of psi energies. Sensing what June was doing,

Melissa did likewise. Both men threw their hands up against their heads and ears, staggering back from the two girls who now lay sprawled on the sofas. "Bitches!" shrieked Tom. He reacted by slapping June hard across her face, stunning her. Ben punched Melissa in her jaw, echoing Tom's sentiments. The two men stumbled out of the side room, leaving the two teens sobbing and gasping for breath.

Still sobbing, they helped each other get up. They could not go back into the Great Hall, not like this. Everyone would know. Instead, they tried a side door, and headed outside into the dark night and found themselves alone on a small balcony. For a time, they just stood there and cried softly. Everything was ruined now. Both teens began to believe that their mothers had been right; all men were brutes, hardly worthy of their attention and love.

Just then, the door opened and two other boys a year older than themselves stepped quietly outside. One spoke softly, "Are you all right? Did they hurt you? Alan, she's bleeding." The boy named Alan stepped over to Melissa and began to dab the blood off her chin, while the other gently took hold of June's hand, asking, "You hurt?"

We can't speak. My face, he slapped my face. Is it bleeding too? June sent him.

"Alan, they can't speak for some reason. No, you've got a bit of a bruise and your makeup is rather a mess, but you'll live. How's she doing, Alan? I'm Henry, by the way. He's my twin, Alan. We have been watching you both since your fancy entrance. You ought to have known that you picked on the wrong men to escort you. That whole bunch is just a bunch of bull- headed third year guards who like to bully everyone. They think that they are hot stuff."

"I'm going to heal her a dab, Henry. Bleeding won't stop unless I do," Alan replied. He focused and his crystal glowed blue for a moment. "There, that ought to do it. Come on. Let's get you two somewhere safe and cleaned up."

Thank you, Melissa sent, still trying to stop crying.

"Here, put your arm around me. We won't let you take a tumble. Those are awfully high heels that you are wearing," Alan said gently. "They look good on you, though."

The two boys led them into the side room and then down a deserted hallway and into another room that had a bathroom in it. For once, June and Melissa were not rushed by the boys, who seemed un-phased by their need for very tiny steps. In fact without saying a word, they demonstrated both gentleness and compassion for the two highly upset young women. "Okay, this bathroom is not used much. We'll stand guard and make sure that no one disturbs you. If you need some assistance, just let us know," Alan said softly. He and Henry let go of the two and moved back to the door, turning their backs on them, giving them even more privacy as they made their way into the bathroom proper.

God, our faces are a mess. How could we have been so stupid? June sent, still sniffling and clearing her nose while looking at her reflection in the mirror. A dim lantern provided the only light, but there were others that could be lit if they chose to have better lighting. They didn't. Mechanically, they began to wipe their once nicely done makeup off their faces and then washed in cold water, hoping the chill of the water would do them some good.

What do we do now? The Brom circles are all at the dance. We can't ask them to send us home, there would be too many questions to answer, Melissa sent, becoming more alarmed by the minute. Now they felt trapped in Brom Manor.

We could contact the Imperial Circle, but then our moms would be asking all sorts of questions that I'm not ready to answer, June replied, looking at the slight bruise on her face. *Maybe we can hide out in here until it's time to go home.*

"Is everything okay in there?" Alan called out.

Now what do we do? Melissa asked, examining her lip that Alan had healed for her. There was still a little swelling where her lip had split, but it was healing fine now.

Stall? June suggested and sent to Alan, *We need a bit more time.*

"Okay, no rush. How about a quite walk? We know some cool places where you can just relax. Later, if you want, we can go back to the dance. You probably ought to do that, you know. By now, people will be wondering what happened to

251

you two. We saw lots of men and women watching you both when you entered. You will be missed sooner or later," Alan chatted from his position by the door.

Melissa began to panic. *He's right. We'll be missed, but I can't face them right now. Can you?*

No! Maybe we ought to take a short walk and calm our nerves. I'm shaking like a leaf in the wind. The two agreed and took as deep a breath as they could, which wasn't much, and holding onto each other, they bravely made their slow way back to the door.

"Ah, you both look just fine now. Come on. Let's take a stroll for a while. You both look petrified," Henry said quietly, but looked them in their eyes, first one and then the other. June nodded and the boys slipped an arm around each woman's waist. "We'll steady you," he whispered.

They went down the hallway and took another unfamiliar exit. Melissa finally realized that they were now behind the manor house. Neither teen had ever been here. Still, the air was chilly and refreshing to them both. Rain was eminent; one could smell it on the winds. As they moved slowly down the cobblestone walk, several dogs began barking.

"Quiet Queen, King, it's just us," Alan called out and the dogs settled down. "We raise and train dogs. Dad taught us. Some are used as sled dogs in the winter. I want you to meet Queen; she's our smartest dog. We've trained her to herd, though our older brother often uses her as a watch dog."

That's interesting, Alan, Melissa sent, thankful for a completely different topic. Soon a black and white medium sized dog came bouncing up to the lads, her tail wagging low to the ground. Alan petted her on her head and Melissa noticed that Queen never took her eyes off Alan's eyes, rather like a staring match.

"Good girl, Queen. This is Melissa and June. They are friends," Alan spoke to Queen as if she were a person. Queen responded and moved over before Melissa and began looking straight at her. Melissa, holding onto Alan, bent down and petted her head. "Melissa can't speak Queen, but she likes you, I can tell." Melissa smiled for the first time since their disastrous encounter. Then Henry did the same with June, introducing her to Queen. Both women smiled and petted the very friendly dog, though they had to hold onto the lads to keep their balance. They could not bend much at all except from their hips.

It's hard trying to stand like this with only our toes on the ground, Melissa sent as an explanation to Alan.

"We could tell that as soon as we saw you both entering the dance. The jerks that brought you haven't a clue about such things. How are you feeling now? You know that you really have to go back in there and dance. If you don't, those jerk-offs win and you lose. We'll be your escorts and make sure that you can hold your heads up to those slime balls," Alan told them.

Melissa felt too embarrassed to say anything, but nodded her assent. "On guard Queen," Alan commanded his dog. Barking once, she dashed off into the darkness. One small lantern provided the only illumination on this rather private walk. Again, the lads kept a secure arm around their waists, miraculously moving at their pace. Now Melissa and June began to notice the boys and how considerate they had been and were. Both were perhaps slightly older than they, identical twins, with curly brown hair, bowl cut, and blue eyes. Each wore an identical light brown pod-silk suit but Alan's neck wrap was yellow while Henry's was light blue. Their faces were youthful but with strong features. Involuntarily, they slipped their arm around the lads as well. As they made their slow way back inside and down the halls into the Great Hall, the two young teens finally felt comfortable and began to relax.

As they again entered the packed dance hall, they tensed up at once and the lads felt that instantly. "Sh. It will be just fine. Ignore those jerks and their pals completely. Focus on us, follow our lead," Alan whispered to Melissa and Henry nodded to June. Both boys gracefully pivoted the two girls around and took hold of them in the proper dance position. They did it as if they were highly trained and skilled dancers, both June and Melissa felt a tingle of excitement or anticipation that they had not felt earlier on the dance floor.

Evidently, the boys were also aware of how difficult it was for them to breathe and purposely kept their foot motions to a minimum, which did not overly tax their shallow breathing. Because of their strong hold on them, they no longer worried about falling or even keeping their balance. As they lost it, they felt just the right pressure being applied to counter their lean. At last, they began truly to enjoy the dance, reflected in their faces and eyes.

During the short break between songs, they also noticed that many women were casting glances their way admiring their extreme look and were aware that they were dancing gracefully in spite of their extreme heels. *I think I am sensing some envy from some of the younger women,* June sent to Melissa. *Can you feel it?* Melissa replied that she did too.

An hour later, Melissa was finally able to cast a discrete glance at the boys who had been their dates. She was just in time to see him feeling up a woman who was probably his own age and got to see her slap him across his face. June turned in time to see his disgrace as well. Both teens smiled. "See, told you that they were jerks," Alan whispered to Melissa. "You dance very well."

My first time in these heels. It is so hard, but you make it easy for me. Thanks, Alan, she sent. He smiled.

"I'd like you to come see our dogs during the daytime. It's fall and the snows will come soon, but the leaves are fantastic for the next few days. Think your mothers will let you come for a short visit, like maybe tomorrow or Monday?" Henry asked June and Melissa.

They smiled. June sent, *We'll try. Tomorrow might be the better day, since we have to help them at court on Monday. Are you sure that you want two hobbled up girls?*

"Who cares about that? You both are smashing and bright. We'd love to show you around. Let's hope it is a nice day. Never can tell this late in the season, though," he explained.

Say, we don't know your last name, June sent.

"del Fuego, but our grandfather was Jake Sikes and our grandmother was Evita del Fuego. She had the katalyein gift, which meant she was like Empress Amy and had no arms, born that way just like our sister, Sally. She's twenty now, and we've had a lot of practice helping her out with things over the years. She's over there in that red gown dancing with her boyfriend. He's in the guards too. Just remember, not all boys are jerks like Tom and Ben," Henry whispered, but both June and Melissa could hear him.

"Right, you two are pretty darn impressive. I don't know many who would do all that you're doing for your mothers. We heard that Emperor Jan lost her arms too. I suspect that they are really having a hard time walking without their arms to help them. I bet they are very thankful that you are there to help them, though I honestly don't understand why they are doing that. Sally has enough trouble as it is without, well you know what I mean," Alan whispered.

Thanks, June flushed a little. *Mom and Jan are having a terrible time, though they never say so. We can tell, but in two years, they will retire and we are supposed to get much of this undone. God, I hope so, but they'll never be able to get their arms back.*

The music ended, and one of the musicians announced, "Musician's break. Refreshments time. Next set in twenty minutes." As the two lads escorted the girls towards the back area now packed with other couples heading there as well, a number of women interrupted them to chat about their new fashions. Of course, the two were unable to speak but did their best to answer them telepathically.

Over and over, they had to explain that it was painless but that getting used to the pipe corset and the toe shoes took a great deal of time and practice and no, they were not very adept at walking yet. Still, they knew that a fair number of these women were seriously considering taking the plunge. All this positive attention continued to extrovert the teens, who relaxed even more, putting the nightmare start of the evening behind them.

When the last dance was announced, servants lowered most of the lights. June and Melissa decided to reward the two boys and gave them a passionate kiss as so many other couples were doing. To their surprise, the boys returned theirs in kind. Later, they insisted on walking them back to the tower, where the late night circle was just gathering. Their first action would be to teleport the two girls back to their tower. Again, the two young couples shared a goodnight kiss and the lads waved to them as they vanished from sight.

"Well, how did it go?" Jan asked Melissa as the two walked slowly into their main bedroom suites, each holding onto the other for support. "Shit! You got hurt! Out with it," Jan spotted the slight swelling on her daughter's lower lip and demanded to know.

"Are you all right, dear? Your face looks a little off and your makeup is gone. What did those boys of yours do to you?" Amy interrogated June. Before either could answer, regretting that they couldn't just speak anymore, Amy added, "I knew it. Those boys couldn't be trusted. We should have never left them go to the dance alone, Jan. Somehow we ought to have gone with them."

Mom, please. We are all right. They were jerks but we're all right. Alan and Henry rescued us and they are really incredibly nice and gentle with us. We really like them. They want us to come and see their dogs tomorrow and the fall leaves. Please, mom, you have to let us go. We really want to see them again. I know. You were right. Some men are total jerks, but they are not all that way. Alan and Henry aren't that way at all. They have a sister, Sally, who was born without arms so they are very sensitive to our needs. She's got the katalyein gift. June sent to both of their mothers.

"Damn men anyway. Most of the universe's ills are due to the evils of men," Jan declared passionately.

Mom, they are not all bad. Some are. Okay, we found out the hard way. Okay, we admit it, but they aren't all nasty and evil. Alan and Henry are really kind and gentle and compassionate. We don't want to be like you both are.

"What do you mean like we both are?" Jan retorted, realizing that she was having an argument with her daughter.

*You know what we mean. Women are supposed to marry men, not other women. It's so embarrassing for us. Have you ever thought about how **we** feel? Everyone thinks that you both are, well very strange, and they think that we are strange too. We want to be normal. We don't want to marry other women like you two,* Melissa burst out what she'd wanted to say for years but had kept her tongue.

Jan and Amy flushed to the roots of their hair, their faces felt very hot. "Damn, Jan. What have we done to our daughters? Honey, we never, ever meant to make you feel unhappy, not ever." She sighed heavily and fought back tears.

Jan, also fighting a rush of conflicting emotions, sensed that Amy desperately needed her support. "She's right. We never wanted you to feel ashamed of us or embarrassed. Look, you are now dating boys. You have to understand what we've been through. Amy and I married because in this whole wide world, we have only truly loved each other. Damn, girls, if we don't teach you but one thing, make it this: marry out of a deep love for the other. Don't settle for anything less. Your mom and I, June, have been in love with each other for close to sixty years now."

Amy sighed. "We've not told you a lot about our past because some of it is hideous and not fit to hear. You want to know why we hate men so, well sit down before you fall down and we'll tell you. Damn, just be careful with men, will you?" The four sat down, and Amy began to relate some rather awful events that she'd endured and Jan added more of hers when Amy had finished. "We've been beaten, raped, tortured by damn near every man who laid his hands on us. We've been battling the wicked evils that other men have caused innocent people all our lives. Ever since I was kidnaped at eighteen, I have had to deal with the viciousness of men and their actions. You are right, I am very bitter towards men. Not one of them has ever shown me the respect and kindness that I deserve. Only Jan has done that ever since we first met."

Jan spoke up, "Melissa, was all this desire to have a pipe corset and toe shoes done just to help you attract men so you could avoid having to marry a woman, like I did?"

Now it was the teens' turn to flush crimson. June answered for the both of them. *Yes. We were terrified that we'd have to marry some woman and we wanted to make sure that guys found us very attractive. I'm sorry, mom.*

"Come here. I can't hug you, but I'd give anything to do so. Hold me. I love you so. I wish that you'd have said something about this to us long ago. Honey, we'd never, ever force you to marry anyone. We want you to fall in love and be loved and marry out of a deep love for your partner, whoever that may be. We know that we are unusual and are looked upon with a good deal of scorn, but we never realized that you also bore some of that as well. Forgive us, will you?" Amy asked. June hugged her mother, while Melissa hugged Jan.

"You have to follow your heart, Melissa," Jan whispered. "Be true to yourself above all."

Does that mean that we can go tomorrow? Melissa asked.

"Of course you can go tomorrow. I wouldn't dream of saying no, as long as it is something that you really want to do," Jan replied. Both teens relaxed finally. "Promise me that you will always talk to us first and not hold something back like you have with this, will you?" she added. Both did and then helped their mothers get ready for bed.

When their daughters were gone the next morning, Venerada Luisa made contact with Jan and Amy. After pleasant greetings, Luisa explained, *As you know, the rulers of the lands no longer keep the tower's venerada informed about their plans. Towers and rulers are now kept entirely separate. Still, I have my ways. I hate not knowing what King Pete is planning. I've just learned that the Midlands and Easterlings rulers met secretly after their meeting with you to discuss what you told them about electing a new emperor and empress.*

Amy replied, *We figured that they would.*

Did you know that they are planning to circumvent the whole emperor-empress thing in the future?

What?

My contact said that they are planning to elect a young couple, one each. The empress will be from the Easterlings and the emperor will come from the Midlands. They will be married before they undergo your modifications and become the new leaders.

Well, that's what we planned, Amy replied.

The new choices are going to be mere figurehead, lackeys, doing what the rulers desire. They are planning merely to buy time until you both die of natural causes. Then, they are going to abolish the whole emperor-empress concept and take control themselves. I thought that you both ought to know. Can they do that?

Probably they can, but if we live long enough and continue having everyone prosper, perhaps they will have a change of heart, Amy replied and Luisa bid them good day, breaking the contact.

"Damn, they could do just that, Amy. After we are gone, what's to keep them from abolishing what we've setup? Has all this been for nothing?" Jan broke down at last. She'd made the supreme sacrifice and now it seemed that she'd done it for nothing at all. The ruling men would merely wait them out and then take over control of Tierra once more.

Amy wanted to throw her arms around her life-long lover, consoling her, but couldn't. "We must continue to do our best to show them that our way leads to peace and prosperity for all and that their way only leads to more destruction." She couldn't think of anything else to say. Somehow, she didn't believe what she was saying either. Maybe they were doomed anyway.

Chapter 18 The Exit

September 1203 finally arrived. Jan and Amy had been busy, but for the last two months, they had little to do. All was ready for the big transfer of power to the newly elected emperor and empress and their advisors and domestique helpers. The Imperial Circle had not been idle either, having doubled the size of the tower and manor, building. They had added both around the existing structures, as well as upwards since their ground dimensions were fixed. The complex was ready for the first inauguration and celebration of the new leaders. Amy and Jan had already moved most all their possessions out of the Imperial Castle and into rooms in Brom Tower.

The newly elected had undergone their body modifications in the spring and during the summer months, Jan and Amy had extensively trained them in the technology of arbitration that Amy had learned on Ataro Prime, a technology that she hoped and prayed would continue to bring peace and prosperity to Tierra as it had during their reign. These newly elected men and women fit the advance warning that Venerada Luisa had given them. Half were from the Easterlings and half from the Midlands. Valen and the entire Westerlings thus had no say in this election, much to their dismay. That they were angry was not lost on anyone, but there was little that they could do about it at the moment, not with their archenemies, Amy and Jan, still around.

Emperor Carl Christopher was twenty-one, a brown haired and blue eyed youth. Amy already knew that he was anything but bright. Jan had complained bitterly that he was a moron and justified that by saying only an idiot would have consented to this horrific body modification. His new bride, Empress Calandra, was a typical Easterlings bound woman, with uncut but braided, long brown hair. She continued to wear her tight fetter skirt, but had to wear a pod-silk blouse. The former made walking extremely difficult for her and she usually had her domestique supporting her when she had to move. She was twenty and fairly cute as well, but also was anything but bright.

Their domestique helpers were another married couple, Dan and Elnora Sheffield. She too was an Easterlings bound woman who also retained her tight skirt and her arms were chained to her waist at her elbows. The advisor to Carl was Carver Welsh, who was also armless now, but his wife, Ada, was not. She acted as his domestique. Empress Calandra's advisor was Felisa Sandro also a bound Easterlings woman, but her Easterlings husband, Aldo, served as her domestique.

Amy and Jan complained to each other that none of these eight were particularly intelligent or quick on the take. Even worse, none of them had the *mentales* gift! The domestique helpers were in for an awful time. Jan grumbled, "Well, what did you expect? Only morons would consent to the body modifications." She was still terribly depressed about having given up her arms for this exit strategy that now had the makings of a dismal failure.

"We can only trust that they will practice what we have tried to teach them and not be the men's puppets," Amy answered grimly. She too had almost lost hope as well. "We'll keep an eye on them. If they don't do well, we will have to make other plans for the future. Somehow, someway, we have to prevent these men from leading Tierra back into vicious wars again. We've got to plan for the more distant future generations that will need our help long after we are gone, love."

"Huh? How are we going to do that? It's hopeless," Jan replied.

"Not really. We can't give up, not now, not after all that we have done, Jan. We've got all our combined equipment and an enormous bank account, to say nothing of our underground contacts. We just have to be smarter than these men, that's all," Amy declared, though at the moment, she too was depressed.

Later, they changed into their fanciest dresses and prepared for their last actions as emperor and empress of Tierra. With their daughters supporting them, they walked into the packed throne room. Imperial Guards lined the room, guaranteeing that there would be no trouble during the ceremony. Amy noted that nearly half of the ruler's wives were now wearing the fashionable pipe corset and toe shoes, clinging to their husbands for support. Before them, their replacements stood, the domestique helpers with their arms around the waists of those that now depended upon them.

At Amy's nod, the musicians began a fanfare, while one by one beginning with Carl, the new rulers and staff stepped up to the disguised bot, which verified that they were appropriately modified for the position that they were assuming. Of course, all were. At last, Emperor Jan spoke loudly and clearly, "I give you Emperor Carl Christopher, Empress Calandra Christopher, his advisor Carver Welsh, her advisor Felisa Sandro, and their domestique helpers."

A huge round of applause followed and their helpers assisted the two new rulers to get to their thrones and properly seated. The Easterlings women in their fetter skirts had a most difficult time of it, but Amy felt compassion for the steel determination of these Easterlings women who were refusing to abandon all their traditions. Emperor Carl spoke loudly, "Let the coronation ball begin." The music began once more and the many couples followed the order. Amy and Jan, supported by June and Melissa, made their way slowly to the tower. Once there, their Imperial Circle teleported them to Brom Tower.

Venerada Luisa was there to welcome them officially to Brom. She led them directly to Angelica's room, where she had the medical machine ready to go. An hour later, June and Melissa regained their voices and Jan and Amy had their feet partially repaired. At least, now they only had to wear the high heels that they'd worn before. Melissa and June had decided not to have their feet restored just yet. Their weddings were scheduled for this very evening and both still desired to remain the latest in fashion, if they could manage it. Both Alan and Henry had agreed to let them see if they could, but all four agreed to have their feet repaired if they couldn't.

Once done, the two brides-to-be were ushered off by Sally and Stella to get dressed for their wedding, while Luisa accompanied Amy and Jan to their temporary room here in the tower. "Are you sure that you want to move out into the city proper? You are most welcome to stay here in Brom Tower as long as you desire," she repeated her offer.

"No, it's time that we begin our own private lives as ordinary citizens once more. Thank you, Venerada Luisa for everything," Amy countered.

"No, it is we who owe you everything. No one has sacrificed so much to bring peace and prosperity to Tierra than you two. Okay, I'll send Lana to help get you dressed for the weddings." She bowed and left the two.

Later and now able to walk significantly better, Amy and Jan walked proudly up to their assigned positions at the front of the Great Hall. Late autumn flowers were nicely arranged and their fragrance filled the air. Musicians began playing and the two twins, whom were nearly impossible to tell apart, stepped into the room taking their places awaiting their brides. Amy and Jan turned to watch their daughters as they began their slow walk up the aisle. Having had two years of practice walking in their toe shoes, both were managing it well. As Jan and Amy caught sight of their daughter's radiant faces, tears of joy and happiness trickled down their cheeks.

Proudly, both brides moved beside their respective grooms and Venerada Luisa Wycombe, now dressed in a white gown, stepped before them. She conducted the wedding ceremony. The only way that she could tell the twins apart was that Alan wore a yellow tie, while Henry wore a black one. She kept the ceremony simple and soon the two couples shared a kiss and the music began once more. Amy noted that both men were being extremely careful to match the pace set by their wives in their toe shoes and that brought a smile to her face. The thought struck her, maybe June was right — all men might not be wicked. Perhaps there were a few good men in the world and it had been their misfortune to have never found any.

The reception and dance that followed was a happy time for all. Jan did notice that quite a few of the women now wore the pipe corsets too, along with the toe shoes. As Carmen had predicted, these would become quite fashionable, but she was more than relieved to have her feet partially restored. Maybe if she still had her arms, then she could manage in those shoes again, but not like she was. Later in the evening, both mothers gave their daughters a goodnight kiss and their husbands gave them hugs as well. After that, Miguel escorted Amy and Jan out to a waiting carriage and drove them to their new home in the city of Brom. He made sure that they got safely inside and that the lanterns were lit before he too bid them goodnight.

"Well, love, here's our new home," Amy stated, looking at the many ornate boxes that held their clothes and personal items stacked in their living room. All their Imperium equipment was already in the secret chamber under the watchful eyes of Angelica and Miguel. "Now at long last, we are just normal people."

"Ha!" Jan retorted. "We are anything but normal people, Amy, or are your eyes going blind?"

Amy laughed, she was not going to debate that detail. "Come on. Let's see if the bed is prepared. I hope that we don't have to make it yet tonight. I'm emotionally drained. Our daughters — they really have married. I hope and pray that they are truly happy."

"I'm sure that they are. Did you see their eyes when they were walking down the aisle?" Both women began to cry once more. Later, they activated the several crystal networks that had been installed providing them with some measure of security. If assassins attempted to break into their home, the crystals would sound an alarm, waking them or alerting them as needed. Jan sighed, "Well, tomorrow the staff that Luisa hired for us ought to be arriving. Perhaps we can get them to help us unpack some. Meantime, let's get some sleep. I seem terribly tired just now. Happy though. We did all right with our daughters, didn't we?"

"Yes, if nothing else, we did do that right, love."

Early the next morning, the two had just gotten out of bed and were dealing with using their psi powers to get themselves dressed when they heard a loud knocking on their front door. "Damn, we aren't even dressed yet," Amy grumbled. For these two, the process was excruciatingly slow; they missed their daughters' helping hands. Still in their nightgowns, they slipped on their heels so that they could walk and headed for the door. Amy used her psi powers to open the door. Two men stood there.

"Miss Amy? Miss Jan?" one of the men said in a kindly voice. "We are your assistants. Angelica Evita e Kaylee sent us. I'm your chef, Stu Tucker, and this is your gardener and handyman Verne Stanford. Angelica said that your pantry is empty so I took the liberty of brining breakfast with me."

"Oh." Amy looked a bit startled. She and Jan were expecting a couple of women to help them with their needs. "But," she started to protest. Her stomach growled, when she smelled freshly baked bread. "Okay, come on in. We are not dressed yet. Not sure where everything is at; we just got here late last night and went to bed. Haven't even begun to unpack though there isn't that much really. Clothes mostly."

Stu smiled, "Angelica told us to expect something like this. Not to worry. Let's get a hearty breakfast in you, Misses. Then, we can see to what needs to be done first." The house was not that large, and they quickly found the kitchen and attached dining room. Their new house was a small stone cottage with a basement. The front door opened into a long hall with their bedroom the first door on their left, while their living room was the first door on their right, where their crates were stacked. The end of the hall opened into the combined pantry, kitchen, and dining room, occupying the back half of the small home.

Verne said, "Misses, you just make yourselves comfortable at the table there and we'll set breakfast. Angelica didn't say what all you would need assistance with, but obviously, you have the gift, same as us. So we'll just let you tell us when you need some help."

Amy detected sadness or grief in his voice, but didn't inquire, replying instead, "Yes, that is the best way. We'll let you know. Thanks." The two women activated their crystals and moved their chairs out so that they could sit down, but Verne was right there, sliding the chairs in for them. He then began setting four places from the second bag that Stu had sat on the table. Meanwhile, Stu had already started taking various steaming pots out of his larger bag, carefully setting the teapot down.

"Well, that was tricky. Just try bringing a pot of tea in a

bag without spilling it," Stu chatted, as if he'd done this many times. However, Amy also detected that he was masking a deep grief as well. He didn't do such a good job hiding it. "Sorry, don't know how you like your omelets, so you are just going to have to take them the way that Mary liked them. She was my wife, died of the rotting disease two years ago now." Now Amy knew what he was hiding.

"I'm sorry. You must have been close," Amy apologized sincerely.

Stu sighed, momentarily halting laying out the breakfast. "Yes, Miss, that we were, close. I couldn't save her, though Lord knows how hard I tried." His voice had a catch in it and he stopped talking and continued serving, silently filling up the four plates with omelets, pancakes, and freshly baked bread. Verne poured out the strong black tea.

Once finished, before sitting down, Stu asked, "Will you need us to feed you? If not, we'll sit across from you."

"We can manage with our gifts," Jan replied. How strange it felt to have two men as their servants and she certainly wanted them sitting across from her where she could keep an eye on them. *What is Angelica thinking of, sending two men to be our servants?*

Both men sat down across from them. Both were probably forty, the women judged. Neither was particularly handsome; they had brown hair that touched their shoulders and blue eyes. Stu's face was somewhat angular, while Verne's was roundish. Verne had a more robust frame and his muscles were more pronounced than Stu's. Jan could not help asking, "How come Angelica asked you two to be our assistants?" She thought better of saying their servants.

Stu answered first. "Well, Misses, I owed Angelica a very big favor, long standing. Years ago, Miss Angelica was a powerful fighter, and she saved my family once. So I owed her and, after my Mary died, I just couldn't go on, not really. You see, we had an inn but without her, it wasn't the same so I gave the inn to our son and his wife. If I am honest, I just sort of sat around for nigh onto two years now trying to figure out how to go on, you know. It's as if I lost the better half of my life. What am I to do now? Anyway, Angelica came to me and called in her favor, and I certainly could not refuse her. I've cared for my wife's needs so I am able to care for yours as well." He looked at Verne, either unable or unwilling to say more.

Verne cleared his throat. "Pretty much the same. I owe Angelica a very big turn. My gift is gardening. I make plants grow and thrive, always have had that knack. Mr. Green Hands, they call me. Lucy and I have two grown children; they're married now. I lost her about three years ago. Montaña beast got her while she was out collecting more wild flowers for me. I should have never let her go off by herself. It's all my fault that she's dead. Been really hard to go on, you know. We were married twenty-two years. She was the orchid of my life and after she passed life's not been the same for me. Been considering going out there myself and sitting around until another Montaña beast comes by and takes me, but Angelica came by last week and called in her favor. I owe her, so here I am. I'll see that you have the best flower garden in Brom, come spring. You wait and see, Misses."

Stu added, "I hope that you will not be embarrassed to have us help you with your private needs, Misses. We told Angelica that perhaps it would be better for you to have two women assistants, and that you'd not be comfortable with men helping you with such, but she was insistent. We could not turn her down, not after all she's done for us. So if you prefer to have women here and not us, just let Angelica know. We understand. I, we are — well, we knew how to care for our late wives, so we do know what you will likely be needing, but well, we've never met, well, you know, women like yourselves, married women." Stu was obviously fumbling to find the right way to say what he meant.

Jan laughed, "Women lovers, eh?" Both men flushed; she'd hit her mark. "Well, just so you know, we've had. . ." She paused. *Do they know who we are?* "Say, do you know who we are or were?" she asked pointedly.

"Er, well not really. Two pretty women with obvious physical limitations and you've just moved into Brom, that's about all that we really know, Misses. I'm sorry. Should we know more?" Verne replied and asked humbly, feeling even more out of place with these two women.

Jan could not help but laugh, embarrassing the two men further. "You are looking at ex-Emperor Jan and ex-Empress Amy."

Their eyes looked as if they might pop out of their heads. "Oh my gosh!" Stu exclaimed.

"Forgive us Misses, er Your Majesties," Verne mumbled.

"Misses will do. We are finished with that whole part of our lives. We are now officially retired from public services," Amy broke in. "What Jan was trying to say, fellows, is that we've have nothing but horrific experiences with men during the last eighty years of our lives. I could get pretty darn graphic, but I won't. For nearly eighty years, Jan has been the only person in the universe that loved me and I, her. We've had no one else on which to depend, and frankly fellows, we have a pretty low opinion of men."

She stopped and realized that both men were now actually recalling the devastation of Bettingham, when the Nuclear explosion went off. Back then, she had made darn sure that every *mentales* gifted persons, save children, fully experienced the horrors of the many deaths. Verne finally recovered and mumbled, "I cannot ever forget that day, not ever. I've been dedicating to making all things grow ever since then, doing the best that I can to heal the earth and people."

"Same here," Stu whispered. "I was just a lad, barely married then. Mary and I were shocked to the core, but after that we always took in anyone who was in need, giving them room and board at our inn until they got back on their feet."

"Wait, Miss Jan, you don't look like you are an old woman. You can't be even forty, unless my eyes deceive me or do you use illusion-based psi powers?" Verne asked, adding quickly, "or should I not ask such things? Forgive me if I shouldn't."

Jan laughed, lightening the suddenly serious mood. "We're ninety this year. We've undergone several of the alien rejuvenation processes. Yes, we look like we are thirty-eight or so, our bodies do, that is. However, we don't plan to use those machines any more. No point, there's not much for us to live for now anyway."

"We've retired, but to be truthful, Stu, Verne, we haven't the faintest notion of what we are going to do now. As long as we are being frank up front here fellows, we are physically limited, terribly so, but our psi powers help us compensate a good deal. All that is really my fault, you see. I had to endure this so that we could get back here to Tierra. We both were abducted by the Rigel-3 aliens when we were about eighteen, taken as telepath slaves to other worlds. Long story, but the only way we could get back here is for me to have my body altered to this mess, and Jan's waist and feet too. It is my stupid fault that she's also lost her arms. Perhaps I made the wrong choice, as it now turns out."

"I'm so sorry for you both," Stu said humbly, "women should never be so ill-treated, not ever. Still, I know what you mean. The world is full of men who have lost their way, just as there are women who've lost theirs too. Honestly, Misses, if you would prefer to have women as your helpers, let Angelica know. Since we owe her huge favors, it is not right for us to ask her."

Amy made an instant decision. Both men seemed kind enough. "Well, let's not be hasty. If Angelica chose you to be our helpers, she must think very highly of you. We'll give it a go. Besides, your omelet was quite good."

"Thank you, Miss Amy. We'll do our best," Stu promised. "We should get you dressed and your hair done. Then, we can tackle sorting out your things and then we ought to visit the market and lay in some supplies."

"Shame that it's fall. I can do some fall prep work on your gardens, but you'll have to wait until spring for the fruits," Verne added.

They returned to their bedroom. "We might as well wear the same dress as yesterday. Everything else is still crated up," Amy suggested. Quickly and gently, Stu began helping Amy out of her nightgown and into her slip and pod-silk gown, while Verne did the same with Jan.

"Excuse me, Miss Amy, but that corset must be terribly uncomfortable and there's so much steel in it, how can you bend?" Stu asked. Both were still wearing their nylons from the day before. They'd been too tired from the day before to

269

deal with them before heading to bed last night.

"Quite true, but when we tried not wearing them, we had way too much back pain and had to continue wearing them," Amy explained, recalling how badly both had felt when they tried to live without them.

"Miss Amy, will you permit me to see what I can do about that? I have healing hands or so my Mary always said. I know that I failed to save her from the rotting disease, but I can try, if you will permit me," Stu volunteered.

Is he trying to get into my pants? Amy wondered. *No, I don't sense that he's getting aroused. Shit, it can't hurt to let him try, though it'll probably amount to nothing, since the medical machines couldn't do anything about the back pains.* "Sure, go ahead and give it a try, Stu."

Carefully, he undid her garters and then untied the highly restrictive pipe corset. "God does that ever feel better. Oh, my! I'm so weak," Amy gushed. Stu helped her lie down on her bed.

"Okay, I want you to feel my hands," he said softly. Gently, he began massaging her back. She felt the warmth of his hands, as they seemed to float over her body. After a half hour, Amy had yawned a good deal and she felt greatly relieved.

"Well, your muscles are going to need time to strengthen, Miss Amy. Things seem to have been moved around some, but we need to strengthen your back muscles bit by bit. Here's what I want you to do." Stu began showing her how to do some simple exercises. "Stop the moment that you feel any pain and let me work that pain out for you. Meantime, allow me to see what I can do for Miss Jan here."

A while later, Jan murmured contentedly, "Stu, that felt fantastic. You have warm, healing hands all right."

"Thank you, Miss Jan. Mary always said I did too. Now then, you do those exercises too. I think that in time and with enough exercises, you can strengthen up your backs enough to no longer need to wear them. We'll work on this several times a day. You didn't get into this shape overnight, and it's going to take time and real effort on your part to get your muscles back into shape. Meanwhile, I'll put them back on you, but not so tightly. If we work at it, Misses, I think that soon you will be free of them. Alas, though, I don't think that I can do anything for your feet. They seem like they are broken and re-healed into their unusual shapes."

"Thanks Stu. Yes, they were. We can get by okay with our feet, but it would be fabulous not to have to wear these pipe corsets any longer," Jan replied, still feeling utterly relaxed.

Shortly, the two were dressed again and now the men gently brushed out their hair, and Amy sensed that each had done this many times for their late wives. She couldn't recall a man ever having such a gentle way with a woman's hair as these two men had. She couldn't resist peeking a little at their minds. She admired what she saw, fleeting glimpses of them and their wives.

"Okay, shall we head to the market first so that we have something to fix for lunch? Then we can start unpacking." Stu suggested, finally fastening Amy's bluebird clasp holding in place the back of her long hair. They agreed and the men found their heavier cloaks and fastened them around the two. "There now, you look like normal women going shopping," he said with a smile.

"Women don't go shopping for food supplies in such fancy heels," Jan pointed out with a childish giggle. The two men chuckled and agreed. Stu put a supporting arm around Amy while Verne did the same with Jan, and they headed out into the streets of Brom.

Although the day was overcast and rain was likely, probably turning to snow later in the day, the streets were swarming with men, women, and children. For the first time since they had returned to their home world, Amy and Jan felt like ordinary women, just walking to the market. Inwardly, they felt pleased at Stu's comment. Indeed, with their heavier cloaks over their shoulders, no one could see what they were missing; they looked quite ordinary, except for their heels that is.

An hour later, Stu busied himself in their kitchen, while Verne handled their unpacking, with the two women merely directing him as to what went where. By noon, he had their few possessions stored. Lunch consisted of roasted rabbit in a spicy sauce accompanied with a good helping of vegetables and of course the remainder of the loaf of bread. Over lunch, Stu asked, "Now then, where do you wish us to stay at night? We ought to sleep here somewhere, in case you need something during the night. If you would prefer to be left alone, we can leave, but we'll have to return early in the mornings to help you dress and fix breakfast."

The reality of their situation struck home to Amy and Jan. While neither liked the idea of having men so close, the practicality of the situation dictated it be so. "Unless you want or need to return to your homes at night, it would probably be best for us if you did stay here," Amy answered for the both of them. Jan nodded her agreement. While they could manage by themselves in all likelihood, it would be difficult.

"We should stay. That simplifies things quite a lot. There's no room for us up here, let's check out the basement. Perhaps we can make do down there," Verne suggested. After lunch, they checked out the basement. A root cellar and a coal bin were all that was down there. They decided that they could make do down there and left to bring a bed and some of their things back.

While the men were gone, Amy and Jan did as the men asked, doing their back exercises. "They really are a kind, gentle pair," Jan mused.

"True, and maybe there is some hope for us and our backs. That back massage of Stu's felt fantastic," Amy added.

"I know, incredible. His hands were warm, and I've never been so relaxed before. Amy, I have to admit that I became slightly aroused. It's been so long since I had hands touching my body like that."

"I'm sorry, Jan. It's my fault that I haven't been able to treat you properly for the last twenty years."

"Hey, no regrets. We did what we had to do to get home. Still, I got aroused a little."

Amy grinned, "I'll admit it, love, so did I. Damn, it felt so good. I guess we can give these men the benefit of doubt and see how it works out. They both are still in grief over the loss of their wives."

"I know. I sense it frequently. They must have really loved them. I felt really normal while we were out shopping. Normal, that's so strange. I've not felt 'normal' for so long that I can't remember when," Jan pointed out.

"Me either. It felt so strange just being a normal person for once. I think I really liked that. Say, what are we going to do now that we have really retired from 'active duty?'" she asked.

"Dunno. Just relax I suppose. I'm sure going to work on these back exercises, though. If we can get free of the corset, we'll have far more flexibility," Jan declared.

Later, the men returned with a bed, some furniture, and some of their clothes and personal items. Once they had their basement room fixed up, Stu got supper going and left Verne to watch it while he gave both women another of his back treatments. "You should be getting these at least three times a day. I'll do better tomorrow."

"Thanks, Stu, not only does it feel fantastic, but it is relieving the pain," Amy validated him.

After a supper that tasted far better than what their cook back in the Imperial Tower served, the men cleaned up the dishes. Stu then asked, "Okay ladies. How about a card game before bed? Or perhaps a Who Done It game? Or you name a game?"

Amy was about to chide him when Jan brightened up and said, "Damn, I've not played cards for over sixty years! Let's! Crap, how am I going to hold or deal them? Well, I'll figure something out. What kind of card game?"

Verne said, "Hey, I learned a new one from a Westerlings descendant a while back. It's rather challenging. It's called 7's. The object is to get seven of a kind, but two's and jokers are wild cards and can be substituted in place of any other one. You get five hundred points if you get seven or eight of one kind, like five's. If you have one or more wild cards to make the seven, then you only get three hundred points." He explained the rules further and they decided to have a go at it.

The four sat around their dining room table and began to play. The women used their psi powers to lift, examine, and move their cards. While it took some effort on their part, they began to enjoy the total relaxation and the table chat. After a while, Verne took a particularly nice discard pile, after Jan discarded a 10 that he needed.

"Say, I thought that you needed 9's not 10's," Jan protested with a teasing smile.

"Ah, I figured that you were peaking at me hand, so I focused on needing 9's instead. Gotcha, Jan," Verne laughed. The others roared, including Jan, who indeed had not resisted the temptation of peeking, using her psi gifts.

Several hours later, they ended for the night. Amy and Jan activated their warning network of crystals embedded in the doorframe of their front door. Then, they allowed the two men to help them get ready for bed. This time, on Stu's advice, they left their corsets off and he gave them both a good back massage, relaxing them completely. "Holler if you need anything during the night," Verne said and the two men headed down to their basement room.

The next morning, the two awoke to the smell of freshly baking yeast bread. Stu was up and at it early. Verne had already stoked the coal fire and the home was slowly warming up. "Sleepy heads. It's morning, got a couple inches of snow outside, but it'll probably melt this time of year. First, massage, then dress. Breakfast in an hour," Stu called out. He again worked on their backs. He had one doing her back exercises, while he used his hands on the other. Then, both men help the two women get dressed. Today, they put on their knee high winter boots that were far warmer than their usual heels. Still the boots had the same stiletto heels as their regular ones. They had no choice in this, since their feet were still rather deformed, but neither complained because they didn't have to wear the even worse toe shoes.

Breakfast done, the four sat around the table sipping their tea. "So now what?" Verne asked. "I would suggest that we acquire a carriage for you and perhaps a sleigh for the winter."

"Yes, probably two horses and two reindeer," Stu added.

"Then we ought to do some shopping. This place is rather Spartan. It could use some things to liven it up a bit,"

Jan added. This time, the men put the women's heavier cloaks over their shoulders. Once more, they looked like normal women going about their morning activities, save for the extreme heels on their boots. As they walked along with the men's arm around them, many others said hello to the two. Both women began to enjoy just being "normal."

After ordering their wagon and sleigh, Verne suggested that they purchase more appropriate clothing. "Look, Brom gets snowed in most of the winter and it gets quite cold. You are both going to be chilled all the time in those light dresses, pretty as they are. We should get you something more Brom-like."

"Right, my Mary always wore warm pants beneath her thick wool dress. Guess you don't need gloves and mittens, though," Stu teased them, bring a grin to their faces.

"We have a difficult time managing pants," Amy countered.

"Well, that's why you have us, your assistants. Trust us, it gets darn cold here. Let us pick out some warmer clothing for you both. If you don't like them or they don't work out for you, you don't have to pay us for them. Okay?" Stu countered.

Their next stop was the dressmakers that Mary always used. Stu and Verne ordered them two sets of heavy pants, tall socks, and woolen dresses. However, the dressmakers had to modify the dresses to accommodate their lack of arms, promising to have them delivered by the end of the week. "Wise choice," one of the makers whispered to Amy as they left. Amy smiled, thinking perhaps these fellows knew what they were doing.

As they walked home, Stu pointed out, "The only complication is that your sizes may change if you can eventually stop having to wear those corsets. We'll see."

As the days passed, the four continued shopping for little things to spruce up their new home. Three times each day, morning, just after lunch, and at night, Stu continued to work on their backs and made sure that they did their exercises. Bit by bit, their back strength returned and by the end of October, they no longer needed to wear them, though they still needed the massages. A month after that, they were pain free at long last, and they abandoned their pipe corsets for good.

Jan insisted that Stu continue giving her massages though, and Amy echoed her. "It feels so good and I am so relaxed when you finish. Besides," she admitted, "I long to feel hands sliding over my body."

"I'm sorry, Jan. I haven't been able to do that for you for so long," Amy realized what Jan was missing now. She'd had the benefit of Jan's hands on her all these years, except for the last couple.

"I know, I never said anything, love. You couldn't do anything about it anyway, so I kept quiet." Jan explained and rationalized. "But I missed it badly."

"Often folks don't know what they are missing until it's gone," Verne stated with a sigh, thinking of his late wife.

"You can say that again, Verne. I miss Mary every day," Stu finally admitted what the two women had long suspected.

"Well, why don't you both rub our bodies for us? We really appreciate it," Jan said.

Stu flushed a little. "Miss Jan, that might be misconstrued. I, er, well, Mary used to get, well you know, aroused when I did that for her. It might not be appropriate. Yet I can feel how badly that you want to feel hands on your body, but we don't want to, well, er, you know, do anything to upset either of you, not that way. It wouldn't be right, since you two are a couple and all that."

"I don't know about you, Amy, but I'm game. Verne do it. I'll let you know if you are doing something I would rather you not do. It is so utterly frustrating that I can't even touch myself any longer. It's not your fault, Amy; don't start crying on me. I know that you feel that way too, and I cringed every night after I lost mine and could no longer rub you. So, have at it, Verne. Trust me. I'll let you know if you do something I'd rather not have you do."

"I'm sorry, Jan," Amy added, fighting back tears as she fully realized how much Jan had given up for her and her exit strategy. "Stu, do me too, please, I'm begging you. I'll let you know, but she's right. It's hell being like this sometimes, utter hell."

All four were telepaths and the slightest touch of their fingers sent waves of energy and pleasure sensations through the women's bodies. One thing led to another. It was not as if suddenly Jan and Amy's love for each other vanished. Rather the opposite, being pleased so reminded them of all the sharing that they had done for over a half century and that had been mostly denied to them the last twenty, particularly so the last few years. Yet, for the first time in their lives, they enjoyed what the men were doing, respected them, and they found themselves responding and begging for more. They made the first moves, kissing the men, passionately. Before long, the four shared an intimacy that only telepaths can experience, four connected as one.

As the four lay naked and panting beside each other in the crowded bed, wholly satisfied, Stu said that he hadn't intended for it to go so far. Amy stopped him, "Sh! Hold me tightly. Yes, like this." She wiggled her head and shoulder over his chest, his arms around her. Beside her, Jan was doing the same with Verne. "I can't begin to tell you how we've missed this closeness," she whispered.

Jan whispered, "Perhaps you men are not all bad after all. It feels so good to snuggle up to you and to feel your arms holding me, Verne. Thank you."

"I have missed it too," Stu admitted how he felt and Verne, likewise.

Later, Amy whispered, "I think that we need to get a larger bed." That big of levity cracked up all four of them, but didn't spoil the moment. Neither women fully realized it yet, but that was their new beginning unfolding.

The next midmorning, Angelica dropped by. "Well, how are these two fellows working out," she asked as the five sat down for tea after exchanging pleasantries.

"Perfect, Angelica," Amy said blushing a little. "At first, I was about to curse you, but then we needed their help."

"Yes, and they need your help too. Losing a loving wife is terrible. Are you two doing better?" she asked the men.

"I thought that you'd lost your marbles or something when we first came here," Stu answered her. "But then I saw that they really did need our help and we did our best.

Somehow, they've made me come alive once more. I didn't think I ever could, you know, after Mary passed."

"I know that, Stu, only too well. Glad that it's working out for everyone. It can be terribly hard to recover."

"I very nearly didn't," Verne admitted sheepishly.

"Nothing to be ashamed of, Verne. I know how deeply you loved Lucy. She was a great woman, wife, and mother. Still, we both know that she would have wanted you to move on and not sit around waiting to die. Thanks Amy, Jan, for helping these two fellows. They are good friends of mine. Besides, how do you like Stu's cooking?"

"Fantastic chef!" Amy gushed. "Three times better than the cook that we had at the tower." Stu looked pleased with her compliment.

Angelica smiled, though her many age lines showed visibly. She sighed, "Well, I came by for another reason too. As you know, we are continually resettling the women from the Arc here in Brom. We've gotten most of them resettled but we are rapidly running out of places to put them up. I've got a married pair of sixty year old women who need a place to stay and someone to not only assist them, but to help get them adjusted to life without their zillion bots. They are Earth kindred, Adora and Agata. I know your home here is on the small size, but could you possibly put them up here? We've already gotten them suitable clothing."

"Sure, Angelica. The guys are sleeping with us now anyway. We can put them in the basement, but we need to fix it up a bit first," Amy replied.

Relief was visible on Angelica's face. "Thank you so very much. It has been quite a challenge finding new homes for five hundred women and children. We have managed not to break up any marriages or families, but I won't lie; it's been quite a challenge. We are down to the last few now. I'll see that they are brought around tomorrow, is that okay?" It was and she then began to explain fully the women's dependence on their bots. "It will be especially hard for them, since they are so old, but go slowly and I think that they will learn to adapt. We all hope so."

Chapter 19 New Life

Spring 1204 brought forth a floral garden in the backyard of their new home. Verne under-represented his gardening skills, Jan said over and over. Adora and Agata adapted nicely once spring arrived. At long last, the two older women got an opportunity to exercise their special skills with the earth. The typically rocky ground found here so close to the solid mountains did not lend itself well to gardening endeavors. Everyone watched as the two set to work. Using their skills, rock seemed to pulverize into dirt as if by magic. In short order, the backyard suddenly had a foot of quality topsoil, and Verne set to work on his many plantings. Agata and Adora constantly assisted him, helping to plan the overall garden.

By May, it was finished. As one stepped outside their backdoor, a trellis with trumpeter vines arched overhead. A cobblestone path followed a winding course around the yard highlighting a different layout of flowers at each bend. "Just you watch, Miss Jan, each month will bring forth a different set of blooming flowers," Verne explained. Agata, Adora, and Verne were quite proud of their accomplishment.

"You will have a variety of fragrances, but they will change month by month," Agata told Jan and they toured their final product. "Verne is a master with flowers," she declared.

"Aye, but you ladies are masters of the earth. Without your great assistance, I'm afraid this would be appallingly less," Verne countered, praising them for their work.

"Well, thank you all! This is an incredible garden indeed. I shall treasure it always," Jan replied, leaning into Verne, who slipped his arm around her waist just the way that she loved.

"It is absolutely beautiful," Amy added, very much impressed with the result. While she'd seen many formal gardens, especially among the very rich who had "owned her" at one time or another, none seemed to compare to this one. Perhaps it was because it was theirs; perhaps it was because of the love that had been put into it. She suspected the latter.

"Well honeys," Adora said — she always called the two

women honeys — "you deserve it. Honestly, when we first stepped into your home last winter, we were scared stiff! How could we possibly survive without all our bots? Then, we saw you two honeys and well our hearts went out to you. You have such a more difficult time with everything than we do. Honestly, we still don't know how you can manage. We have so much more of our arms than you do, so we set our minds to it. Of course, we treasure all the help and patience of your men. We just wanted to give you deserving young women something back of beauty. My, this is the finest garden that we've ever had the pleasure of helping create."

"Thanks, Agata, Adora. It is fabulous," Jan praised the two older women. "I've heard that soon you will have your own home. Verne has promised me that he'll help you get your garden going too." Both women looked pleased.

"Yes, honey, we have heard that too. Honestly, we never believed that would be possible for us, but now anything is possible. We've learned that from you two," Agata replied. "Now if you will excuse us, Adora and I want to sit in the warm sun before it clouds up and rains. You certainly do have an inordinate amount of rain here."

They all laughed. "Yes, you can say that again. Good for the ferns though. My favorites," Verne replied. The four went back inside, leaving the two older women sitting in a pair of chairs in the center plaza, surrounded by numerous flowers that had just opened only the day before.

Inside, Stu and Verne glanced at each other and took deep breaths. Amy and Jan noticed their strange antics and wondered what was up with them. Was there more than just the garden surprise?

Stu broke the ice. "Miss Amy, I can't begin to tell you how much you mean to me. Will you marry me?"

At the same time, Verne announced his feelings for Jan, asking her to marry him. Stu added quickly, "We do not want to in anyway interfere with the relationship that you have for each other, so if you will consent, we four ought to continue to live together. I can't imagine life without the both of you in it. You've given me back my life."

"But Stu, Verne, you don't know about our dark past.

We're assassins, really," Amy said hastily. She and Jan had not really told them about their sordid past. "We've done really terrible things across the galaxy out there. Look, we allowed Bettingham to be destroyed and made you two and all the others with the gift feel the horror and pain of those who died. You two are the nicest men that we've ever met. We are not worthy of you."

"Look, Amy. The past is the past. Life is in us four today; the future is all that really matters. I love you and I know and can feel that you are at least fond of me, Jan and Verne, likewise," Stu countered.

"Damn, Amy, he has a point. That's behind us now. Even trying to rule Tierra is behind us. I never thought that I would feel this way about any man, but I do and I know that you feel that way too, Amy. Life's still in us, so for once in our lives, let's just live it. Verne, I accept, as long as we four live together. I can't part with Amy, not ever," Jan declared. "For once, Amy Blackwater, you listen to me, will you?"

Amy flushed. "Okay, love. I give in. Stu, I accept too. Same conditions, we have to stay together. I will never, ever abandon Jan." The two men threw their arms around the women and gave them a most passionate kiss.

Amy pulled back slightly, "But there is one thing that you have to realize from this moment forward — that is that Jan and I are still part of the Tierra Underground. We still have all our equipment and machines. With the help of others, we are keeping an eye on both the Rigel-3 aliens and the new emperor and empress. We are not about to allow any more bad things to happen to Tierra, not as long as we live."

"Of course, just let us help as we can. I know that we are not much at spying or fighting, but let us help as we can," Stu answered her.

That afternoon, they invited Angelica and their daughters and their husbands over to see their new garden. All four planned to surprise them with their exciting news. Alan and Henry brought the three women there in a nice carriage and helped all three down, while the four watched from their front steps. June had told them that they were arriving and they had come out to greet them.

Both June and Melissa looked radiant and very happy, the two mothers noted. Both young women still looked the height of fashion, wearing their pipe corsets and toe shoes. They definitely needed the supporting arms of their beaming husbands as they made their slow way up the short cobblestone walk to the front door. Both wore Elegant Fashion Inc gowns, June in a light blue satin, Melissa in a darker blue.

They'd barely reach them when June burst out, "Mom! Great news! I'm pregnant! You're going to be a grandmother this year."

Melissa exclaimed jubilantly, "Mom, me too. Pregnant. You're going to be a grandmother too! Isn't this fantastic?"

Tears came involuntarily and they hugged their mothers, who chatted over this exciting news. Angelica smiled, though she coughed a little, not a good sign, Amy thought. "Sorry mom. We had it all planned out how we were going to surprise you and all that, but I couldn't help myself," June admitted.

"Wonderful. I am so happy for you. It is the miracle of life," Amy replied as Stu gently wiped her tears for her. "Okay, come on all you, you just have to see the garden that Verne, Adora, and Agata have created. Honestly, we've seen none finer in the galaxy. This one has love built into it."

Amy noted that it took nearly three times longer to get through their house and out into the garden. While their own heels slowed them down, they were speedy compare to their daughters. June did whisper, "Mom, you are right. In time, you do get really used to walking in them. We do fine now, well mostly. Sloping ground and snow are a bitch though." Amy smiled and chatted.

They met Agata and Adora, who were still sitting in the garden, though it was already starting to cloud up. After introductions and many superlative compliments, Amy finally said, "We asked you here not only to show you our new garden but also to tell you that Stu and I are getting married and Verne and Jan are also."

June shrieked. Melissa gasped and very nearly fainted. Then they both threw their arms around their mothers and began crying. "Mom! I am so utterly happy for you!" June exclaimed. For a time, congratulations flew about.

Then, Angelica spoke up, "Well, this worked out as I had planned. Now, please, do an old woman a favor and get married before my body passes away." Of course, this brought two opposite ideas to head. First, they all wanted to know about her "plan." Second, they found out that Angelica was deathly ill and beyond the healing skills of the tower.

Angelica explained, "It's one of the things that old women can still do. We can see what others really need, though they often cannot. I put you four together to see what would happen. I got one of the things that I wanted which was to get these two men over their loss. Now, I have even more. Just please get married soon, I would love to witness it."

Unwilling to take any chances at all, they held the weddings the next day out in their new garden of love. Stella was Amy's bridesmaid, while Sally was Jan's. Alan and Henry stood up as the men's best man, while Venerada Luisa performed the ceremony. Angelica, Adora, and Agata served as witnesses. June and Melissa merely cried nearly the whole time.

Afterwards, June whispered to her mother and giggled, "You know, you are not too old to have another baby."

Amy flushed. "We'll see, June, we'll see. First though, I need to get some lessons on how to be a proper grandmother. Luisa, little help with this!" Everyone laughed, including Angelica, though her coughing was worse this day.

Later after everyone left, Jan took Amy aside. "You know, love, if there are still some good men in this world, then maybe our grand plan for peace and prosperity for Tierra will work out after all."

For the first time since they met the new emperor and empress to be, Amy felt that Jan might just be right. Maybe there really was hope after all and not everything had been in vain. She hoped so and now had a reason to believe it might just happen.

Carmen Valen was not idle either. Her newest victories were now taking broad hold — namely the body modifications that allowed women to wear her pipe corsets and toe shoes and now toe boots for the cold winters. She knew that to achieve her goal of having them widely adopted across Tierra, she could not continue to have the women coming directly to Exchange City and her Elegant Fashions Inc to have the modifications done. For a broader acceptance, she had to take the process out to the larger cities.

Thus, she ordered a large number of the needed medical machines and machines to build the pipe corsets, toe shoes, and toe boots, the latter of her own design specifically for the winters of Tierra. First, she setup satellite Elegant Fashions Inc stores in each city that had a tower. One section of these new shops contained the Preparation Machines, as she called them. While they were primarily medical machines able to handle most all known medical emergencies via a complex set of menus all written in Imperium Standard that she could read, she only wanted certain procedures to be utilized.

Thus, she found an able computer specialist at the spaceport to make her modifications. While she could not disable the countless procedures built into these medical marvels, she could alter the program's menu items. When her bribed specialist finished, each of these machines displayed single menu items and no longer the lengthy series of choices to be programmed. This single button press approach made it extremely simple for anyone to operate them. Of course, there were no longer choices that would undo any of those that could be repaired. The items that could be selected were to remove arms, remove ribs and adjust for pipe corsets, alter feet to fit the toe shoes, and tie off vocal cords. The first and last were to handle future emperors and empresses, the middle two would become her workhorse menus.

By spring of 1203, she had eight new storefronts established in all eight cities where the towers and rulers were located. She had dozens more planned, and within a few years, she'd have these in every town whose population was at least five thousand. Carmen sat back and grinned, "Revenge is so utterly sweet!" Then she mused further, "You know, I wonder if I can also get men to wear the pipe corsets and toe boots, emulating the fashions of the emperor and his advisor?"

Now she set her mind on how to achieve this new challenge. Men were fighters, but in pipe corsets and toe boots, they simply could not and thus would not consider these changes. Still she thought of an angle: the emperor and his advisors. "Rulers ought to set a good example by emulating their supreme ruler." She wondered if she could somehow sell this idea to those men? "Ah, a real challenge," she said to herself with a coy grin.

The End.

Other Books by Vic Broquard

Without Warning (fantasy)

The Trident Series: (fantasy)
      Volume 1 The Trident and the Book
      Volume 3 The Trident and the Scepter
      Volume3 The Trident and the Resurrection

The Adventures of Elizabeth Stanton Series: (science fiction)
      Volume 1 The Evolution of the Path
      Volume 2 The Great Messiah
      Volume 3 Of Kings and Queens and Troubadours
      Volume 4 Chaos in the Aftermath
      Volume 5 Power Plays
      Volume 6 Age of Exploration
      Volume 7 Abducted
      Volume 8 The Emperor and Empress
      Volume 9 A Job Worth Doing
      Volume 10 Degradation
      Volume 11 The Second Crusade
      Volume 12 When Worlds Collide
      Volume 13 Dark Ages

The Lindsey Barron Series: (fantasy)
      Volume 1 The Rod of the Apocalypse
      Volume 2 The Board of Governors
      Volume 3 The Crown of Moses
      Volume 4 Dominus for President
      Volume 5 The National Health Care Program
      Volume 6 States Justice
      Volume 7 Cross and Double-cross

Zoran Chronicles Series: (fantasy)
      Volume 1 A Dragon in Our Town
      Volume 2 Dragons, Power, Courts, and War

Planet of the Orange-red Sun Series: (science fiction)
>   Volume 1 When Kingdoms Fall
>   Volume 2 Dark Ages
>   Volume 3 Age of the Towers
>   Volume 4 Difficillis Exitus
>   Volume 5 Age of the Lords
>   Volume 6 The Renegade Tower
>   Volume 7 Rebellions
>   Volume 8 The Aliens Return
>   Volume 9 Power Struggles
>   Volume 10 Guilds, Genetics, and Gods
>   Volume 11 Magi, Witches, Swords, and Superstitions
>   Volume 12 The Voyage of the Eagle's Seed
>   Volume 13 Justifications
>   Volume 14 Responsibilities

The Return of the Wizards: Twelve Companions – The Making of Wizards (fantasy)

www.ingramcontent.com/pod-product-compliance
Lightning Source LLC
Chambersburg PA
CBHW060857250626
47159CB00008B/2782